# HAVENWOOD FALLS
# VOLUME SIX

## A HAVENWOOD FALLS COLLECTION

BELINDA BORING    C.J. PINARD    DANIELLE BANNISTER

# ABOUT THIS BOOK

Three paranormal fantasy novellas (books 18, 20-21) in this multi-author shared world of Havenwood Falls, home to sexy men, strong women, and neighbors who bite.

### *The Lurkers Within* by Danielle Bannister

Spirit Agent Tasha Young has never fit in. Her talents as a modern-day ghost buster make her a loner by necessity. Her job is an easy one. Enter a haunted house, remove the misbehaving spirit, collect the cash, and move on to the next city. When she and her team are invited to Havenwood Falls for a special case, she quickly discovers that this retrieval isn't a simple bag and tag.

### *Addicted to You* by Belinda Boring

Sequel to *Nowhere to Hide*—As Havenwood Falls' resident bookstore owner, empath Sedona Mathews is surrounded by a swirling mess of feelings—both fictional and real. But until now, they'd always belonged to others. Then sexy angel Micah Westbrook walked into her bookstore and her life. The trouble with emotions, however, are in the space of a minute, they can twist and change—complicating life in a heartbeat.

### *Affliction Mine* by C.J. Pinard

From *USA Today* Bestselling Author C.J. Pinard— At his cousin's pleading, Karson Kane returns to Havenwood Falls to help with his elven uncle, who's about to be released from supernatural prison. Karson has no idea what awaits him in the mysterious mountain town, but he feels strongly he's meant to go. Within the first twenty-four hours, Karson's cousin gets thrown in jail, too, and Karson ends up in the ER, leaving him to think he may have made a mistake coming to the magical town. Until he meets Scottlin Glover. The gorgeous, auburn-haired breath of fresh air treats his injuries, but leaves him wanting more from her, as he can't seem to take his eyes off her.

# HAVENWOOD FALLS BOOKS

*Forget You Not* by Kristie Cook

*Old Wounds* by Susan Burdorf

*Fate, Love & Loyalty* by E.J. Fechenda

*The Winged & the Wicked* by T.V. Hahn & Kristie Cook

*Alpha's Queen* by Lila Felix

*Ink & Fire* by R.K. Ryals

*Lose You Not* by Kristie Cook

*Tragic Ink* by Heather Hildenbrand

*Nowhere to Hide* by Belinda Boring

*Flames Among the Frost* by Amy Hale

*Rock Me Gently* by Susan Burdorf

*From the Embers* by Amy Miles

*Defying Gravity* by Kallie Ross

*Break Me Not* by Kristie Cook

*How the Dead Lie* by Stacey Rourke

*The Lurkers Within* by Danielle Bannister

*The Collector: Awakening* by Kristie Cook, R.K. Ryals, Belinda Boring & Nadirah Foxx

*Addicted to You* by Belinda Boring

*Affliction Mine* by C.J. Pinard

*The Ward & the Wanderers* by T.V. Hahn

*Toil & Trouble* by Melissa Wright

*Of Salt and Stars* by Seven Jane

*Redefined* by Morgan Wylie

*Betrayal Among the Frost* by Amy Hale

*Forever Loyal* by E.J. Fechenda

*Fate's Demand* by Emily Cyr

*The Wu & the Wand* by T.V. Hahn

*A Demon's Redemption* by JD Nelson

Also try the YA line, Havenwood Falls High; the historical paranormal line, Legends of Havenwood Falls; the darker, sexier side of town, Havenwood Falls Sin & Silk; and the local supernatural college, Sun & Moon Academy.

Stay up to date at www.HavenwoodFalls.com

# THE LURKERS WITHIN

## DANIELLE BANNISTER

~ A Havenwood Falls New Adult Novella ~

# HAVENWOOD FALLS

# THE LURKERS WITHIN

## DANIELLE BANNISTER

## ALSO BY DANIELLE BANNISTER

*Pulled: Book 1 in the Twin Flames Trilogy*
*Pulled Back: Book 2 in the Twin Flames Trilogy*
*Pulled Back Again: Book 3 in the Twin Flames Trilogy*

*Short Shorts*
*The ABC's of Dee*
*Enigma*
*Doppelganger*
*Must Love Coffee*

*Netherworld: Book 1 of The Hallowed Realms Trilogy* with Amy Miles
*Hollow Earth: Book 2 of The Hallowed Realms Trilogy* with Amy Miles

*This one goes out to my mom, Sharon Estes, who is my one and only alpha reader. She has to love me no matter what crap drafts I send her way. She reads them all—every single version—to help me find my "oopsies." Love you, Mom!*

# CHAPTER 1

"*W*ant me to take point?" Adam asked. His trap was raised high, like you might raise a gun going into a drug bust. His muscles flexed, showing delicious chocolate biceps. There were no two ways about it—that man was fine, but also not on my radar. Poor boy wanted some quaint Christian girl. That's definitely not me.

"No need," I said. "It's only a Class C spirit. It's not going anywhere."

Generally speaking, Class C spirits were harmless and confined to the places where they died, unless they were way older than this dipshit ghost, who chose to spend his afterlife tormenting a politician. We had him right where we wanted.

I was the last thing a pissed off ghost wanted to see, for good reason, too. I was the best spirit agent around. When a spirit felt me walk into a room, they knew their time was up. What can I say? I was infamous for being a bitch in both the human and spiritual realms. I wouldn't apologize for my skills. Or for being the best in my field. I was paid quite well by the feds for handling these "classified" cases. My job was simple: enter a haunted house, remove the misbehaving spirit, collect the cash, and move on to the next city. The world was none the wiser as to just how many ghosts they walked the earth with. Most were harmless. I only went after the ones that became a problem.

My team was called in this morning to remove a less-than-friendly Casper. This one was trapped in the attic. In a matter of minutes, the job would be over, and I could go back to the hotel, where I planned to sink into their hot tub. It really was the world's easiest job.

More often than not, I got assigned a Class B spirit. Those assholes became strong enough to emit sounds but were mostly harmless. Sure, I might end up with a scratch or two from the older ones, but those went away by the end of a day. Because they were so powerless, demonic spirits specialized in the psychological mind-game damage they could do to the humans they'd been forced to live with. This type of auras wrongly blamed humans for the reasons they were trapped between realms. These were the douchebags I specialized in. Grumpy spirits who liked to bite. That didn't scare me. I was into the rough stuff.

"Room is clear. Waiting on your call, Agent Young," the voice in my headpiece said. Ah, Winston was on today's mission. How wonderful. He was scared shitless of me. As he should have been.

"We go in when I say we go in, Winston."

Winston bumbled an apology, and I focused back on the door.

Beside me, Adam and my other team member, Eduardo, were all business, their traps poised and ready. They were so serious on these missions. For them, I imagined, this was pretty scary shit. Going up against a spirit wasn't as simple for them, mostly because they couldn't see them the way I could. The imagination was always worse than reality when it came to fear. I could see what I was after, so ghosts didn't frighten me in the least. The rest of the world was less fortunate.

To be clear, I couldn't see a ghost in the same way I could see a human. Spirits were not of this realm anymore, and therefore didn't hold the same shape as living, breathing humans. Instead, I saw the fragments of what was left of them—their auras. Their souls. It was sort of like looking at humans with heat-seeking glasses. A blob of pulsing energy. It wasn't crystal clear, but it was enough to be able to aim a trap accurately.

This baddie in the attic would be a cake walk. Normally, I wouldn't be called in for such an easy bag and tag but when this spirit took up residency at a VIP's place, my team was called in by the feds. Of course, if the FBI was asked about its Soul Searcher program and my place on it, it would deny any and all knowledge of me and the other spirit agents. Such was the risk of a confidential job. I was like a ghost myself. Now you see me, now you don't.

Only a few dozen teams like mine existed around the world, though most of them didn't have a team member like me. They had to rely on malfunctioning gadgets and incompetent tech to bring a spirit down. They didn't actually remove the spirit permanently. They simply pushed them somewhere else, but that wasn't my concern.

There were only five of us that the feds had in their employment who were also Recoverers. There were likely dozens more, but none of them wanted to be controlled by the bureaucracy. I didn't mind. It paid well. Being a Recoverer was another special skill of mine. I could bring back the recently crossed over. Well, I could bring them back if I could get to them within a few hours. I couldn't bring back anyone long dead like Elvis or Prince, though I totally would if I could.

Hell, a lot of those "near-death experiences" you read about? Nine times out of ten, it wasn't a miracle. It was a Recoverer sent to bring the soul back to the human realm. These souls weren't fully dead. They were stuck in the spirit realm and hadn't officially crossed over. Like purgatory, I guess. We snatched them out of the waiting rooms of death to live another day. I'd like to say why we brought back who we did had to do with noble reasons like true love, or they had the formula to cure cancer, or some shit like that, but it was usually because they owed money to the mob or were a family member of someone important. The feds charged a pretty penny for a recovery and only those with power could pay it.

I was recovering more souls than I trapped these days. It's like all the Recoverers decided to go on vacation at the same time. Lazy fuckers. No one had a strong work ethic anymore. But that was just fine by me. I'd happily take their fees.

Just then, Eduardo lifted his trap as he winked at me. Unlike Adam, he got off on this part of the gig. He knew the men on this team were there only for show. I was the star, and he liked seeing me in action. Well, Eduardo liked seeing every aspect of me.

I don't say I was the star player merely because of my ability to see the spirits and bring back the dead, though those were pretty kick-ass skills. No, I was the leader of the team because I was the only one who could actually use the trap properly. I don't know if they were just slow on the trigger, aimed wrong, if their guns weren't calibrated right, or what. Whatever the reason, whatever the job, my traps were the only ones that took the spirits down. Adam and Eduardo were basically my backup dancers. I didn't need them at my side, but it sure made an intimidating picture to the spirit.

Nodding, I gave Adam the signal to kick down the attic door. Did we need to break the door to get to the spirit? Hell no. Breaking shit was for the politician's benefit. Might as well make him believe it was harder than it looked, right? Smoke and mirrors. That's all ghost hunting and politics were, after all.

Adam went in first, followed by Eduardo. Each of them shouted for the ghost to show itself. This was really quite a ridiculous thing to say to a ghost, especially with me on the job, but it made them feel useful and masculine to yell.

The ghost was there, plain as day to me. Eduardo and Adam watched my face to follow where I was looking, so they would know where to aim their traps. Usually, I had to walk around to find the thing cowering in a corner, but this spirit was hovering right in front of me. Almost as if it wanted to be found. In fact, I swear it cocked its head when it saw me.

"Why, hello," I said with a smirk.

Adam and Eduardo raised their traps to where I was focused, but my trap remained at my side as I studied the boldness of the spirit. This was unusual behavior for a spirit. They were typically more skittish when they knew their time was up. Color me intrigued.

"Fire?" Adam whispered when I stalled the command.

"Not yet. I need to check on one thing first," I said, tapping against my earpiece. My eyes never left the aura. Though I couldn't see actual eyes, I had the sneaking suspicion its focus was directly on me as well.

"Go ahead, Agent Young," Winston said in my earpiece.

"Is my room ready at the Ritz?"

"Yes. I have booked a king bed, just like you asked."

"Good," I purred. "Eduardo and I plan on making good use of it later." There was a silence on the other end of the com, which assured me I had made poor Winston blush. I knew full well all our conversations during missions were recorded. I didn't say such things to torment Winston, but to annoy my commanding officer, Agent Duncan. He didn't care for the fact that Eduardo and I were screwing around. It was jealousy, pure and simple. They all got that way when I tired of them.

"I suppose it's time to trap this spirit and go play, eh, Eduardo?" I whispered into his ear.

His lips curled into a mischievous smile for a half a second, but then he refocused on the mission, like a good boy.

I lifted my trap in one fluid movement, waiting for the spirit to make a run for it, but it didn't move. It held its ground in front of me. Smart spirit. It would have been wasted energy trying to escape from me.

"Your time is coming," the female-sounding spirit said, though only I could hear it. I raised my eyebrows, impressed in spite of myself. They normally couldn't communicate. It took too much energy. Those four words likely drained her completely. She was easy prey now. Not that she wasn't before.

"Yeah, yeah, we all meet our maker soon enough. Right now, though, it's your turn," I said, before walking right up to her. I pointed the gun to where her head was and pulled the trigger. My wrist singed a bit from the kickback of the gun, but it was a small price to pay.

"Target acquired."

I handed the trap to Adam, who held onto it like it was worth more than gold. Spirits fascinated him. He longed to be able to see them as I did. He always took meticulous notes after each capture, begging me to describe each spirit in as much detail as possible. Apparently, saying it looked like colored smoke wasn't enough for him. I wished he could see an aura, just once, so he'd get off my back about them.

Eduardo was less professional about the completion of our mission and opted to grab my ass instead. He pulled me close for a congratulatory kiss. I wasn't about to object. That man knew how to use his tongue.

"Get a room," Adam groaned. Eduardo and I did this sort of

thing all the time, so you'd think he'd be used to it by now, but his prudish ways always left me feeling a little dirty. In the good way.

"Great idea," I said. I'd had enough work for one day. It was well past time to let off some steam. Eduardo was the perfect way to do it, too. We left the attic, arm in arm, leaving all thoughts of the job behind.

# CHAPTER 2

*T*hree months and nine captured spirits later, I still wasn't tired of Eduardo, which was a record for me. I don't know if it was because he was Latino and knew how to treat a woman, or if I might have been falling for him. It had to be the first option. I didn't fall for anyone. I left them too soon to allow for that. Eduardo made me break my own rule of no more than two dates. Working with a guy you were also sleeping with, however, complicated that rule. It wasn't as though I could just disappear from his life, like I did with every other guy. It was easy to ditch guys I met when we traveled. Our team was never in one spot for more than a few days. Eduardo was a harder man to shake because he was paid to follow me.

This thing with him was getting out of hand, though. I had to cut this off. I couldn't be the monogamous partner he wanted. That just wasn't me. I was too much of a flirt. After our Thanksgiving break, I'd call it off. It wasn't fair to him. I'd spend the week screwing his brains out, then I'd toss him to the curb. It was a solid plan.

That's when I felt his hands press warmly against my breasts. The way he breathed hot against my neck alerted me to the fact that our morning coffee was about to be postponed.

"You're up early," I teased, reaching my hand around to help him achieve his full potential.

"I say we skip the gym and do our morning workout in bed," he murmured.

"You riding me sounds so much better than me riding the elliptical," I said in my husky voice that drove him wild.

For the next half hour or so, we "worked out" so hard it would have made even Jane Fonda proud. When we had finished, he rolled off me, slapping me on the ass as he did. He was still frisky. Good.

"Hey, Tasha, how many scales do you have filled in now?" Eduardo asked, running his hand along my back, which displayed an outlined tattoo of a Mexican King serpent. It really was an impressive piece of work. My torso held much of the snake's body as it wrapped twice around me. The tail ended at my hairline on the back of my neck while the black head of it disappeared into my 'Garden of Eden.' The individual scales, numbering over a hundred, were outlined and waiting to be fully inked in. A full-body tat like this would likely take twenty or more years to fill in. In its outline form, however, it still made for an epic piece.

"How many? Um . . . a lot." I laughed as I watched his eyes rake over my naked body. I'd lost count of how many were completed, since I started with the ones on my back first. I hated needles and really didn't want to watch it being done, so being face down for as much of the process as possible was ideal. For someone not keen on needles, perhaps a full-body tattoo was stupid, but the idea of it came to me in a dream one night. The fact that I had a birthmark that looked a bit scale-like cemented the design for me. I hated those ugly birthmarks, and they seemed to keep cropping up more often as I aged. This design disguised them perfectly. Even the tattoo artist thought it was pretty badass. Hurt like a motherfucker though.

I craned my neck in an effort to see the scales he was staring at, but it was useless. I wasn't as bendable as I was in my twenties. "I'm guessing there's probably like twenty-five by now?"

Eduardo shook his head. "That looks like a lot more than twenty-five. I'll have to count them one day," he said, leaning over to lick one, "with my tongue."

"You always were a stickler for actual data," I replied.

He slid off the bed then and tossed a sheet on me, so I wouldn't get cold. He was thoughtful, that one. "I'm gonna hit the shower."

"Mmm," I said, hugging the sheet around me. His cologne was intoxicating all on its own. Still, not a reason to keep a guy around.

After this break, I'd need to be reassigned to a new team. Again. Maybe I'd try the London office. Lots more pasty-looking guys with bad teeth there. Less temptation.

"Hey, Tasha, get your ass in here with me!" Eduardo yelled over the noise of the rushing water.

"I'll be there in a minute." I grinned. No harm in enjoying him while I could. Though I needed to check in with work. I still hadn't gotten the official "you're clear for vacation" message, even though I put in for the time months ago. Sure, the work was easy, but the constant travel was weighing on me. I was looking forward to parking it in one place for the week.

Yanking the sheet off me, I yawned and walked, buck-naked, over to my phone. It was tucked into the back pocket of my pants.

As soon as I turned it on, notifications started pouring in, which was unusual. I didn't have friends or family—at least, none that knew this number—so I knew something big at work must have gone down overnight. Especially when all fifteen messages said the same thing.

**AGENT YOUNG, CALL THIS NUMBER ASAP.**

"So much for being off next week. Asshats." Blowing out a breath, I glanced at the number. It wasn't my normal FBI contact, but that happened now and again. An undercover op would need help, so they called my team in. The feds were the only ones with my number, so it had to be legit.

Tossing the phone on the bed, I went to join Eduardo. Whoever it was, they could wait ten more minutes. Maybe twenty.

*Forty* minutes later, thank you very much, I sent Eduardo down to the lobby for coffee. I hated the crap they pawned off in the room. Tasted like caffeinated cardboard. I missed my own four-cup coffee pot, ironically. I couldn't remember the last time I slept in my apartment back in Soho. Was it weeks now, or months? Ultimately, it didn't matter since the feds picked up the bill, but there was something about having a space of your own. A space you could claim. With each passing year, I found myself longing more and more for that elusive word—home.

Sighing, I punched the number given me into my cell and plopped on the unmade bed. The smell of our morning adventure still lingered on the sheets as I lay down, waiting to find out where I was being shipped off to next. This, by far, was the worst part of the job. Always leaving.

# CHAPTER 3

"*H*avenwood Falls?" I asked, pulling out my laptop to search for its location as my contact prattled on. "Where the hell is that?"

"It's a small town in Colorado. Don't bother looking it up. It's not on any map. Remote town with lots of mountains. Pack layers. November may be warm in Jacksonville, Agent Young, but it won't be in Havenwood Falls."

I closed my laptop. "How did you know where I am?"

"I just know, Agent Young. Can we skip the fifty questions?"

Well then, Captain Dickhead wasn't a chatter. Great. I worked with men like this all the time. Alpha types who felt they needed to talk down to the female of the species. Damn it all if I didn't usually find men like that sexy.

As Dicky spoke, I did a mental inventory of the few clothes I had: Two pairs of black pants, three white button-up dress shirts, two black bras (because why wear a white bra when a black one through a white shirt could be so titillating), three pairs of shoes—two of them heels—and one black leather jacket. I'd likely need to grab something warmer when I got to the airport; something easily left behind on the plane ride back when I left. I traveled light. Lived light. Everything I owned fit in one travel suitcase. Necessities only. That's the reality I knew.

"Agent Young, your flight leaves in four hours. There will be someone waiting to pick you up from the airport. I trust that will be enough time to get your team ready?"

I pulled my thoughts out of my carryon and back into the conversation.

"Yes. Absolutely."

"The tickets are being left with the front desk of your hotel. Your fee has already been wired to your account. Any questions?" he asked. Now that the details were sorted, he sounded bored.

"Yeah. Just one. Who are you?"

Agent Duncan usually called my assignments in. Not that I minded not hearing from Duncan. He was a snore-fest. This guy, while arrogant as fuck, at least sounded sexy as all get out. Hell, this guy might be just the thing to get my mind off Eduardo.

"I'm the guy paying you to do your job, Agent Young."

Well, well, well. I was annoying him. Good. Men like him needed playing with.

"I meant, what is your name?" I asked, matching his arrogant tone.

"You'd better start packing, Agent. Let your team know we're counting on their A game for this capture."

Great. This was going to be one of those top-secret missions the feds sent me on where everything was need-to-know, including who was in charge.

"It's the only way I play," I said.

"So I've heard." With that, there was a click and the call was ended.

Eduardo came in just then with our coffees and two bagels perched precariously on top. I relieved him of one set.

"Eat fast. We've got a mission. Flight leaves in four hours."

"I thought you were off next week?"

My phone vibrated then, alerting me of an incoming wire. I showed him the screen. He gave a low whistle. I nodded. "For this fee, I'm available."

Eduardo nodded. "I'll call Adam."

Adam was staying on the floor above us. He learned the hard way to never be below our room. Eduardo and I were too noisy. Adam was always ready to leave at a moment's notice, so I had no doubt he'd be here within five minutes, which was a good thing. Four hours wasn't a lot of prep time, but our cover stories always remained the same: Adam played my husband, and Eduardo, because of his baby face, played our bi-racial son. *Leave It to Beaver* had nothing on our motley crew.

Playing Adam's wife was easy, because Adam was a fine piece of man. Standing at six foot one, he had dark cocoa skin and bicep muscles for days. He was uber religious, though, so he had no interest in me and my "whorish" ways. He harped on me a lot about all the men I slept around with, but I knew he secretly wished I'd find someone and finally settle down. He had a good heart, that one. He was going to make some virginal woman very happy one day. It just sure as hell wouldn't be me.

At each new assignment, we adopted our roles and played house for a few days until the spirits got close enough to trap them. Older spirits could move around more than the chick we bagged in the attic a few months ago. As awesome as I was at trapping spirits, I couldn't walk through walls. Playing chase with a ghost was not my idea of a good time. Hence the cover. If we went into a house with Class B spirits with traps blazing, we'd never get as close as I needed to be to bag them. I had to literally be right on top of them in order for the trap to work. Sneak attacks were the only way to land these assholes without all the Tom & Jerry–style chasing.

"Where are we headed?" Eduardo asked after he hung up with Adam.

"Havenwood Falls. Ever heard of it?" I asked.

He shook his head, making his lush curls bounce as he did. "Should I?"

I shrugged. "No. I guess it's somewhere in West Bumfuck, Colorado."

"Great. Adam and I will blend right in." He smirked, showing off not only his cute-as-fuck dimples, but his golden Puerto Rican skin.

"That town will be crazy jealous of the white chick with two colored studs on her arms."

He grabbed me by the waist and pulled me to him.

"I'd do her," he said.

I laughed. "You have. Twice just this morning. Unfortunately, we don't have time for round three. We have to get to the airport."

"Party pooper," he said playfully, but promptly went to pack his things. I watched his backside as he walked to the dresser. *I think we'll need to squeeze in a mile-high-club visit.*

# CHAPTER 4

$\mathcal{W}$ hen my team was picked up at the airport in a cheesy-looking tourist bus that would have put the Mystery Machine to shame, I couldn't help but think that bus was going to be the weirdest thing I'd see all day. I was so, so wrong.

After a four-hour drive, the little bus that could managed to haul our asses up the windy, snow-covered, and fog-ridden mountainside. We were driven into a town that looked like a replica of Mayberry. Not even joking. For starters, the center of Havenwood Falls looked more like a movie set than a real place. It just looked too perfect. Magical, somehow.

In the middle of town was a squared off section that held a park area with a fountain dead center and a gazebo off to the right of it. Like a proper, old fashioned gazebo. What town still had those? It wasn't even Thanksgiving yet, and there were Christmas decorations everywhere. No respect for Thanksgiving. I wanted to hurl. Towns like this were so not ready for the likes of me and my crew. I dug out my cell to check the time, and only then did I realize what day it was —Black Friday. That's why there were so many people out and about. I missed Thanksgiving completely while traveling here to this bullshit assignment. How pathetic was I that I forgot a major holiday like that? It was just one of the many ways my job consumed every aspect of my life.

"Hey, we missed Thanksgiving," I said to Eduardo.

He shrugged. "I don't really like turkey anyway. Besides, this place makes up for it. Check out those slopes!" His eyes were still focused outside the window on the mountain beyond. I was about to scold Adam for not reminding me, but then I remembered he was Canadian.

Surrounding the square was an odd assortment of businesses. Your typical things like coffee shops, town offices, and hair stylist and such, but they all had hippy-dippy names like Into the Mystic and Shear Magic. I knew cannabis was legal in Colorado, but these store names were out there even for a pothead.

That's when we passed by the Haven Saloon.

"Praise Jesus. We're saved. They have a bar," I said, to no one in particular. Eduardo and Adam were too busy looking at this bizarre little town with far more wonder than I was. I wasn't sure what it was, but something about this town felt very, very wrong, while at the same time, a little bit right.

"There's a ski shop! Tasha, we *have* to go skiing," Eduardo beamed.

"Um, we're only here for a week. I don't know how much skiing time there will be." I looked up at the mountains, though, and was surprised to see whitecaps when there were only a few inches on the ground. "Have you ever been skiing?" I asked Eduardo, raising my eyebrow.

"No! Which is why we should try it!"

Adam and I exchanged a glance. Eduardo, though he was great in the sack, was not known for his athletic prowess outside of the bedroom.

"Let's just focus on the assignment first, shall we?" Adam said, taking the pressure off me to tell him no.

"Fine, but then we are so all going!" he said, bouncing up and down in his seat like the teenager he was about to portray. It made me laugh despite the surroundings of this bizarre little town.

The small group on the bus filed out one by one. Adam and Eduardo grabbed our gear while I looked around for where the hell we were supposed to go to now. Dicky hadn't exactly been clear, and he wasn't returning my texts.

"Agent Young?"

I spun around and saw a man dressed in black holding a sign with my name on it.

"That's us," I said.

"Right this way." He gestured to his black car with tinted glass that screamed FBI. Way to be inconspicuous and likely blow our cover, jackass.

"Damn, girl. We're being treated like royalty," Eduardo sang as he hopped into the car. "Who is this dude, anyway?"

"No clue. Someone who clearly doesn't understand the concept of working undercover."

Adam and I exchanged a glance. He felt it too. There was something unusual about this mission. We never got wined and dined this much. Something was fishy.

As our driver took us out of the center of the town, we realized he wasn't going to speak to us. Every question we asked went unanswered, which meant he must have been given specific orders to keep quiet. Fine by me. The sooner we got there, the sooner I could find out the assignment, finish the job, then get the hell out of dodge. This place was making my skin itch. It was too perfect, which meant it was hiding a secret. It didn't help that all the tourists and hippies were gawking at us, I just knew it. Didn't matter where I went. People always stared at me. Yes, I am a freak. Move on with your lives, people!

We made a left on Thirteenth Street, which seemed fitting considering the supernatural twist to our jobs. We stayed on that road until the car pulled up beside a light sage-colored house. It didn't look like a haunted house you might imagine in a book or movie, but houses with the most demonic spirits didn't. They looked like normal, cute little houses.

Just like this one. The hairs on my arm went up. This was bad. Very bad. Whatever was in that house wasn't something we'd been up against before.

Once I got outside of the car, my suspicions were confirmed. In that moment, I knew *exactly* why our team had been called in. My stomach lurched. This was no Class B spirit.

"Tasha? You okay?"

Adam had a bag in his hand, while Eduardo was pulling out the rest from the trunk. The driver stayed in the car, the engine still running. He must have known what we were up against, because he had no plans to stick around.

"Everything's hunky-dory, babe," I said, making direct eye contact with Adam to make sure he understood. "Just got a little carsick is all."

*Hunky-dory* was a code word. It warned the team that all was not, well, hunky-dory. It told them that I'd felt the presence of intense dark energy. There was something predominantly evil oozing out of that house. If my senses were right, and they always were, there was far more than one baddie inside, to boot.

"You have the key, *Mom?*" Eduardo asked, slipping into character and letting me know he got the message. Normally, we didn't have to put on our act until we got inside, because ghosts couldn't see that far, but this was old energy, possibly the oldest I'd ever come up against. The older the spirit, the farther they could see.

I took the small carryon Adam had, which held one of our five traps. They were hidden among our belongings for ease of access. They had to be close by, but also hidden, lest we spook what we were hunting. I had a sinking feeling that what we were packing wasn't going to be enough. Whatever spirits were lurking within were a patient group. They were gathering for something. Something big.

My muscles tensed in anticipation as I put on a plastic smile. We were being watched. Better make it convincing. Since our contact wasn't providing me with the information I needed to formulate a plan, I would have to figure it out myself, which meant seeing exactly what we were up against with my own eyes before I called headquarters and reamed someone's ass out for sending us in here so unprepared.

"Let's go see our new home for the week," I said, sounding way more chipper than I felt.

# CHAPTER 5

From all outward appearances, the inside of the house looked like any other you might find listed in an Airbnb ad. The appliances were new and all stainless steel. All the surfaces had been dusted. The path to the house had been shoveled and sanded. The sun beamed inside through large bay windows, doing its best to remove the shadow that hung over the place like a living, breathing beast.

Everything inside looked like it had been handpicked by an interior designer, save for a creepy-ass wooden doll perched on the mantle. She had on a green dress from what looked like the 1700s. The paint had chipped on the nose and neck, making her look like she'd been smudged with dirt. The dress she wore had yellowed from the sun. She had an apron and bonnet over the dress. A servant. Not the sort of doll you'd usually see kept over the years. It was the eyes that made her creepy, though. No color to them. Just black orbs that seemed to follow me as I walked. I had to turn it around. It gave me the heebie-jeebies, and I didn't scare easy.

Eduardo gave me a weird look when I turned around from the doll. I tried to communicate with just my eyes to use extreme caution in this house, but Adam and Eduardo were already on the defensive. While still trying to keep up the cover of a happy-go-lucky family on a ski vacation, they clutched their bags tightly, ready to take out their traps the moment I gave the order.

"Cool digs," Eduardo said in his best teenybopper voice. "I'm going to go check out the bedrooms."

"I'll go with you," Adam said. "No way are you claiming the biggest room, kid."

I nodded, understanding they were really doing some surveillance. Not that it would help. Eduardo and Adam wouldn't be able to see anything out of the ordinary. Not like I did. Sometimes they could feel a temperature shift, though, if a spirit was old enough. My guess was they'd be covered in gooseflesh by the time they came back, if the upstairs was anything like the downstairs view.

My mouth fought to stay closed and conceal my true horror while I looked at what appeared to be an empty living room to human eyes. In reality, I was in a living room that was filled with no less than six spirits, each one circling around me. They weren't attacking or trying to latch on to me. They seemed to be patiently observing. I had no doubt there would be more in the bedrooms.

Poltergeist was my first thought. We must have been on an ancient burial ground, or some shit like that. Why else would there be so many spirits in one spot? Then another thought struck me. Had there been a mass murder here? That was a high possibility, too. My contact hadn't mentioned anything about what we were up against, but I was racking my brain for logical reasons so many spirits would be in the same house. Spirits weren't as mobile as movies made them out to be. They couldn't just travel around from house to house. They were tied to the space where they died. So what the hell happened here?

I thought back, trying to remember all the case files I'd read from other spirit agents about mass spirit gatherings, while I placed my bag on the floor. The only one that came even close was one from Sweden about ten years ago, when a spirit agent discovered four souls in the same house who had somehow merged themselves into one spirit. The case was dismissed by other spirit agents as unsolved. Other than that, I couldn't think of any other case file that had this many spirits in one place.

Keeping up my disguise, I plopped down on the couch and scanned the room, appearing to appreciate the view from the bay window, but I was instead assessing the color of the auras in the room.

Spirits gave off different colors based on their mood. Yellow meant they were at peace and content. Those were, by far, the easiest ones to capture. The blue auras were confused spirits. They didn't understand why they were in between worlds and often didn't believe they were dead in the first place.

A confused spirit was what most people came across. They caused minimal damage in that they mostly only scared the shit out of their owners with their moaning and floor creaking. They were more annoying than harmful, but even spirit pests needed an exterminator.

Red auras were the worst. They were the pissed off baddies. The most demonic ones. They hated the human realm and the fact they were stuck in it. They would hurt anyone they could. It took massive amounts of energy and years as a spirit to be able to leave any sort of physical mark on a human, but it still fucking hurt. That said, red auras were rare. In my years as a spirit agent, I'd only come across a handful of them. This room alone held six of them.

How the hell was I supposed to trap this many demonic spirits with only five traps? We couldn't. We literally couldn't. In fact, it was extremely dangerous for any of us to be here. I had to get my team out, now.

"Hey, Mom?" Eduardo asked suddenly from upstairs. There was a thread of panic in his voice. Adrenaline rushed through me as I wondered if I was too late.

I ran up the stairs to find Eduardo standing over Adam's limp body. Adam was sprawled out on one of the beds, his eyes closed. There was no blood, no sign of foul play; it simply looked as though Adam had decided to take a nap, which we both knew was not what was happening.

"What's wrong, peanut?" I asked, highly aware we were being watched. I didn't want to spook them into doing anything else rash. I rubbed Eduardo's shoulder hard, trying to hide my panic.

"Um . . . I think Dad passed out," he said, clearly as freaked out as I was but trying hard to maintain the cover. "I went to check out the other room, and when I came back, he was like that."

My blood began to race as I walked over to Adam. I pressed my hand against his forehead, like a wife would do for a potentially sick husband, and watched closely for signs of life.

"Oh, honey, Daddy's fine," I said in a whisper. He was still breathing, but his skin was colder than it should have been. *Shit.* "I think he's just exhausted from the trip. Jet lag is a real thing. It can knock you right out." I took one last look at Adam then turned my attention back to Eduardo. "Why don't you and I go for a walk, check out the town while your dad sleeps? There looked like some great lunch options to try out."

Eduardo was tense, but he nodded, looking back one last time at Adam. I knew he wasn't okay with leaving Adam in this condition, but he would listen to my orders. I'd fill him in as soon as we got clear of the house.

"Yeah, okay. We should come back later. Let him rest."

"Good idea, kid," I said tousling his hair.

I looped my arm through his and led him as casually down the stairs as I humanly could. We needed to get out of this house stat and contact headquarters. Someone needed to tell us what the hell was going on here.

For a half a second, I thought we weren't going to be able to leave as I noticed all the red auras following us to the exit, but when I put my hand on the knob, it opened, bringing with it the freedom of the cool afternoon air.

When we had walked several blocks, to be far enough that I couldn't feel the spirits watching us anymore, I dug out my cell phone. Agent Duncan was going to get an earful from me. I wanted to know who the hell called me and why. I didn't trust my contact as far as I could throw him. When I tried the line, however, the call never went through.

"Damn it!" I held up the phone and tried again. Still nothing.

"What just happened back there?" Eduardo asked, rushing to keep up with my stride. While he couldn't see what I had, I was sure he knew that whatever went down wasn't good.

"They took Adam, that's what's happened," I shouted. I was pissed.

Eduardo stopped walking. None of our team had ever been taken into the spirit world. In fact, it had only ever happened once in my time as a spirit agent. Only a Recoverer, like myself, could bring back a taken soul, but only within twelve hours of the attack. After that, they were stuck in purgatory while their body lay in a coma. Brain dead, doctors called it. More like soul-sucked.

"Someone has some serious explaining to do," I said as I tried my contact's number instead. At first, I didn't think it was going to go through, then the line finally connected.

"Agent Young. I didn't expect to hear from you so soon. Done already, are you?" my contact said on the end of the line. He seemed amused. I was about to wipe that smile off his smug face.

"Cut the shit. I need to know what the fuck my team is up against."

There was a silence and some shuffling noises, like he was trying to find a private place to have this conversation.

"What happened?" he whispered.

"They've taken one of my agents, that's what's happened! There are at least a dozen demonic spirits in that house. Now we're up against a clock to get Adam's soul back, which means I have to drag my ass back in there, so I need you to tell me what the hell is going on!" I yelled, garnering some stares from the joggers on the other side of the road. Fuck them. I couldn't care less about my cover right now. Adam's life was hanging in the balance.

"Meet me in town square. There's a coffee shop called Coffee Haven. I'll explain what I can."

It was my turn to stop walking.

"Wait. You're *here?* In Havenwood Falls?" We didn't have any spirit agent FBI branches in Colorado. Who the hell was this guy?

"Ten minutes, Agent Young."

The call ended, and I stared at my cell for a moment.

"Something is seriously messed up here," I said to Eduardo as he approached me.

"Ya think? Why didn't you recover Adam back there? You said he was taken. Why didn't you just pull him back into this plane? Why did you make us leave? What aren't you telling me, Tasha?'

"There wasn't time to recover him. Not without one, or both of us, being taken next. We're not up against one spirit, Eduardo. It's a fucking legion."

Eduardo stopped walking as he let that sink in. He'd never taken down a legion before. None of us had. It wasn't what we were trained for, so our contact had better have a damn good plan and explanation for all of this, because I was officially out of ideas.

# CHAPTER 6

*W*e didn't need ten minutes to reach the center of town. I would have been there faster if Eduardo hadn't been slowing me down by asking me a million questions I didn't have the answers to. No, I didn't know how they took Adam. No, I didn't know why there were so many in the house. No, I wasn't sure how we were going to save Adam. All of my answers started with "No." I had no fucking clue what was going on. Add to that the fact that walking in heels, in the winter, with just my thin leather jacket meant not only was I pissed at being lied to, I was also cold. I was in a foul mood. I almost felt bad for our contact. The hellstorm he was about to endure wouldn't be pretty.

"I hate snow," Eduardo said beside me, trying to stomp out the snow from the treads of his sneakers once we made it to the center of town. Eduardo hated any temperature below eighty degrees, so this place wasn't rubbing off well on either of us.

"Says the guy who wanted to ski earlier." I snorted.

"Skiing and walking around in sneakers in four inches of snow are two very different things, chica."

"Yeah, well nothing about this mission is making me warm and fuzzy either," I said, pulling my jacket around me tighter.

Our meeting spot was easy enough to find once we made it to the center of town. The smell of caffeine permeated onto the sidewalk. Coffee Haven was on Main Street, wedged in between a massive book store called Shelf Indulgence and a consignment store of some kind. Two types of stores I never frequented. I hadn't read a book since high school, and I never bought anything used.

Eduardo was still peppering me with questions as I yanked open the door of the coffee shop harder than I needed to. The small bell above the door chimed, making me roll my eyes. Of course there was a damn bell on the door. This town was too perfect. I didn't trust it. My eyes darted around the room, looking for my contact, or someone who looked like they might be, but found that it was deserted, save for an older couple in the corner sipping their drinks. I glanced at my phone to check the time. We were early.

"Should we get a coffee?" Eduardo asked. Finally, a question of his I could answer.

"I'd rather have a shot of whiskey, but I suppose caffeine will have to do."

He nodded. We were both caffeine addicts, and with Adam taken, I knew this was going to be one long-ass day, so I'd need to keep my eyes and brain alert, which meant strong coffee. And lots of it. The air here was messing me up and giving me a wicked headache. The caffeine would need to do double duty today.

"I'll get it." I gestured toward a table near the window for him to sit at. I shrugged out of my coat and handed it to Eduardo, who took it and moved to the table I indicated without saying anything else. *Good boy.*

As I walked up to order, I was taken aback by the massive marble counter. I highly doubted it was the real thing, given the size and the budget a shop like this might have, but nevertheless, it was still impressive for a joint like this.

I checked out the rest of the shop while I waited for the barista, who had his back turned while he was on the phone. The ambiance here was bizarre. There were plants everywhere, as well as artwork, and random crystals placed in every nook and cranny. It was a hippy-lover's dream.

While I waited, I placed my elbows down, being sure to squeeze my breasts together to give the guy working the counter the best view. I had a nice rack. Seemed a pity not to show it off whenever I could. Plus, I loved how it messed with guys' brains. Flirting was something that came naturally to me. Even in times of high stress like this. It was a coping mechanism to be sure, but what a fun one to have.

The barista finally hung up and then turned around. When he saw me, his eyes became unavoidably glued to the show I was offering. I smirked. He cleared his throat as he approached me and pushed up his dark rimmed glasses. I couldn't help but notice him play with his wedding band. Guilty conscience much?

"What can I get ya?" he asked. His voice shook a little, letting me know how nervous I made him. Good.

"How about a name, for starters?"

"Um, I'm. Um. Davis. My name is Davis. I'm the manager here. How can I help you?"

I loved his obvious discomfort.

"What's good here, Davis?" I batted my eyes for good measure, 'cause why not?

"We make a mean latte."

"I'm sure you do." I licked my lips nice and slow. "Two coffees. Black. I like my drinks dark and strong. Just like my men."

His eyes widened again, but he quickly came back to reality.

"Right away," he said, turning to grab two mugs, seemingly grateful to get away from me.

I turned around and leaned my back on the counter, waiting for our drinks. Eduardo had his cell out, probably trying to get a signal. It didn't seem to work outside of local calls, since my contact was the only one I had been able to reach. It made absolutely no sense. Or, more likely, something was seriously messed up about this town. There had to be a reason I couldn't contact the outside world, and I was betting it had nothing to do with faulty cell towers.

"Here ya go," Davis said from behind me.

I turned back around and noticed the start of a tattooed compass on his hand. The bulk of it disappeared up the sleeve of his shirt. How cute. He was a tat-tease.

"Nice ink," I said, ready to do a little toying of my own.

He glanced down at his hand. "Thanks. I got it at Tragic Ink right there on Eighth Street, if you're interested in getting one yourself." He pointed out the window to a building on the square, but I didn't turn to look.

"Oh, I think I've got enough ink, don't you?" I asked, lifting the bottom of my shirt to expose the massive snake coils wrapped around my waist. Davis's eyes nearly fell out of his head. "I'd show you where the head is, but I'd get arrested for indecent exposure."

I bit my bottom lip. Playing with men was just too much fun.

"Thanks for the coffee," Eduardo said, suddenly at my side. He pulled my shirt down for me.

"Oh, are you jealous?" I snickered as we walked back to the table.

"I'm not the jealous type, but overt flirting like that is going to get you in trouble one of these days," he said.

"I'm counting on it."

As soon as we sat down, our contact walked in. It had to be him; otherwise, I would be very disappointed. Mr. Tall, Dark, and Handsome himself walked into the shop, sticking out like a sore thumb against the granola decor. There was no way he was FBI. People that good-looking didn't work for the feds.

I tried not to drool as I took him in. He wore a dark gray overcoat, which he removed and slid over his arm with a practiced ease. The dark silk suit and crisp white undershirt he wore, paired with gorgeous stubble across his jaw and no wedding ring, had me drooling. *Lickable. So very lickable.* Maybe this mission wasn't such a bust after all.

"Special Agent Young. Agent Lopez." He nodded to each of us as he sat down across from us without revealing his own name.

"Davis," he said, not taking his eyes off me, "I need a witch's brew."

"Sure thing, Mr. Bishop."

I clasped my hands and put them on the table.

"Bishop? So that's your name. Funny. I'm not familiar with any Bishops in the Bureau," Eduardo snapped. He was jealous. They needn't fight over me. I'd gladly share.

That observation garnered a glare to my partner.

"Tell your lapdog to go fetch something outside. Then we'll talk," Bishop said, turning his deep blue eyes back on me. *Damn.* He was sexy.

"Whatever you need to say to Tasha, you can say to me," Eduardo said, putting his arm around me, effectively marking his territory.

Agent Bishop leaned back in his chair and looked at me, clearly indicating this conversation was going nowhere until Eduardo left.

He knew he held all the cards. I had no choice. I had to play his game. For now. Adam couldn't wait for this pissing match to play out.

"Why don't you go take a walk?" I asked, turning to Eduardo, trying to placate him with my eyes. I'd make this up to him when this nightmare was over.

His displeasure was written all over his face.

"Oh, is that how it is, is it?" His tone spoke volumes about how pissed he was at me, but there was little I could do, given our current situation.

"I don't have time to play games with this guy, Eduardo. Adam needs our help, and this dipshit may hold the key." That seemed to soften the blow a bit, because he nodded once.

"Fine." He stood up fast, grabbing his coat and coffee. "I'll be right outside." Eduardo and Bishop had a mini staring contest, but Eduardo eventually backed down and huffed his way outside.

"Threatened by a little boy, are we, Mr. Bishop?"

He leaned across the table. "I don't share. Anything."

I matched his inward lean with one of my own, being sure to showcase the girls.

"Well, you've got it. Now, would you mind telling me what the fuck is going on in that house, or do I have to whip it out of you, Mr. Bishop?"

His eyes seemed slightly amused. "You couldn't get me to do anything I didn't want to, even if you were down on your knees, Agent Young."

Oh, he was good. Playing hard to get too. I smirked. "Call me Tasha."

I extended a hand, but he didn't take it, as though proving his point. Maybe he didn't want to play with me. That would be a first for me.

"Roman," he said when I took my hand away. "Well, Tasha, as you've probably deduced, I am not with the FBI."

"No shit. Everything about this mission hasn't smelled right, starting with you. Now why don't you tell me why you brought me here?"

Davis arrived just then with Roman's drink. It looked like a regular black coffee, but there was a definite shimmer to it. Like there was oil in it or something. Probably coconut oil or some healthy shit.

"What the hell is that?"

"It's mine and, therefore, not your concern."

"You know what?" I said as calmly as I could. "You're absolutely right. I don't care about you, or the sewage you're about to drink. I only care about my partner, Adam. Who took him, and why did you bring us here?"

He smiled. "That's more like it." Roman picked up his cup and took a slow and careful sip before he answered my question. "I invited you here because I've heard you're the best in the business."

My eyes narrowed, and I licked my lips. "I'm the best at *everything* I do."

He smiled as though that was exactly the answer he was expecting. "I'm counting on that." He took another sip as though we weren't under the gun for recovering Adam's soul. "Ms. Youn—Tasha, have you ever heard of the Indrori?"

"That another one of your fancy coffee drinks?"

He closed his eyes for a moment, as though he were trying not to scold me for being insolent.

"No. An Indrori is an agglomeration of spirits. One demonic ghost who has figured out a way to absorb the spirits of other ghosts around them, giving it strength unlike anything the world has ever seen."

"Well, that's where you're wrong. The world has seen it. Well, a select few have. My agency knows all about these soul clusters," I hedged, trying to remember more information on that one case file I was thinking about earlier.

He pushed his cup aside. "I'm sure your 'agency' has seen a few feeble couplings peppered here and there. I, however, am referring to something far more aggressive."

I'd play along, if only to get a clearer picture about what I was up against. "Go on."

"We believe that this Indrori has a hundred souls or more currently within his control. He appears to be able to merge and unmerge with these souls at will, according to our source."

I blinked at him, fighting the urge to roll my eyes. The guy was clearly yanking my chain.

"A hundred-plus souls . . . all under the control of one aura? That's not possible. You should have stopped at ten. I might have believed you then." There was no way. No way was a thing like that possible if I didn't know about it. "I would have felt it if there were that many souls in that house."

"Perhaps. If they were all in the house at once. My source tells me that the Indrori seems to be able to move in and out of places, separating souls and joining them together at will."

I rolled my eyes. "Well, forgive me if I don't trust your source. I'm in this field, Mr. Bishop. I know what spirits are capable of. And what you're talking about is impossible."

"My source also tells me that there was a breach in the Infernum not too long ago."

I raised an eyebrow. *The Infernum?* It sounded like a nightclub, but somehow, I knew if I said that, he'd be Mr. Grumpy Pants with me, so I let him continue. He seemed to like to hear himself talk. Hell, I did, too.

"It's a prison, of sorts, for immortals, and also home to some not-so-friendly ghosts," he clarified.

"Let me guess, these hundred or so spirits did the breaching?" I said, waiting for the punchline.

"Not necessarily. We don't know how many may have escaped, but there was most definitely a massive energy shift in our town."

"I think it may be time you lay off the wacky tobacky, Roman."

My comment made no impact on his deadpan expression.

"Fine. Don't accept my information, but don't expect to recover your partner without it."

I glared at him. He had me by the short hairs, and he knew it.

"Tick-tock, Tasha," he replied. Though his tough exterior showed he was firmly in control of the situation, there was an edge to his eyes. A pleading, almost. In spite of his confidence, I got the distinct sense that he needed my help just as much as I needed his.

"Fine. Tell me what you know."

His lips curled into a smile. "That's a good girl."

# CHAPTER 7

orty minutes later, I had heard everything about Havenwood Falls and the thing that was living in that house. What he told me left my mouth hanging open, and not in the good way.

This entire town was made up of supernatural creatures and humans alike, all of them intermingling with each other as if nothing were out of the ordinary. One of the waitresses in this coffee shop, for example, was a witch, but the manager I flirted with was a human. The owner of the shop was a fae. Naturally.

"What kind are you?" I asked Roman when I was able to form semi-coherent thoughts.

Roman leaned across the table, waving his hand around almost like he was trying to swat away a fly, and then clasped his hands in front of him.

"I am a warlock."

"Naturally," I said, though nothing about him being a witch was natural at all! I eyed him again and reconsidered his hand movement.

"Did you just cast a spell?"

His eyes narrowed.

"I merely muffled our conversation from prying ears," he said, as though that were the most natural thing on the planet.

"How are the people—humans, I should say—not freaked out

that they are next door neighbors with a vampire, or shifter, or whatever the hell might want to eat them for dinner?"

"That would never happen. The Court of the Sun and the Moon, the true governing body of Havenwood Falls, ensures things don't get out of hand, and we don't end up eating each other. Well, much. The Court knows all. Sees all. Yes, Tasha, even you will get a visit from them, soon enough. Well, besides me, that is."

"Me? Why?" I didn't like the sound of people keeping tabs on me. Especially in a place like this, where there might be eyes everywhere.

"Like I said, we keep tabs on everyone and everything. Especially the tourists. Plus, we have magical wards and protections in place. That really isn't your concern at the moment. Taking care of this Indrori is. You are the only one who can fix this."

"You keep saying that, but you don't seem to comprehend my point. Yes, I'm the best in my field, but what you're asking me to do is impossible. Not with the equipment I have," I repeated for the third time since he told me about the Indrori. I was like a broken record he refused to listen to.

He stood up, buttoned his suit jacket, and slid his coat on.

"Ultimately, the choice is yours, Tasha. Try my plan, as outlined, and bring your partner back to this realm, or leave altogether. But I can guarantee you this: nobody will save your partner if you choose to leave. Our town is currently up against a formidable force that this Indrori may be just one small part of, and saving all of the people of this town comes before one person nobody even knows is here." With that, he took one final sip from his mug, pulled a fifty-dollar bill from his wallet, and tossed it on the table before he left me alone to consider my options.

Eduardo came back in as soon as Roman left. He'd been watching our discussion from outside like a hawk ready to pounce if he tried anything funny. It would have been a sweet display of jealousy if we weren't so royally fucked.

"So? What was that all about?" he asked as a few new people entered the shop. They were happily chatting with each other, warming their fingers with hands cupped to their mouths. Completely oblivious to the hell that lived a few blocks away.

I stood up. "Not here. We've got eyes."

I glanced over to Davis, who was chatting with his new

customers. How much did he know about the town he lived in? Was he one of them? Or was he one of the poor saps left in the dark?

Spooked, I put on my coat. Eduardo nodded once, and we left Coffee Haven. We walked toward the center of the town square. I ignored the blast of cold air hitting me from all angles, suddenly unable to feel the chill against my skin. It was all I could do not to throat punch the kids on the corner singing Christmas carols.

"Tasha, slow down. Talk to me. What did that asshat say to you?"

I slowed my pace and stood in front of the fountain. My eyes glassed over a bit.

"Did you ever read any fantasy books when you were a kid?" I asked, still trying to process everything Roman told me.

Eduardo looked at me funny, but answered me anyway. "Do comic books count?"

I nodded, though my mind was a million miles away.

His hand caught my shoulder, forcing my mind to stop spinning.

"Tasha, what's all this about? What did he say that has you so rattled?"

"It's all real," I whispered, focusing on the fountain a few feet away. "All of it. Vampires, witches, shifters. It's not just ghosts that walk among us. There really are terrible things that go bump in the night." I wasn't so sure why it was such a leap to believe in all the rest, when I knew full well that ghosts were real. But I'd grown up seeing ghosts. Today was the first time that I'd ever spoken to a witch . . . that I was aware of, anyway.

"What are you talking about? Babe, you're freaking me out."

I stood and watched the fountain, which was still running even in this weather. I tilted my head as I watched what looked like flecks of something shiny in the water. I took a step closer to be sure I was really seeing what I saw. Of course they had a fountain that rained gold. Hell, the water probably wasn't even water. It was probably unicorn tears.

"There's no time to explain it all right now, but," I said, shaking my head, "I know what took Adam."

Eduardo stiffened. "What are we up against?"

"Something we've never trapped before. A super spirit of sorts called the Indrori," I said, as I turned away from the fountain and headed back toward the house. "So we have to hurry."

The sun was starting to set as we raced back to the house. It cast an eerie shadow across everything the darkness touched. The last thing I wanted to do was go back into that house again, especially now that I knew what I was up against, but Roman's plan was just crazy enough to work. I had to try, for Adam's sake.

Eduardo ran after me, quickly matching my stride.

"Tasha, what the hell is an Indrori?"

"According to Roman—"

"Since when are you on a first name basis with our contact?" There was no mistaking the jealousy in his tone. This was not the time to have this discussion.

I needed him to follow orders. "He's not FBI. We were tricked into coming here because of our unique skill set—well, *my* skill set. Roman is one of the guys in charge of this town. He seems to think I'm the only person who can defeat this thing and save Adam."

"What, you wanna go back in there?"

I nodded. "I have to, Eduardo. According to Roman, the Indrori is like a ghost cluster. One soul absorbing the spirits around him."

"Like that case in Sweden?" he asked.

"Yeah, except this one can manage more than a few spirits. Over a hundred. And possibly one more, now that he has Adam."

Eduardo stopped walking for a second.

"Hold up. Since when can a ghost absorb that many spirits?"

"Since about four hundred years ago. Apparently, there are legends of such a beast existing that far back. There was a mass breakout from the prison that held all these spirits. That's when we got the call." My feet were flying back to the house as fast as my words were coming out of my lips. I had a plan, a long shot at best, but it just might save Adam, if I hurried.

"Tasha, wait up," Eduardo yelled, catching up with me. I was on a mission. I needed to get back to the house.

"What prison?"

I stopped walking and faced Eduardo.

"Look, there isn't time to repeat everything Roman told me. Just trust me on this; we are up against the most powerful thing I've ever seen. There are five traps to go up against hundreds. Every second I waste explaining how any of this is possible is a second we lose trying to save Adam."

"What's your plan then? Just bust in there, traps blazing, and hope for the best?" he fumed. I knew he was frustrated. I was too, but there just wasn't time.

I started walking again. "No. I'm going to use myself as bait."

A moment later, he was at my side again. I pulled out a bottle of pills from my pocket.

"What are those?" He reached for the bottle, but I shoved them back inside and continued walking.

"Roman gave them to me. They're placebo sleeping pills. When I get back to the house, I'm going to pretend to be exhausted and pop a few of these to 'nap' alongside Adam. He says they won't be able to resist such a good target. They'll merge into one, and when the fuckers get close to me, I'll bag 'em."

"Tasha, will you stop for one second? Jesus!"

Exasperated, I spun around.

"What?" I snapped.

"You aren't thinking rationally. You just told me that we're up against a demonic coven all rolled into one mega badass boss and you just want to waltz in there with a weapon that has no hope of bringing that many spirits down?"

"First off, *we* aren't doing anything. You're no longer on the mission. Not one foot back in there. Do you understand?" He started to protest, and I held up a finger. "That's an order. You are powerless against what's inside. You can't see them like I can. You won't be able to escape if they come for you, and I'm not risking you being taken, too." I could see his macho-man argument coming, so I tried to soften my tone. I ran my hand across the side of his face. "I can't lose you, Eduardo. I don't know if I'll be able to get Adam back, but I won't risk you. I won't. You are not to step one toe on that property."

"So what am I supposed to do? Just wait outside?" Eduardo was clearly pissed. I'd never taken him off a mission before.

"No. You're going home. Go back to Coffee Haven. Roman has arranged for the bus to pick you up and drop you at the airport. Your ticket info should be in your email soon."

"This is bullshit, Tasha. I won't leave you."

I took his hand, defusing his anger, and pressed my lips against his gently. "You will, because this is a direct order. Go. Now."

His expression changed when he heard the pleading in my voice.

It was a manipulative tactic, sure, but one I had to use. The only way to get him to safety was to make him believe he had my heart. I couldn't help it if he was foolish enough to believe I had one to give.

Leaning in, I gave him one final kiss and walked away. Eduardo didn't follow me, as I knew he wouldn't. He wouldn't disobey an order, even one as impossible as the one I'd given. He was a soldier first and foremost, and I used that to my ultimate advantage. This was between me and the shitstorm waiting for me back at the house.

Reaching into my jacket, I touched the pills again, clutching the bottle in my hand as I went over the plan in my mind. Once I rounded this block, I'd have to pretend that nothing was amiss. I needed to go back inside, cool as a cucumber, and act like Adam was still sleeping, and then quickly join him.

One nagging problem was that I had no idea how they had taken down Adam so fast. Normally, a demonic spirit attacked only at night when we were at our weakest. Even then, it's a bite or claw mark. They sucked Adam's entire soul out in a matter of seconds in full daylight and with Eduardo in the next room! Then again, we'd never dealt with this many souls all at once. Apparently, they could do things I couldn't even fathom.

The hardest part of the plan would be sneaking a trap into the bed with me before they tried to attack, but I had something in mind for that. These assholes may be able to merge into one supreme being, but there was one thing I had that no one could resist, dead or alive.

Back at the house, I unlocked the door and let myself in, humming lightly as I did.

"Adam? You up yet?" I asked, closing the door behind me. Three red spirits entered through the walls to watch me. "I'm afraid we've lost our son to the slopes," I said, faking a laugh. "Although it may have been the snow bunnies he was interested in more than the trails." I reached into my jacket pocket and grabbed the pills, then threw the coat onto the couch. I aimed it directly at a spirit, who didn't move as it came down on him. The jacket worked its way through him like a cloud of smoke, my phone spilling out on the cushion next to it. A moment later the spirit had reformed. That was not good. Spirits I was familiar with usually took hours to reshape themselves when disturbed like that. This one did it in a matter of seconds. These guys were strong. Far stronger than I had anticipated.

Trying to steady my nerves, I ventured up the stairs as fast as I could without actually running. Clearing the landing, I made my way into the bedroom with my red shadows following close behind. In the hall, I was joined by two others.

"I told him to have fun, and I was gonna come back to the house and," I walked in to discover Adam still flat on his back, "pass out." I chuckled, keeping my disguise up.

I glanced at the clock beside him. Almost two hours had gone by. Fuck. I had to work fast.

"Napping sounds like a great idea," I whispered. Adam's bag, which held one of my traps, was at the foot of the bed. "But first, a shower."

Grabbing the bag, I went into the bathroom. I could feel the spirits following me. A total of eight now, by my count. The ruse of a shower had worked. There was an eagerness in the air that hadn't been there before. Spirits, much like humans, were horny things for the most part, and I was counting on that for my plan to work. My body was going to have to be my ace in the hole.

Closing the bathroom door, I opened the bag, thankful to find two of my traps waiting. Each was about the size of a gun with a rectangular barrel. The only way out of this was to get them to combine. One shot to take down many. I might not get them all, but I had five tries to take down as many as I could. It might bag enough to drag Adam out of the house before they could stop me. It was a long shot, but I had to try. I wasn't going to leave a member of my crew behind.

Hence the shower. I needed them distracted. I wanted their eyes on my assets, not the sleight of hand trick I planned to play on them. Emboldened, I walked over to the shower, which had a glass door. Perfect. Turning the water on, I unbuttoned my blouse, one button at a time, feeling the energy in the room shift. I swore half of the demonic spirits I caught were just sexually frustrated auras. They had nowhere to put that much pent-up energy, so they took it out on the humans they were stuck living with. I planned to use their frustration today to my advantage.

As the water warmed, I removed the elastic band that held my French braid in place, working my fingers slowly through my hair to release it into black ribbons down my back. Shrugging out of my shirt, I kicked off my heels as my blouse fell to the floor. I shimmied out of my pants, leaving me only in my black lace bra and panties. They were watching me, and they were pleased.

Might as well give them the full show.

Unhooking my bra, I let it fall next to my blouse and then pulled down my panties slowly, making sure to give them the best view as I bent at the waist to take them off.

Sliding open the shower door, I stepped inside, letting the water saturate my hair and run down my back. Through half-closed eyes, I saw the spirits draw nearer to take in my fully exposed body. So far, so good.

I took as quick a shower as possible. I was well aware that Adam was waiting. I had to work fast. Turning the water off, I grabbed a towel and dried off my hair. Letting the rest of the water trickle down my naked body, I walked over to the bag. Time to make my move.

This was Adam's travel bag, so the traps were mixed in with his clothing, for reasons just like this. I dug around inside until I found one of Adam's T-shirts. Perfect.

I yanked the white shirt over my still wet body. Though the view was now obscured, the shirt clung to my damp skin. *Eyes on the peep show, boys.* Flipping my head upside down as though to finish drying it, I positioned the towel over the bag and "accidentally" dropped it directly over the trap. A moment later, I picked up the towel, with the neatly hidden trap nestled safely inside it. Step one done.

I made my way to the bed with the towel at my side as though I was merely bringing the towel with me to finish drying off my hair. I placed the bundle on the pillow next to Adam and then went back to retrieve the sleeping pills from the bathroom.

"I am dead tired. I hope these sleeping pills help make up for the jet lag," I whispered to myself, but loud enough for the spirits to hear. I popped open the cap and swallowed a handful, dry. I tried not to gag as they went down. I'd assumed they'd taste more like sugar than sand paper.

As the placebos worked their way down my throat like mini razor blades, I tucked the trap under my pillow, then finished towel-drying my hair. I faked a yawn, tossed the towel to the floor, and pulled the sheets over me. I turned onto my side, away from Adam and facing the spirits. One hand over the top of the sheets, one hand under the pillow. My finger on the trigger.

*Come on, you dirty bastards. Join up so I can knock you all out at once.* If Roman was right, there was a very good chance not all of the spirits were even here. His theory was that the Indrori moved around and absorbed souls at will, so if I could take out these eight, it might buy me enough time to recover Adam and get the hell out of dodge. Screw Havenwood Falls. They could find someone more qualified than me to take on this mess. My priority was Adam. Being bait to save him would be worth it.

*Any second now . . .*

The tick of the clock went by painfully slowly. Each second sounded like a drum in my ears. Twenty minutes of trying to keep one eye slightly open was mentally exhausting. Remaining motionless proved easier, however, the longer I lay there. I was growing anxious, ready for them to merge. *When were they going to strike?*

After thirty minutes, I had to shut my eyelid because it started to flutter, which would give me away, but before I did, I saw one of the red spirits disappear. *Finally!* They were merging.

My finger was still on the trigger as I waited. In the warm cocoon of the duvet, I inadvertently let out a large yawn. I chided myself for allowing it to escape, but so far, the spirits hadn't backed off. In fact, I swore they merged again, because there was a definite shift in the temperature. When a second yawn ripped through me, however, a slow onset of panic set in.

I tried to open my eyes, but I couldn't. They were heavy. Like lead. In fact, my whole body felt numb. My head swam like it was drifting in and out of consciousness. I could no longer feel my finger on the trap. I couldn't feel any part of my body.

All at once, reality came crashing down. Roman hadn't given me placebos. I'd been given the real deal. He set me up.

I tried to remember how many I'd swallowed. A few I could probably fight, but I easily took six or seven, maybe more. What had it mattered? They were supposed to be fakes. Jesus. *Why would Roman do this to me?*

My mind spun as I felt the temperature of the room turn to ice. That could only mean one thing. More had arrived. Paralyzed by the sleeping pills, I could do nothing now. I was helpless. I was the one who was trapped and about to be taken into the spirit realm.

# CHAPTER 8

*I* had been told countless times what it was like to die by the souls I'd managed to recover over the years. The stories were so similar that I knew their accounts must have had at least some shred of truth to them. Even with all that knowledge of existence beyond the living, I was still not prepared for what I saw.

The transition began on my lips, like a kiss from a lover who had been out in the cold. The chill then webbed slowly across my face, giving me the sensation of having my head submerged under icy water. All warmth drained away as the feeling traveled down my neck, then spread out to each arm. I was conscious, suddenly, only of the heat within my toes, curled tight under the sheets, until they too succumbed to the pull of the spirit realm.

When I opened my eyes anew, it was with the eyes of a ghost. I had been taken to the other side of the living. Just as Adam had been.

Turning my head around, I could tell that I was still in the house, but everything was dark and blurry, as though I were stuck in dense fog. Looking down at my body, I noticed that it still looked like me, except for one key difference. I was translucent. That actually brought me comfort. It meant I wasn't dead. Not fully. Not yet. If I was a full spirit, the edges of my form wouldn't be quite so defined. I would appear more blob-like.

I was between worlds, so my physical body was still on the bed, while my aura lay trapped here. Wherever here was. I was on the clock now, too. Only now, there was no one around to help.

*Think, Tasha.* Who else could help Adam and me? That, by far, would be the largest hurdle. There were only a handful of people on the planet who recovered souls, and as far as I knew, not a single one was in the United States. The FBI intentionally spread us out on each continent, save for Antarctica, because anyone stupid enough to go there deserved what they got. It made sense logically to be spread out, so we could make sure a Recoverer could arrive at any place around the globe within hours, since time was essential in recovering a soul. However, that also meant the others wouldn't be able to get to Adam and me in time, even if they knew where we were, which they didn't.

That realization hit me like a wall. No one knew where we were. Roman had tricked my team into coming here, so my division had no idea I was even in Colorado, much less trapped in purgatory. Plus, I was scheduled for a vacation anyway, so they wouldn't come looking for me for at least a week, which would be too late. I'd sent Eduardo away, which meant the only person who knew about our situation was the one person who had sent us here. Roman Bishop.

I cursed. We were screwed. Getting us out of here alive was entirely up to me. How, I had no idea. The first thing I needed to do was to find Adam. Maybe he had an idea. After all, he was the logistical one of the team. He'd had a lot more time to think about our situation than I had.

Spinning around, I realized that my movements in this reality were effortless. I looked down and noticed that my feet no longer touched the ground, but hovered about an inch above it instead. This helped to confirm that I wasn't fully dead yet. If I was a true ghost, my movements would be coming harder and slower than this. While I continued to exist in both worlds, it seemed I would retain the physical properties of both realms. It was my only advantage that I could see. As the hours ticked on, however, my ability to move would likely be reduced. This was the sort of problem Adam would love to solve. I had to find him.

Floating around the bed, I searched for any sign of him. While I knew he was on the bed in the human world, here in the spirit world, the bed beside me was empty. He had either moved or had been taken elsewhere.

"Adam!" The sound that came from my throat sounded foreign against my lips. It was more like a moan than an articulated word. I called out his name again around a tongue that was having a hard time making the right noises.

As I floated through the room, I noticed that, while I wasn't completely see-through yet, my aura did have a light blue tinge to it. The aura of a confused spirit. Talk about hitting the nail on the head. Not only was I confused about my actual state of existence, I was confused about how I planned on getting back. I had no traps, no game plan, and absolutely zero clue of how to escape.

*Wait. I did have traps.* They were in this very bedroom.

Determined, I floated toward the pillow I'd hidden the trap under. When I tried to lift the pillow up, however, my hand disappeared straight through it.

"Shit!" I hissed. My voice came out slow, like maple syrup. I should have known I wouldn't be able to manipulate objects here. From my understanding, it took spirits years before they could so much as move a lace curtain, and I was trying to pick up a heavy trap?

An overwhelming sense of dread filled me. I didn't know what to do. I was in a different world, and I didn't know the rules. How was I going to get out of here if I didn't fully understand where *here* was?

That's when I heard a moan that wasn't mine. A voice that was deep and low but laced with agony.

"Adam?"

I floated down the hall, searching for where the sound was, checking the second bedroom and bathroom. I found nothing but dark corners. The cry came again, and this time, I could tell it was coming from below me. I made my way down the stairs and into the living area.

Heading downstairs was harder than I expected. I had to focus hard to move downward versus just hovering straight across the stairwell. It was maddening not being able to get to him faster. When I finally figured out how to point my aura in the direction I wanted to go, I rushed into the living room.

Gone was the bright sun and winter landscape from the bay windows of this morning, and in its place was more darkness. There were no street lamps, no Christmas decorations glowing from neighboring houses. The only thing that stood out in the shadows was a faint blue glow coming from the far corner of the room. It was Adam.

The second I made a move to go toward him, however, the color of the room shifted. Through the floorboards, a deep purple haze seeped through the cracks. Instantly, my training kicked in, suspecting a nerve gas attack, but then I stopped myself. *Nerve gas wouldn't do anything to a spirit.*

With my guard up, I watched as the fog continued to enter the room, this time from every angle—through the walls, around the window frames, down from the ceiling. The smoke converged into one centralized area directly in front of Adam.

I knew, without any shadow of a doubt, that this was the Indrori. In silent awe, I watched the sheer size and color of this thing as it formed into one giant mass. It was unlike anything I had ever encountered in all my years as a Spirit Agent. The color too—dark purple, ominous and chilling—was unlike anything I'd ever seen before. The smoke began to swirl around Adam like a vortex.

"Leave him alone!" I shouted, although the sound that came out was surprisingly weak.

The Indrori did nothing to stop the descent on Adam, so I rushed over in my useless form, ready to fight. When our auras connected, however, I felt the true power of the Indrori. In an instant, I was knocked backward, clear across the room, as though an explosion had gone off. My side actually felt like a shard of metal had pierced me.

The vortex stopped spinning around Adam and changed course— toward me. I held my hands over my head in a feeble attempt to ward the beast off.

"I knew you were a fighter, Agent Young, but I didn't expect you to be foolish as well."

I whipped my head up, realizing that thing had just called me by my name. It knew who I was.

The voice of it was neither male nor female, but somehow a combination of both. The Indrori was communicating with me, but not through any mouth that I could make out. In fact, there was nothing resembling a human form, save for vague skull-like shapes that danced within the smoke. This, more than anything else, confirmed for me that there was definitely more than one soul inside him. There were too many skulls for me to count as they swirled in and out of the smoke.

"Leave him alone," I said again, barely able to see Adam's aura through the Indrori's.

"Or what? You'll swat at me again?" The ripple of different people's laughter danced around the room.

"Take me instead," I shouted. "Let him go and take me!"

"Oh, such chivalry for the man you're not even screwing. I would have thought you'd save that loyalty for the one you are. Where is the boy-toy, Eduardo, by the way? And don't lie to us again and say he's skiing."

"How . . ." I couldn't even form the sentence. *How would the Indrori possibly know about my relationship with Eduardo?* We'd only used our cover stories at the house. How could the Indrori know we were more intimate?

"Oh, Tasha, we know everything about you. Right down to the way you like to be fucked."

My mouth opened to speak, but I couldn't find the words. The confidence with which it spoke made me believe it knew that and more.

"We have been watching you since your birth," It said. "One or more of us have been following your journey very carefully."

They had been stalking me. That wasn't at all freaky.

"Why?"

"Why? Oh, come now, Agent Young, surely you know why the spirit world would be interested in you." The voices echoed around me in chorus.

Despite my very unstable situation, I found myself getting defensive. The work I did was noble, when you got right down to it. I was helping rid the world of harmful spirits.

"Look, I don't know what your problem is, but whatever it is, it's with me, not my partner. Now let him go."

Laughter filled the room. It came from every side, like a souped-up version of surround sound, except this really was all around me.

"You honestly don't know why we have a problem with you?" They asked. "You, a being who has the ability to eradicate our very existence? You who, with a simple pull of a trigger, can destroy decades' worth of work a spirit fought for? You can't fathom why we might take a vested interest in you?"

The truth was becoming uncomfortably clear.

"Agent Young, you, and those like you, are creating the genocide of my kind, and you mean to tell me that you don't understand why we want the problem eliminated?"

And there it was. My crime laid out. I was the ghost world's Hitler, and they wanted to end me.

The only trouble was I saw no way to prevent the Indrori from doing just that.

# CHAPTER 9

The Indrori moved as one giant mass as it circled me from all sides. I could feel the hatred from the spirits within pouring onto me. They wanted to finish the job they started by removing my soul from my body. To a human, the worst they could do as a demonic spirit was leave a few claw marks on the flesh. Together, as one united form, however, they had enough combined energy to literally remove my soul from my still-living body. It left me vulnerable to whatever torment they had in mind next.

"Stop!" Adam's barely audible voice said from behind the Indrori.

"He's taking a rather long time to die, don't you think?" The Indrori sighed. "It's been annoying listening to him whine, but we needed a reason for you to stick around and not run away. We knew you wouldn't be able to resist saving your partner. Even if it meant sacrificing yourself to get here."

*Wait. They think I came up with the plan to be taken on my own? Does that mean Roman isn't working with them?*

"Now that you are finally here, however, we have no need for your partner."

The Indrori's energy left me then and began to swarm around Adam.

"No! Stop. Your issue is with me!" I shouted. "Take me instead."

At that, the Indrori paused. "All in due time, Agent Young."

The purple haze grew thick and dark as it circled Adam. There was one scream of agony from his lips, then it was cut off. The mist from the Indrori flowed into Adam's aura until it dissolved into the dark violaceous haze of the Indrori. In a matter of seconds, Adam was no more.

"No!" I screamed, but even as my lips parted to make the words come out, I knew it was too late. Adam's soul had been consumed by the Indrori.

"What are you waiting for?" I cried. "You brought me here; you've eliminated anyone who could have helped me escape. Just kill me already!"

They seemed to be dragging this out. Likely to make me suffer. Assholes.

"All in due time, Tasha. For now, I must rest. One does get full after a big meal, doesn't one?" Their laughter surrounded me again.

Just like that, the dark cloud around me dissipated and drifted back through the cracks from which they came. For a moment, I didn't move. I thought their disappearance was a trap somehow, but I didn't feel them anywhere in the house. They really had left me alone.

Time was not on my side. I had to find a way out of this house and fast. I had no idea how long of a "rest" he would need before coming back for me, so I needed to escape while I could.

In my semi-transparent state, however, doing anything fast was problematic. Since I didn't have feet that touched the floor, the only way to move was to float, and I had yet to figure out the speed control in this plane, which was maddening all on its own.

Logically, the first place to try was the front door. I had no idea what I'd do once outside, but I couldn't just wait around and be a sitting duck. Maybe I could find Roman and haunt him or something until he figured out a way to help me.

When my hand reached for the door, however, the handle didn't budge because my hand went right through it. Of course it did.

"Fuck. Okay. That's fine. I don't need to use a door. I'm a ghost now. I can float through shit."

Closing my eyes, I moved toward the door, and to my delight, my body easily manifested itself outside as though there was nothing in my way at all. First there was a door, and then, when I opened my eyes, there wasn't.

"Cool."

There was an intense feeling of relief that I was no longer inside the darkness of the house, even if the outside looked just as dark as the inside. I wasn't sure if that was because it was night or if everything in the spirit world was dark.

The first logical thing I needed to do was find a way to reach Eduardo. Maybe the bus hadn't picked him up yet? If he was still around, he could reach out to the Bureau and try to get a Recoverer here in time. I had no idea if I would be able to make a journey that far away, though I had to try. A six-minute walk was nothing for a human, but light-years for a spirit.

When I tried to float down the sanded walkway, however, I discovered that I was unable to move any farther. It felt like I was caught on something.

Glancing behind me, I saw that my lower half was still stuck inside the house. I was half in and half out.

"What the fuck?"

I tried moving forward, but my aura did not come out any farther.

"Shit."

I was tethered to the house.

I chided myself for thinking that because I was only a half spirit, the rules wouldn't apply to me. It was only ancient and demonic souls that had found a way to merge outside of the space they died in. Even then, it wasn't more than a few hundred feet, which meant that wherever the Indrori went, he wouldn't be that far away. That's why he had no issue with leaving me unguarded. He knew I would still be trapped.

Yet I refused to believe that I was helpless. There had to be something I could do. Some way to make the traps work. Some weakness the Indrori had that I could take advantage of. I couldn't be a sitting duck. I just couldn't be.

A wave of rage swept over me as I screamed into my prison.

"Hey, Universe! I could use some fucking help here!" I shouted to no one in particular. I was a firm believer in karma and evil always losing, but right now that picture wasn't looking so good. "Do you hear me, world? I need help!"

*"Stop shouting already. I can hear you, Jeez Louise!"*

My head whipped around, trying to find where the female voice came from. Was the Indrori back? If so, why was it only one voice I could hear?

"Who's there?"

*"My name is Harper Sinclair. I'm a spiritual scribe. You called out for help. Here I am."* The girl's voice sounded bored. Like she's said this speech a hundred times before. *"Wait. Who are you? You don't sound like a demonic spirit."*

"A spiritual what? And demonic? Where the fuck are you?" I floated from room to room, trying to figure out where the voice was coming from. I refused to believe it was coming from my own mind. Was this a trick of the Indrori?

*"My location doesn't matter. Look, I'm just trying to help. If you're not a demonic spirit, you must be damn close to one, because that's the only kind of spirit I can talk to. Unless you're an angel. Are you?"*

She thought I was a demonic spirit, or worse, an angel. That must mean she was human, and a psychic of some kind.

"Look, I'm no angel. And I'm not a ghost, either. Not fully anyway. I'm a human." I looked down at my figure, well, through it. "Sort of. It's complicated. Where are you right now?"

I could hear her exasperation in my mind.

*"If you must know, I'm in the woods and was about to take a picture of a nesting red-tailed hawk, but you keep shouting in my head, which is super weird and uber annoying. I've never actually heard anyone before, not like this. My abilities have never worked like this. You are kind of freaking me out. So can you tell me what the heck is going on?"*

I decided it mattered little that I couldn't see this voice or that I had no idea what a psychic scribe was. At the moment, she was the only thing around that might help me figure this mess out. I'd asked the universe for help, and this was what it gave me. I was going with it.

For the next several minutes, I tried to explain, as succinctly as I could, the events of the last few hours, which even I was having a hard time believing.

*"Wait. You're up against an Indrori?"* came Harper's stunned reply when I had finished.

"Yeah," I said, relieved that she seemed to know what I was up against. "What do you know about the Indrori?"

*"I'm the one it contacted first. I told the Court about it as soon as it happened. Are you Tasha Young?"*

"The one and only." This Harper must have been the source Roman kept referring to. "Great. So we're on the same page. How the hell do I defeat it?"

There was no answer to my question, which I didn't take as a good sign. Surely, if there had been an easy way to do it, she would have rattled it off just to be done with me.

"Harper? What do I do?" Still no answer. "Harper?"

Great. She probably knew I was a goner.

*"Sorry. I'm back. I needed to get another journal. I tore through the last one."*

"A journal? Why do you need a journal? Are you writing down my final words or something?"

*"No,"* she said. Her voice felt rushed. *"It's a long story, but it's how I communicate with the other side. By writing. Usually, I talk and the spirits answer through writing. You are different. This is backwards for me. Maybe because of where you are. Are you . . . dead?"*

"No, I'm not dead," I said with more conviction than I felt. I *wasn't* dead . . . yet.

*"Of course. Sorry. I don't really understand the logistics of how we are talking right now. This is all very strange for me,"* she apologized.

"You and me both, kid." Though I had no idea what Harper looked like, I sensed she was young. I was guessing early to mid-twenties. My entire fate rested on a girl who spoke to spirits with a pen. I was fucked.

*"Tasha, listen to me very carefully. I need to know where you are right now."*

"I'm in the house hiding from that thing!"

Harper's voice became agitated. *"You're inside the actual house on Thirteenth? The big green one? Alone?"*

"Yeah. That's where Roman sent me."

*"This was not the plan. I'm on my way!"*

At those words, a reckless plan formulated in my head. I could teach her how to use the traps. So what if no one but me had ever been able to use them successfully before? I'd be right beside her. I could tell her where to aim it. It was an option. The only one I had.

*"Oh, and Tasha, try to stay hidden as best you can, though up against an Indrori that's kind of impossible,"* Harper added.

"Gee, thanks for the vote of confidence."

*"This is no joke,"* Harper warned. *"I got a glimpse of this Indrori when it first reached out, and it's nothing like the other demons and spirits I've worked with. I don't know how the hell you ended up there alone, but I need to let the Court know. We'll need backup, for sure."*

"I'm not so sure they would help, considering one of their own set me up. That rat, Roman Bishop, is the one who drugged me," I spat. If I got out of this, his was the first neck I was gonna wring.

*"That makes no sense. Sure, the Bishop boys like to stir up trouble, but this is insane, even for them. Look, let me handle that. You just stay hidden."*

Her voice sounded so small against the enormity of the situation.

"Thanks, kid. Hope to see you soon."

Just like that, the connection I had with Harper was severed. It felt about the same as a door being shut in my face.

Still, there was good news. Harper was on the way. Possibly with backup from the Court. What a bunch of suits were going to do I had no idea, but then, nothing about Havenwood Falls made much sense.

For the moment, there was hope. I clung to that small shot in the dark as tightly as I did to the sliver of my humanity.

# CHAPTER 10

*I* tried not to count the seconds since I last spoke with Harper. Just like I tried not to jump at every sound I heard. So far, I was failing on both counts. The Indrori could be back any time, and without Harper, there was no hope of escape. I was a mouse in a cage, waiting for the snake to pounce.

My fingers ran absently along my waist to where my own snake tattoo was. I could almost feel it wrapping tighter around me, squeezing the life from me . . . much like the Indrori wanted to do.

I had no idea how big Havenwood Falls really was or where Harper was coming from within it. I was banking on her arriving in enough time for me to teach her how to use the trap before our giant purple people eater came back to dine on my soul.

"Please, God, if you're listening . . . Thanks for sending Harper . . . Now, if you get me out of this mess, I'll . . . stop drinking. No. I won't. You and I both know that's a lie. Um, I'll stop sleeping around. As much," I amended.

That's when I heard a noise. A telltale ringing of my cell phone. Was God calling me on my cell? Curious, I went back inside and into the living room, where I saw it on the couch, face up, where it had fallen out when I ditched my coat before I was forcibly removed from my flesh.

It wasn't God. It was Eduardo. Instinctively, I went to pick it up, but, of course, my fingers went right through the cell and into the couch beneath it.

"Damn it!" What a frustrating place to be in. I was utterly useless and defenseless.

Because the phone was face up, I could at least read the text message.

**Eduardo: You know, the guys all warned me. They told me you'd burn my ass. I was convinced I was gonna be the one to change that. Guess I was just another notch on your belt, huh?**

I stared at the words illuminated on my screen, hating the truth behind them. While I hadn't quite finished playing with Eduardo, I would have sent him packing soon enough. After a while, I cut them all loose. So why did his words sting so much?

**Eduardo: You could have just told me you were done with me, you know? I never took you to be a liar. That's cool. Whatever. Give my regards to Roman. And tell him to wear a hat.**

Of course he thought he'd been dumped for Roman. He wasn't totally off. If I hadn't been in this current mess, I may have pursued Roman. I'd be pissed at myself for going after the bastard, but I probably would have.

Ugh. Roman. That slimy bastard. If I ever got out of this, I was gonna cut his dick off. He'd be lucky if I didn't do worse after he threw me in this trap. I didn't care what Harper thought. Roman was involved in this somehow. I just knew it.

*"Tasha? You still alive?"*

My head whipped around toward the front door. A female voice was calling out from behind it.

"Harper? Thank God."

I floated back through the door and got my first look at the person I had only been able to hear in my head. She wasn't at all like I was imagining, aside from the young part. That, I got right. She was in her early twenties, but she was way more casual than I had presumed. She had on jeans and a ratty old sweatshirt, which nearly swallowed up her petite frame. She wore her long brown hair tied back in a messy ponytail and had on massive hiker boots that looked two sizes too big.

When I looked back up, Harper was focused on a journal, writing something down. She didn't seem to notice me floating literally two inches in front of her.

*"Tasha, where are you now? Is the Indrori back?"* I saw her write on her pad.

"I'm fine. I'm standing right in front of you."

Harper looked up at me and stared right through me before she frowned.

*"Ah, there you are. Sort of,"* she wrote. *"You're like a shadow."*

I nodded my head. "Well, I only see translucent-like auras in the spirit world, but I can see that you're solid. Guess that means you're still alive," I said.

Her eyebrows crinkled, and she went back to the journal. *For the moment.*

This was one bizarre conversation—me speaking and her writing —but I was more than thankful to have someone here who might be able to help me.

*"So . . . what's the plan?"* Harper asked.

"You come in, I show you how to use the spirit trap, we capture this jackass, and somehow get me home in the next four to five hours."

*"What happens after five hours?"*

"Oh, nothing major. Just that I can't come back to the land of the living after that. The brain doesn't function away from the soul after that long. So we're kind of on a clock here. Let's hope I didn't lock the door when I came in, or you'll have to break in."

*"Right."*

She tucked her journal under one arm and placed a hand on the door. If I had breath to hold, I would have as she turned the knob. Mercifully, it opened without issue.

"Finally, something goes my way," I said as Harper walked into the house. Her eyes were wide as she scanned the place, probably expecting to find the Indrori.

*"How long do you think we have until it comes back?"* I could hear her fear inside my head. This wasn't fair, me dragging her into this. It wasn't her fight, but without her, I was defenseless. I wasn't able to save Adam, but I was going to make sure that Harper wasn't hurt. Somehow.

"The gun is in the bedroom. Through the living room, top of the stairs," I said, knowing we had little time to play with.

*"Gun? You never mentioned a gun. You said trap. I don't know how to fire a gun!"*

Her writing was shaky. I was freaking her out. I couldn't have her bolting on me. Not when I didn't have any other options.

"It *is* a trap. I shouldn't have said gun. Bad choice of words. It works sort of like a gun in that there is a trigger to pull, and I guess it's sort of shaped like a gun, but you won't be killing anyone with it."

I wasn't sure if I made it worse or better.

*"Okay, right. I can't kill anyone because they are already dead."* She bit her bottom lip as she looked down at the words.

I didn't mention that she could kill me if she didn't succeed, but that likely wouldn't help her nerves.

"Exactly. You'll trap the Indrori, and I'll bring them back to the feds, and we'll dispose of them properly."

Harper looked at me funny. *"Dispose of? You can't get rid of a demonic spirit. It's not possible. You have to send them back to Hell or the Infernum. It's the only safe place for a spirit as evil as the one after you."*

"'Cause that worked so great before."

*"I know it's hard to believe it, but the Court will help make this right again."*

"How long have you lived here?" I asked.

*"I was born here,"* she said, putting down her pen and then holding up her wrist. On it was a tattoo of a writing quill. I nodded, remembering what Roman had told me about the town branding not only their supernatural people with magical tattoos, but their visitors, too. The quill seemed fitting for her power.

An errant thought slipped through my mind. What kind of tattoo would I get and where would I put it? I chided myself for the thought. A tattoo being placed on me required that my soul wasn't going to get sucked out *and* that it found a way to get back into my physical body. Two things that seemed beyond hope. At best, I could try to take this thing down so no one else would be taken, or at the very least, weaken it until someone from the Court could.

"In all seriousness, Harper, what makes you think this thing won't just break out again if we find a way to cage it again?"

*"That's up to those with higher pay scales than us to figure out,"*

Harper wrote. "*Getting them back there is going to be the tricky part. I can command demons, a few at a time, but I don't know if I'm strong enough to control that many spirits, so let's hope your trap works.*"

"Control demons?" I asked. "You know what? I don't wanna know."

"*So, this gun—trap thing—I just point it at the Indrori, and that's it?*"

"Yeah, point and shoot," I said. It was a good thing she couldn't see my face, or she would have seen the lie there. It was a tad more complicated than that, but the less she knew about the odds of it working, the better. A nervous trigger finger didn't help anyone.

"The traps are up the stairs. In the bedroom, first door on the right."

Harper nodded and headed for the stairs. I followed her, trying to urge her along faster, but also trying not to freak her out.

"There should be one in the bag right near the bed," I instructed when she made it into the bedroom.

"*Oh my god,*" Harper wrote, stopping once she saw the bed. She was looking at Adam's face-down, limp body. Mine was lying beside his.

"That's my partner. That thing under the covers beside him? That's me." It was weird seeing myself outside of my own skin. Though it was only a lump under a duvet, I knew if I pulled back the covers, I'd see my own lifeless body. "Adam is still alive, in that his organs are still functioning. He's breathing in and out . . . but his soul —" I fought back my emotion. It was still too hard to think about. "He's never going to come out of that vegetative state. They took his soul. The thing that made Adam, Adam." It was so hard to think I was never going to be able to talk to him again. "That's what is going to happen to me if the Indrori has his way."

"*Right. Let's not fail, okay?*" Her shoulders rose back as though she fully understood the stakes now.

Letting out a breath, Harper went over and unzipped the bag with ease. She lifted a trap up and shifted it to her other hand.

"*Wow, it's heavy,*" she scribbled with her right hand, as the trap remained in her left.

"Yeah, you're gonna want to grab a second one. One for each hand. Just to be safe."

Harper lowered the trap and looked in my general direction. Her eyes landed about a foot lower than where my eyes really were. A spot I was accustomed to men staring. She wasn't ogling me, even though her eyes were wide. She just didn't know how tall I was.

*"You think I'll need two of them?"*

I didn't have the heart to tell her she'd need to likely fire fifty of them at a time to take this thing down. That's when it hit me how big the stakes were for Harper. All this time, I'd been focusing on this being the only way to stop the Indrori, but what about her? I was sticking her in the same situation Roman had put me in. This was a bad idea. I couldn't do it. I wouldn't put her life on the line.

"You know what?" I said. "I've changed my mind. This is too dangerous. You need to get out of here before it comes back."

*"I'm not leaving you. I can help. I've been working with demons for almost a year now. Besides, I have these traps. I'm not some defenseless kid, Tasha. I can do this."* She dropped her notepad to the ground, effectively cutting off our communication.

"Harper!" I shouted. "The plan won't work, okay? Even if you hit this thing dead in the center with both guns—it won't be enough. I was a fool to drag you into this. You need to get out of here before—"

At that moment, I felt a shift in the air. I knew Harper could feel it, if not see it too, because her posture stiffened.

"Get out of here. Now!" I hissed.

She stood there, like a deer stuck in headlights for a long moment. She held only one trap in her hand. Her entire body trembled as she lifted the gun toward the vibrant violet aura that merged its way into the bedroom from all around us.

"Sorry to keep you waiting, Agent Young," the Indrori began. "I had to make a quick trip to the bus stop. Couldn't let your boy-toy miss out on all the fun. He was delicious."

No. Eduardo. The fucker took him, too. He was tracking down anyone that was close to me.

"You bastard!" I shrieked. I felt my insides rattle against the pent-up rage. I was about to lurch for him when Harper shouted.

"Get out of the way! I got this!"

The Indrori shifted slightly to my left to take in Harper. The trap was raised between her two shaking hands.

"Agent Young, you brought me a snack. How delightful. But

really, after devouring you, I'm not sure I could eat another bite." The laughter rose from the Indrori and reverberated across the room.

"Leave her out of this!" I yelled, essentially sealing her fate. It was a fatal slip of the tongue. I had just let the Indrori know who he should go after next.

"Harper, put the gun down and get out of here," I shouted at her. Couldn't she see how much danger she was in?

She ignored me and lifted the gun higher. Though she likely wouldn't be able to make out the exact shape of the Indrori as well I could, she must have seen its general direction, because the gun was pointed in the right spot. She closed her eyes and shot.

# CHAPTER 11

*H*arper stood there, arm outstretched, eyes pinched tight, likely too afraid to open them to see the reality of the situation that I saw all too well. She had missed her mark by a mile.

"God damn it, Harper, run, now, or I'll kill you myself," I spat, at the exact same time as the Indrori moved in on her.

I forced my aura in front of the large mass. It halted as though amused.

"Rule number one: You don't get to touch my friends," I said.

"Friends? Oh, Agent Young, you don't have any friends." It was a childish retort. One that would have normally bounced right off me, but for some reason it stuck there like glue. The monster was right. I'd never had a friend. Not a genuine one. Ever since I discovered my gift as a child, people have only wanted what I could give them back—a loved one's life. I had gotten used to being used and, as a result, became suspicious of anyone who wanted to get close to me.

How could the Indrori know that I had always been a loner, though? Their tone indicated that they had intimate knowledge of my life.

"Tasha, get out of the way. I can handle this," Harper said. Her eyes were narrowed. Thin fingers danced through the air as though she were writing on an invisible sheet of paper. She was writing words that I couldn't decipher, but it seemed to be doing something, because the room grew darker then. Shadows appeared from the corners, and I began to panic, thinking the Indrori was doing this.

"Foolish girl. You can't control us. One demonic soul, perhaps, but united, we are too strong for you."

Harper didn't seem deterred. She continued to write in the air as more shadows emerged. It was only then that I realized Harper was summoning the shadows.

"What are those, Harper?"

"Spirits," she grunted through her efforts. "I'm summoning them to help from the Infernum."

"Spirits? Harper, no! You can't—this thing *absorbs* spirits! You'll just make it stronger!"

"I've got control of them, Tasha," she strained. "Now stay back."

But it was clear to me that this was a losing battle. Already I could see violet tendrils reaching out to the dark shadows, wrapping themselves around the spirits Harper had summoned. Within moments, the shadows were gone, and the Indrori was even larger.

"Enough games!" the Indrori shouted. A wave of energy rocked through the room, bouncing Harper and me backward.

"Are you okay?" I asked. The energy blast had knocked her straight off her feet.

"It's too strong. I need to find Desi. I'll be back, Tasha. I'll bring help!"

A moment later, she was on her feet and bounding down the stairs. I didn't have time to ask her who Desi was, but I knew that whoever it was, it would be too late. There would be nothing left of me to save.

Scrambling to get my aura centered, I followed after Harper. I knew I couldn't escape the house, but I was stalling for time. I needed to think of something to do to weaken this bastard, and right now the only thing I could think of was trying to force it to use energy to chase after me. This was a game of cat and mouse that I didn't want to lose.

Downstairs I stopped in the living room. I heard the front door slam. Harper had made it out. That was a small comfort. Though we barely knew each other, I felt like we were friends. She hadn't wanted anything from me. In fact, I had been the one using her talent.

It didn't take long for the Indrori to drip down from the ceiling. The purple aura looked no worse for wear despite my efforts. Figures.

"Looks like it's just you and me now, *Beetlejuice*."

The thing was stronger than ever now, thanks to Harper's help. I had no idea how I was going to get out of this alive. The only thing I could think to do was try to stall for time. My mouth got me out of plenty of sticky situations. Maybe I'd find a way to talk myself free.

"Before you take my soul," I began, "I have a question or two."

The Indrori stopped its advancement toward me and hovered as though curious what I might want to know. I took it as permission to keep going.

"What's your end game? You take my soul and then what? Your revenge is over. Whatever will you do with your time? Off to the Bermuda Triangle, are you?"

"I'm disappointed, Tasha. I would have thought you had figured it out by now."

I didn't answer, because I didn't have a clue as to what he was getting at. He was playing a mind game. I just didn't know the rules. Still, I wanted to keep up the talking to give Harper as much time as I could to get far away from here.

Seemingly frustrated by my stupidity, his aura came closer. So close that I could feel his energy forcing itself against my own.

"You're the last of your kind, Tasha. The last Recoverer in the world."

I had no idea where he was getting his intel, but he was wrong. "No, I'm not. There are at least five of us, dipshit."

A small laughter surrounded me.

"Actually, there were six of you. *Were* being the operative word. Now, it's just you. Naturally, I saved the best for last. You are the end of an era."

"Bullshit," I hissed, but I couldn't help but wonder if they were right. I had no way of knowing if they were lying or not. Recoverers were so spread out, in different time zones. It's not like we kept in touch. We all had our own missions, but if they were all gone, surely, I would have heard something. Right?

I shook my head, blurring my aura as I did. I was fading. The Indrori's proximity was draining me.

"Fine, so you put an end to bringing back a few dead, so what? There are other spirit agents. We can still take you down!"

The Indrori split apart just then. Gone was the purple mass, in its place a sea of red with a few blue auras still clinging to what little humanity they had. I realized then, it was this combination of the demonic and the confused spirits that gave the Indrori its coloring.

"Your Spirit Agents can handle one of us at a time, Agent Young," the Indrori screamed, "but as one, we are unstoppable." A moment later, the auras were assembled again. Their power was in their numbers. I had to find a way to break them apart.

"Our teams are smart. They'll figure out a way to stop you."

More laughter. I was really getting sick of that sound.

"If they live long enough."

I couldn't help it. I let out a chuckle of my own. "What? You're going to take down every human spirit agent, too? There are literally thousands of us, with more being trained by the minute."

His reply came all at once, hot against my ear as if he was standing in the flesh beside me.

"You underestimate our power. We'll get every last human who wishes us harm. Once you are gone, there will be no one to stop us. After you, the endgame is simple. Every single person in Havenwood Falls. And then every single supernatural in this world, including the one known as the Collector. Their days of imprisoning our kind for merely existing are over."

Before I could react, their aura pulled away from mine as they circled what was left of my spirit in the same tornado-type motion they had done before they took Adam. I wasn't long for this world, whether the Indrori took my soul or not. There was no way out of the end game. No way to warn anyone else what the Indrori was up to after he took me down. I could only hope that Harper got herself out of Havenwood Falls before he had time to carry out his plan.

Wait. Maybe she could warn the others.

"Harper!" I shouted, knowing she wasn't here in the house, but praying she would hear me again. She did before, and I hadn't even been knowingly trying to reach her. "If you get this—get out of the town. Get everyone out! I can't stop it. The Indrori is going to take you all! Run!"

"It's too late, Tasha. Much, much too late."

His anger pulsed through all of their auras, causing the air around me to grow hot. It felt like I was at the gates of Hell. The cold of the spirit realm had become hotter than a sauna.

"Before we finish this, don't you know why we saved you for last? Why we didn't rip your soul out from your mother's womb thirty-two years ago when we first felt your presence?" the Indrori asked.

"Because that would have been impossible?" I spat.

"You underestimate our power!" the Indrori shouted as the spirits circled around me again and again. My head felt dizzy watching the skulls dance around me. "You humans always have," he went on. "What you fail to realize is that spirits know the *moment* their destroyer is made. It's a twist of cruel fate that we are not strong enough on our own to do anything about it. But together, as one united front, we've been able to stop any new Recoverers mere weeks after conception."

"What?" I gasped. That couldn't possibly mean what I thought it did.

"Oh, don't give me that look. Miscarriages happen all the time."

This thing really was evil. While I didn't care for kids myself, I would never want to harm them, let alone smother them completely.

"Why would you care about Recoverers?" I gasped. "We *help* humans stuck in the spirit realm! We save them from becoming lost between two planes for the rest of their existence. Why would you want to prevent us from that? I can see why you'd be pissed at us for trapping your ass, but why would helping save them from a life in purgatory tick you off?"

The Indrori pulsed with what I could only assume was anger.

"Did it never occur to you who might be pulling those lost souls to the other side in the first place? Souls stuck in purgatory are the easiest for us to manipulate. They require minimal energy to absorb. It's how we grew so strong so fast. Each one you rip away is another strike against us!" the Indrori raged.

I wasn't about to be intimidated. Not when I was already a goner. I would get my answers one way or the other.

"All right, fine, so why didn't you do the same to me? Why didn't you take me while I was still in the womb?" I shouted.

The swirling of the vortex slowed, but the grip on me didn't lessen.

"Because you, dear Tasha, are special. You have an aura that has been virtually impenetrable to us since your conception. Every time we've tried to take your soul, we have failed."

"How many times have you tried to kill me?" I heard myself ask.

"Three hundred and eighty-seven."

"Jesus," I whispered. That rattled me and gave me hope all at the same time.

"What makes you so confident you'll succeed this time, jackass?"

It probably wasn't smart to taunt this thing, but maybe this wasn't the end for me. Maybe I was stronger than they were?

"Why will we succeed this time?" the Indrori asked, forcing my attention back on the swirling spirits. "Because we finally figured out what the issue was. Your bloodline was too strong."

The Indrori's auras danced close to me again. Though they weren't physically touching me, I felt like I was being pinned down by a cement truck.

Just then, the Indrori's shape changed. A long branch broke away from the rest of the mass like a smoky tentacle.

"Sorry, this might hurt a little." The Indrori laughed.

Unable to move, I watched in horror as the tentacle slinked its way around my waist, mirroring the pattern of my snake tattoo. The smoke against my aura felt like a branding iron everywhere it touched. I let out a scream as intense pain enveloped my core. The tendril tightened around my spirit, and I heard a loud crack, followed by another. From the location of the pain, I knew it was breaking my ribs one by one. Because I was within two planes of existence, I could feel not only the heat of the aura's touch, but the physical pain of my human form crushing within its grip.

"I can destroy you now, Tasha, because I have absorbed your bloodline."

If I hadn't been in so much agony, I would have asked him what he meant, but as it stood, I was little more than a ragdoll. I couldn't see anything against the blinding white-hot pain. My thoughts were splintering, just like my spirit.

"You thought you could keep your parents safe from me, simply by cutting ties to them? Or maybe you just didn't know?" The Indrori waited for me to reply, but there was no way I could speak. I was in too much pain. I just wanted the pain to stop. *Please, make the pain stop.* "Foolish girl. Did it never occur to you that you inherited your dual ability from someone?"

I knew they were messing with my head now. My parents weren't like me. Far from it. My dad was a mailman, and my mom was a librarian. You couldn't find two more boring people on the planet. They didn't have the ability to bring back the dead. And they sure as hell never saw the spirits I did.

"It's rare, you know, to have a Seer and Recoverer marry, but to have both mutations passed down to their child? Unheard of. It's what set you apart, Tasha. That's what made you untouchable all these years. You had both of their DNA to protect you. We were most displeased."

I made a pathetic attempt to escape the vise grip I was in, but it made no difference.

"Think of it this way—at least you don't need to send them a Christmas card this year."

I shook my head violently, refusing to believe their words. My parents were fine. This was just a way to break down my spirit. Yet, at the same time, I knew the Indrori was telling the truth. It was the only thing that made sense, in a sick and twisted sort of way. My parents never really freaked out about my visions. They only told me to keep it secret. They never even took me to a doctor to get my head examined. Could they possibly have known what I was, because they had similar abilities?

"No!" I cried. A wave of anger shot through me, and the Indrori's grip suddenly lessened just enough so I felt a bit of relief.

"Interesting," the Indrori said. "You're stronger than we imagined. Even with the help of your parents' spirits inside of us, you are still proving to be a worthy foe."

The tendril squeezed around me one more time, and I knew it had just cracked another rib.

"Well, this is embarrassing. You seem to have drained us. Another soul to feast upon should do the trick, though. Perhaps someone strong and youthful, and good with a camera?"

Harper.

"No!" my raspy voice choked out, but it was too late. The Indrori had already dissipated through the floorboards, leaving me as emotionally drained as if I had been gutted like a deer.

The Indrori was taking away everything that mattered to me before it took my life. They were making me suffer the way they felt my kind had made them suffer. And there was absolutely nothing I could do about it.

# CHAPTER 12

*A*lone in the house once again, I waited for a surge of energy to kick in. An adrenaline rush or something. This was my last opportunity to get out of here and try to save Harper and everyone else in Havenwood Falls, but I couldn't move. It felt like I was sitting in a pool of mud up to my neck. Their touch had drained me, much like I had drained them.

This was what Adam must have felt in his final moments. He, too, just sat there and let the Indrori take his soul. I understood now that it wasn't because he didn't want to fight the Indrori off, but because he literally couldn't. The hold that single tendril had on me was too strong. I couldn't imagine the pain of the Indrori's full form on me. I felt as though I was being burned alive. Even now, my skin was still hot where the tendril had coiled around me.

"*Tasha!*" A small but mighty voice pierced my mind. It was so faint, I thought I'd imagined it.

"Har-per?" My voice was thin. "Stay . . . away. Get . . . out." There was so much I wanted to say, but I didn't have the ability to do it.

"*Save your voice. I heard your screams. I know you're hurt. I got your message loud and clear. I've been trying to get back into the house, but the Indrori is making it really hard. I might not be able to get back in just yet, but I can still help you from out here. The Court is rallying supernaturals. Right now, we have to get you out of there. I tried to cage the Indrori on my own while it was attacking you, but I couldn't make him budge."*

I tried to reply, to tell her that she needed to stay far away from here. She seemed to understand what I was about to say, because she answered my unspoken protest.

*"Don't worry. I'm not anywhere near the house, but my ability—I can force demonic spirits to do my bidding, but this thing—it's too strong. The only way to save you is to get you out of there. But I need your help. How do you recover a soul? How do we bring you back to the human realm?"*

If I had been able to laugh, I would have. The only way to recover my soul was with the help of another Recoverer. And the Indrori had wiped all of them out.

"Not possible. Save your . . . self," I gasped. Didn't she understand the danger she was in? That they all were in?

*"Maybe Octavia can help?"*

"Who?" I'd never heard of a Recoverer by that name, so it must have been one of her people, though it did sound vaguely familiar in some far away way.

*"Octavia. She's a necromancer. She can bring back the dead. She's on probation, and she's not supposed to use her powers, but the Court could make an exception."*

"No. Leave me. Save . . . self."

*"I'm not leaving you to die! Roman will be there soon, Tasha. He'll know what to do. Stay with me."*

I tried to shake my head even though she couldn't see the gesture. Roman wasn't going to help; he was the jackass that wanted me gone.

"Roman, traitor. In on it."

*"You think Roman Bishop wanted you killed by this thing? He's an asshole, sure, but he's on the coven's High Council. He's been helping more than anyone to try to figure out a way to get you out. He went outside our original plan, because he has zero patience, but if he sent you in there alone, he had to have a reason."*

As she spoke to me, the pain around my torso intensified. My flesh felt like it was burning. I cried out in pain. "Ah, God! Help me." I panted between waves of agony. "It's burning."

*"Burning?"* I heard Harper screech. *"Where is the fire? What is burning?"*

"Me. Skin. Burning. Everywhere. Harper. Hide. He's coming . . . you." I tried to focus my brain on getting Harper to safety, but the pain was too great. I tried to pinpoint what part of my body was hurting the most, but it really did feel like it was all over. My torso, my back, the base of my neck, even my Garden of Eden was burning. Wait. *The pain mirrored the exact location of my tattoo.*

What the hell?

I looked down at myself and noticed distinct orange glowing inside my aura. In fact, it looked like about ten scales of my tattoo along my midsection were glowing. Judging by the pain in other places, I was willing to bet there were glowing scales there, too.

"Harper," I croaked. "My tattoo . . . is glowing."

For several minutes there was no answer from Harper as I stared at the vibrant scales etched into my skin. Trying to focus on each spot of pain, I was guessing there were about twenty or so glowing patches spread around my body, but all within the confines of the tattoo. Was the Indrori branding me? Burning their dark energy into my flesh? Was this how it was going to end? In a blaze straight into Hell?

*"Tasha,"* Harper said. *"Listen to me carefully. When did you get your tattoo?"*

When did I get my tattoo? What the hell did that have to do with anything? I was used to people asking about my ink because it was so unique, and because I had a knack for showing it off, but I couldn't see how knowing when I got it made any difference.

*"It's probably nothing, but Roman is on the phone with me, and he's asking."*

"Long time ago," I spat out between throbs of pain. Jesus, this hurt.

*"Tasha . . . Roman said . . ."* Her voice shook, which meant it couldn't be good news. *"He said* you *are the trap."*

I must have been losing my mind, because that statement made no sense. This was the end. It was likely a matter of minutes now before my brain turned into mush.

*"Tasha, listen to me,"* Harper urged, trying to hold my attention, but it was waning by the second. I was so drained. *"Roman needs to know why you got your tattoo."*

These were probably my last moments left in this world, and Roman wanted to talk about my tattoo?

"To . . . cover gross . . . birthmarks," I said through gritted teeth. "More each year. Ah, fuck, this hurts!"

That's when I saw the telltale purple of the Indrori seep into the room. They were in the house, just below me now.

*"Those weren't birthmarks, Tasha. Roman says they were ghosts you trapped. Wait, what?"* I heard the confusion in Harper's voice as she relayed Roman's message to me.

"No. I used traps." I couldn't believe these were going to be my final words, an argument about the fundamentals of how I did my job.

*"He said, 'Then why can no one else use the traps but you?' Tasha! You sent me in there knowing the trap wouldn't work for me?"* she asked.

Whoops. Wait, I hadn't told her about the trap issue. Or Roman for that matter. Only my team members and Agent Duncan knew that. Roman must have bewitched Duncan or something to extract the information. Of course he did. Fucker.

*"Tasha . . . those dark spots that showed up on your skin . . . Roman said they aren't all ink. The scales are the souls you've captured. They are trapped in your skin. You. Are. The. Trap."*

As more and more purple smoke wafted into the room, I pondered what she said. Was it true? Is that why Adam could never figure out where the souls went from my traps? Was that why my skin felt like it was on fire now, because I had just absorbed some of the Indrori's demonic spirits?

I watched as the Indrori formed into one mass and couldn't help but notice that it didn't seem quite as large as it had moments ago. Maybe that was just my mind latching on to one last shred of hope.

Still, if I really was the trap, then this game was about to get interesting.

"You must be quite proud of yourself, Agent Young," the Indrori spat as he merged closer to me.

"Very," I said, my voice surprisingly strong now. If what Harper told me was true, this jackass was about to go down. If not, I was. Either way, this was going to end. Now.

"How did you warn the girl I was coming? I'm *dying* to know your secret."

"Guess that's just one of the many surprises there are about me that you will never know."

"Agent Young, there is nothing that I don't know about you. And once you are merged with me, there is nothing that will stand in our way. Not even your precious Collector."

I didn't know anything about a Collector, and right now I didn't care. All that mattered was how much I could egg this thing on and get it closer to me.

"You talk a big talk for a dead spirit floating."

The Indrori moved closer to me. Its form split again into a long tendril, and I suddenly realized I had no idea how to fight this thing.

"What do I do?" I shouted to Harper. In all the confusion and acceptance that I might be the weapon Roman said I was, I didn't actually think to ask *how* to use it.

*"Tasha, he doesn't know. That's why he sent you in with the Indrori in the first place. He wanted to see your power in action. He wanted to know how you did it himself."* I could hear the tears in her voice. *"I am so sorry. Look, I've left a message with Addie. She can help. I'm on my way with or without her. I'll be there as soon as I can."*

Great. I was to be a guinea pig for Roman's twisted sense of curiosity. Why didn't that surprise me? He was exactly the sort of guy who would throw me into a death pit to see how I'd manage. Jackass. And now Harper was on her way into this mess, and dragging another stranger in, too, but it would be too late.

"What do you do?" the Indrori asked, echoing the question I had posed to Harper. "You die, Agent Young. You die."

With that, the tendril coiled again around my aura, covering the faded blue of my aura with their own evil hue. All at once, I was paralyzed again. My soul was bending to their will. Crushing pain. Burning. Agony. I knew, even without looking, that I was glowing again. There was one difference, though. I wasn't scared anymore. This time, I understood the reason for the pain. Like I never had before.

In the past, whenever I took down a ghost, there was always a "kickback" from the trap—a heat that radiated off the gun. I realized now that it wasn't the gun. It was me. I was absorbing the aura's soul. Their energy was burned into my flesh. Just like Roman said. I was the trap. It hurt so much now simply because I was absorbing so many souls at once.

The longer the Indrori held me, the faster they would be caged.

That knowledge sent a surge of energy through me. I didn't need to do anything but accept and receive their souls into my flesh.

"What . . . what are you doing?" the Indrori sputtered after a few minutes. They must have felt the shift in energy.

"Winning." I smiled.

The Indrori seemed to sense what I was doing, because he tried to release the tendril, but he couldn't. Unbeknownst to me, I had latched my own aura onto the Indrori. I was in control now.

Whatever I was doing simply by staying in contact with the Indrori was working, because his coloring was growing less intense by the minute. The sheer size was diminishing as well with each passing second. What used to fill up the entire bedroom now only commanded a fourth of it.

Now that I wasn't closing my eyes against the pain, I could see what was happening. Soul by soul, they were leaving the Indrori and filling the spots on my skin.

"Stop! Let me go!" a voice cried out that wasn't the Indrori, or at least, not the same voice I'd been accustomed to. This was one singular voice. An older woman, by the sound of it.

Her blue aura was screaming at me, and I realized her soul wasn't demonic, but there was nothing I could do to reverse what my body was doing on its own.

"What is happening?"

"Don't send me back!"

"Wait! No! Please!"

"Tasha!"

More pleas came, each time a different voice. Some were hostile, and some were confused, many of them victims in a game they wanted no part of. Some were evil through and through, judging by their color, but others—I could sense some were innocents. I felt conflicted about trapping them, but there was nothing I could do. Another force had taken over, and it wasn't going to stop until the job was done.

"Leave her alone!" a voice boomed. It was Harper. Beside her stood a massive lion. Like, a legit lion. With fucking wings on its back. The roar of it rattled the room.

"Meet Desi," Harper said.

Lion or not, neither of them was a match for this much energy.

"I . . . got this," I gasped. "Get out!" There was no way I could stop what I was doing to save Harper or her pet. I needed her to save herself. The Indrori seemed to swell against the challenge. It was too late. I could feel my grip weakening.

I screamed out to warn her as a bright flash of light filled my eyes. It turned the whole room white, and then there was nothing. Nothing left of the Indrori. Nothing left in the room. And most troublesome, nothing left of Harper. Unable to hold on to rational thought, I felt my eyelids close, and my body fall hard against the floor.

# CHAPTER 13

When I awoke, it was to the sound of voices spoken in hushed tones. There was an odd buzzing in my ears, as though I'd just been through an explosion, or had been dropped on my head from a great height. Everything hurt.

"Hey, I think she's waking up." I felt a hand wrap around mine and knew without opening my eyes that it was Eduardo. I'd know the feel of those strong hands anywhere on my body. I felt my lips curl into a smile. The Indrori didn't kill him. It was a bluff. *Thank you, God.*

"Tasha?" I didn't recognize the female voice.

My eyes squinted open as the brightness of the sun blinded my senses. Jesus, it was bright in here. When I was able to focus, I looked down at Eduardo's hand in mine. I could *feel* his hand in mine. It was warm as it held me. His touch was warm. I was warm. And solid.

"How—how am I touching you?"

Eduardo smiled, but looked over to the girl sitting on the other side of me.

I turned to her, as though she could make sense of it all. Was I no longer in the spirit realm? Was I dead? Was this Heaven? It certainly was bright enough to be, though I would have thought Heaven would have come with a lot less pain. "Who are you? Where's Harper?"

"I'm Addie—Addie Beaumont. I came as soon as I got Harper's message." She gave me a weak smile that didn't reach her eyes behind black-framed glasses. Like Harper, she wore an oversized hoodie and jeans. Unlike Harper, she had a piercing in her nose, and tattoos peeked between several bands of bracelets and where her sleeves rode up. Something about her made me like her instantly. "We were worried about you."

"Where is Harper?" I said again, this time slowly. I still didn't know who this woman was or why she was here or how I was even back in the human realm without the aid of a Recoverer.

"We were hoping you could tell us that?" a deep voice asked. Roman appeared beside Addie, and I tried to lunge for him. I instantly regretted it as pain shot through my rib cage.

"Easy, babe," Eduardo soothed. I let him push me back into the bed, not because I agreed that I needed to rein it in, but because I had no other choice. I was dizzy from the pain I'd just caused myself. The way my head was currently spinning, I would likely fall to the floor if I tried to stand up.

As I lay back, I noticed I had been changed into my normal clothes. Black slacks, black bra, and my white blouse. Eduardo must have helped me, because I didn't remember dressing myself. I didn't remember anything after latching myself onto the Indrori.

"What happened? Why am I so weak?" I croaked. Every muscle in my body felt swollen. No. That's the wrong way to describe it. I felt full. To the point of exploding out of my skin.

"Well, I'm guessing you have several broken ribs and extensive internal bruising, but I think your discomfort is a result of more than your physical injuries," Addie said.

Eduardo and I looked up at her, waiting for her to explain.

"I've been trying to communicate with some of the spirits trapped inside of you—" Addie began.

"Wait, you can hear them—inside my skin?" I looked down at my shirt and pushed it aside to look at my tattoo. Every single scale on my skin appeared to be filled in. "Holy shit," I whispered.

"Not in the same way Harper can. I'm a witch and a hellhound shifter, and since the spirits are denizens of Hell, I have other ways. They're confused and angry—that's all I can discern. Judging by your color and weak pulse," she said, leaning in to check my complexion, "I'm going to guess that having this many souls trapped on you is not great for your health."

"Ya think? God, I feel like I need to be juiced, like that Violet kid in *Charlie and the Chocolate Factory*." My head was spinning from all this new information. Like what the hell a hellhound was.

Roman let out a huff. "That's it. She needs to go to the Infernum and release them," he said.

"Oh, now he cares about saving me," I said, flopping back onto the bed, feeling nauseous. "Seriously, guys. Where is Harper? She was there trying to fight off the Indrori one minute, there was a flash of light, then poof—both she and the Indrori were gone, and I somehow am back here feeling like a beached whale. What the fuck happened?"

"We have people working on Harper's whereabouts. Trust me, we are just as curious about where she went as you are. Right now, we need to worry about you."

I looked up and saw a woman walk into the room. She was an older lady, dressed in a dark business suit, her blond hair in a chignon.

"You found us," Roman said.

"Of course I did," the woman replied.

Roman huffed and turned his attention back to me.

"Look, Tasha, I know you're still pissed at me for tossing you in that house with no knowledge of what you were up against, but you were in no real danger. I had a handle on the situation. As planned, the hellhounds were on standby to bring you back if things got too bad, but I had to let you try. I had to know if you had the gift the Court believed you did." I glared at him. I didn't trust Roman in the slightest.

"Choose your words carefully, Roman. Just because we knew what she could do does *not* mean we condone the way you handled the situation."

Roman waved away her comment like an annoying fly.

"What if you had been wrong?" I asked.

Roman growled. Fucking growled. If I wasn't so out of it, I might have jumped him right then and there. It was hella hot. "If you failed," he said, "the Indrori would have been handled in other ways, but it wouldn't have worked for long." He came over to the bed. "Tasha, with the power they held, there would be no way to contain that much energy. Eventually, our tricks to hold them back would have failed. If your unique ability to separate an Indrori back into single souls again was real, we needed to know that. You were our last and only resort from that thing truly escaping the Infernum, if not today, then in the near future, especially if the Collector has anything to do with this."

Addie and the other woman both threw death glares at him. This Collector person kept coming up, but it was clear from their stares I wasn't about to pry any information out of them. Clearly, this was a town concern and sure as hell not mine.

"So why didn't you tell me that?" I said as vehemently as I could in my weakened state. "Why not be honest? Why not arm me with that information to protect myself?" My head spun just then, causing me to lose my balance, and my eyes rolled back in my head for a second.

"Tasha, you need your rest," Addie said, trying to get me to settle down. Eduardo had stood up, ready to punch out Roman if he so much as took a step closer to me.

I took comfort in that, even if Roman would likely flatten him if it came to blows. Eduardo was built, but Roman was a warlock, and he didn't play fair. Still, it was nice of Eduardo to stand guard for me, if only as a show of testosterone. He was trying to be the alpha. Silly puppy. He had no idea what he was up against.

"Telling you the truth would have slowed things down immensely. We're dealing with too many threats at once, so I took matters into my own hands with this particular one." He glanced at the woman beside him, who glared at him again. "Yes, yes, I know. We'll talk later, Saundra. Consider me properly hand-slapped," Roman drawled to the woman.

"This discussion is not over," she said. "For now, we need to get Tasha to the Infernum. I'll call the hellhounds. Addie, you can lead her there. The others will be waiting to help you."

Addie nodded, then Saundra left without allowing Roman another word.

"Addie is helping me, but who is helping Harper?" I asked, sitting up, though feeling like I was going to hurl. "Where did she go?"

Roman lowered his gaze, cutting off an answer he might have given me. Addie reached out a hand to me. It was hard to read her expression due to the tinted glasses she was wearing. "We have several of our people looking for her. I'm sure she's fine. Harper is still learning about her abilities. Her mace may have even pulled her out."

"Her what?"

"She has a mace—the weapon, not the pepper spray. It's a little like Thor's hammer. It can get her out of pickles. I'm guessing that's what happened, and she'll turn up soon enough. But for now, we really do need to get you taken care of." She reached out a hand as though to help me stand, which was the last thing I wanted to do.

"We should let her rest," Eduardo said, trying to push Addie away with just his glare.

"She can rest after she's shed those souls," Roman said. He walked over to the bed and took hold of my arm. "Let's go."

"Stay away from her!" Eduardo attempted, and failed, to swat his hand away. Roman looked at me for a moment, then adjusted his jacket and flared his nostrils ever so slightly. His left hand twitched. He'd better not pull any magic shit. I wouldn't stand for that. I needed to calm the situation down.

"Hey, babe?" I said, turning to Eduardo. "I'm so thirsty. Could you make me some tea or something? There should be a peppermint tea in the bags we brought." I tried to bat my eyes in the way that got me anything I wanted with him, but I was just too damn tired to pull it off.

"Of course." His eyes focused on me intently. "I'd do anything for you. You know that, right?"

My throat tightened at the emotion that suddenly got stuck there. I nodded once and watched him walk by Roman, his chest puffing as he did.

"Fine. After your tea, you'll shed." Roman walked over to the wingback chair in the corner, unbuttoned his jacket, and sat down in a way that indicated he was not happy with having to wait on me.

"Quick question," I said, closing my eyes against the bright sun for a moment. "Why do you keep saying I need to 'shed'?" I opened my eyes in time to see Roman glance at Addie, who exchanged an unspoken dialogue with him. They were holding something back. "Addie, what is he talking about?"

None of this was making any sense, but Addie was a friend of Harper, so I was hoping that meant she could be trusted to tell the truth.

"Fine. I'll tell her," Roman said with reluctance. His hand pressed against his lips in a tent formation as he seemed to consider his words. "There have been stories of someone else with your exact abilities. *One.* He died centuries ago, but he also 'wore' the souls of the dead on his skin. There are no pictures of him from that time, no printed records, only the stories passed down over the generations. They say he was marked in a similar way to you. He didn't have a tattoo so to speak, but he did have strange markings all over his body."

I sat up a little, suddenly very intrigued.

"The legends mention him only as The Lizard Man, because of the scale-like patches and his affinity for the desert. Twice a year, he would have to shed his gathered souls. He had no access to Hell or the Infernum—no reapers or hellhounds to help him—so the story goes that he went to the desert to release the souls as far away from civilization as possible. In all truth, The Lizard Man is an enigma." Roman clenched his jaw a few times. "We don't know if any of this is true or if it was just a ghost story people told to keep children from wandering into the desert."

Roman stretched his neck from side to side, showing off neck muscles exposed from where his shirt was undone at the collar. I resisted the urge to find that as sexy as it was.

He picked up the creepy-ass doll on the mantel and looked at it absent-mindedly before returning it back to its face-down position. "When I heard the rumors that another soul shedder was alive and in the United States, and working for the feds, no less, I had to find you."

"Soul shedder?" I raised an eyebrow, even though the term did sound kind of badass.

Roman didn't seem to hear my question, because he rattled on. "I had to see it with my own eyes. We were desperate, Tasha. The Indrori had breached their prison and for some reason, came here to

Havenwood Falls. Our town didn't know how much danger it was in. We have other pressing issues—"

"Like this Collector dude?" I asked.

"Precisely. This Indrori business was the last thing we needed. There was no way to know that the Indrori was looking for you specifically."

"You should have stuck with the plan," Addie admonished, glaring at him. The way she stood up to him made me like her even more. I could see why Harper trusted her.

"When we found out you were a soul shedder, the Court was definitely intrigued. But their plan was cumbersome. Too many people involved. Too many ways for things to go wrong. Too much planning and ensuring everyone was safe."

"In other words, they had a sane approach to Tasha going up against an Indrori," Addie said, folding her arms in front of her chest.

Roman took a few steps toward her, but she didn't retreat. It was a power move for him, and one I was quite sure he got away with a lot. But not with her. He wouldn't have with me, either, if I were able to get out of this bed. Asshole.

"Back off," I hissed, hating that I was too tired to clock him over the head.

He turned his focus on me instead. "We didn't have time to waste, Tasha. They were too powerful. Who knows what damage they could have done to Havenwood Falls if I hadn't forced your skill?"

"So you didn't tell anyone that I was coming?" I stared him down, daring him to lie to me.

"I was planning on telling them. Eventually," Roman confessed.

I wanted to lay into him about how selfish it had been of him to risk my life and Harper's that way, but I found that I was too tired to fight with him. It really did seem as though I was carrying hundreds of souls on my skin. I could feel my flesh straining from the pressure of their auras. I was suddenly quite nervous. I wasn't sure how much longer I could hold onto all this energy.

"So what is the plan, then? I'm just supposed to go back to the Infernum—the place they escaped from, mind you—do the hokey-pokey, and all the souls come off me?"

Addie looked at me blankly, and I wondered if it was because of how insane I sounded, or if she was too young to know what I meant by hokey-pokey.

"I honestly don't know how you do it," Roman said. "How did you absorb them all?"

I thought back on it all. "I didn't do anything. I just sort of held on," I said.

Roman nodded as though that made complete sense. "I suppose then all you have to do to release them is to let go."

It sounded so easy and so impossible all at the same time.

# CHAPTER 14

"*This* will help with the nausea," Roman said, dropping a white powder in the tea when Eduardo brought it in.

"Hey, she's not drinking anything you poisoned, asshole. You've already drugged her once!" Eduardo shouted.

Eduardo wasn't wrong. He did get me to take those sleeping pills. Still, the way my stomach was lurching, I was willing to try anything. Even more sleeping pills. Anything to make the feeling subside.

"Give me the fucking tea or I'll hurl on your face," I said. Addie snickered at my side.

Eduardo looked between me and Roman before he sighed and relented.

After I sipped the tea that Eduardo made me, that I really didn't want, Addie told me that she was going to take me to a cemetery to gain access to the Infernum.

"Wait. Hold up. The entrance to the prison is in a cemetery?"

Addie shifted her glasses. "Yes, and the only way in is with me, so do not let me out of your sight."

"Says the lady who wants to take me for a stroll in the cemetery," I winced.

Roman grunted. "Hurry up and drink your damn tea. We need to leave."

"She'll take as long as she needs, buddy," Eduardo said.

In a flash, Roman snapped his fingers, and Eduardo's head fell onto his chest. Loud snores erupted from his lips as though he'd been asleep for hours. If I wasn't so pissed I'd actually be impressed with how fast the spell worked.

"What did you do to him?" I shouted.

"He's fine," Roman said in a bored tone. "He can't come with us. Humans aren't allowed in the Infernum. Addie can only take you. Let's go."

I glanced at Eduardo, who seemed quite content.

"Roman's right. He can't come. He'll be safe here," Addie assured me.

Just then a roll of nausea swept through me.

"Oh God." I held my hand to my mouth for a moment. "I thought this tea was supposed to help this?"

"It is," Roman hissed. "But even that won't hold long. We have to leave. Now."

I suddenly didn't want to test Roman's theories about how much worse I might feel if I didn't shed these souls. I swung my feet out and tried to stand, but I had a hard time supporting all the energy on me.

"Grab her arm," Roman ordered Addie. "If anyone looks at us, she's drunk. We're taking her home to sleep it off. Got it?"

Addie nodded. Secrets had to be kept, after all. Even if I was carrying over a hundred souls on my flesh, to the outside world, I was reduced to a lush. How lovely.

A few seconds later, we were in a car, driving. I wasn't sure how long we drove before we stopped, and they pulled me out. I kept fading in and out of alertness. The tea was definitely wearing off, and the waves of pain were getting more intense by the step.

"Where the hell are we going? I don't know how much longer I can take this," I gasped as they dragged me down a cement walkway. My head bobbed up and down as we went through the cemetery. I was trying really hard not to pass out, but this constant jostling around made that difficult. Everything went dark for a moment, like we were going through a tunnel, or maybe I blacked out. I couldn't tell if what I was seeing was real or if I was hallucinating.

Roman shifted my weight. "It's right up ahead. I can't go any farther. Addie, can you handle her?"

I didn't see her answer, but I felt her taking my weight fully against her side.

"Liam and Savage are waiting for you . . . below," Roman said to Addie.

If she replied, I didn't hear. I just felt my body being dragged along the grass past graves that danced in the moonlight. We stopped in front of what looked like a mausoleum.

"What's happening?" I said, trying my best to hold onto focus.

"Okay, Tasha, Liam and Savage are hellhound shifters. They'll take us into the Infernum. Whether they're in their human forms or in their hellhound forms, you can*not* look into their eyes. Understood?'

"Why not?"

"Oh, no biggie, really. It's just that their stares could kill you if you do."

"Commencing eye closing," I said, snapping my eyes shut.

"Hang onto me, and don't open your eyes. You're going to feel like you're falling, which you are, but trust me, you won't be hurt so long as you keep your eyes closed and hang onto me. Got it?"

"Hold on. Eyes Closed. Copy that. If you were a guy and you had a blindfold, this might actually be kinda kinky." I tried to laugh, but my stomach rolled. "Let's just get there," I groaned.

Addie's arm wrapped tight around my waist, and I closed my eyes. That's when we took a step off what I could only envision as a cliff. It took everything in my power not to open my eyes against the sensation of falling. I swear, we fell for miles. I couldn't even begin to imagine what could be this deep.

"Almost there. Hold on," Addie said over the wind.

And then, all at once, we weren't moving.

"You can open your eyes."

I took a moment to catch my breath before I risked a look. There was very little to see. Darkness surrounded everything. In the distance were hulking figures coming toward us. They carried with them the only light I could see. Bright yellow light seemed to radiate off their bodies. From this distance, they looked like wolves on steroids. It was the sound, though, that did me in. It brought me to my knees. Screams. Thousands of screams coming from every direction. I couldn't tell if it was coming from the darkness or from the souls trapped inside me.

"Okay, time to close again. The hounds are coming."

I did as instructed, mostly because I needed to escape from the reality I was in. I just wanted the pain to stop. For the screaming to stop. For the darkness to finally be lifted.

"We're inside the Infernum. The hellhounds will help trap the souls you shed. So just do your thing. We'll take it from here."

I wanted to ask more questions. I wanted to know the specifics of how it would all go down, but without warning, a wave of pain came over me. All my muscles constricted. I heard myself scream, but in a voice that wasn't my own.

"Tasha?" Addie said. I felt myself curl into a tight ball.

"Stay back," I whispered in warning.

"Let go, Tasha. It's safe here." I wasn't sure if Addie said that, or even if I had uttered the words myself. All I knew was that the phrase felt like the turning of a faucet. This was a safe place. I wouldn't hurt anybody. I didn't need to hold on anymore.

Laying on the ground, I clutched at my stomach. It felt like the worst menstrual cramps of my life, but spread out over every scale on my skin. The pain was worse than when I'd absorbed them. Jesus Christ! I hadn't anticipated shedding to be this painful. Then again, I was about to birth some pretty pissed off souls.

A scream tore through me as I opened my eyes and watched the first soul leave my skin. It emerged wisp-like, from the fabric of my waist band. It glowed red, and I could hear the voice of the aura shouting in time with my own cries. Before the spirit could travel far, there was a golden flash of light, and the sound of growls as a hellhound bounded after the released spirit. I didn't have time to consider the mechanics of how any of this worked, because a scream from both myself and the aura began anew.

On and on this went. Pain, hellhound, repeat. I heard the screams of each soul that came out of me. Several cursed my name and vowed to find me, but I knew they were empty threats. Even if they got out and did find me, I'd trap them again. There was some comfort in that.

"Tasha?" It was a voice I recognized.

Adam's voice pierced through the pain. I opened my eyes and saw his aura floating out of my side. The panic in his voice rattled my bones.

"Adam!" I reached out to try to grab him, but his aura was already being pulled away by a hound.

"No! That's my partner. Stop!" Another wave pulled through me, causing all thought of Adam to leave my mind. Blinding pain radiated from above my chest as another soul was close on his heels. How much more of this could I physically endure? I felt like I was going to split in two. One shed merged to the next until it just became nothing but agony.

The one voice I expected to be the loudest, however, never came. The Indrori's voice was silent. That voice was the amalgamation of souls that spoke for the whole. Once I separated them, their control was no more.

When the last soul had been shed, I could tell. My body felt like my own again, though very, very tired. I closed my eyes. I needed to sleep, for like a thousand years. This cold, dirty ground would do just fine.

# CHAPTER 15

*W*hen I woke up, it was to a strange room. I expected to awaken in a hospital, or the morgue, truth be told. Definitely not in a cozy-looking bedroom. Sitting beside me, with her back ramrod straight in a chair near the door, was the woman Roman had called Saundra.

"Ah, she's awake at last," she said as I pushed myself up into a sitting position. I expected to feel groggy or in pain, as I had been prior to my shedding, but to my surprise, I felt quite agile and full of energy. Even my ribs felt better. "We haven't been properly introduced. I'm Saundra Beaumont. I sit on the Court of the Sun and the Moon and the High Council of the Luna Coven. I'm sorry to have met you the way I did. I want to extend my sincere apologies for the unfortunate way you have been treated. However, we are here to help and protect you now. As we should have done from the moment you arrived."

"Where am I? Why don't I hurt?"

"You're at Whisper Falls Inn." She shifted in her seat. "I had Dr. Underwood tend to your injuries."

I didn't know who Dr. Underwood was, but I had to assume he was a supernatural if Saundra called on him. I was no expert, but I knew cracked ribs weren't something that healed overnight, so magic must have been in play.

Glancing around the room, I noticed that, while the room was homey, there were no giant stuffed animals or flowers laid out, which meant Eduardo hadn't been here yet. He liked to spoil me whenever he got the chance.

"Guess Eduardo and Harper haven't been here yet?" I asked.

Something in Saundra's eyes flickered. "No one knows your location but me and Michaela, the inn's owner."

My eyebrows shot up, instantly questioning her motives for keeping me hidden away. I didn't know her at all and had no idea if she was good or evil, truth be told. She seemed to follow my train of thought, because she put up her hands briefly in surrender. "It's only so that you could recover in your own time without a million people hovering over you. You needed peace and quiet, so I saw to that."

I relaxed a little. "Well, thank you for that, I guess. How long was I out?"

"Three days."

At that, I bolted upright. "Three *days*?" That's when I noticed the IV attached to my arm.

"I'm surprised it was only that long," Saundra said flippantly. "I would have expected at least a week after your ordeal, but then again, you are a bit of a mystery."

It was hard to believe I'd been asleep that long, but after what I'd endured, I was surprised I wasn't dead.

"Eduardo," I said, knowing he was probably worried about how I was doing, too. "I need to see him." He was probably tearing up the town, trying to find out where they had taken me.

"I'm afraid that will be quite impossible."

"And why is that?" I asked, not enjoying the finality of her tone.

"The Court met, and it was decided it was best that Eduardo's memories of Havenwood Falls—and of you—be wiped clean."

"Wiped clean? What the hell are you talking about?"

She placed her hands on her lap in a slow and methodical way.

"It means just what you think it means. And before you think about it, even if you were to find him, which you won't, he wouldn't remember you, or anything about his time in Havenwood Falls."

I stared at her for a few moments, waiting for her to tell me that she was joking or that I'd misheard her, but it became clear that she had really sent him away. She'd erased him from my life.

"Who said you could do that? You don't have the right to—"

"Actually, I do, Agent Young. This is *our* town you're in. We have full say who stays and who goes."

My nostrils flared in anger.

"And my partner was a threat to your stupid little town?"

Saundra's upper lip twitched at the insult, but she kept her composure. "Your human 'friend' was never a threat among a town of supernatural beings, Tasha. He was, however, a threat to you."

She wasn't making any sense. Eduardo wouldn't hurt me. Not possible.

"Please, enlighten me," I snapped.

Saundra pursed her lips, seemingly annoyed that she had to explain her rationale to the dumb human. "Do you love him?" she asked.

"He's my partner."

She frowned. "Yes, I know. That wasn't an answer, though."

"I fail to see how my being in love or not with him has anything to do with why you sent him away!"

"It has everything to do with it."

I opened my mouth to ream her out for daring to assume how I felt. How dare she say I didn't love him. She didn't know anything about me or our relationship. But I couldn't articulate a proper argument. I cared for him, had fun with him, and we fit together perfectly, but I would never love him. I was just too wild to be tied down. At least, not yet. I knew he was falling for me, and I had done nothing to discourage him. It had been cruel of me to lead him on. Truth was, I held on to him so close because he was the only person I had whom I had ever considered a friend. It was selfish of me to hold on to him when my ultimate goal was going to be to let him go. Saundra had done him a kindness by erasing me from his memory.

"No, I didn't love him," I admitted at last. "I'm not capable of loving anyone but myself."

Saundra nodded. "That is precisely why I sent him away. He had fallen for you in ways that human men fall for beautiful women. But you are not normal, Tasha. You never have been. You're gifted, even among the supernatural. Your ability to absorb souls won't go away. There will always be lurkers within your flesh. You will always be tied to the spirit realm. You can't expect a human to be able to deal with such a burden."

As much as I hated to hear it, she was right. I wasn't normal. Why did I think I'd ever be able to have a normal relationship with a guy?

"Besides," she went on, "a puppy-dog crush would get in the way of the work we need you to do here in Havenwood Falls."

I couldn't help it. I laughed straight in her face. "You want me to work for *you*? After the shit your town pulled on me? Dragging me here without telling me the truth, allowing one of my best agents to be killed, imprisoning his aura, and then sending away a guy I was seeing?"

Saundra sighed. "What happened to your partner, Adam, was unfortunate. However, we were able to retrieve his aura during your shed. He has been released into our custody and supervision within Havenwood Falls."

"Wait? Adam is alive?" I asked, not daring to believe it.

Saundra shook her head. "No. Not in the way you're thinking. Too much time had passed for that. His vitals were weak back at the house. He was brain dead, as I'm sure you knew. The only way to salvage the best part of him was to allow him to cross over. We provided him with the option to stay here or to wander the earth. He chose to stay."

Adam's aura was intact. His soul had been saved. My eyes overflowed with emotion. I'd be able to see him again, even if he was only a spirit now.

"Can I see him?"

She nodded. "Soon. He's here, actually. In the inn with Madame Luiza, another spirit. She's giving him the tour."

"I wonder what color his aura is now?" I whispered to myself.

"Color?" Saundra asked.

I shook my head. "Nothing. I see an aura's color. It matches the mood they are in. He was blue the last time I saw him. Confused."

Saundra seemed bewildered by this. "Oh, well, I'm sure you'll find Adam looks very different now that he is no longer confused. He's a striking man. It's no wonder Madame Luiza is monopolizing him. She's a wicked flirt."

"Wait. You can *see* Adam?"

"Of course. He's more translucent then he was when he was alive, but his features are still quite present."

I stared at her for several minutes. Was this what happened to a spirit when they got to choose their fate? Was I only able to see auras in a state of distress? Or could she see ghosts differently than I could? There was so much to process.

"We're quite pleased he has chosen to stay. He will make an excellent addition to Havenwood Falls. I'm hoping you'll choose to do the same, Tasha. We could use your abilities here," Saundra said.

Pulling my emotions back in check, I turned my attention to Saundra.

"I hate to inform you, lady, but I already have a job. One that pays quite well. I get to travel on someone else's dime and rid the world of asshole souls at the same time. Why do you think I'd want to stick around a dump like this?" I asked, ticked at her audacity, thinking I'd actually stay here after everything that happened.

Saundra stood up and walked over to the window and pulled back the drapes. The sun had gone down, but I could see the streetlamps and Christmas lights twinkling in the darkness. "Because I know what you want, Tasha. What you really long for, more than anything else. It's something money and a million air miles could never grant you, but we can."

"Oh, really? What's that?"

She turned around and clasped her hands in front of her again. "A place to call home."

I stared at her blankly, unable to articulate my response. How the hell could she know that's what I longed for, when I'd never mentioned it to another living soul? I wondered, suddenly, if she could read my thoughts.

"Think it over," she said, before she crossed through the room and left me alone.

Damn it all. She was right. I had been searching for years for a place where I fit in, where I was accepted for my oddities. Now that I'd discovered my true identity as a soul shedder, I was going to have a ton of questions. Questions only a town like this had any hope of providing answers for.

For several moments I sat in silence, trying to process everything that happened. Just when I was ready to get out of bed and hunt her down to ask my questions, there was a knock on the door. The person on the other side didn't wait for an answer before they opened the door.

Addie walked in, wearing a black hoodie with a pentagram on it, jeans, and knee-high leather boots.

"Hey, how you feeling?" Addie asked, shutting the door behind her.

"About a hundred souls lighter. You?"

"I'm feeling a lot safer now that those spirits are back where they belong. Thank you, Tasha. That could have gotten really ugly."

I laughed. "I don't know, it was pretty rough from where I was lying."

"Right. Sorry."

I shook my head. "It's okay. Hey, did you find Harper yet?"

Addie's expression shifted, her gaze dropping. "No. We haven't given up, but . . . she's just gone. We can't find any trace of her. Her mace, Desi, has been hunting for her nonstop. It's like she disappeared off the face of the planet."

"Was she pulled into the spirit realm?" If she had been taken by the Indrori before I took it down, then maybe she was just between planes. I could recover her. "If she's in the spirit world, I could—" That's when it struck me how many days I'd been asleep. Too much time had passed. I wouldn't be able to recover her.

"I don't think she's passed on," Addie said, stopping my train of thought.

"Well, what happened to her then?"

Addie took a breath, as though debating how much to tell me.

"Please. She . . . she helped me when no one else would. If I can help you figure out where she is, I have to try," I plead.

"I shouldn't be telling you this. You aren't even a ward of the town."

"But I was with her when she disappeared. Maybe there is a piece to this puzzle I can help with," I argued. I wasn't just going to give up on Harper. She didn't give up on me. Even when her life was on the line.

"The Court thinks that the Indrori and the Collector may have been working together."

"You keep mentioning the Collector. Who is he?"

Addie stood up and walked over to the window. She seemed to gaze outside for the longest time before she spoke. "We don't know much, really. Someone who calls themselves the Collector has been threatening people in our town. Including Harper. The fact that Harper showed up in this house with the Indrori makes us think that they were working together to take Harper down."

"Wait, so you think Harper was the target?" I shook my head vehemently. "No. The Indrori clearly wanted me dead. They told me point blank their plans to destroy me."

"I know. Which is why I think the Court may be wrong on this. I don't think they were working together. I think the Collector saw an opportunity to take Harper and used the distraction of the Indrori to his advantage."

"It would be the perfect setup. But how would the Collector even know Harper was there?"

Addie turned around. "There is a lot the Collector knows that we can't figure out." She lifted her hand and tugged absently on her shirt.

"What aren't you telling me?" Nervous twitches were a dead giveaway when a person was trying to be secretive.

"It might be nothing . . ."

"Tell me."

Addie came back to the chair and sat down. She bit her lip for a moment before she spoke.

"When we were in the Infernum, Liam, one of the hellhounds you saw, said when returning some of the souls you shed to their prison, some of them . . . their signatures smelled different when he returned them to that section of the Infernum. He couldn't pinpoint what was off about it, but it was different than any of the other souls he'd dealt with. It might be nothing."

"Or it could be everything," I said.

"How so?" Addie asked.

"I don't know. It's just . . . Harper said something like that, too. That her powers—they were working differently with me. She said it was like everything was backward somehow."

Addie shrugged. "Harper's gifts are still emerging, though. That might just be her growing into new gifts. I'm sure we'll figure it out. We just have to keep thinking."

"I could help," I heard myself say. "I could go back to the house. See if her spirit is there . . . I mean, maybe she's trapped. I wouldn't be able to bring her back, but I might be able to find her, at least."

Addie smiled, then patted her black bag. "If you're sticking around, you're gonna need one of these."

"One of what?" I glanced at the bag.

Addie rolled her eyes. "Saundra didn't explain what I do, did she?"

"Besides saving my ass? No."

That prompted a laugh. "When I'm not out being a badass hellhound, a witch, and saving your ass, I'm also the town's resident tattoo artist."

I should have guessed she was a witch. That's why she and Roman seemed to have a shorthand I couldn't pick up on.

"Oh. Do you work at Tragic Ink?" I asked, remembering the shop Davis at Coffee Haven had told me about. Her working there would be cool, but I wasn't sure why she was bringing it up now.

"Nope. I work for the Court. I'm the business manager and responsible for the Registry."

She sat down beside me, placed a black leather bag on my bed, and took out several tattooing instruments.

"Um, are you giving me a tattoo?" I asked.

"Yep. That's why I'm here. Saundra really didn't tell you anything about this?" She sighed as though she was used to having to do the dirty work. "It's my job to mark the residents and visitors of Havenwood Falls. It's how the Court keeps tabs on the supernaturals. Makes sure we're not breaking any rules, stuff like that."

"Yeah, Roman Bishop told me a little about it. They act like an ankle monitor, right?"

"Yes and no." She dug into her bag again.

"Does it zap us if we get out of line?"

She stopped rifling in her bag to look at me. "Of course not. That's not how we are. It only works with the wards on the town. If there's trouble, the Registry gives us an idea of who we need to track down for the cause of it. See, I infuse the ink with magic that connects with the energy of the wards, so we know who comes and goes. But we only care if there's a problem. Otherwise, we don't pay any attention. And the magic also gives everyone a benefit. So it's a mark of freedom, in a way. It's a symbol that we belong. That we are a community."

I hadn't thought of it that way. When she said it like that, it seemed like the tattoos were a badge of honor. Something to wear with pride, not shame. I sort of liked the sound of that.

"Although, you've got a killer tat already," Addie said nodding toward my torso. Smiling, I reached down, lifted my shirt, and showed her the snake coiled around my body. The scales were no longer filled in.

"Woah," we both said at the same time.

"They're all gone," I whispered, running my fingers over the thin black outline of the scales. I really had shed them. "These were all black before," I said in wonder. "I wear demonic spirits, apparently. Until I get full, and then, I shed—like a snake—and off to the Infernum they go."

"You have a wicked gift." Addie didn't even bat an eye at how bizarre the statement was. Instead, she seemed . . . impressed.

"Yeah, it's kind of wild." I laughed, realizing how comfortable I felt chatting with Addie.

"A snake is such a fitting tattoo, given your abilities," she said, admiring the handy work.

"It is?" I would never in a million years attach spirits to snakes.

"Well, sure," she said, pulling on a pair of gloves. "I mean, a snake has long been used in medical logos, for good reason."

I paused to remember the snake and staff images on my own medicines in the past. Why *did* we use a snake logo for medicine? I'd never stopped to think about it. Addie seemed to realize I was clueless, because she gave me a small smile and went on.

"Greek mythology has long believed that snakes are sacred beings. Their venom was used for healing rituals and such, but their skin— the shedding of their flesh—that was a symbol of renewal and rebirth. Just like a life cycle. We live, we die, we are reborn as spirits. It's also kind of like you right now. You get a chance to reinvent yourself here, in Havenwood Falls."

I didn't answer her as my fingers traced over the outline of my tattoo. I eyed her bag with interest. She must have seen my eyes wander, because she brought the bag closer.

"You can pick any design you want," she said, "and you can choose anywhere you want it. I can make it visible or invisible, that's your call. The only question I need to know before we start is, am I making you a visitor tattoo or a resident one?"

I stared at her for the longest time, hoping she would pick for me. Did I want to go home, well, back to living in hotels and dating strings of men who would never fill the void in my heart, hiding away my gifts from anyone outside the FBI? Or did I want to give this rinky-dink town a shot, with their promise of accepting me for the freak show that I was? Did I want to shed the old me and step into a new place? A place that held the promise of home . . .

Addie looked up at me with expectant eyes, and I smiled.

"Resident."

# ABOUT THE AUTHOR

Danielle Bannister lives with her two children in Midcoast Maine, along with her precious coffee pot and peppermint mocha creamer. She is a writer of all things swoon-worthy, angsty, and snarky. She holds a BA in Theatre from the University of Southern Maine and her master's degree in Literary Education from the University of Orono. Her writing includes a collection of short stories called *Short Shorts*; The Twin Flames Trilogy: *Pulled*, *Pulled Back*, and *Pulled Back Again*; *The ABC's of Dee*; *Enigma*; *Doppelganger*; *Must Love Coffee*; and *Netherworld* and *Hollow Earth* with co-author Amy Miles.

# ACKNOWLEDGMENTS

I want to thank Kristie Cook, R.K. Ryals, Randi Cooley Wilson, and E.J. Fechenda for letting me play with their characters and locations. I offer my apologies to them for the million and one questions I asked them in order to make sure I was getting their ideas correct. It is challenging to write in a world where so much has already been established, but these ladies helped me immensely until my romance brain slowly learned how the fantasy world worked. I am ever humbled.

# ADDICTED TO YOU

## BELINDA BORING

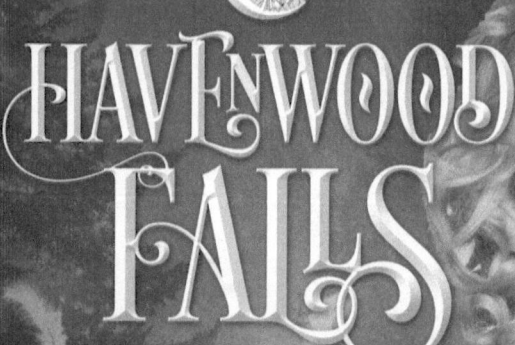

# HAVENWOOD FALLS

## ADDICTED TO YOU

# BELINDA BORING

# ALSO BY BELINDA BORING

**THE MYSTIC WOLVES SERIES**

The Mystic Wolves

Forget Me Not

Testing Fate

Forever Changed

Savage Possession

Darkness Unleashed

Last Wolf Standing

Blood Oath

A Very Mystic Christmas (Collection of Christmas Memories)

**DAMAGED SOULS SERIES**

Bittersweet Melody

Bittersweet Symphony

Enchanted Heart

Loving Liberty

Broken Promises

**HAVENWOOD FALLS TITLES**

Nowhere to Hide

Addicted to You (Sequel to Nowhere to Hide)

Blood & Damnation (Legends of Havenwood Falls)

The Collector: Awakening

Short Story Anthology 2018

*To my dear friend and fellow author, Kristie Cook.*
*Thank you for inviting me to join this incredible world.*
*You helped me find my joy and voice again. Love you!*

# CHAPTER 1

"The sooner you hire someone, the sooner things can go back to normal," Maxwell's gruff admonition broke the silence. My ghostly friend had been studying me all morning, and now he was peering around me to the ignored paperwork by the bookstore's computer.

It had been a long, grief-stricken four weeks since the psychic fair and the attack afterwards. Just one short month since I'd been shot and betrayed by someone I'd trusted so completely that I hadn't seen it coming.

I still hadn't brought myself to enter the storage area.

I still hadn't found the courage to sort through the pile of applications stacked on the counter beside me. I wasn't going to rush it. I prayed that my faith could be bigger than my fear, and so far, it was working. One step at a time.

Micah was the one who put away orders as they came in, and he was the one who worked on the to-do list I created each morning. I saw the worry in his eyes whenever I handed it to him, the way his lips kind of parted as though he was about to speak but thought better of it. He understood that I was processing things in my own way, in my own time. The consideration made me love him just that little bit more.

Love could be deadly for an empath.

I knew that painfully well, having lost both my parents to heartbreak. It was a mantra that I'd repeated over and over inside my head, but since meeting Micah Westbrook, there was an even louder voice in my head trying to convince me that it would be one hell of a way to go.

Micah.

The man made it worth the risk.

Maxwell, on the other hand, was not as kind or sympathetic.

I let out a weary sigh and covered the job applications with a magazine.

"Out of sight, out of mind," I countered, not ready to deal with him either today. There was no question that my friendly ghost was struggling as well in the aftermath. His sense of helplessness had been etched across his furrowed brow as he recounted how much he hated not being corporeal. I'd listened to his furious diatribe about Austin, and the only way his temper had been somewhat placated was knowing that Austin had been banished from Havenwood Falls. He'd simply wished for a chance to exact his own justice—the wringing of the traitor's neck.

His words. Not mine.

He'd felt the betrayal keenly because he had stepped in to fill my late grandfather's shoes and watch over me. After I'd discovered the Dunlap Broadside in one of his trunks up in the attic, the truth had come out that not only had my friend been there at the first printing of the Declaration of Independence, but he'd then gone on to fight alongside General George Washington in Yorktown. There was no doubt in my mind that he'd seen all manner of brutality fighting against the English, and had he been able to, he'd have killed Austin with his bare hands.

It had revealed a savagery in him that I'd never witnessed before. I felt like I was meant to be scared of him because of it. Instead, I felt safer. Ghost or not, Maxwell was not a man to be meddled with.

"So you're back to sticking your head in the sand. I see." He didn't bother camouflaging the disappointment in his voice.

My hand hit the top of the counter a little harder than I intended.

"What do you expect me to do?" I asked, my voice filled with exasperation. "I'm not a robot. I can't just experience something . . ." A large lump formed in my throat, making it difficult to swallow and speak. I cleared my throat and tried again. "I can't just bounce back like nothing happened, Maxwell. Why can't you just let me do things in my own time?"

Compassion flooded his gaze, and I could see he desperately wished he could wrap his arms around me in a hug. "Girl, I wish I could. I wish I could say we lived in a world where nothing bad happens and good people live happily ever after. Would you rather I lie to you?"

He peered deeply into my eyes until I could feel him touch my soul. His honesty helped soothe some of the jagged pieces still too raw to mend.

I glanced at the applications again. Here was my opportunity to be equally as candid—to share what was truly at the root of my hesitation.

"What if I make another mistake? What if I don't see the danger and next time it's more . . ." I struggled to finish my sentence.

"Fatal?" The man had read my mind perfectly.

I nodded. "I'm not being morbid or anything, but if it were just me at risk, it wouldn't be too big of an issue. But Holly was there. Micah and I are together now, so she's always going to be around. Micah had tried warning me about the threats he was protecting her from, and I contributed to it." The words came tumbling out with such a force, I was breathless at the end.

Micah's voice surprised me. "Is that what you think?"

Somewhere in the back of my mind, I'd heard the tinkling of the doorbell, but I'd been so wrapped up in my thoughts and conversation with Maxwell that I'd missed Micah entering. The very sight of him made my heart race a bazillion miles an hour, and without thinking, I licked my lips in anticipation.

Kissing was the last thing on his mind, however.

Right now, he pretty much mirrored the exact same expression the ghost did—incredulous shock.

I guess I hadn't confessed that small tidbit to them—my feeling that the attack was my fault and that somehow I should've been able to prevent it.

I shrugged my shoulders, not ready to face both of them about this. "Austin was my employee, my responsibility. It was my store. *I* provided the chance for him and Holly to meet. *I* encouraged their friendship and study dates. How much clearer does it need to be?" I'd gone over the details countless times in my head, often while I lay awake at night, staring up at the ceiling in my apartment. "You know I'm right."

Micah actually scoffed, making a sound that was a cross between a snort and a grunt. "I know you are wrong. One hundred percent, emphatically wrong." He took a step closer, so he could cradle my cheek with his palm. "Sedona, please tell me you don't honestly believe that."

As much as I savored the warmth of his touch, I knew in this moment, with these guilt-riddled feelings churning inside me, it didn't feel right to accept such kindness. Reluctantly, I stepped back and broke the contact.

Micah stared down at where I'd just been standing, a serious look of sadness crossing his handsome features. I hated the fact that I'd been the one to put that expression there. I just didn't know how else to explain what had been bottled up inside me until now.

Maxwell disappeared once he realized this was a private moment. His only parting gift was to mouth the words *listen to him.*

Micah reached for me again, and I skirted away.

"Please don't do that, Sedona. Don't close yourself off from me."

I couldn't help it. I burst into a laugh that bordered on hysterical. "This coming from the man who walked through those doors practically a blank slate, a man with so many secrets that I'm surprised you're not drowning in them all." I could feel my skin heat from the emotional outburst, but I didn't suppress it. "Even now, after everything we've been through, you still keep parts of yourself shielded from me."

There was a hint of frustration in his response. I could feel him trying to be patient and understanding, but like every other man on the planet, he couldn't see it from my perspective.

"This isn't about me, though. We're talking about you." And with all the skill of a ballroom dancer, he sidestepped around my retort, and waltzed me back to where the spotlight was back on me. "Help me comprehend what's going on in that beautiful head of yours." He offered me a gentle smile to try to soften the mood, but it was too late. Everything I'd kept stuffed inside was rushing to the surface, ready to explode.

"Don't flatter me!" I exclaimed. Part of me knew it was unfair to unleash on the man I was dating, the man I was falling in love with. Another part egged my own impatience on, telling me to purge until there was nothing left but the echoes of an empty heart. Surprisingly, there was another voice that had recently emerged. It was that voice that whispered if there was ever a person I could completely confide in and bare my soul to, it would be Micah.

"I'm sorry," he murmured and reached for me again. This time I didn't shrink away.

"Don't you think it's ironic that you expect such transparency from me, yet you keep everything within you tightly wrapped up in some impenetrable fortress?" When he nodded, not speaking a word in response, I took courage. "I may be an empath, but I'm also human, Micah. How else am I meant to feel? Tell me, how am I meant to process this? What must I do so we can all go back to pretending like the world is wonderful and filled with rainbows and butterflies?" I stared up into his deep blue eyes, the challenge thrown. When he didn't reply, I let out a loud, unladylike grunt. "That's what I thought."

Scooping up the damn applications, I gripped them in one hand as I grabbed my keys and threw them at him. "Lock up after yourself. I can't stand being here a second longer."

With one last look over my shoulder, I fled Shelf Indulgence, not waiting to see if he'd follow.

So much for me being okay with what happened and being strong.

Being an empath wasn't as fun as it sounded. It was taxing—both emotionally and physically—and often when I slipped up and invaded someone's feelings (by accident), the consequences resulted in me feeling like an outcast.

Micah had offered to help heal those emotional wounds with his own angelic grace, but I'd politely declined. Every time he used his powers—for whatever reason—it sent out a beacon to those who were hunting for him and Holly. I was grateful that he'd given me a small vial of his divine essence that I wore around my neck, under my clothing. It replaced the black tourmaline pendant I used to wear, but had given to Holly to help ground her after Austin's attack.

Micah's gift was precious to me, and I didn't need to think too hard to know that given time, scars would fade, and it would almost be like my young employee's betrayal had never happened.

Almost.

I could deal with almost.

I'd spent so much time hiding away in my bookstore, sheltering the town from my troublesome gifts, that I'd forgotten just how powerful I could be. Looking down the barrel of the gun Austin had pointed at me, threatening to take Holly away, I'd made a silent vow that should we survive, I would never make myself that vulnerable again.

But that was then and this was now.

It seemed like I was surrounded by lies at the moment, but none bigger than the ones I was telling myself.

I wasn't doing fine.

I was falling apart, and for the life of me, I couldn't stop the tears that finally started to fall.

# CHAPTER 2

*I* didn't get too far before I heard someone calling out after me. It wasn't Micah, because I was pretty sure he was still rooted to the spot in the store, stunned over the tantrum I'd just thrown, his gaze flickering between the door I'd stormed out of and the keys I'd thrown at him.

Embarrassment warred with the guilt that had taken up residence inside me. It took every ounce of willpower for me not to turn around and begin apologizing profusely. I'd acted like a jerk and taken my insecurities out on him.

But I didn't stop. Tears streamed down my cheeks, big salty drops hanging from my top lip before falling. They tasted like regret and fury. Now that I'd lifted the lid on the box that was my own feelings, there was no stuffing them back in.

"Sedona. Please. Don't make me chase after you in these shoes. I won't ever forgive you!"

Callie.

I'd run past the consignment store, and of course, she'd seen me racing by, a complete mess. She wasn't someone who gossiped, and I didn't need my empathic gifts to recognize her intentions. She was worried, and her chasing after me came from a place of compassion.

Slowing down, I shortened my stride and gave her a chance to catch up. A few moments later, her arm looped through mine, and

121

her friendly energy reached out calmly. It was enough to bring me to a complete halt.

I didn't deserve this kindness.

Not now.

Not today.

A lie started forming in my mind. The last thing I wanted was to have a complete meltdown in the town square instead of going somewhere more private, like I'd hoped.

But there was no holding back my emotions now as I sniffled, tempted to wipe my nose on the back of my hand, grossness be damned. Luckily, Callie had come prepared with not just one tissue, but the entire box.

"Here. Knock yourself out." She didn't study me too hard, and I was grateful for that. We stood there together—side by side—before I started walking again. This time it lacked the frenetic pace from before. The anger and bluster had ebbed, and like the tide, it swept back out from my heart.

"Sorry," I murmured, picking a spot on the ground to focus on. That was the thing about holding someone's gaze. If you knew what you were looking for, you could read a person's mind and get a sense of what they were feeling. You didn't need to be magical or an empath. You just needed to be patient enough for the truth to reveal itself.

Callie understood.

I wasn't ready to be that vulnerable with her.

Taking a deep breath, I blew my nose again, and attempted to steady the riot that had exploded inside me. I felt chaotic. All it had taken was a small tap-tap at the wall, and a crack had appeared in the dam around my psyche.

I hated feeling like this—so out of control and uncertain.

"You're going to think I'm being stupid," I began, hoping she'd believe the fib I was about to give her. "It's this freaking purple pig plate design I've been working on." Casting a quick sideways glance at my friend, I silently hoped she wouldn't ask too many questions.

"You mean for Plate Painting in the Park?" Callie asked, her surprise showing. "That's the reason you're rushing down the street like someone kicked your dog?" The strength in her stare almost unraveled my nerve. "Sedona, it's all about having fun. I'm sure your plate's going to kick ass like usual."

For a second there, I thought she was talking to someone else, because while I had many talents, artistic skill with a paintbrush was not one of them. I'd be lucky if the traditional pig even resembled one.

"I'm surprised the witch hasn't come back to haunt me." A few more fat tears rolled over my cheeks, and I snorted. "Her plates sucked souls into the painted scenes. Mine just suck."

There were many traditions here in Havenwood Falls, and despite my exaggeration, I actually enjoyed the plate painting event held in April. I'd been doodling for the past few months, hoping that inspiration would strike, and maybe, just maybe, this was the year *my* design would be featured. It hadn't happened yet, but a girl could dream.

Callie stood there silently, studying me.

She cut straight to the chase. "Liar."

"Excuse me?" I fired back. The sinking sensation in my gut told me she'd seen right through my story. I couldn't lie to save my life.

"You heard me. I don't believe that's why you're *this* upset." Callie refused to break eye contact with me, and my resolve weakened.

"I'm an empath," I blurted. "I feel things passionately and deeply." My cheeks were starting to tingle from the cool air hitting them. Whereas most of the country was beginning to warm up, with spring melting away the last effects of winter, the weather in Havenwood Falls was still quite brisk. The forecast app I had on my phone had warned me not to expect anything higher than forty degrees today, so I'd dressed warmly. Right now, I wanted to wrap my black crocheted scarf around my face.

"I think we need to go on an excursion." Callie spoke so matter-of-factly that I didn't argue. Instead, I let her guide me around the town's square until we stopped in front of Eloise's shop, Into The Mystic. It housed all kinds of new-age things, including psychic readings.

My tears had finally abated, and I rubbed at my tired eyes, wishing we were standing in front of my apartment door instead. The sudden need for the privacy of my own home was overwhelming, but when I went to step back, Callie clicked her tongue in disapproval.

"Be brave, dear friend." And with that, she pushed me through the door, the smell of white sage incense hitting me square in the face.

"But," I began, trying to explain that this was the last place I wanted to be. Memories of the fair and the events that happened afterward tugged sharply at my heart, and more tears filled my eyes. Eloise had organized the fair, and while it wasn't her fault, everything associated with that night and my being shot made it tainted for me.

Callie stopped guiding me, and instead turned me about so she could face me. Her eyes were more hazel today than the green they usually were. There was such a confidence bursting from within them that I wished I could somehow reach down inside her and claim some for myself.

"Do you trust me?"

I was slow to answer, purposely trying to avoid eye contact. "You don't . . ."

She cut me off, not wanting to hear the excuse I was prepared to deliver. "Yes or no, Sedona. Do you trust me?"

This time I threw aside the fear that had controlled me and boldly kept her gaze. "Yes."

"Then believe me when I say you need this." She wore that same expression again—the one that said she was one hundred percent certain that what she spoke was truth. She'd read my cards at the fair, and while a lot was just teasing, there had been tidbits that struck close to home.

Like my growing love for Micah and my worry about getting my heart broken. Tarot had counseled me to take a risk and dare to fly— that the only thing holding me back from finding the happiness I craved was myself.

I let out a pent-up breath and nodded. "Fine."

I looked about the store, noting the new Van Morrison poster Eloise had hung up by the cash register. Every book Shelf Indulgence had ever sold about the Irish singer and songwriter had been ordered just for her. In fact, I recognized the lyrics to his song, Into the Mystic, which was oddly fitting, considering the store's name.

"What am I looking for?" I asked, trying not to sound like a petulant child. What I also didn't admit was that I was already feeling better. It meant there would be no wallowing at home with a large glass of wine and a book, hiding under a blanket fort in the living room. My emotions were no longer clouding my judgment.

I was back to feeling more like me.

"You need another talisman," Callie replied promptly, and with a sweeping gesture of her hand, she pointed over to one of my favorite parts of the store. "Go find the one that calls out to you."

Crystals.

Gems.

Stones.

It didn't matter what you called them, it was the energy and magic that was contained within them, a small piece of Mother Earth to hold and keep close.

"We could be here a while," I whispered softly, wonder now filling my voice as I slowly began tuning everything else out. I felt lured to the neat shelves and baskets that contained the different stones. There was an ever-so-slight tug at my aura—that telltale sign that what I was looking for was also seeking me.

I lightly touched a beautiful green stone and read the card in front of it. Malachite, a stone that had incredible healing properties to the one wearing it. Electricity zapped at my fingertips, revealing its power, but it wasn't the one calling me.

Callie nodded as I moved away from her, the movement caught in my peripheral vision. "I'll be here whenever you're ready."

And with that, she turned her focus to the tarot and oracle cards that were arranged on a nearby shelf.

We were both content to explore.

Quartz.

Citrine.

Snowflake Obsidian.

Selenite.

Each of these crystals caught my eye and warmed my hand as I held them. Snippets of information filled my mind—lessons where I'd learned how one helped reduce stress while another was good for canceling out negative energy. I remembered my grandfather telling me that selenite was a great stone to include in my collection because it didn't require charging from the full moon, adding his warning that should I submerge one in water, it might dissolve.

Selenite had always intrigued me. The one before me had been cut and polished to resemble a unicorn horn, and I could already feel its cleansing energy brushing across my aura. It held the ability of promoting clarity to a troubled mind, yet when I picked it up, closing my eyes to see if it was the *one*, I felt sadly empty.

It was only after walking down a few feet and looking to the left that I found it—the stone that beckoned like a siren, its frequency pinging hard against my own.

I didn't need to read the neatly written card to know its name.

Labradorite, or what I affectionately called it, the galaxy stone.

To some, under a certain light, it appeared to be a dull piece of rock, somewhat transparent with a greenish, black color. But when you held it a certain way, the most gorgeous flashes of color burst outward. Greens, blues, yellows, and sometimes, if you were lucky, you could find purples and pinks.

I tentatively reached out to the palm-sized stone, marveling at how it fit so perfectly. As I curled my fingers around it, appreciating the bold flashes of blues and greens, I felt the most incredible heat flow through my veins, sweeping throughout my body until it burst out the top of my head.

I felt energized.

I felt grounded.

I felt it caress the wounds I'd received to my spirit and gently heal them.

I'd found my new talisman.

"Excellent choice," Eloise interjected from behind me. It didn't bother me that she surprised me. Nothing else mattered but the soothing feeling that all but encompassed me, acting like a salve on my bruised heart.

Callie had made her way back over to me as well. "Labradorite. I should've known. It's all about persevering through the changes and learning to trust your intuition again, Sedona."

Eloise nodded, her graying auburn hair pulled back into a soft bun. The Swarovski crystals in her dangly earrings caught the light from above and glittered. "You'll find the answers you seek. Don't give up."

Satisfied with her contribution to the conversation, she excused herself to help the other customer who was perusing. That was Eloise Sinclair for you. She was eccentric, and psychic, and you might not always understand her meaning, but when she said something with that prophetic tone, you listened.

"Feeling better?" Callie asked, nudging me with her shoulder. "Is it working its magic?" Her eyes dropped to the crystal I now held up to my chest.

I laughed. An hour ago, I would've thought such a response impossible. I'd been consumed by pain and fear. While it wasn't all rainbows and sunshine yet, I was definitely seeing clearer.

"Thank you."

Callie shrugged it off. "What are friends for?" It was then that she revealed what she was holding. A bundle of white sage leaves wrapped with twine. "I officially declare this excursion a success." She returned to guiding me, knowing that I wouldn't be handing over the crystal, my fingers still wrapped around its smooth surface. "Eloise, could you put this all on my tab?" Callie raised the sage and pointed to me.

"No," I started, shaking my head. "You don't need to do that, Callie. I can pay for it." I was already reaching for the debit card stashed in the front pocket of my jeans.

She actually looked like she was ready to scold me. "Consider it a congratulations gift." She dared to wiggle her eyebrows at me, her eyes twinkling. "And no, I'm not going to tell you what I mean. You'll know soon enough."

Damn psychics with their cryptic comments.

There was no arguing with her. "Then, thank you again." I offered her a watery smile, my eyes filling this time with grateful tears. I started laughing again and quickly wiped them away. "I'm such a mess."

"But you're a cute one," she countered. Handing me the small brown paper bag that held the smudging bundle, she waved goodbye to Eloise. I followed quickly after.

We slowly walked back toward her consignment store and my bookstore in comfortable silence, and I relished the peace that had settled within me.

True peace.

Welcomed peace.

"Do you need me to come in with you?" Callie asked as we reached Shelf Indulgence. The lights were out, which told me that Micah had closed everything up like I'd requested—demanded. Guilt tugged again at me for my rudeness toward him, and I was glad that he wasn't still there waiting for me to return. I needed a little more time to pull myself together, and I wanted to do this next part alone.

It was long overdue.

I shook my head slowly.

"I've got this," I said, my voice growing stronger and more self-assured. Suddenly I turned and threw my arms around her. "You knew exactly what I needed, Callie. Thank you so much." I squeezed her one more time before releasing her. "I . . ." I was at a loss for words again. "Did you know the Beatles released their song 'A Little Help From My Friends' on the tenth anniversary of International Friendship Day?"

A knowing smile curled her lips. "And you'll always have mine, Sedona."

Before it became too awkward with me standing there reciting more facts instead of expressing how I felt, I patted the side of my jeans, groaning out loud.

"Micah has the keys, doesn't he?" She said it more as a fact than a question.

I closed my eyes momentarily before remembering I'd stashed a separate key just in case I ever found myself in this predicament. I tried not to kick myself too hard for forgetting.

"You're way too trusting, Sedona," Callie exclaimed behind me as she cautiously looked about to see if anyone had seen me retrieve the spare. I'd have to find a different hiding spot again.

I turned the key in the handle and entered the bookstore. "You're not the first person to tell me that." My response came out in a grumble, and my friend laughed.

"Then I agree with him. Just don't tell him that." Him being Micah. "Never tell a man that you think he's right. It sets a very dangerous precedent, and they become unbearably arrogant after that." There was a knowing gleam in her eyes that told me she spoke from experience.

"Duly noted." I glanced about. Everything looked normal and the same. I waited for the sensation of dread that often rose up and threatened to suffocate me, but it never came. "I think I'm good now."

And I was.

We exchanged one last hug with the promise to have lunch some time later that week. Watching her leave reminded me of the importance of not completely shutting myself off from the world. That sometimes the risk of letting people in and truly seeing who you are was worth it.

Lifting the sage to my nose, I took in a deep breath.

"Time to clean."

Then, with the lighter I found in the top drawer of the front counter, I got to work smudging away the trauma of the past.

# CHAPTER 3

*I* knew exactly where he'd be, and after successfully smudging every inch, nook, and cranny of the store, I locked up for the second time that day and made my way to him.

Nerves coursed through me as I mentally rehearsed the conversation I was about to have. It was hard not to shrink away from admitting I'd acted like a complete loon. I wasn't used to losing control like that. Trusting that he'd forgive my momentarily lapse in judgment, I walked through the white picket fence gate and trudged up the steps to his door.

*Piece of cake*, I muttered softly to myself, taking in a fortifying breath of courage. This was what it meant to be a responsible adult. Emotions were often complicated, expressing them sometimes difficult. But that didn't mean a person got a free ticket to act as they wanted and not face the consequences.

This was my walk of shame of sorts. Thankfully the only person who knew how I was feeling right now was securely inside the house, on the other side of the door I was knocking on.

The sound of footsteps heightened my anxiety, and I gulped hard. Without thinking, I slipped my hand into my pocket and found the labradorite crystal I carried. The heat sizzled against my skin, and I smiled with a little more confidence.

Tomorrow I'd send Callie her favorite bottle of wine from

Soothing Sips. That or a fresh order of Mexican goodies from Tacos for Daze. I didn't think she realized just how much her small intervention this afternoon had helped. It was the difference between night and day—calm and chaos. Standing there in Eloise's new age store had helped unknot my abilities so I could focus.

The door swung open, and my stomach dipped. Thankfully I didn't gasp out loud like an idiot. I didn't know what had happened, but the sight of Micah standing there in just a plain white T-shirt and dark denim jeans made my heart race a little faster and my mouth water.

I never wanted that feeling to go away.

"Hey," I whispered, a sudden shyness taking over.

He leaned against the door frame, his arms folded across his chest. Someone else might've read his body language as being apprehensive or cautious, but I wasn't paying attention to any of that. My gaze went to his arms and the sight brought back the memories of how safe and secure I'd felt in his embrace. There was nothing intimidating or scary about this man. Even with the knowledge that he was a warrior amongst angels didn't dim or erase that growing attraction between us.

"Hi." A dimple appeared as he offered me a warm smile. God, how I loved making that appear.

"Can we talk?" My request came out rushed, as if the words themselves worried that I wouldn't utter them. "I need to explain." It was tempting to purge everything right there and then to babble and ramble like I was prone to do. I wanted to do this right, however, so I gestured over my shoulder. "It's a nice night. Want to go for a walk with me?"

Micah nodded, and disappeared into the house, no doubt warning Holly that if she dared to step a foot outside the house and the protective warding he'd established, he'd ground her for fifty lifetimes. Right now, that was his favorite threat whenever she was feeling rebellious.

Not that his young charge purposely tested her limits. Austin's attack had scared the bejeezus out of her. She'd also gotten it into her head that she wanted to go to Havenwood Falls High when they had registration for the new school year. It meant she'd have to prove she was reliable and could follow the lengthy list of rules he'd no doubt insist she agree to.

I was silently rooting for her. She was a good kid having to deal with a shitty destiny. It wasn't her fault who her father was or that there was a price out for her death. Details about their life before coming to Havenwood Falls were still elusive and fiercely protected by Micah. He was firm when he said that the less I knew, the better. What I did know was enough to make me worry. I couldn't imagine the pressure of always looking over my shoulder, studying the shadows for a constant threat. It was hard enough dealing with the repercussions of being an empath.

Micah returned, and I stepped aside as he locked the door.

"Can't be too careful, right?" I added, trying to find a way to bridge the conversation from politeness to what was pressing against my heart.

He simply nodded. I didn't like quiet Micah.

"Did you know that flamingos bend their legs at the ankle?" I continued, keeping my tone light and open. "They basically stand on tiptoe." As if to demonstrate, I stood on mine and looked at Micah, hoping against hope that I'd be rewarded with some kind of indication of what he was thinking. When we'd started dating, one of the ground rules had been that I would try not to use my abilities on him without permission. Relationships were about trust, and I'd been adamant that he wouldn't ever have to worry about me trying to gain an unfair advantage. I still remembered that conversation where Aunt Millicent had given it away that she'd asked me to spy on him. The hurt in his eyes and voice was something I never wanted to see again.

"Interesting." It was all he said.

I took that as a good sign.

"Did you know that rollercoasters were invented to distract Americans from sin?" That made his eyebrows raise. I licked my lips and smiled. "Yeah, I think that guy's name was something Thompson." I briefly paused as I searched my memory. "Marco . . . Marcus . . ." Then it came like a lightning strike. "LaMarcus. That's it. LaMarcus Thompson. It was his way of giving New Yorkers a more wholesome pastime than visiting saloons and brothels." My face reddened. "Not sure why he thought there was a comparison." My cheeks flushed as heat crept over my skin. Now my mind was on sex . . . sex with Micah.

I could tell he was stifling his need to laugh, biting the insides of his mouth. We started walking, side by side, his shoulder brushing against mine.

"I know which one I'd prefer." His answer caused me to stumble, and I reached out to steady myself with his arm. Micah said nothing else. At least he was consistent.

There wasn't really any kind of destination as we strolled down the street, turning at one corner, only to head in a different direction at the next. More facts tumbled about in my head. It wasn't what I wanted to talk about, though. I felt like there was this giant proverbial elephant sitting in the room between us—the memory of my arguing with him earlier.

I bit the bullet before my impatience broke and slapped me hard.

"Micah?" I ignored the way I asked him timidly.

He didn't answer as we rounded another corner, and right as I was about to grab his arm and force him to look at me, he took charge and pulled me into him. No words were exchanged as I peered up into his stormy expression. There wasn't just one emotion simmering within his gaze. I had to force myself to blink before I got swept away in the hurricane.

"I'm so sorry," I uttered, hoping that it wouldn't come across as feeble. I didn't get a chance to add anything else before he crushed his mouth to mine, tightening his embrace around me.

He was kissing me.

He wasn't being silent anymore because the smoldering kiss he was delivering was saying everything for him.

I didn't resist.

I didn't stop him, so we could talk about our feelings and what an idiot I was.

I let his lips press against mine, and when his tongue stroked the seam of my mouth, I opened up completely. The groan that erupted at the first touch of his tongue almost buckled my knees. There was no uncertainty in the way he kissed me or how, with a simple caress of Micah's breath at my throat, he could be so dominant and masterful. This was the kind of kiss that I read about in books—the type that laid claim and laid bare. Micah was telling me that all was forgiven. He was showing me that nothing had changed. He was proving, once and for all, that I wasn't alone . . . that I had him.

I wrapped my arms around his neck, not wanting this moment to end. Not because it would mean I still needed to apologize, but because, just like the crystal in my pocket, it filled me with a delicious heat that made me feel invincible. It filled me with light—one that blasted away the doubt that had been lurking there.

His fingers tangled in my hair, sending chills through my body, prickling my scalp. Everywhere he touched obliterated the worries I had about us. I just couldn't shake the doubt that whispered the attack was my fault.

"Micah," I murmured, barely able to get his name out.

"It doesn't matter," came his response, his own breathing a little ragged. "I believed you that night when you came to stop me from leaving with Holly."

My mind raced to remember. Then suddenly it was there.

*"I can't promise what tomorrow holds, but we'll face it together."*

I'd meant every word when I'd said it a month ago. In that moment, I'd felt so brave, so unbelievably confident that there was nothing that could stand in our way to happiness. I'd been so naïve.

"Do you still believe that?" Cradling my face between his hands, his thumb brushed back and forth over my cheek. Each caress left shivers in its wake. "Please tell me you still believe it."

Did I?

Did I still feel that conviction, especially in the wake of my suppressed guilt?

I wanted to say yes, but for some reason, I couldn't get it to leave the tip of my tongue.

"But how can you trust me?" It came out so soft that Micah had to lean in to catch my question.

Taking hold of my hands, he brought them to his mouth, kissing the backs of my fingers. "Because I know your heart, Sedona. Because I know you would never wish Holly or me harm." When he saw I was about to argue and push my point further, he brushed the pad of his thumb lightly over my bottom lip before leaning in to feather an even lighter kiss over my mouth. "Sometimes bad things happen. Sometimes they happen despite every precaution taken. All we can do is face each challenge when it comes."

I started to shake my head. "It can't be that simple, though. We're not talking about a small oversight here, Micah. I brought someone into your lives who had every intention of kidnapping Holly. This Collector person is a real and genuine threat. Not some perceived threat. Not some distant phantom wailing and rattling its chains."

"And we thwarted that attempt."

"That bullet could've easily killed her." This was an admission that lay right at the foundation of my guilt. I didn't care that I'd been the one who got shot. My entire focus was on that sweet teenager whom Micah had sacrificed so much to protect and keep hidden.

"Yes, and thankfully, it didn't." He stroked away the single tear that had escaped from my eye. "It wasn't your fault, Sedona."

I lowered my defenses and made myself vulnerable to him. Standing there in the street where the town continued about its nightly business, oblivious to the two people struggling to find a balance in their relationship, I closed my eyes and rested my head against his chest. I could hear his heart beating, and slowly, my own matched it.

"How do you do that?" I asked, not moving.

"Hmm?" His response rumbled against my ear. "Do what?"

"Make things calm while standing in the midst of a storm." I was tempted to sneak a peek at his face, but that would require moving, and I was feeling too comfortable and safe in his embrace. This was all so new to me still.

I felt him shrug. "I don't know. I guess I try to stay as true to myself and what I believe as I can. The love I feel for you is real, so I focus on that."

Butterflies fluttered in my stomach at the sound of him saying he loved me. "You make it sound so easy, though."

He finally laughed, the sound filling the night air. "It's far from easy, but worth the effort. You decide what you give your attention to. I choose the silver linings." His next words thrilled me. "I choose us."

"I didn't mean to lose my temper with you today. I could hear the words coming out of my mouth but did nothing to stop it. I was feeling insecure, and once I started, it came out like verbal diarrhea." I cringed at the last word. Definitely not conducive to talking about love. "You must've thought I was crazy."

His hand was firm at the small of my back, and he added a little pressure there. "Want to know what I thought?"

This time I stepped out of our embrace and really looked into his kind face. There wasn't a trace of annoyance or frustration. His were the features of a man who was being open and honest.

"Yes, please. Makes it easier than guessing."

*And getting it wrong,* I added mentally.

"I wished I'd known you were carrying such a heavy burden, something that was never yours to begin with." He kept his hands where they'd fallen to his sides, his fingers moving ever so slightly, like he was trying not to reach out and touch me. "I can't change what happened. I felt helpless this afternoon as I watched the dam you've been using to keep everything inside crack and crumble. You were hurting."

"That doesn't excuse me lashing out at you, though, Micah."

He nodded. "It doesn't, but it helps me understand better. Plus, I knew once you calmed down, you'd come so we could talk. Time has a way of healing wounds, Sedona. Space does the same, but I can't seem to keep myself from reaching out and holding you close." And with that last confession, his arms were back around me, and this time I didn't try to step away. I reveled in the warmth from his body.

"So we're good?" I asked, just to make sure.

"We were never not good," he replied. "As long as we can talk through it, we'll be able to get through anything. Just don't shut me out, okay?"

"Right back atcha," I answered, feeling lighter. He laughed at my teasing.

"Let me get you home."

We walked again in comfortable silence, holding hands as the sounds of cars passing by finally filled my ears. I'd basically tuned everything out except us. I hadn't noticed that people were still out and about.

As we reached the end of the street, someone came around the corner, bumping into me as they passed by.

I didn't pay them any attention, my focus still on the miracle that was me and Micah.

We'd overcome another hurdle—this one of my own creation. Unlike my earlier doubt, today had somehow made us stronger as a couple. I could feel it all the way down to my toes. Everything felt . . . right.

And the heated kiss we exchanged at my door just proved the thought that once again floated to the surface.

Life was good.

Love was good.

So very, very good.

# CHAPTER 4

*N**ever let somebody's drama determine the outcome of your day.*

The desktop calendar of daily quotes was spookily accurate today as I caught sight of the last person I wanted to see this early in the morning.

"Any more words of advice, Mr. Terry Mark?" I asked out loud, staring hard at the square printed paper as though it would magically add an extra quote or two. Unfortunately, magical powers or not, I wasn't Harry Potter talking to Tom Riddle's journal.

Sometime in the future, I was going to need to fix this tension between my aunt and me. As an empath, I got an inside advantage to how she viewed the world—to how she saw our relationship. Buried deep beneath her pride and driving need to be useful lurked her love for me. I couldn't fault her for constantly pushing me toward using my magic more. With no children of her own, she saw it as safeguarding our family's legacy and ensuring that her knowledge didn't fall by the wayside.

What I struggled with was her inability to even acknowledge my own needs. That same thirst for power didn't run through my veins. When ambition was handed out in Heaven, I was busy reading or something, and missed out. She saw it as a character flaw to desperately squash. Once my parents died, and then my grandfather, the pressure fell even harder on her shoulders.

For the most part, we danced around each other, our game of tug of war often ending in mutual frustration.

It didn't help that I antagonized her. I considered it payback for the countless lectures she delivered, her voice droning as she talked about family honor and my lack of respect.

And here she was again, about to grace me with her presence. The look of determination that filled her features didn't betray her purpose for the visit. Neither did the haughty scowl she offered when she entered.

"Good morning, Sedona. I trust that everything is well with you." Her greeting was almost dismissive as she strode past where I was sitting at the counter, her focus directed toward the back of the store.

*So she was here for that*, I mused. It was going to be *that* kind of social call.

Secreted in the far back wall, beyond the entrance that led to the store room, was a door that led to the upstairs apartment. My grandfather had lived up there until he took his last breath, and it was where the pull-down ladder was kept for the attic.

No one had cause to go up there. Going up to the attic to find some window display inspiration was the last time I'd ventured that way, and honestly, it hurt my heart too much to be surrounded by all the items that represented my beloved grandfather's life.

"What can I help you with you, Auntie?" I asked, forcing her to stop in her tracks and talk with me. If she was wanting into his apartment, she was going for one reason only—the extensive library of magical tomes and paraphernalia he'd collected and inherited.

That I'd inherited, according to his will.

There was no mistaking her exasperation. "I need to find a certain volume from the *family* collection." I didn't miss the heavy emphasis placed on *family*. "Unless you're ready to step up and do your part." A smug smile briefly curled her lips before she returned to her normal expression.

I didn't take the bait. "Wait until I'm finished with this." I gestured to the pile of paperwork I'd been successfully ignoring up until now. "Then I can let you in and get it for you." I threw her one of my own grins, feigning interest in the electricity bills.

"I wouldn't want to rush you, niece." Her foot betrayed her false patience, tapping twice.

I rested my hands on the top of the counter and pushed my chair back. "What were you looking for in particular?"

Part of me really didn't want to ask, because she would see it as a foothold into berating me about my shameful reluctance.

Aunt Millicent was nothing if not predictable. "Important research for the coven." Peering over her glasses so she resembled an eagle looking down on the world, she started speaking the words that began most of the arguments we had. "If you didn't squander your gifts, you would know. The coven is always needing the support of powerful witches like you, Sedona." She even had the same tone of shame and disgust. "You have no idea how embarrassing it is to see others bring their family members into the fold, and yet I remain alone in my duty."

I was careful to keep my own sigh quiet as I continued up the stairs. "Yeah, I imagine it's got to suck."

That was the wrong thing to say. "Sedona Mathews, that's enough of your sarcasm, thank you very much." She grabbed my arm and squeezed harder than anticipated. I squeaked from the brief flash of pain as her nails dug in through my light sweater. When I added a loud *ow*, she finally released her grip. "You know I do this because I love you. I wouldn't push if I didn't recognize what great potential you have. Not just as your birthright, but also because I believe you can achieve anything once you put your mind to it."

This was the closest she ever came to praising me. As with any of our conversations, there was always a major *but* at the end of such small compliments.

"But?" I prompted, wanting to speed this up. I still had bills and applications to ignore.

"Why must you try my patience?" she exclaimed, sounding more and more like she was the victim of some horrible verbal assault. "All I've ever wanted was to see you succeed, Sedona. Is it wrong for me to want greater things for you?"

So help me, if she sniffled or feigned any kind of emotion, I was going to stop, go back downstairs, and leave the store. I wasn't in the mood for her brand of encouragement.

"Sorry, Aunt Millicent," I mumbled, choosing instead to not add fuel to the flames between us. We finally entered into the small living room area in my grandfather's home. A heavy coating of dust covered every surface, all except for the large pieces of furniture I'd thrown sheets over to protect.

It seemed she had something else to say. "Why do you still keep that tiny apartment over at Havenwood Village when you could easily move into here?" She scrunched up her face as she looked like she was about to sneeze. "I'm sure he would be pleased knowing you were close."

Turning about in the room, I took in all the familiar sights that still pulled at my heart and memories. We spent countless nights sitting in front of the now abandoned fireplace—both he and I with our books opened, a comfortable silence enveloping us as we read. Many discussions had been shared across the small dining room table —some that would cause my aunt's eyebrows to rise so high that they'd fall over the top of her head and down her back. My grandfather always nurtured my love of facts and learning. There was never a topic we couldn't tackle together, and some of my earliest childhood recollections came from the tidbits he shared over a meal with me.

I shrugged, not really knowing how to answer her. It had always been an expectation that one day I'd make the decision and move everything over. It made a ton of sense, considering I worked downstairs. Maybe that was why I hadn't made the leap yet. It was nice having a separation between business and personal.

Besides, the grief I still harbored over the loss of a most beloved patriarch hadn't faded enough for my liking. In the back of my mind, I still held the belief that he was tinkering around while I worked downstairs. I wasn't ready to let go of the fantasy.

I eventually pointed over to the closed door. "Help yourself." Wrapping my arms around myself tightly, I was ready to just leave her up here to figure it out. "I'll see you back downstairs."

"You're not going to assist?" My reluctance to stay was nothing surprising. Her gaze sharpened as though she could somehow break me by sheer will. Then something completely unexpected happened. I would later wonder if I'd imagined it.

Her facial muscles relaxed, and I caught a small glimpse of whom she might have been.

"Sedona, I know I'm not the most pleasant to be around, but I ask that we put aside our differences long enough so I can find the answers I'm seeking." There was a foreign tone to her plea. It was with a gasp that I realized she was being one hundred percent sincere. "Please."

It was with that same earnestness that I heard myself replying I would.

I hadn't entered my grandfather's magic room since his death, and now I was willingly following my aunt inside.

Hell must've frozen over.

That or the purple pig had sprouted wings and was now circling overhead.

For whatever reason, there was one thought that stuck.

Aunt Millicent had said please.

Holy crap.

"CONSIDER WHAT I SAID CAREFULLY, Sedona. That's all I ask."

To say the past few hours upstairs with my aunt was like visiting the Twilight Zone would have been an understatement. It had been hard to trust the softer side she showed me—that niggly voice in the back of my head warning me that this was some kind of trap intended to manipulate me.

But over the course of three hours, I'd laughed more with my aunt than I could remember ever doing before. I caught myself opening up and sharing some of the memories I had with my grandfather. Where I expected some snide comment or caustic remark, Aunt Millicent was attentive and genuine in her reactions. It was as if some kind of temporal shift had happened, and this was a new reality where we actually got along.

As we walked back downstairs and toward the front door, a sense of regret filled me. I didn't want this visit to end. I actually liked the woman my aunt could be—that is, if she ever stopped nagging me.

So when she turned one last time and asked me to ponder our discussion, that old familiar feeling of frustration flared back into existence. Her new personality had run its course, and today would slip into the shadows again, something I would later count as a fluke.

I nodded reluctantly, already regressing to our old, familiar patterns. "Sure."

Compassion filled her gaze. Maybe I hadn't imagined this afternoon. "Things are stirring up in town, and we all must be prepared. That's another reason why I push you so hard. I want you to have every chance of surviving it." There was a small, sharp inhale as her expression turned to panic. She'd disclosed something she shouldn't have. "You have so much of your mother in you."

I scrunched my forehead. That was a weird subject change.

"She was this stubborn?" I fired back, already knowing the answer.

It was something that my grandfather celebrated, and one of the many character flaws my aunt liked to point out. I always felt a tinge of pride at the reminder that I was my mother's daughter.

There was that look of exasperation I'd been waiting for. With a slight eye roll, Aunt Millicent shook her head like she wasn't quite sure what to do with me. "Yes, but my point was that she failed to accept the power she held and the responsibility she shouldered in wielding it."

I hated that every conversation seemed to devolve into the same argument.

"It's called a choice," I answered, annoyed that after all this time, she still couldn't accept this fundamental truth. "We get to decide what's best for us. What makes us happy. What we want to pursue, and what we'd rather let go of. We decide the priorities and important things in our life."

Gone was the soft undertone from my voice as disappointment followed with the realization that this . . . *this* would always be the relationship we had.

"I never pictured you the coward." Her abrupt judgment felt like a slap in the face.

I swung open the front door and stepped to the side. "And I didn't imagine someone who claimed to love me would actually hurt me." I gestured outside. "I think it's best you leave now."

"You always were overly dramatic. I suppose that's what comes with spending your life with your head in the clouds and nose in a book." She stood in the doorway, peering down her nose at me. "Forgive me for thinking after all you suffered with Austin and the questions your boyfriend keeps asking, you'd be begging for my help in sharpening your abilities." She had the nerve to tut and shake her head like she was the victim here. It was even lower for her to try to manipulate me using Micah and the mysterious Collector.

Micah had said he was trying to find out information about the one I truly held responsible for Austin and the attempt to kidnap Holly.

"Enough," I blurted out as my eyes began filling with tears. "I need you to hear me. I am not the Sedona you have all these expectations for. I'm not some pawn to control. I'm not your doll to dress up and play with. I'm sorry that I'm not this perfect niece that you can show off around the water cooler. I'm sure it's a source of embarrassment, but I am who I am. If you can't accept that—accept me—then maybe it's time we finally end this charade and call it quits."

My chest tightened. My heart ached. I loved my aunt, but there came a point where enough was enough.

"Confidence. That's all you're lacking."

The sense of utter letdown was suffocating. She hadn't listened to a single word.

"Good night, Millicent." Closing the door on her, I slid the lock into place, and turned around with my back against the frame. Tears streamed down my cheeks. My body felt as though I'd just been hit by a freight train, exhaustion setting in.

I don't know how long I stood there quietly crying. At some point I felt Maxwell appear and saw him from the corner of my eye, but then he disappeared. I was grateful for the ghost's reluctance in finding out what was wrong, because I still had no idea of the right way to explain the rollercoaster of emotions I was going through.

How could I say out loud that I would never be anything more than a tool to be used by the only immediate family I had in town?

How could I acknowledge the truth that I'd kept buried inside— that even after all the many hurtful actions and comments, I still harbored the secret desire to one day be a true family?

This last discussion had shattered that fragile hope I'd somehow managed to keep protected all these years. It was time to grow up and face reality.

It was time to let go.

# CHAPTER 5

*I*f it wasn't for the fact that I knew Havenwood Falls wasn't capable of insanely hot temperatures, I would've bet my life I was experiencing a heat wave. It had started when I'd peeled off my sheets and comforter this morning and had steamrolled through my day until I was forced to resort to using a spray bottle filled with the iciest, coldest water I could find.

The temptation to run upstairs and stand in front of the freezer was crippling, and as another trickle of sweat rolled down the center of my back, it was everything I could do not to yell out that the bookstore was closed.

It was stifling and unbearable.

It was also embarrassing, because nobody else had any idea what I was carrying on about. Micah's thick flannel shirt made me want to shred the garment from his body. He was wearing too much, and just the sight of him made me feel claustrophobic in my own skin.

I spritzed myself again.

And again.

Damn, it was nauseatingly hot.

"Maybe I should take you to the doctor?" Micah asked, for what felt like the millionth time. It didn't matter that he could heal me with a mere touch of his hand. He'd declared the thermometer I'd stashed in the first aid kit was faulty, even as the tiny display screen revealed that I wasn't running a fever.

"Other than the heat, I feel fine." I plastered a smile across my face like it would convince him. "Why waste the doctor's time if it's just a twenty-four-hour thing?"

"Perhaps you're going through the change," Maxwell announced, choosing this moment to appear. "Although you are a tad too young to be affected by such a malady."

I wanted to throttle the ghost for even suggesting it. "This isn't menopause, you ill-mannered pain in my butt!"

If it was even possible, I felt my cheeks grow hotter. I pressed my hands against my warm skin. That was the other conundrum.

I was hot from the inside, but normal to the touch.

Micah reached out and felt my forehead for himself. "I don't like this," he murmured. "Maybe you should go home and rest. I can watch over things here if you're worried about the store."

While lying about on the couch with a book in my hand seemed heavenly and inviting, my extra-long to-do list wouldn't allow it.

"Which brings me to the real reason why I asked you to come today." This next part was exciting, and I couldn't help the butterfly feeling in my stomach. New things and projects always gave me a good case of nervous jitters. I picked up the top piece of paper from the flyers I'd just finished printing out.

I held it up to show him and Maxwell. "What do you think?"

Micah's eyes moved back and forth as he silently read the information. "You want to host a book swap here at the store?"

My nod was a little too enthusiastic, but I didn't try to curb it. I couldn't help my passion for reading.

"Yep, well, actually out in the street, but yeah. I've already gotten the town council's approval, and I know it's short notice—" I paused as panic rose up my throat mid-sentence. When the idea had come to me early this morning while I was showering, I'd worried that three days wasn't enough time to make arrangements and organize the event. It wasn't until everything started falling into place that I gave myself permission to believe. Hopefully, it would be the first of many.

"It is, but I have faith you can do it, my sweet girl." Maxwell had tossed aside his usual sarcastic comments, and instead wore a look of pride. "Give you something else to focus on besides that witch whom I won't mention." For someone I'd only really known for the past few years since I started running Shelf Indulgence, Maxwell was fiercely protective when it counted. Phantom tears had filled his own eyes when I'd entered this morning. He'd heard it all last night, and it had pained him to witness it. "You've got this one to help as well, although I don't think he can hear me." So far, Micah hadn't acted like he saw the resident spook. I didn't bother questioning it. Their relationship was an odd one.

"The ghost is right," Micah added, finally acknowledging him.

"Ooooh, so he does see me!" That seemed to put the proverbial firecracker beneath Maxwell as his ghostly eyes flashed brightly.

For the first time today, Micah turned to where Maxwell was standing with a smirk. "I have no problem seeing you. I just choose not to."

I burst out laughing, which in turn made the guys smile wider.

"Play nice." I reached out and slapped Micah across the chest. The movement caused a ripple of desire to flood my body. He was like a walking contradiction—he was all muscles and hardness, his physique in what could only be described as glorious shape. But I'd also experienced what others might consider the polar opposite—in his arms, I could feel the softness of those same muscles as he wrapped me up in his protective embrace.

Soft and hard.

My gaze dropped for a moment as the word *hard* echoed and bounced around inside my brain. It wasn't the first time my thoughts went to a slightly more intimate place. There was so much about Micah I didn't know about yet, but there was one thing I was pretty certain about.

I was excited to explore new possibilities with him.

*I'm ready to explore him,* came my low, lustful voice.

"So you want me to go hand these out and spread the word?" He had no idea that I'd been quietly undressing him in my mind. That ignorance made me blush, making me wonder if I'd ever be brave enough to act on my inner brazenness. We'd had some pretty intense make-out sessions, but Micah had wanted to take things slowly.

His request had all but blown my mind. Usually I was the one throwing on the brakes when the guys I dated headed straight to the bedroom. The fact that he was the one to slow it down simply intrigued me more. He was different. I loved that about him.

I quickly nodded when I realized they were both waiting for my answer. "Yes, please. The sooner people know, the better I can breathe and stop telling myself I'm crazy for doing it."

Micah read over the flyer again. "You worry too much. I think this is an awesome thing, and after you work your magic, it'll go perfectly." He grabbed my hand and squeezed it. "Plus, maybe it'll clear up some space for new inventory."

This time I did know my cheeks reddened. I wasn't used to someone being that attentive and remembering random outbursts and comments I made. I'd said some off-the-cuff thing about wanting to bring in a whole new collection of books and updating the store's online catalog. Of course, Micah would remember and bring it up right when I needed to hear it.

I refused to let his hand go. "That's the hope." That's when a pang of sadness returned, and I cast a sidelong glance at the applications I'd been ignoring. "I shouldn't have procrastinated. If all goes well, this place will be too busy for just one person." When Maxwell cleared his throat, I added, "And ghost." He winked his gratitude at finally being included.

"Actually, that's the perfect segue into something I wanted to run by you." Micah was doing his best impersonation of the Cheshire Cat. "How would you feel if Holly took over Austin's position?"

It was so not what I thought he would ask.

"I've thought about it too many times to count and disregarded it, because I know how cautious you are with her. Why?" I zeroed in on him and studied his body language. Just out of curiosity, I reached out with my empathic skills to see what he was feeling. Nothing. Even here, alone, he wouldn't—couldn't—lower his guard.

He caught me in the act. "Ask me, Sedona. Don't try to sneak it out of me."

There was enough of a hint of amusement in his voice that I knew he wasn't too mad at my being nosy.

"I'd hire her in a heartbeat, Micah, but I honestly can't have you standing in the corner, or stalking customers throughout the store because Holly is helping them. How many books do you think we'll sell if people don't want to come anymore?" I narrowed my gaze at him. "Be honest. As much as I love having you here, your bodyguard warrior mojo façade will only make her uncomfortable."

Squeezing his hand again, I finally let it go.

I expected Micah to argue with me. Instead, he smiled even bigger. The look he wore rivaled even the happiest child on Christmas morning. You'd have thought he'd just met Santa.

"I found the perfect compromise. A way that Holly can get a tiny taste of independence." There was the guardian I knew. "And you can rest easier knowing that you can toss those resumes in the trash. In fact, let me do that for you." With one swift swipe of his hand, Micah snatched up the pile, and with a grand flourish, deposited them into the bin.

I hated being the Debbie Downer. I didn't always look at the negative, but life had thrown some pretty painful curveballs lately. I was trying not to be too naïve. "Problem solved, huh? Just like that."

His excitement was contagious. It made me want to take his face between my hands and kiss him senseless. His aura glowed brightly— the golden light shining in the flecks of his eyes.

"Maxwell!" Micah all but boomed out his name. "How would you feel about doing a special job for me?"

Again, my boyfriend surprised me. He wanted a ghost to babysit Holly? A being that had no corporeal body and had only recently managed to leave the store.

I was glad to see I wasn't the only one shocked. "While I'm flattered, Micah, I do believe I'm the wrong person for the job." He'd understood the meaning as well.

Micah looked like he couldn't be so easily dissuaded. "I know it sounds crazy, but hear me out. I wouldn't be suggesting this if I didn't believe one hundred percent that it was a viable option. Maxwell," he turned to the older gentleman, "you have your own special bond with Holly, so I believe you will always put her first. She spends most of her time here or at home. As much as I have loved being here and helping, there's going to come a time when I can't. It makes sense."

He now turned his attention to me. "Wouldn't you like to go on a date or spend time alone together? I know how fond you are of Holly, but I also know you want to be wooed and romanced."

Yet another example of him listening to me. I was always telling him about the stories I was reading, swooning over the main characters and their happily-ever-afters.

"True," I agreed tentatively. "I won't lie and say it wouldn't be nice, but never at the expense of Holly and her safety. You're not the only one who takes mental notes. You've made it crystal clear that our relationship can't ever overshadow your main priority of hiding her." There was no resentment in my tone.

"Do you trust me?" For the briefest second, I got a flash of Aladdin offering his outstretched hand to Jasmine. He wanted to show her the world. Micah was asking me to consider the one he was trying to create—a world where he could see a way to both have his cake and eat it, too.

I didn't hesitate. "Absolutely."

"Then let's try this. I wouldn't have suggested this if I hadn't already played out every possible scenario in my head." Maxwell and I still weren't completely convinced. "Fine. Test me."

"What if someone comes in here and has a gun?" It wasn't a hard thing to imagine. There was no point dodging the truth. This had happened.

Micah grimaced. It was still a fresh pain for him as well. "Then you will work your magic, and Maxwell will come for me immediately."

"What if that person leaves with Holly?" It was the ghost's turn to ask.

We continued to grill him for another five minutes, and each time we asked a new question, he came back with a solid answer. This wasn't just some random plan. Micah had given it a lot of thought.

"I can't believe I'm having to convince you about this." He laughed, shaking his head.

"And I can't believe you're willing to loosen that tight grip you've had when it comes to her well-being," I countered.

"Then let's take it day by day. On a trial basis." All humor drained from his face as Micah turned serious. "Trust me. This is the only solution."

He then turned back to Maxwell. "What do you say?"

The ghost studied him thoroughly. Seconds ticked by, and I wondered if Micah could feel the specter's scrutiny clear down to the soles of his feet.

Maxwell fiddled with the end of his moustache, deep in thought.

"Well?" The whole idea was contingent on his agreement.

"If it means I don't have to witness any more of your groping and kissing around here, I say why not." Beneath the fake expression of disgust rose a happier one. He was glad to see me happy and making plans again.

"I'll take that as a yes, Maxwell," Micah said, and he picked up the pile of flyers. "If there's nothing else, I'd better get started on these. I'll have Holly help while I explain the new arrangement."

We all looked over toward the far-right corner of the store. Shelves and displays hid her from our view, but Holly had headed in that direction when they first entered the store. She had no doubt tuned out the world, escaping into the book she'd been carrying.

"Before you go," I blurted, coughing when I heard how weird I sounded. "There's something I need from the attic." I pointed to the ceiling like the gesture would reveal my intention. Or like they needed to know where it was. I was nervous.

Micah nodded. "Then let me know what it is, and I'll grab it for you. Who knows how long these will take to distribute." Rolling the stack into a loose tube, he followed behind me. Any excuse to check out my butt.

The second I heard the door leading upstairs close behind us, I whipped around, and launched myself at Micah. My arms worked their way around his neck, and the kiss I'd been daydreaming about happened.

The flyers dropped to the floor, forgotten, as Micah returned my urgency with that of his own. He didn't hold back. He didn't try to take over or control the aching desire that seemed to explode out from me.

I couldn't get enough of him.

His touch.

His taste.

The sound he made—that guttural groan that just screamed sex.

Everything about my angel was intoxicating, overwhelming, and unbelievably addicting.

I'd told him that once—that he was like that first sip of coffee in the morning, that first chapter in a book that reaches out and whisks you away on an adventure. Books often described it like a drug, but I'd never experienced that. All I knew—all that I was familiar with— was the way his energy set my own on fire. I couldn't keep my own moans from passing through my lips, and some were there simply because I couldn't bear for the kiss to end.

I wanted him.

Wanted all of him.

Right here.

Right now.

My hands dropped to his belt like they'd been doing it forever. There was no feeling awkward or shy. This was where we usually stopped, but I was tired of waiting. Suddenly, I didn't care that we were dangerously close to having our first time in a narrow stairway.

The only thing I could think, that flashed over and over in my mind, was how good this felt, and how natural the next step was. I was by no means a virgin. But these emotions that Micah stirred up in me were definitely new.

The thought made my fingers tremble and slip. His belt was proving to be an obstacle.

Unfortunately, it was enough of a slip that Micah took hold of my hand to stop me.

His breath came out ragged. "Wait."

I stopped and watched as he wet his lips. God, I needed to kiss those lips.

"Why now?" he asked.

"I don't know," I whispered. "It just feels like the right thing to do."

He took my face between his hands and brought his mouth to my forehead, kissing it ever so lightly. "Heaven knows I want this, Sedona."

I tried not to laugh at his choice of words.

It was my turn to sigh as my heart thundered in my chest. I was positively thrumming with desire. It was both terrifying and exhilarating. "So let's take that next step." I peered up into his blue eyes. "I'm ready."

He brushed his thumbs across my cheeks. "Then not like this. I don't want this to be our first time."

Reality crashed around me, and I finally laughed. What the hell had just come over me?

"How about you come over tonight? I'll cook us some dinner, and we'll take it from there." I rose up on my tiptoes and briefly pressed my lips against his. He held my head in place, deepening the kiss until I was back to being aware of only the two of us. I could see why falling in love could be dangerous for empaths. I wasn't just feeling my own emotions. For microbursts of time, I caught his. It was like trying to snatch sparks of light from the air. Just when you think you've captured one, you open your hand and your palm is empty.

I could also see why Micah worried about becoming involved with me. It required a level of trust he wasn't used to. In order to focus on me, he ran the risk of blocking out his focus on Holly. It was enough to make me want to pull back and break the kiss.

If I could.

If I had some kind of choice—my heart overruled my brain this time, willing to drown in desire and excitement.

Micah was the one to do it. "I'd better go." He didn't move, though. It was as if he didn't want to break the magic of the moment either. "Any minute now."

My arms began to drop from where I'd had them around his neck again. Placing my hands on his chest, it was safe to say I'd never been so torn in my life. All it would take was a word, and a few more steps up into the apartment, and it would happen. Micah and I would have sex, and it would be everything I'd ever imagined it to be.

Sometimes being responsible sucked.

I created some much needed distance between our bodies.

"Go. The sooner we get done, the sooner we can start our evening." My voice sounded so needy and guttural. Micah's eyes widened. He liked what he heard.

"I'll let Maxwell know our new plans." He took a step back as well, bumping into the door at the bottom. "Well, not all our plans, but that he'll be watching Holly tonight at my house. I've got plenty of wards there to keep them both safe until I show up."

"Are you sure?" A new wave of concern blasted the last of my desire.

Micah bounded up to where I still stood. He kissed me again, hard and fast. "Positive." He didn't wait for my response. With a wave over his shoulder, he exited through the door. I didn't follow.

Instead I sat on the step, gingerly touching my swollen lips.

Tonight, then.

Tonight, everything would change.

# CHAPTER 6

*Y*ou could cut the sexual tension with a knife.

Never in my life had I experienced this intensity personally, making me wonder how I'd ever lived without it. I knew that sounded cheesy, but it took everything I had to breathe through the emotions that filled the air. It had nothing to do with being bombarded with other people's lust and desire.

No, the sensations that were wreaking havoc over my psyche were emanating from me. Part of me wanted to ask Micah if he was drowning in it as well, but every time the words formed in my mouth, I chickened out.

Dinner was almost ready, and the mouthwatering aroma coming from my oven was one of my favorites. I made a mean lasagna when I felt inspired, and staring at Micah as he sat on the other side of my kitchen island had been all the motivation I needed. I wanted to impress him with my culinary skills.

Heck, those were just a few of the skills I was hoping to show him by the end of the night. Wringing my hands in front of me as I studied the timer, I just hoped I didn't let my nerves get the better of me.

*Be confident!* I inwardly cheered. *It's not like it's rocket science.*

That was the thing, though. It might not be as technical, but with my heart invested, it could end up being just as complicated. I didn't want to wake up tomorrow morning with a heavy dose of regret because we really did make better friends than a couple. Sex wasn't everything, but it was. At least it felt like that right now.

"You're quiet again," Micah said. He'd lit the candles I had gotten out for tonight. The flames flickered against his skin, lighting him up from beneath with a glow that made it impossible to deny. Of course, he was an angel. It should've been obvious from the beginning, if I hadn't been so hung up on how attractive he looked. Maybe it was because I'd been granted a closer look—a sort of peek behind the curtain—that I could truly see his aura.

It was gorgeous.

He was gorgeous.

"You're making me nervous now, Sedona." His voice was soft and gentle. Micah hadn't taken his gaze away from me. "If you're having second thoughts, then all we'll do tonight is eat."

I gulped a little too loudly, drawing attention to my nerves. It wasn't that I was questioning our decision. At least, not like he was thinking. Part of me knew that once we crossed this bridge, there would be no going back. Everything would change. It would be harder to untangle from each other if something went wrong.

"You're not worried?" I asked, grateful for the distraction when the oven's alarm sounded. Grabbing two oven mitts, I carefully removed the hot casserole dish and placed it over the burner to cool off. I didn't see his face when he answered, but I almost lost my grip on the kitchenware at the last minute.

"About us having sex?"

His response shattered any anxiety I'd been wallowing in. When I turned about, it was to find him sitting there, the picture of innocence. It was his cheeky grin that gave him away. He'd done it on purpose.

"No," I laughed, realizing that I hadn't been clear about where my thoughts had strayed. "I'm not worried about *that*." Without thinking, my gaze dropped down the front of his body, resting just below his belt buckle. I had no doubt that tonight would be every bit as magical as I imagined. I just couldn't shake the feeling that by lowering our guard, there was a risk of something bad happening. "I meant us leaving Holly with Maxwell so we could be alone."

Sliding the spatula around the edges of the lasagna, loosening the burned parts from the pan, I immediately felt a new emotion settle in the air. It was the one I best associated with Micah and called his "no nonsense" energy.

"I trust them both to follow my orders." There was a slight twitch in his left eye that gave the truth away.

"How many times have you called Holly or texted her?" Dinner was momentarily forgotten while I leaned across the island to stare deep into his eyes. He couldn't lie to me then. There was no way he was this calm, not after I'd seen some of his past reactions.

His gaze dropped to his phone that was beside him on the countertop. The screen was face down, and I wondered if it was because he didn't want me to see that he was troubled.

"Um," he answered slowly. He leaned in as though he was about to expose some dark secret. I did the same until our faces were mere inches apart. "I plead the fifth." And with a smugness that shot licks of heat down my front until it pooled between my legs, Micah crossed his arms across his chest and sat back.

"Are you even American?" I retorted, slapping my hand down on the island's granite surface. "As an angel, aren't you meant to encompass all of mankind?"

He simply nodded. "Something like that."

His gaze followed me as I began pulling plates out so we could eat. I could feel it—hot and driven—as if he was memorizing every move and nuance.

*God help us. How are we going to survive dinner?*

"You disappeared again." Sure enough, I'd stopped mid-dishing out the lasagna and been standing there like an idiot, daydreaming. "You do that a lot."

"I do?"

Micah reached out and with the top of his finger, wiped a few drops of the marinara sauce from the plate I'd placed in from of him. "You get this faraway look. I often feel guilty for speaking up, because you look so content."

I rolled my eyes, handing him a fork. After quickly filling my own plate with a smaller slice of lasagna and a healthier serving of green salad, I came around the island, so I could sit on the stool beside him. "I'm not that bad. I just sometimes get distracted and squirrel."

"Squirrel?"

I loved it when I used words in a way he'd never heard before. "It means that my attention can split easy. One minute I'll be scrolling through a publishing house catalogue, and the next, I'm ten pages deep on Pinterest, searching for finger puppet patterns." That was the best way to describe it. "And it all depends on the day and what's going on. It used to make my grandfather laugh and tease me. I would come into the store when I worked part time there after school and find acorns by my name badge, or on the plate of cookies he left out. It was our own personal joke."

"Because squirrels like nuts."

"And my grandfather had a soft spot for squirrels." I felt sheepish for sharing such a personal memory with him, but it also felt right. This was what normal couples did. I wanted us to be that—regular, normal, reliable, predictable. No drama meant that the chemistry that continually built between us couldn't come to an end.

"I'm quite partial to them, too." The tone in his voice had deepened. Micah was no longer playing with his food, using his fork to push the cucumber drizzled with ranch dressing back and forth through the pasta sauce.

He was looking at me so intently that the odd feeling came back —the one where my surroundings started to grow hazy as my focus on Micah became brutally sharp and clear. He was all I saw. He filled my vision.

"Micah," I murmured, not completely sure what I was trying to say. My mouth opened slightly. I closed it back up.

He caressed the side of my face before tracing the outline of my lips. "What do you need?"

He searched my eyes for some indication of where my head was. I was done thinking about it—fantasizing about it. I was a grown woman, and there was nothing wrong with confessing my wants. No, my needs.

I turned in my seat and placed my hands on his upper thighs. The jeans he was wearing were a frustrating barrier keeping me from what I wanted—to feel his bare skin. To be able to feel him all over. I wasn't sure where these new brazen urges came from, but for just once, I didn't try to rationalize them away.

"You. I need you."

He had the decency to not tease me in return.

He slowly rose to his feet, pushing the stool away with the backs of his legs. Extending his hand to me, he helped me up to join him. Up close and personal, he smelled so good, and without thinking, I buried my face into his chest and inhaled deeply. My hands fisted up in his shirt.

It was getting harder to think clearly.

I wasn't complaining.

"Hold on." In a move that rivaled those in the romantic comedies, Micah scooped me up in his arms, and carried me to my bedroom. He kicked the door closed, and then with an endearing tenderness, he carefully lay me down.

"No one's going to walk in on us, Micah," I joked, the idea of someone watching not altogether unwelcome. "We're completely alone." I sat up and rested back on my hands. "Just you and me."

His smirk was sexy as hell. "And Lavender. I don't want any surprises, so she can hate me later for evicting her from her favorite spot. She can deal with sleeping on the couch tonight." There was that streak of humor he had that always left me feeling good.

Then it hit me.

He was nervous.

The jokes and trying to lighten the mood were his own attempts to keep calm.

That made him even sexier for trying.

"I'm sure she'll understand." I scooted forward until I was at the end of the bed, sitting in front of him. I stroked the sides of his legs before resting my hands at his belt. As I slowly unbuckled it, Micah's breath hitched with each sharp tug I gave. When his belt finally gave way and I'd popped the top button, my finger slowly traced over the zipper's teeth.

He groaned with impatience.

I was surprised I wasn't wanting to rush things either. This moment was all I'd been thinking about, and now . . . now it was going to become a reality.

The zipper made a slight noise as I lowered it.

With a quick jerk, Micah's jeans dropped to his ankles. Seconds later they were kicked across the room. His shirt then joined it in a crumpled pile, leaving him naked. In front of me. Boldly. Proudly.

"Sedona." My name came out husky and raw. He'd asked me

what I'd needed earlier, and it was clear to me now exactly what he was needing. The feelings were mutual.

He fingered the neckline of my top, showing incredible control because he hadn't already ripped it from me. I didn't need to read him to know that's what he was thinking. His desires were plastered across his face, revealed in the way he bit his lower lip. His hands trembled a little.

He made me feel fragile. He hadn't even touched me, and already I felt precious to him.

"Let me," I offered, and then, pushing him back so we could swap places, I shoved him on top of the bed. I had an idea, and tonight was already full of magic. It was the kind of night where nothing was impossible, and there was no fear of crashing if you chose to free fall into the moment. It made me brave.

I was the center of his attention, and I reveled in it. I savored how good his gaze felt on my body, how easy it was to imagine his hands touching me everywhere.

First, I inched out of my skirt, holding it up before dropping it to the floor.

Next, I removed my new favorite shirt. It was so silky, and it had felt delicious against my skin all day—like a lover's caress. I tried not to shiver when I felt his breath blow gently against my hip. I tried not to crumble as he followed up with his tongue—the maddening swirling pattern he made enough to snap my patience.

His finger looped under the side of my panties, pulling them down so he could kiss where they'd been. I was a riot of emotions— each one battering against my resolve to savor our first time together. I wanted it to be tender, slow, romantic.

Instead, all I could focus on was the desperation building. I didn't know how long I could hold out, especially as Micah's mouth moved. My knees buckled, and I toppled forward, landing squarely on top of him. My mind instantly recognized the hardness pressed against me.

"I need you in me." I hadn't meant to say it out loud. I rocked my body gently, watching to see how he would react. "Now."

I didn't waste any more time getting undressed, tossing my panties and bra in some direction. All I could see was Micah, the hunger in his eyes, and how ready he was for this to happen.

Somehow, while watching me get naked, he'd managed to find a condom.

When he went to get up, I shook my head, my hair loose around my shoulders. "Do you trust me?"

He gestured for me to continue, and I pushed him back until we were both spread out across my bed. I felt an odd sense of satisfaction and pride seeing him there surrounded by my pillows and bedding. He belonged here with me. Fate or not, there was no denying the rightness of the moment.

As I slowly guided him, sliding down his length until he filled me, something clicked inside me. Like a door unlocking after finding its key. There was nothing left to think or feel. All that existed was the desperate need to move.

Micah's hand spanned my waist, holding me as we both found the tempo that curled my toes and had him uttering my name over and over. Suddenly I couldn't wait. I was done keeping that maddening pace, and as I flicked my hips forward, I picked up the speed, and deepened the stroke.

Micah's eyes rolled back right before I couldn't hold his gaze. Thrusting. Rocking. I gripped on tightly before throwing myself forward and collapsing on his chest. The orgasm that ripped through me was unlike any I'd ever experienced—even the ones I gave myself. What made it even more excruciatingly blissful was the sound Micah made the instant he had his own release.

With ragged breath and heaving chests, we clung to each other, and for the smallest of moments, I felt him—Micah with no protective barrier to hide behind. He'd lowered his guard. There was no telling whether it was by accident or intentionally. I basked in the light that radiated from deep inside him.

I'd said he was beautiful. God, what an understatement that was. He was Divine.

We lay like that for a while in silence.

Our bodies were pressed together, yet neither of us moved. Instead, our eyes locked. It was incredibly intimate and vulnerable. It was as if with each breath we took, we bled more into each other, the boundaries between our auras blurring until there was no longer two but one.

If I hadn't believed in magic before, I did now.

When a small voice finally broke the quietness of my mind, I didn't argue. I simply obeyed.

"Micah?"

His breathing had steadied to the point I thought he'd started falling asleep. The crispness of his response told me he was far from that. "Yeah?"

"Again."

The night had only just begun.

# CHAPTER 7

*J* stared at myself in the mirror.

Nope, I was still Sedona Mathews.

I'd had sex before, so being with Micah hadn't "popped my cherry," so to speak, but as I peered closer over the vanity cabinet, I half expected to be glowing . . . or different . . . or someone else.

Because while I'd had good sex in the past, that wasn't how I would define last night.

That hadn't just been great sex—it had been phenomenal.

Every single cell in my body still vibrated quietly as if they were basking in the sweet afterglow. I hadn't been able to stop smiling, and there was definitely a twinkle in my eye.

The hot shower I'd just enjoyed had done wonders on my sore muscles, and I couldn't quite decide if I was happy not to limp today or not. I kind of liked having the reminder that my world had been thoroughly rocked.

And I'd held my own.

In fact, there had been a point where I'd taken over, surprising even myself by claiming exactly what my body demanded. For an angel, Micah hadn't blinked an eye. There was nothing saintly about the way he'd worshiped my body, and I would've sold my soul to the Devil himself to keep Micah working that magic with his mouth.

While I hadn't woken up with birds chirping and woodland creatures surrounding my bed, there was a pep in my step as I finished dressing, grabbed the last slice of toast I'd made, and headed out the door.

I felt different.

I felt new.

I felt . . . incredibly . . . horny. I couldn't remember the last time I'd actually physically hungered after someone else. The craving was so strong that I was all but running toward the store, hoping that Micah would drop by before running his errands.

I was already calculating the time it would take me to arrive and whether or not I could open the store up a few hours late, when I bumped into Callie coming out of her consignment store. Fortune was shining down on us, because it was the first time I'd seen her without a coffee in her hand this early in the day. I liked to tease her that she was a "double fister," and that one day she'd get in trouble carrying two hot items in her hands. That had earned me a smirk and a muffled response that was dirty and gutter-worthy.

I'd blushed back then, but now as the memory rose, I wondered what the logistics would be to perform it. The image in my head was enough to scandalize the morality of even the most liberal members in Havenwood Falls.

"Whoa, Sedona!" my friend exclaimed, instantly reaching out to steady herself. "Where's the fire?"

*In my pants!* I wanted to reply. It was honestly on the tip of my tongue, and by some miracle, I managed to stifle the urge to blurt it.

Callie gave me a quick once over, that look that told me she was trying to assess the situation with her own gypsy-demon gifts. If I thought life was tough as an empath, I knew it was equally sucky for her. She saw things—often events she'd rather be ignorant about— and people weren't always receptive to being told their secrets.

Where I let their judgments hurt me, Callie shrugged it off. That's what made her so badass in my eyes.

"Sorry." I laughed, doing my best to convince her I wasn't crazy. She hadn't stopped studying me, and it wasn't until a huge grin spread across her face that I realized she knew.

Maybe I was wearing a massive neon sign over the top of my head that flashed: *I had amazing sex last night! Woohoo!*

Callie didn't warn me. She tugged sharply on my arm, with the forceful "get in here now" command that I knew better not to ignore.

Her grin was contagious, and when she shoved her finger right in front of my nose, I knew I was in for it.

"Explain yourself, Sedona Mathews. Right now." She folded her arms across her chest. "I mean it."

I decided to feign ignorance. "I'm sooo-oorry?" I drew out, pretending not to know what she meant. "I wasn't paying attention to where I was going. I'm running late." I added that last bit as an afterthought.

"Baaaah." She cupped her hands around her mouth and made a loud, obnoxious noise. "Wrong. Try again."

I tilted my head to the side. "Um?"

She poked my chest this time. "You. Had. Sex. Which means . . . You. Had. Sex. With. Micah." She used her finger to add extra emphasis. Not once did she let me look away. "Go ahead and try to deny it." There was that smug grin again. She knew.

"Well . . ." I was having fun drawing out my confession. I was filled with relief that she'd stopped me, because I was desperate to tell someone about it. The longer it bounced about in my head, the easier it would be to convince myself it was merely a dream. "If you want to know the truth . . ."

Excitement flared in her eyes. "Wait!" Then, after dragging me through the store, she gestured for me to sit in one of the chairs while she grabbed her cup of coffee. "Okay. Now spill the beans!"

I picked at the hole beginning to form at the knee of my jeans. "Did you know that if you're having a hard time orgasming, it might be because your feet are cold. Put on some socks and see if it helps."

Callie sprayed the mouthful of coffee she'd just taken all over.

"Sedona," she blurted, unsure of where to wipe first. Using the cuffs of her sweater, Callie swiped the soft fabric across her mouth first. With an annoyed look, she tossed a cloth to me. "What the hell?"

I kept up the pretense and gave a nonchalant shrug. "I read it somewhere and figured it was my civic duty to pass that helpful nugget of knowledge on."

It was my turn to study my friend. Right as she moved to take another sip from her ceramic mug, I let another truth bomb slip.

"Also, did you know latex condoms are made with a milk protein? Do you think this means vegans can't use them?" I tried to wear the most innocent expression I could muster, but as her eyes grew wide and she almost choked, I couldn't hold it a second longer.

I burst into laughter and threw the cloth back at her.

Callie was speechless. She kept staring at me like I'd suddenly grown two or three heads. I didn't flinch when she lashed out, grabbed my arms, and gently shook me. "Who are you? And what have you done to my sweet friend?"

I felt her magic brush up against my aura. She honestly thought something was wrong with me.

"It's me, silly," I answered, the muscles in my stomach sore from laughing so hard. "I was just messing with you." I still hadn't confessed the truth about Micah, but right as I went to, something else caught my eye. "Oh. My. God. When did that come in?"

I slid off the chair and grabbed the metal hanger on the clothes rack. It was as if the heavens had opened and set a spotlight on the most beautiful dress I'd ever seen.

If it could even be classified as a dress. It was definitely the most risqué thing I'd ever considered buying. Usually, I would look wistfully at such items and immediately talk myself out of adding it to my conservative wardrobe. While I didn't wear pant suits and such, this showed more skin than even my bathing suit.

It was perfect.

"I'm trying this on!" I announced, and without waiting for Callie to argue that I was still ignoring her most pressing question, I headed toward the fitting room. I was already stripped off and stepping into the black, tiny, stretchy dress by the time I heard her outside.

"Sedona?" She sounded hesitant now. "Is everything okay?" I could almost imagine her biting her bottom lip as she fielded my response. "You don't seem like yourself."

That made me scrunch my brow and temporarily forget why I was in the small enclosure. "I'm who I've always been. I'm still me."

I glanced back at the floor length mirror.

Was I really different now?

Had being with Micah really changed who I was?

Did it matter?

Poking my head through the door, I flashed her a happy grin. "Unless you're referring to the mind-blowing sex I had last night."

And with that, I promptly closed the door and waited for the explosion.

Callie all but kicked the door open and stood with her hands firmly on her hips. "You brat! How long were you going to string me along, Miss Casually-Drops-The-Truth-Like-It-Was-Nothing?"

I could see her warring emotions clearly: excitement for me, annoyance at my teasing, curiosity about what I thought, and a healthy dose of disbelief. The last time we'd even touched the topic of when my first time with Micah would be, I'd neatly sidestepped it.

"You can't blame me for the ruse. It's too much fun teasing you." I'd seen all that I needed with the dress. It fit like a silken glove and would feel incredible if I wore it without any underwear. Perhaps I'd model it for Micah later. The idea made my insides heat and smolder. "I'm going to buy this now."

She nodded.

To show her I hadn't meant to deceive her, I gave her a tight hug. "It was beyond anything I'd ever hoped for."

There was a wonder that colored my words—an amazement that revealed how I truly felt. I was still needing to pinch myself.

"Is it true what they say about angels?" Callie wiggled her brows at me suggestively.

My nod was filled with enthusiasm. "Absolutely."

We were back by the cash register, and Callie was folding the dress to drop into a bag. "Really? I always wondered."

I did a quick look over my shoulder to make sure there weren't any customers lurking too closely to overhear us. Even though the store had only just opened, I was still surprised to see I was the only one in here. Most of us knew if we wanted to find a great deal, we needed to get here first thing in the morning.

"The bigger the hands . . ." I held mine up and wiggled my fingers. "The bigger the wings!"

She slapped me hard. I deserved it. Callie was one of the few people who knew about Micah. While I hadn't confided why he'd brought Holly to Havenwood Falls, I had sworn her to secrecy about him being an angel. As much as I loved having Maxwell as a confidant, it had been a godsend becoming close friends with Callie.

After paying and getting everything squared away, I finally owned up to the real reason I'd bumped into her. It was purely hormones and lust.

"I've never been prouder." She wiped away an imaginary tear and beamed with pride. "I won't keep you, but promise me you'll give me all the juicy details tomorrow at lunch."

"Well," I started, threading my fingers through the bag's handle and lifting it from the counter. "When a man and a woman love each other very much . . . "

"I swear I'm going to forget I like you and kick your ass, Sedona." She shoved me good naturedly. "I'm not used to this sassy new you. Who would've thought all you needed was the right guy."

"And the right dick," I blurted, the filter in my brain short-circuiting. It was my turn to gasp out loud at my beyond bold comment. "Damn, I said that out loud."

Callie was all amazement. "I didn't even know you knew that word."

Before I could retort with something sarcastic, a sharp pain exploded in my head, causing me to stumble backward and bang into the counter. The room began to spin, and as Callie's scared features filled my view, I struggled not to throw up.

Something was wrong. This hurt worse than the usual beginnings of a headache or phantom pain.

"Callie," I uttered, groaning through clenched teeth. "Go find him. Tell him." I was now having to breathe through the rapid bursts that had traveled down into my neck. I wouldn't be able to keep upright if this didn't stop.

I missed seeing Callie leave.

Sprawled out on the floor, not caring how it looked, I let out a long groan, and closed my eyes.

The only thought left was this: if this was how I was going to die, at least it was after spending the night with Micah.

Cliché or not, at least I'd be going out with a bang.

# CHAPTER 8

*I* couldn't keep my eyes off him.

In all fairness, Micah hadn't been able to tear his gaze away either. The dress I'd bought from the consignment store had been worth the investment. I felt absolutely sexy in it. Like I could conquer the world. I couldn't remember the last time I'd worn something that showcased my curves so perfectly.

It was decadent.

Much like the rich, chocolate cake I was eating painstakingly slowly, hoping that it was driving him crazy. For the first time in a long time, I was having an amazing time on our date, and there wasn't anything nagging at me for my attention. I felt brazen sitting beneath the soft glow of mood lighting, the spaghetti strap of my dress having dropped from my shoulder again. This time I didn't bother fixing it.

I wanted Micah to imagine unwrapping me when we got back to my place. Maxwell had agreed to watch Holly another night at her home, so I had my boyfriend all to myself again. I was feeling a little jealous about having to share him, which was strange because that so wasn't who I was.

Yet that feeling swirled about inside my head, messing with my heart. When our waitress had lingered a little longer than I'd liked, batting her eyelashes at Micah, I'd wanted to plunge the spoon deep into her chest. When my fingers slowly wrapped about the silver cutlery, I could see it so clearly in my mind.

The gasp.

The pop that I imagined would happen once my spoon broke through her skin became all I could focus on.

That and the sense of satisfaction.

Instead, I took a large piece of the cake and crammed it in my face.

I was a lover, not a fighter.

I would just ignore my wayward thoughts. Perhaps they weren't even mine, and I'd somehow locked onto someone else's emotions, which was terrifying. Who was here that would delight in stabbing someone?

I glanced around nervously, hoping that I'd get some kind of revelation that I wasn't going crazy.

Just crazy in love.

"You're quiet," Micah murmured softly, leaning forward to grab my hand. The mere touch of his fingers sent chills trickling through me. He traced a circle with his thumb, shooting fire down to my toes, all while staring at me, watching for even the smallest of hints.

"I'm just enjoying my dessert," I answered with a smile that I hoped resembled something seductive. "Unless . . ." I was about to be the boldest I'd ever been and pushed away my plate. "You'd rather just go back to my place now and cut to the chase."

He took it in stride. "I've never seen you not finish something sweet."

I locked gazes with him and stretched my foot out underneath the table. I traced the tip of my shoe up his leg until I reached his knee. "There's a first time for everything, right?"

My comment must've confused him, because I didn't get the smile I was hoping for. "Are you sure you're feeling fine? You haven't pushed yourself too much with coming out tonight and planning for the book swap?" He studied me until I squirmed in my seat.

"I've never felt more alive in my life." It was the truth. Sure, I'd just collapsed a few hours ago, but I didn't want to focus on the things I couldn't control. There was no doubt I could conquer the world if I simply set my mind to it, and right now, I was all about conquering the man in front of me.

Hell, forget what I wanted. I *needed* to wrap myself up in him and forget the outside world existed.

Scooping up a dollop of the icing, I savored the taste that flooded my mouth. "Maybe we should get the waitress to box up the entire cake, so we can take it home."

Micah waved to the nearest staff member and made our request. Moments later, the box was at our table, and the check was being paid. He had understood my meaning. I was done with being out and about. I wanted to be home.

Immediately.

The air's chill felt like heaven against my heated skin. It was a beautiful star-filled night in Havenwood Falls, and I craned my neck back to stare up at the sky. Everything was perfect.

"Let's get you home," Micah whispered in my ear after kissing it. He threaded his fingers through mine, and our hands swung between us.

Chocolate and sex. I wondered if Callie had seen that in my future way back at the fair when she'd read my cards.

"You're still quiet." Damn, the man was perceptive. "You'd tell me if anything was wrong, right?" He squeezed my hand. I loved how affectionate Micah could be. Right now, it was driving me insane, because we were still quite a walk from my apartment.

As we passed by the town square, I caught a glimpse of my store. So much had happened in such a short period of time. Taking over the store had made sense back then. It was somewhere safe that I could be free to be myself. I was able to surround myself with the words I loved. I could hide away when reality became too tough and retreat into books.

For a moment there, I'd worried that the incident with Austin had tainted my little niche here in town. I'd been terrified that I wouldn't be able to look past the trauma and reclaim my power. I didn't want to be a victim all my life, and I sure as hell didn't want everyone else viewing me like that either.

Through it all, I'd managed to find a confidence that lit me up from the inside. It was finally my turn to live happily ever after. Tonight was just more evidence that my life truly was magical.

"I promise you I'm fine," I answered, plastering the happiest smile on my face that I could. "In fact, I'm more than fine." A hint of a breeze danced with the hair at the back of my neck. It sent a tickling sensation down through me until it stopped in the pit of my stomach. Then it burst into molten desire.

I tugged on his hand, making him stop. An urgency had taken over as lust drummed a steady beat within my veins. All I could think about was Micah with his mouth all over me, and my mouth—my lips—all over his skin.

"Desperate times call for desperate measures," I mumbled, taking a quick scan of the square for any other pedestrians. It was a quiet night in town. Thankfully, most people were at home, relaxing after a hard day at work. This might work, and I'd be able to cross something off my newly formed bucket list.

Micah stared at me, wearing a quizzical expression. "You're starting to worry me, Sedona."

I placed my finger over his mouth and shushed him. "Trust me. I just had a wicked idea." I slowly started leading him across the street to one of the alleyways that cut between streets. People usually kept to the more well-lit areas in town, and for the most part, the alleyway was reserved for deliveries and dumpsters.

And in this case, a quick pitstop because with each step I took, I felt like I would combust. Something was stirring inside me, and it made me want to scream.

To his credit, Micah didn't argue, and seemed willing to see what crazy plan I was plotting. When we were deep enough in the dimly lit corridor, I whipped about and pushed him hard. I kept pushing him until he backed up against the wall—eyes wide, expectant.

"Sedona." My name on his lips felt like a prayer. He was the only one who'd ever been able to make me react this way from simply speaking my name. It made what I was about to do all the more urgent and necessary.

I took a few steps toward him. "I can't get enough of you, Micah."

His gaze dropped to where I'd placed my hand over his chest.

"There's been something I've wanted to do all evening."

He nodded slightly and licked his lips. I wet mine, too.

"Sedona, I don't think this is the right place for that." He stopped looking at me and peered back to the opening we'd just come from. "Someone might walk past . . . see us. What if the police get a report?"

Sheriff Kasun was a wolf shifter, as were some of his officers. They'd definitely be able to smell the sex in the air.

I didn't care.

"Let them watch."

I waved my hand through the air and uttered a small spell. It was a basic cloaking shield to keep us hidden from prying eyes. It was enough to appease Micah's caution. What I didn't disclose was it didn't prevent those with preternatural senses from knowing something sexual was going on. They could hear.

I silenced Micah with my mouth, my tongue tracing the seam of his lips. Any questions he might have had evaporated into thin air as he snaked his arm around me, anchoring my body to his. The kiss was hot and intense, his fingers digging into my hip. The pain sizzled through my head, and I welcomed it with an outpouring of desire. Every second pushed me closer and closer to losing my mind.

Sex.

It had never been this exciting. It was as though I'd never experienced it before Micah. Perhaps it was his angelic nature, or the fact that I could finally just let go and embrace the moment.

I ground myself against him, feeling him harden beneath my hand as I slid it between us. I couldn't stop myself as I unzipped his pants and freed his erection. The sight of him standing there with his pants to his knees, a hunger blazing from his face, made the risk worth it.

"I came prepared." Lifting the hem of my dress, I revealed a surprise I'd been dying to reveal.

Micah whistled low and long.

I wasn't wearing any panties.

"Sedona." There was so much longing in that one word. "Are you . . ."

I didn't let him finish. With our lips locked and my arms around his neck, I wrapped my legs around his waist. Micah then turned me about so my back was against the cold brick wall.

"Please," I asked.

He answered with a grunt as he slid into me.

We were a perfect fit.

"Don't hold back," I gasped, needing him to throw his protective nature to the side. I wanted to chase this sensation and see where it could take us. Feeling his thickness inside me, I needed him to move. "Now's not the time for gentleness."

I gripped him tightly and rocked forward. Micah's eyes widened, and when I repeated the motion, I witnessed the exact moment he threw caution to the wind as well.

He was magnificent.

As we found the rhythm, the air stilled around us and our muffled cries grew louder. It became easier to forget where we were. The harder and faster he pounded into my body, the more fevered I felt. I relished the soft noise from our bodies hitting each other. It was the most beautiful sound I'd ever heard.

It soon became too much. Titling my head back, I gave in to the magic he was weaving, and held on for dear life. This was transformational. It was epic. It was being etched so deeply into my psyche that I would never forget even the smallest details.

The slickness of his body and mine.

The feel of the bricks against my exposed butt.

The way he leaned into me like I was his salvation.

The way I clung to him like I was drowning.

If this was what addiction felt like—that incessant need and hunger for the one thing that left you feeling alive—then I was addicted to Micah Westbrook.

"Hold on," he warned, before finding some source of energy that had him thrusting harder than before. It was intoxicating. It was exhilarating. It was surreal.

I shattered so hard that there was no catching my breath. I couldn't speak if my life depended on it. All I could do was rest my head forward, completely sheltered by Micah's body. I prayed to God that I wouldn't have to move and place my feet on solid ground again. I didn't want this to end.

"Wow."

It took me a good five minutes to muster the strength to utter it.

"I agree," Micah countered. I loved the wonder that filled his voice. "We can't stay here forever, though. Not like this, at least."

As if to prove his point, a moving shadow caught my eye from my peripheral vision. There was someone paused at the alleyway entrance. "We'll wait for them to leave."

Micah cussed beneath his breath. "You're going to be the death of me," he countered. He slowly lowered me to the ground, careful to make sure I had my balance.

The shadow moved, and whoever it was disappeared from view.

I straightened my dress. "Tell me you don't think this was worth it." I loved teasing him, which was strange, because never in a million years did I think this would be me—completely sexed up in the side street.

Micah grabbed my face and cradled it between his hands. "You will always be worth it." He feathered one more kiss against my lips. "Let me get you home."

Adrenaline coursed through me as we snuck out of the alleyway and continued on our way back to the apartment. The second the door was locked behind us, my dress dropped to the ground. It felt empowering to be naked and carefree.

Micah pulled his shirt off, his eyes never once straying.

He was close enough to catch me when another familiar wave crashed through me.

Pain.

And with that came a scream.

# CHAPTER 9

*T*he day had arrived.

Micah and Callie had both tried to tag team me—both equally adamant that no one would be upset if I moved the book swap event back a week. I'd been watched like a hawk after waking up in my apartment, tucked into bed. I'd found a worried boyfriend sitting on a chair he'd dragged in from the kitchen so he could monitor me. When I argued that he could've easily supported me lying beside me under the covers, he'd kindly refuted that it wasn't the time for jokes.

I'd been completely serious. While I had no clue what had taken over my body, I did know how good I would feel with his pressing against mine. He had exactly the right cure for what ailed me. He didn't agree with that, either.

I refused to let their worry sour my excitement. I'd always wanted to do something like this as a way to get the community reading and visiting Shelf Indulgence. In a day and age where books often had to compete with video games, favorite TV show binging, and movie franchises, I needed every advantage I could take.

The imagination was a gift not to be squandered.

As I took care of the last minute details and made sure I had a wide variety of books to choose from, an idea surfaced that actually made me laugh out loud. It would remain a secret that only I knew about, and it would be my gift to the town I loved.

Now the day had arrived, and I was bursting with eagerness. They'd be talking about this small event for years to come. Even the library had offered to donate some of their outdated stock—pairing together with my store to make it a grander affair.

"Sit down for a moment," Micah urged, pushing a glass of water toward me. He was all about keeping me hydrated the past few days. I think that's where we'd kind of landed in diagnosing the pain I'd experienced. While there had been flickers of nausea and dizziness off and on, I'd kept those moments to myself.

It had passed.

Today was a new day, one that I hoped ended with Micah finally seeing that there was no danger, so I could seduce him back into my bed again.

Now that I'd had a taste, I was insatiable.

I tipped the glass backward and drained it. I was tempted to open my mouth and stick out my tongue to prove I'd swallowed it all. There was a layer of annoyance that I couldn't quite shake—I didn't like the attention and people wanting to take care of me.

"Satisfied?" I cocked my brow at him and then returned my focus to the checklist I'd created. Everything was in place. All that was left was officially starting the event. "I gotta go and welcome everyone."

People had started forming groups outside in the town square while they waited. It had warmed my heart to see them holding books, and some had even brought bags filled with them. It was with that confidence that I quickly pecked Micah's cheek and headed toward the door.

My lips were still tingling, my stomach fluttering with nerves.

"Wait, one more for good luck!" Whipping around, I grabbed Micah's face and kissed him hotly. My tongue didn't wait for him to part his lips. It dipped inside, and I moaned, squirming against him. "Okay, maybe two."

My fingers threaded through his hair, curling so I could tug a little. My god, the sensations that coursed through me were intoxicating.

"I'm addicted to you," I murmured against his mouth. "I can't get enough. Is it always like this?" The last part was more for me than him. I didn't really want to hear that he'd had sex like this with someone else. There was a good chance I wouldn't survive the intense jealousy that would follow.

He leaned down until our foreheads touched. His voice was filled with . . . reverence. "I don't think so, Sedona. I think this is just for us."

For us.

Those two words sent my stomach tumbling again, my need to kiss him returning.

A sharp rap at the window broke the moment.

Holly was peering inside, her hands cupped to block out any interfering glare. She pointed to her watch and motioned that it was time.

"Raincheck?" I whispered, grabbing hold of his belt loop.

"Raincheck." He kissed my brow and threw his arms around me for one more hug. "Until then, behave yourself." Micah slapped my butt and led the way to the store's entrance. "And have fun."

"Oh, I plan on it." My gaze shot over to the books I'd wrapped in brown paper and displayed on a large wire shelf.

Then, stepping outside, I welcomed the crowd to Shelf Indulgence.

∾

"Umm, Sedona?" Holly looked like she was terrified as she inched toward me. One of the brown covered books was in her hand, and it looked like it had been hastily rewrapped.

*So it begins*, I mused. I was surprised it had taken over an hour before someone had brought it to my attention. I wasn't ignorant to the different emotions that swirled about Havenwood Falls. The town had its fair share of scandals and risqué behavior. I also knew that there were some who were a lot more frigid in their views. It was to this group that I'd wanted to cater.

Kind of my way of welcoming them to a world where vanilla was only one flavor in the midst of many.

"What's going on?" I asked, thanking the customer I'd been serving and handing her the bag. We'd had a steady stream of people perusing in and out of the store, and I was ready to call the day a success. My gaze dropped to the package in her hand. "Something wrong?"

"I'll say there's a problem." The screeching voice belonged to Irene Beckett, which was interesting. I'd expected a reaction from one of her cohorts, not her. Irene had always come across as a lady with a colorful past. I'd imagined her huffing and puffing at first, only to drop the book back in her bag before heading home for a night of guilty pleasure reading.

"You didn't find what you wanted?" I looked around them to see if there was anyone else needing my attention. Micah caught my gaze from across the room and mouthed, *you okay?* I waved him off. This wasn't something to worry about.

"What is your excuse for tricking good, upstanding, virtuous members of the community into purchasing such . . ." She sneered at the paper-covered book still in Holly's hands. "Smut." To prove her point, she snatched it out from the young teen's grasp, and held up the cover for all to see. "I heard all about what happens in this story. I'm shocked that you would offer it, Sedona Mathews."

*Sixty-Nine* by Maddison Grey.

I'd specially ordered them and paid an insanely high price to get them here in time.

The story was one filled with debauchery and erotic pleasure. I'd flicked through the pages last night, which resulted in me using the novel as a fan. The author had spared no description as she told the tale of a young woman coming into her sexuality, exploring the darker, more sensual side of BDSM.

It was the perfect story to open the eyes of the naïve.

It was an intense read that challenged the rigid beliefs some readers held regarding sex and their bodies.

There was no doubt in my mind that Mrs. Beckett hadn't read it yet. She'd taken one look at the sexy cover of a scantily dressed couple in an intimate position and instantly passed judgment. While it wasn't as tame as the covers displayed in the romance section of a chain store, it didn't deserve the tongue-lashing I was having to listen to.

I took the book and brushed my hand over the front. "I still don't see what the issue is. The sign stated clearly that if you were ready for an adventure, the book was for you." I stared back at her. "You agreed to swap."

Her mouth flapped open and closed. Open and closed.

Holly finally chimed in. "Perhaps we can give Mrs. Beckett her book back? Would that make you happy?" She quickly rushed over to the table piled with completed transactions. When she returned, Holly looked to me for approval. "Okay?"

I shrugged my shoulders. "That's up to you, Irene. I quite enjoyed the book, but if you're not ready to take a risk, we'll totally give you your own book back." I all but shoved it at her. "In fact, I insist."

I'd never been so rough with a customer before. I'd had my fair share of difficult people who would take their frustrations out on me, but I'd never crossed that line.

That was, until now.

Micah must've seen me, because one moment, he was across the room, answering questions, and next, he was by my side, his hand firmly at my elbow.

"How about you help Mrs. Beckett find another book, Holly? I need to talk with Sedona about something, and then we'll take care of those." He used his head to point to the discarded title.

He hadn't even finished that when Willow from next door came in, craning her neck until she saw us. She had a brown paper-covered package with the telltale rip showing she'd seen what it was protecting.

"Hey, Sedona, I think there was a mistake made?" She waved the parcel up beside her head.

"I never thought you to be a prude," I blurted out, moments before Micah's hand landed firmly over my mouth.

"Ignore her. Yes, there was a mix up, and we're in the midst of fixing it." He didn't miss a beat, even as I twisted about in his embrace, his other arm snaking around my waist to keep me from breaking free.

Willow eyed me closely. "Is there something I can help with?" She sensed something wasn't right, with her fae abilities that were similar to mine. Despite the chaotic emotions exploding inside me, a small piece of me acknowledged it too.

Did I really just lick Micah's palm?

He didn't flinch.

"Actually, can you help Holly while I figure this out? I just need someone to remove the other wrapped books and make sure no one else has them." He squeezed me hard, hoping it would stop me from squirming. It didn't.

He moved fast, and before I knew it, we were close to the back wall where the door leading up to the apartment was. He didn't go through it, however. Instead, he dropped me back to the ground. His embrace had lifted me up, so it was good to stand on my own again.

"Did you have to?" I asked, straightening my clothes.

"I thought you might need some privacy." The second he realized the way I'd interpreted his comment, he corrected himself. "No, that doesn't mean so we can make out. You're not acting like yourself." This time, when he grabbed the tops of my arms, he wasn't gentle. He stared at me so intently that it made me feel like I was naked.

That thought didn't help matters.

"Why are you always seeing the threat in everything?" My voice rose with frustration. "What's wrong with finally feeling confident?"

"Is that what you call it, Sedona?" Micah pointed over his shoulder in the direction of the entrance. "You purposely antagonized Irene Beckett. You wrapped up an erotic romance book with a misleading invitation. You're not acting like yourself, sweetheart." His tone turned to one that held tenderness. It was easy to see the worry in his eyes.

"I don't know." And that was the truth. I wouldn't deny that things were a little strange, but I still wasn't convinced that the change was unwelcome. I liked the way I'd been feeling. "I really do feel fine."

He was at a loss for words.

I placed my hands against his chest and rose up to kiss his cheek. "I appreciate your concern, though." When I inhaled, I caught a hint of his cologne. There was no stopping me then as I buried my face in his neck, breathing him in deeply. "Thank you."

I feathered a light kiss against his skin. That kiss led to another. Then another.

"Sedona." There was a firmness in the way he said my name that I didn't like. It was a tone that said he wasn't easily distracted.

"Come on. No one will know." I took hold of his hand and pulled him with me. Each step I took backward brought us closer to escaping upstairs. My fingers were already unbuttoning the top of my jeans.

"Stop!" Micah thundered. His command echoed in my mind. I stopped. All I could do was look up at him with a dumbfounded expression. "This isn't you."

Something inside me snapped. A volcanic heat that began in the tips of my toes and unfurled up through my body until it buzzed loudly against my skin.

"This is me!" I exploded with an anger that was both familiar and foreign. It came from a small place that I pretended didn't exist—a box where I shoved everything I didn't want to share—the dark parts of myself that I refused to acknowledge. "I decide. No one else."

The next part happened so fast that I would later admit there was no possible way I could've stopped.

Stamping my foot in defiance, what I could only describe as an energy wall pulsed out from inside me. The force of the magic blasted over nearby bookshelves. It knocked Micah off his feet, slamming him into the wall that separated Shelf Indulgence from Coffee Haven.

Horror slapped me hard in the face—waking me up from whatever craziness possessed me.

Blood oozed out from the large gash at Micah's temple, but that wasn't what had me screaming.

Somehow, I'd blown a large gaping hole in the wall. Customers who had been enjoying their beverages and pastries were now looking around with confusion. In the midst of heavy dust clouds settling in the air, a flabbergasted Willow appeared.

"I know I joked about you owing me one for helping just now." She stepped through the newly created doorway into my store. "But this wasn't what I had in mind."

That's when I realized that all eyes were on me. The whispering that was gradually growing louder and louder was about me. No one was interested in the book swap anymore. The show I'd just given everyone was far more entertaining.

"Get me out of here, Micah," I uttered, panic descending.

Something was very, very wrong. The confidence that I'd just been basking in had shriveled into the doubt that now consumed me.

Pain had me doubling over.

I emptied my stomach, the violent retching bringing me to my knees.

Everything went still, and the fear that Micah wouldn't help me became unbearable.

Would he ever be able to trust me again?

"I've got you, sweetheart." His touch sent a wave of calming energy throughout me, and I relaxed into his arms as he picked me up. "I've got you."

That was the last thing I heard as I closed my eyes.

I was safe.

# CHAPTER 10

*T*he room was blissfully dark.

Unfortunately, that was the only good thing about being in my grandfather's old bedroom. Micah had chosen to bring me upstairs instead of pushing through the crowd to take me home.

I couldn't really remember much after that. The pain that had taken over everything and stolen my focus was a cruel master. Fiery whips blistered against my skin, making it impossible to do anything but writhe and moan.

Everything hurt.

Existing became intolerable.

The world seemed to press down over me—every thought and feeling screeching to be seen. Nothing made sense. I was suffocating beneath the weight being an empath brought. So much noise. So much suffering.

It blared in my ears and grated over my aura, leaving dark smudges over my psyche. There was no escaping it. Something had broken inside me, and there was suddenly no protective bubble that kept me sheltered from the outside. My own personal warding had been obliterated. It was as if I'd never cast the spells that would help keep me from drowning in the sea of emotions here in town.

A breeze appeared out of nowhere. My body spasmed, and my back arched up off the bed in agony. My skin was beyond sensitive now. I was slowly losing my mind.

"How can I help?" My heart hurt to hear the depth of helplessness in his hushed question.

*I need him to touch me. Only he could soothe the savageness.* I balked at the thought. I could barely stand the air caressing my body.

The need was persistent.

"Hold me." The plea was pitiful to the ears, but it was all the strength I could muster.

With painstakingly slow movements, Micah finally relaxed enough beside me, so it didn't feel like I was next to a plank of wood. It took another few seconds before he trusted himself to release his breath.

I stifled the cry that almost escaped when he wrapped his arms about me and pulled me in closer. He knew it had hurt anyway. Where my mouth had obeyed me, the muscles that clenched and trembled had revealed the truth.

"It's okay. It's okay," I repeated, again and again. The mantra matched the one I'd been reciting in my head. Slowly, the pain receded somewhat, enough that I could relax as well.

"Let me heal you."

I let out a tired sigh, wishing I could move so I could look at him properly. I needed him to see how sincere I was. "This is enough, Micah. Just let me lie here with you a little longer." I released the yawn I'd been holding. "Just hold me."

"At least use some of the grace I gave you." This wasn't the first time he'd made this suggestion. It wouldn't be the first time he heard me reply the same.

"No. That's for an emergency, not now. I think all I need is sleep, and I'll be okay. No need to worry." I steeled myself as a short tremor went through me, like the aftershock waves that happen after an earthquake. At least, that's what I told myself.

"Can we talk about what happened downstairs then?"

"No." I shook my head, wincing when my headache flared. "I have no idea how I'm going to face everyone after today. Maybe I should go ask the coven if they could give me a mercy memory wipe or something so I can forget. I'm so mortified."

"I've already taken care of it."

That brought my pity party to an abrupt end. "What do you

mean you took care of it?" I asked sharply. "There's a huge freaking hole in the wall of my store, and everyone saw me do it."

"I might be fairly new to town, but I know how these things work. Magic happens, and the coven steps in to cover it up. You might want to thank your aunt for how quickly she got the ball rolling. I might not agree with how she talks to you, but that woman is efficient. The damage is repaired, and memories are being wiped." He gently grazed the side of my face. "The only one who remembers now is you, me, your aunt, and the members of the coven she talked with."

Gratitude crashed through me in waves. He'd stepped in and taken over without me having to ask. This was what it must feel like to be in a relationship with someone who genuinely cared.

He let out a loud groan. "I don't like being this helpless. Not with you. I don't like when unexplained things start happening around those I love."

"You love me?" I asked, teasingly. He'd said it before, but I never tired of hearing it. My lips curled into a soft smile.

Micah chuckled, his chest rumbling beneath my ear. "Focus."

His finger softly brushed across the top of my arm, and the sensation sent goosebumps flaring all over my skin.

As much as I hated being responsible, he was right. Now wasn't the time for distractions. "Raincheck?"

He nodded. "Raincheck."

It was becoming our thing—a way for us to acknowledge something needed to be addressed, but later.

His finger drew a light circle over my bicep.

"Please don't." It had slowly dawned on me that the pain had gradually been fading away. The only thing I could think of being responsible was Micah. "I know what you're doing. You're using your powers when you shouldn't be."

It didn't matter how many times Micah tried to explain he had a little leeway before others would sense his divinity. He argued that it was justifiable, and I countered that unless I was dying, he was never to risk exposing Holly for me that way.

"I'm not, sweetheart." It still thrilled me every time he called me that. "I'm just moving energy about. Trying to see what helps." He hadn't stopped moving his fingers back and forth. Now that I knew, I could definitely feel a pattern emerging.

My moan this time was one of relief. I sunk into the magic his touch was creating, allowing the energy to move about freely. With this new awareness, I could sense how with each stroke of his finger, the more balanced and centered I became. I no longer felt the rawness of pain, or the blistering heat of lust.

I could finally breathe.

"Better?"

My reply was muffled. "Mm-hmm."

"Sedona?"

I was barely awake, sleep tugging at me. "Mm-hmm."

"I protect what I love." There was that word again.

I snuggled into him.

"What happened downstairs wasn't some weird coincidence."

More truth.

I took in a deep breath and then slowly released it.

"I don't think it was, either." I finally admitted what I'd spent days arguing about, desperately trying to convince everyone that all was well. "Something's not right inside me. I can't explain it." That was the thing that sucked. I hated not understanding things.

"I need to find out if this is somehow connected to this Collector person Austin was working for. I know you'd rather just forget everything and move on, but something—or someone—came for Holly, and you got in the way. What if this is some type of payback?"

His response baffled me. "How did you make that leap?"

I watched as his gaze narrowed on me—the way it felt as though he was looking beyond the façade I showed the world and studying something only he could see. I hadn't even considered the person responsible for the attack on Holly and me. Yet, Micah had somehow put two and two together—and came back with five. It made no sense.

I didn't like the way he paused before answering. Only people with something to hide measured each word they said, careful to not reveal too much of their thoughts. I expected this kind of response from Aunt Millicent or those who were merely my acquaintance.

Not the man I loved.

"This isn't going to work between us if we're keeping secrets," I whispered. There was a crack of emotion in my voice—one that hadn't been there before—because all I could think of now was that Micah still didn't trust me enough to confide in me. He'd returned to hiding.

My accusation surprised him. "No, I do trust you, sweetheart. That's not why I mentioned it."

There was no holding back as more doubts filtered through my mind. "Then why did you just hesitate if you weren't trying to censor how you answered my question?" I wasn't going to let this go. "Why do you think the Collector is involved with this? People feel sick all the time, Micah. Maybe I ate something weird, and that's why I feel like this." My hands rested over my stomach as though the mere mention of being ill would bring the symptoms rushing back. "Not everything's an attack."

There was nothing but compassion shining in his eyes now, and he grinned somewhat sheepishly. "Call it an occupational hazard, then. I've been on the run for so long with Holly, always staring into the shadows for hidden danger, that I forget not everyone anticipates threats around every corner."

He took hold of my hand and squeezed it gently. The gesture was meant to be comforting, and it helped a little to settle my rattled nerves.

"I can't imagine what it was like for you to always be looking over your shoulder."

Micah nodded. "You stop seeing the world as your ally, and begin acknowledging that everyone around you holds the potential to become your enemy. I've kept Holly safe so far because I no longer consider the inconsequential or smaller reasons behind things."

It was starting to make more sense. "So you just instantly go for the worst case scenario."

His smile lit up his face. "Exactly. Chances are that ninety-nine point nine percent of what's happening to you right now can be resolved with a simple explanation. I *have* to entertain that point one percent, however."

"And that's the Collector?" Just mentioning the name of the mystery threat made my skin crawl. I tried to ignore the fact they were still out there somewhere—possibly watching. "So this could be a second attack?" It still felt weird to make that assumption.

He nodded again. "Possibly."

An even more horrifying thought surfaced.

"What if it is, then?" Now that we were talking about him, the thought sat like a heavy rock of dread in my gut. The very notion that I was a pawn in this mysterious being's game sickened me.

Tears began to fall.

"I'm going to demand a meeting with the Court again tomorrow, and I won't leave until they answer my questions. Every. Single. One."

"And if they don't give them to you?"

"Let me worry about that. Close your eyes again and try to sleep some more." I could feel him moving my energy around again, his touch now filled with magic.

"We'll figure it out," I murmured.

Hope filled my heart, but not before a sliver of fear wormed its way in.

The Collector.

Was I losing my mind or was there really someone out there seeking retribution against me?

Like always, the answer danced out of my reach—taunting me.

In my dreams, it haunted me.

# CHAPTER 11

$\mathcal{S}$ helf Indulgence remained closed the next day.

As far as I was concerned, I never wanted to step foot outside the upstairs apartment. Even with Micah trying to convince me that it wasn't as bad as I imagined, I was content to ignore the world outside.

Thoughts about my outburst piled up inside my head until I wanted to scream for the noise to stop.

Micah had remained by my side, only taking breaks to ensure Holly was still okay out in the living room. She'd come upstairs once the crowd had dissipated, locking up the store while the Court took care of magically fixing the damage I'd caused. No one had asked her to. Instead, she saw a need and filled it.

Micah had just finished the last energy treatment in balancing out the power that came and flared like the tides submitted to the moon. I was already beginning to feel edgy—the benefits of his touch fading away faster today. The pain that remained was manageable.

The lust . . . it was torture to have him so close and not be consumed by him.

There was a tiny tap at the door to warn me I was about to have a visitor. I'd refused everyone so far, and I didn't hide my surprise when Holly popped her head through the crack in the door. "Someone wants to talk to you." She seemed twitchy—antsy.

Before I could question her, my aunt pushed her way past, dismissing Holly with the order to close the door.

"What are you doing here?" I asked. She was the last person I wanted to see right now. Her very presence grated against my skin, creating a new wave of pain. She'd broken my heart with her refusal to see me as anything other than someone to manipulate.

"What's happened to you is no excuse for such rudeness. If you can't speak to me with respect as your family, then you will show me it because of my position within the coven." There wasn't a hint of compassion in her words. Once again, she'd waltzed in and with all the condescension she could muster, made herself the victim.

I was the one being rude.

I was the one causing her distress.

If I had the strength, I would've stood up and tossed her out of my home on her ass. Rage sprung to life as I remembered every disagreement we'd ever had. All the cruel words she'd said for my "benefit."

She was spared from any confrontation by Micah's return. The moment he saw her standing there in front of me, he rushed in and made her step back. He wanted her nowhere near me.

"I don't think this is the time, Ms. Mathews," he began, forcing her toward the door by taking a step toward her. He could be extremely menacing when he chose to be.

"While I can admire your willingness to protect my niece, I'm not here on personal matters. I come on behalf of Saundra Beaumont. She felt, considering our familial relationship, it would be better if I come and investigate the magical mishap from yesterday. I thanked her for her generosity." Millicent watched me like she expected me to agree or profess my love and loyalty to the witch. I hated seeing the know-it-all shine in my aunt's eyes. She was itching to say it.

I could feel it.

"If you could kindly invite Saundra to meet with me, I'll gladly answer any questions she might have." It was Micah who answered. "In fact, I'll be willing to sit down and have a conversation with anyone who might answer my questions."

"This doesn't concern you, Mr. Westbrook. I thank you for taking care of Sedona, but this is a family matter now. You're welcome to come back in once I've finished my discussion with my niece." She had the audacity to look down her nose at him.

Micah took one more step toward her. "Everything that concerns Sedona concerns me. So I repeat, please arrange a meeting between Saundra and myself. I understand you're just doing your job." He said the last few words as though he mocked them. "But I don't believe in passing notes back and forth with a messenger."

She actually spluttered, spittle flying from her mouth. "Watch your tone, Mr. Westbrook. I am not someone you'd want to make an enemy of."

He didn't budge. Instead, Micah inclined his head in acknowledgment. "I would give you the same warning. I am older than you think. I have wielded power beyond your comprehension."

Aunt Millicent didn't shrink away. If anything, she grew taller, standing her ground. "Is that a threat?" Whenever she got excited, her voice rose a few octaves, sounding higher pitched than usual.

Like right now.

Dogs could've heard her from miles away.

She was used to intimidating people and had finally met her match with Micah. He didn't cower when she pulled out her phone and started dialing a number. No matter how hard she glared at him, Micah didn't falter.

It was beautiful to watch.

"He's requesting an audience with you." The person on the other end answered quickly. "I explained that." She nodded. "Okay. Thank you."

The conversation lasted thirty seconds max.

"Ms. Beaumont asks that you answer the questions I have, and once she's read my report, she'll arrange a meeting. Not a second before."

Something told me that her response had everything to do with her annoyance at Micah trying to summon her, and less because she didn't have time. People very rarely talked to the high priestess of our coven that way.

He turned to look at me. "Are you up to this?"

Peering around him to my aunt, I wanted to tell him no. I would never be okay talking with this woman who was hell-bent on always misunderstanding me.

But this was town business—at least the large hole was. The sooner we had this conversation, the sooner she could leave.

I nodded. "Just don't leave me here alone with her." I guided his hand to my thigh as he came to sit by me on the bed. If he could help me manage my outbursts by moving about the energy, then I'd be okay.

I wouldn't suddenly act on my need to blast away my aunt.

There was that anger again.

"Micah," I croaked. The flares were happening more often now.

Aunt Millicent completely ignored the brief interaction. "We need to talk about what happened yesterday, Sedona." Before I could interrupt her, she waved her hand dismissively. "And no need to thank me. It's what family does . . . we step in and clean up messes."

Oh, she was especially snippy today.

All I could do was hope my honesty would soften her demeanor. "I honestly don't know. I've been feeling off for the past few days. I remember that I was angry, and then Micah refused." I glanced sideways to where he was listening. Thankfully my aunt didn't ask me to elaborate on what his refusal meant. "And the next thing I know, everything goes flying and boom! A hole."

If she pursed her mouth any harder, her lips would've snapped off completely. "People don't just expel that level of power and magic by accident without some kind of reason. Have you been tinkering about up here in your grandfather's study?" There was a flash of pride in her eyes. "Did you finally take my advice and start honing your skills?"

That reason seemed to please her the most. It was almost cruel to shatter her newly found hope that yesterday was simply a case of a spell gone awry.

"No." I didn't mince words. "And that's exactly what I'm saying. It was an accident."

Micah coughed.

"I suppose you have something to add." I was embarrassed by how patronizing she sounded talking to Micah. Her position within the coven had made her arrogant. She was talking to someone who held more power in his pinky finger than she did in her whole body. She'd either completely drank the special brand of Kool-Aid—loyal to a fault to Roman Bishop and his fellow cronies—or she had no sense of self preservation.

Micah let her superiority complex slide off him like water off a duck's back. "I believe she's being attacked, or at the very least, targeted."

She openly mocked his statement. "By whom? Who would be interested in Sedona? She's a young girl who runs a bookstore. She has nothing to offer. What potential she has, she squanders."

This time I did wince. "I'm sitting right here. I can hear you, Aunt Millicent."

She brushed me off with a wave of her hand. "I'm done mincing words with you. I've done all I can to help you, and you reject each of my suggestions and attempts. I ask for honesty from you and return it to you in kind. So again, I ask what happened yesterday. I need something to report."

Micah began to stand and defend me, but I couldn't bear for him to break contact with my skin. He was what was tethering me to the sane part of my psyche. If he stopped, I wasn't sure I could hold my temper back.

"I already told you. I've been feeling weird the past few days. At first, I didn't think much of it. I was actually enjoying feeling stronger." That wasn't the word I meant. "No, it was more than that. I felt confident."

Her face went white as the blood drained out of her cheeks.

"Confident?" There was a slight hitch in her voice.

"But it was more like confidence on crack." That description would have to do. "It just kept building and building until it had nowhere else to go but out." I made an explosion gesture with my hands. "There were other side effects that came along with the new feeling." My cheeks were already starting to flush. "Didn't really have a problem with it."

I winked at Micah. The smile he gave me in return lifted part of the weight that I felt pushing down on me.

"Describe these side effects." She was poised to write them down in the notebook she'd pulled out from her bag.

I didn't answer.

She repeated the question. When I kept quiet, she turned to Micah. "What am I missing here?"

Confusion blazed across her face.

"Sex," I blurted. "One of the side effects was sex. Lots and lots of amazing sex. Do you still want details?" I threw the challenge down at her feet. I didn't have the patience to side step her attitude.

Millicent stopped writing. "That wasn't necessary either, Sedona."

There was one word written on the page, and with an angry scribble, she wrote over it. Then she grew quiet—too quiet.

"What are you thinking?" It was Micah who asked. He moved his hands, and I loved the way the heat from his touch followed.

I wished we were alone, so I could have him touch me all over.

I wanted to touch him.

My breath caught, and I whipped out to grip his hand tightly. I couldn't have these feelings right now—not when I couldn't trust myself to control them long enough not to put on a show for Millicent.

"Just breathe through it," he whispered softly in my ear. "Don't forget I've got you."

"I believe I know what caused this." Her words brought everything crashing to a halt. Even Micah stared at her with disbelief. "And before I explain, please know I did it with the purest of intentions."

A sickly feeling filled my stomach.

I didn't want to hear whatever she was ready to confess. It couldn't be anything good.

"I'm listening." There was a steely menace in the undercurrent of Micah's response.

I closed my eyes. If I couldn't see her speaking, in my tired brain, that meant it wouldn't hurt more. God, I needed this all to stop hurting.

"I cast a spell."

The room felt like even it took a gasp of shock.

"Excuse me?" I asked, just to make sure I'd heard her correctly. "You cast a spell on whom?"

*Please don't say it. Please don't say it.*

I'd read somewhere that one of the best ways to deal with hearing bad news was to not avoid its existence, but to repeat your exposure to it. At the time it had made sense, but that was the opposite of what I was thinking right now.

I didn't want the truth to come out.

I didn't want to hear the dangerous lengths my aunt would go to just to prove she was right.

She'd cast some powerful magic.

She'd enchanted me.

"Whom?" Micah pushed, no longer trying to hide the anger he was feeling.

"After our last argument, I went home and cast a confidence spell on your behalf." She made sure to rush out that last piece of justification quickly, as though it would somehow redeem her shitty actions. "It was with the best intentions. I wanted to show you that I'd heard you when you said you weren't as confident as everyone else when it came to your powers. I knew you wouldn't try to find a cure for those doubts, so I wanted to help you along."

"So you turned me into a raging nympho?" Everything about this conversation was surreal.

"No," she exclaimed equally fast. "I meant no harm."

"Then explain the hole in the wall." Micah sat calmly beside me. I wondered if that was also for my benefit, because he was still trying to manage my own imbalance. "Explain why she can barely tolerate other people unless I'm right there beside her . . . grounding her."

Aunt Millicent's gaze dropped to where his hands were. "It wasn't meant to do that." She shook her head, confused. "I was very specific that my spell and magic helped Sedona face and conquer her greatest fear."

"And you assumed that was my powers?" It was slowly starting to make sense.

"Isn't it?"

She *still* didn't get it. I wasn't afraid of my powers, because I didn't plan on using them. I was content to be empathic and leave the rest for anyone else who was interested. The town wasn't short on magic. There would be plenty of others who would fill the void I made by not embracing the full extent of my magic.

"No. My greatest fear at the moment is being with Micah and taking the next step in our relationship." I turned to face him. "I've been worried about ruining what we have with each other by rushing things. I worried that I wouldn't measure up—that somehow I would disappoint." I shrugged my shoulders with the hope that it hid my embarrassment. It was hard enough telling this to Micah, without my aunt listening in as well.

He gently kissed the back of my hand. "You think too much."

His smile was my reward for being brave and sharing how I felt. I didn't pretend that every thought and feeling I had was completely rational.

"Oh." That's all she would say.

Micah didn't have such problems. "Remove the spell now. Whatever you did, reverse it."

This time, Aunt Millicent didn't resist his demands or reply with some snotty remark meant to put him in his place.

"I'm going to need a candle."

When he returned with a small white pillar, Millicent had finished scribbling something on a piece of paper.

"She's going to need a lighter or matches so she can use the candle's flame to burn her spell." I knew which one she'd used and how to counteract it. Millicent had tweaked it enough, so she was the only one with authority to break it. So simple.

The air stilled. No one said a word. When she was finally ready, she began uttering out loud, her voice gradually growing stronger and stronger. The flame danced about as if it eagerly awaited its chance to burn. It wasn't until the last fragment of paper crumpled into ash that I felt another shot of pain.

Scratch that. An avalanche of agony that never relented, never subsided. Instead of making everything better and ending this nightmare, whatever spell she'd cast had backfired horribly.

"Micah!" I screamed, as the energy inside me reached a dangerously fevered pitch.

"Get down!" he yelled in return, throwing his body over mine.

Time stood still.

The energy reached its crescendo.

It became all I could feel, see, hear, and smell.

I became it.

And then everything fell apart.

# CHAPTER 12

"*S*omething struck back!" I couldn't quite catch my breath with my lungs burning for air. There was no escaping the pain as I frantically clawed at my throat. It felt like someone was shredding my insides Freddy Krueger–style.

"Tell me what's happening." It was Aunt Millicent who filled my vision.

"You're trying to kill me!" My voice was raw and guttural. It took everything in my diminishing power not to hurl all over her. "You fried my circuits and broke me!"

"Always so dramatic," she complained, as she hovered her hands over my body. Electricity crackled between us, but nothing she did seemed to help. If anything, it made things worse. Like a bear woken from hibernation too soon, whatever magic coursed through my veins had created a monster—one that roared in fury for being disturbed.

"Get out." I was done. Grabbing Micah, I begged him to kick her out. She had caused this, and if she didn't quit judging me, I was going to unleash my temper at her. It was white hot and ready to scorch the world.

"You need me." She hadn't even budged, ignoring my demand. "You've neglected your powers, so you're useless to help." She just kept talking, oblivious to the way it felt like daggers in my heart. Her words wielded more damage than the chaos whipping my psyche into a frenzy.

"You're wrong," Micah barked. He wore a grim expression as he cradled me in his arms, hoping that the more he touched me, the more he could soothe the pain. I saw him tug at the leather cord around his neck. It was a Celtic carving that was shaped into a sigil. He hadn't taken it off in all the time I'd known him, and the energetic juice that radiated from the piece told me that it was used in hiding his divine nature.

The strap snapped, and I gasped in horror.

"No!" I exclaimed, surging forward to refasten it around his neck. "Don't you dare, Micah. Don't you dare take that risk."

His hand burned bright as a yellow glow started emanating from his palm. "I won't lose you. Not like this." And without any warning, he pressed his hand firmly over my forehead, his fingers gripping my temples. "I'm sorry, Sedona."

Then he blasted me with a shot of angel grace—his healing touch sweeping into my body, purifying me as it flowed. All the while I murmured how much I needed him to stop. He couldn't jeopardize Holly's safety by putting my needs above hers. It wasn't about being a martyr or wanting to die.

I just couldn't stand the idea of something happening to my sweet young friend.

The fear of the consequences should the worst truly happen felt overwhelming. Micah would never forgive himself. I would never forgive myself for my role in it. It would sit between us—the large, angry, painful wound that would destroy whatever relationship remained.

I couldn't live with that.

With what little strength remained, I pried Micah's fingers back and shoved him away. At least that was what I'd planned on doing if something else hadn't moved him for me.

He yelled in surprise as he slammed backward, a few feet away.

"Micah?" Aunt Millicent called out to him and wore the same grim expression he did. "What happened?"

There was a muffled groan from his direction.

My aunt doubled her efforts in trying to end my suffering.

I began to writhe. Without Micah's help, I was left open and vulnerable to the continued attack.

And then, just like that, it was over. If it hadn't been for the way my muscles throbbed and ached, the pulsing tempo in my head, and the slick coating of sweat over my skin, I'd have thought I'd imagined the past ten minutes.

Micah came to with a start. I didn't know who was more confused —him for waking up and being across the room, or me and the new wave of blissful relief that took over my body.

"You okay?" I croaked, desperately trying to wet my lips.

"Yes, you?" It didn't take him long to return back to his normal self. When he gingerly went to lift me so he could hold me, I stunned him further.

"I don't hurt anymore," I whispered. There was a niggly fear that if I said that any louder, it would jinx whatever blessing I was enjoying. I was scared that the mayhem would return.

My aunt studied me closely, pushing her glasses back toward her face. There was no mistaking her look of skepticism. Unlike her, however, I didn't want to look the gift horse in the mouth.

"We should still try to figure out what happened, Sedona," she said, staring down at her hands. "I can't take credit for your respite. We can't guarantee that the pain won't return."

I closed my eyes in denial, hoping I could ignore her logic. I was tired—exhausted from the relentless battering I'd just withstood. I was emotional from being so raw. All I wanted to do was go home and climb into bed with my boyfriend and forget this ever happened.

"I agree." That was the last thing I'd expected Micah to say. Apparently, Aunt Millicent felt the same. "Don't look at me like that. I'm only saying that I'm not comfortable with celebrating just yet. We still need answers."

His explanation was meant to keep her from acting pious and smug.

"I will need to inform the coven. We should be able to uncover the cause with their aid." Once again, her response was to take over and place her faith in those who watched over Havenwood Falls.

I didn't have that kind of loyalty. "No, I don't want to involve them."

She scolded me. Like honest to goodness, shook her finger at me. "It's not up to you, Sedona. They're better equipped to handle something like this."

I tuned her out and turned to Micah instead. "Take me into my grandfather's study."

An idea had floated its way to the surface of my mind. Like the inspiration had been heaven sent from him, a memory tickled at my senses.

Micah didn't argue with me, something I was incredibly grateful for. As he gathered me up in his arms, not letting me stand on my own, I motioned for him to stop for a moment. "Here's the deal, Millicent. You can either come with me into the study and do our best to figure out what the hell you did so we can fix it—"

"Or?" There was a touch of defiance in the way she held my gaze.

"Or you can leave. Not to bring the coven back here. Simply leave. If you choose not to be part of the solution, you become part of the problem. I'm done fighting with you. I don't have the energy anymore to battle with you over the dumbest things. So decide." I nodded to Micah. "Let's go."

I didn't wait to see if she'd get up and follow. In my heart of hearts, I'd already dismissed her because my aunt was nothing if not consistent. Her loyalty to me as her niece would be once again pushed to the side. The truth that always lay between us was that she felt more loyalty to her own deluded sense of importance than me.

For as long as I could remember, she'd used her connections with the Court and coven to badger and belittle me over my life choices. Whenever I chose not to follow in my aunt's footsteps and show her the exaggerated respect she believed she deserved, it had been one judgmental comment after another.

I was never good enough.

I would always be a failure in her eyes—ignoring my supposed family legacy within the coven by neglecting my gifts.

I was only now ready to accept the fact that there would be no pleasing her—ever.

Once inside the study, the enormity of what had just occurred sent convulsions through me. Hot tears streaked down and over my cheeks. Sorrow and grief burst outward in the form of loud sobs. After trying so hard to keep it together and prove to myself—to others—that I could overcome whatever life threw my way, there was no more pretending.

I didn't hold it back or push it down so I could ignore it.

I cried for myself.

I cried for my grandfather who had left a hole in my heart when he died.

I cried for Micah and Holly—the life they'd been forced to live in order to survive.

I cried for Austin, who had been banished from town already, his memories stripped.

And I cried for my aunt, the one person who couldn't figure out that true power, lasting power, was found in the bonds you created with others. Family. Friends. Not merely connections with those who held the coveted influence and authority.

Micah continued to hold me, rocking me gently as his hand rubbed my lower back.

In the quiet minutes that followed, his tender touch was enough.

THE TIME HAD COME.

I could already feel the heated sensation building inside me again. Aunt Millicent's spell had been removed for a solid hour, and we'd hoped that with it, all the craziness would be gone. But something had pushed back. Another spell. Something.

My body screamed in protest as I moved, my muscles wanting to hold on to the peaceful respite Micah's arms had provided. He hadn't left my side the whole time. I hated knowing that he was worried, because he already had so much to focus on. The sooner things went back to normal, the better.

"Rest some more." Micah's deep voice filled the study.

He reluctantly released me from his embrace, and I slowly stood up and stretched.

"It's stirring again, so I need to find out what it is now." Helping him stand, I let out a lengthy breath. I knew the ritual needed. The inspiration had come earlier while I was resting, and it would be a doozy. I didn't even know if I held enough magic to perform it. It was usually a spell that called for two or more witches.

"Okay, how can I help, then?" He left my side to go look at one of the six bookshelves that filled the room. It wasn't just the love of Shelf Indulgence that I inherited from my grandfather. I'd also shared his deep passion for the written word. He'd spent his life accumulating these powerful tomes filled with our family's history, and kept the family's book of shadows. That was the volume I looked for now.

"There's nothing much you can do," I admitted, flipping through the book Micah had handed me until I found the incantation. A few summers ago, my grandfather and I had been talking about some of his experiences growing up. He'd mentioned a spell he'd been part of that helped the coven find out the truth in a bitter argument between two coven members. It was this spell that I was now trying to read and understand. "Usually this is done with more than one witch. One person says the words and uses the others to help channel as much power as possible."

We were at a disadvantage, and he knew it. "Will having an angel with you help?"

It was the question I'd dreaded. "If you weren't currently hiding from some big bad and protecting an adorable teenager, I'd totally suggest we give it a try." I winked at him with the hopes it softened my sarcasm. "Thanks for the offer, though."

"Then tell me what will happen if you don't have enough juice to fuel this spell."

My mouth went dry. I didn't want to answer him with the truth, because then he would fight for me to abandon the plan.

"She doesn't need to worry about that. She has me."

Speak of the Devil, and she comes.

"I was serious before," I countered, not wanting her involvement if it meant she couldn't let go of her unrealistic expectations. "I don't need or want your help if it comes with conditions."

Aunt Millicent lifted her hands in surrender. "You can't do that spell alone. It'll kill you."

Micah's nostrils flared in surprise. "Sedona? Is she right?"

I felt the pressure to answer like a ten-ton weight pressing against my chest. "Well . . ." He wasn't impressed at all by my nonchalant shrug.

"No," Micah thundered, flashing me a glare filled with the power he held as an angel. "Absolutely not. I'm not going to let you risk yourself that way."

"You're not going to let me?" I threw back, just as forceful. "Last time I checked, Micah Westbrook, I didn't need your permission for anything." I stood with my hands on my hips, glowering.

"You know that's not what I meant, sweetheart." Gone was his anger. "You told me we were in this together, so let's stick with that plan. There has to be something else."

Aunt Millicent had remained uncharacteristically quiet up until now. As she turned through the pages of our family's book of shadows, I could sense a longing I'd never felt from her before. I would almost call it homesickness. Before I could see where the emotional tether would lead, she spoke up.

"I'll ensure she's protected, Mr. Westbrook." She turned to me with a look of determination. "I'll get the supplies needed. You need to ground yourself before you start." Then she walked about in search of the candles, crystals, and herbs needed.

Micah watched her go and then grabbed me by the arm. "Explain it to me. The ritual. Tell me what it involves." He didn't trust my aunt either.

"It's simple enough," I started, hoping to minimize his concern. "It requires me to untether myself from this reality and in spirit form, conjure up what I'm asking to see. I want to see why I've been feeling so strange and whether it's a byproduct of my aunt's interference."

I heard her grunt quietly. I still didn't know how I felt about her using her magic against me.

"And why do you need others to help, if it's that simple?"

"Because magic always comes with a price, and if I'm found unworthy, then my abilities might not be enough to bring me back." I grabbed his hands and squeezed them reassuringly. "I don't know any other way that can give me the answers I need so quickly."

Aunt Millicent chimed in. "Go before the coven and ask for their help." She'd placed the last of the white candle pillars at a point in the pentagram that was permanently etched into the study's wooden floor. "Put aside your pride and insecurities, Sedona. I can even come with you if need."

Micah went still as he thought. "I don't trust you." His sole focus was now on my aunt. "If you use this in any way to hurt her, I will destroy you."

She had the common sense to look shocked by his blatant threat. "You don't scare me, Mr. Westbrook."

"I don't care. Are we understood?" Micah would never back down. He looked every inch the avenging angel right now as he stared her down. "You protect her like the aunt you *should* be and we won't have an issue."

There was a tiny nod from her. "You have my word."

My chest was starting to hurt, and it made me audibly gasp. If I didn't get to chanting, the next wave of pain would hit. I was done feeling like crap.

"Stop. I'm ready to begin. Micah—" I gave him a quick hug, kissing his cheek. "I need you to guard the door just in case someone decides to interrupt." I waved my hand through the air, and the flames from all the candles in the room burst to life. "Aunt Millicent, I need you to join me in the pentagram."

We both sat inside, our legs crossed, and I held my hands out for her to hold. I stared hard into her eyes, drawing on my empathic gifts to see if there was any kind of ulterior motive behind her willingness to help.

Nothing. She was being honest. Knowing this made it a little easier to relax.

"You know what to do, right?" I asked, needing to make sure we were both on the same page. A lot could go horribly wrong with this spell. "Don't break the connection between us once I start. You're going to feel that sharp tug on your magic. Don't resist it."

She actually snorted at me. "I know the incantation, Sedona. I've been doing circle magic and rituals long enough, I could perform them flawlessly in my sleep." When she realized how snarky her reply sounded, she smiled to soften it. "Sorry, old habits die hard." Gripping my hands tighter, Aunt Millicent nodded. "I'm ready."

Words began to spill from my lips. Summoning the elements to bless the spell came next, and I took comfort as I felt each one present itself to my circle. I called on my ancestors, my grandfather in particular, to give aid to my request. When I felt the familiar energy of my mother, tears formed in my eyes.

It was now or never.

Electricity sparked in the air above us and like a portal from another world, a glowing oval appeared above me. The more I chanted, the bigger it became, until it resembled the television screen I had back home. It kept growing the more power I fed the spell.

"It's working," I whispered, so the others would know. "All that's left is to ask."

The two-verse incantation lay before me as I quickly read from the page. When I finished, a mighty blast passed through the room, and for a tiny second, I was worried my aunt would let go of my hands.

"I've got you," she countered through clenched teeth. Sweat formed at her brow before trickling down the side of her face. Strain filled her features. The price was already being exacted for my request.

My own body was under attack as the pain came rushing back. What started as a whimper became an unbearable moan, my body trembling to maintain control of the magic.

"Sedona," Micah called out, checking to see if I was okay. Before he could take a step toward me, I told him to stop. It was too late to go back now.

"Show me," I asked, tilting my head back to the ceiling. "Show me the cause for the pain that racks my body."

Time slowed down, and a hush descended upon us. At first, I couldn't make anything out from the vision that was forming within the cloud above me, but then it became crystal clear.

I instantly recognized the scene of me and Micah walking along the street together. I remembered the moment, the discussion we'd been having. It wasn't until something caught my eye after bumping into someone that I grew excited.

"There. Did you see that?" Without letting go, I leaned closer to my aunt. "That person. It's not a spell."

"No, it isn't," she whispered back, stunned.

"Is that . . . ?" Even Micah was dumbfounded.

It hadn't been my aunt's spell backfiring.

The stranger I'd passed in the street was responsible for the hell and agony I'd been through.

That, and the magical marking they placed on me.

I'd been tagged with something powerful.

I was in deep trouble if I didn't figure out how to remove it.

Immediately.

# CHAPTER 13

"Get it off her," Micah demanded, his anger aimed toward my aunt. Even though the spell had revealed the person had transferred their own branding spell separately from her interference, he was holding her responsible for the attack.

If looks could kill, she'd be six feet under already.

"While I appreciate your anger," she fired back, her eyes never straying from me, "I need to concentrate on helping my niece." Hearing her support tugged at my conscience. Perhaps our relationship could be redeemed. "Focus, Sedona. How are you feeling?"

I tested my energy reserves and nodded. "I'm good. Why?" I was out of my depth now.

"Because I'm going to help you get rid of the mark without it killing you."

It was a night of constant shocks. My by-the-book, rule-loving aunt was suggesting we bypass seeking the counsel of her beloved coven. It was enough to make me look at her differently.

She'd begun turning me about, looking for the physical evidence that I'd been tagged. "You're going to need to take your shirt off. It'll be small . . . perhaps something you'd glance over or not even see." Her fingers roamed roughly over my skin—not because she wanted to hurt me, but because time was of the essence. "Help me, Micah."

The shocks kept coming.

"I don't know what to do," I confessed, bracing myself for the lecture that usually followed after such admissions.

There was none. "I do, Sedona. It's going to be extremely tricky, but we can do this together." She smiled at me. An honest-to-goodness genuine smile. That was a miracle in and of itself.

"This," Micah finally exclaimed, and they both went quiet as they leaned in. I could feel their warm breaths over the bottom of my left shoulder blade, tickling a little. "At first I thought it was a large freckle, but it kind of zapped me when I brushed my finger over it."

Aunt Millicent released a soft mm-hmm. She gingerly scraped at it with her fingernail. "This might hurt, Sedona."

With her palm placed firmly over the would-be freckle, I heard her whisper a short incantation seconds before an excruciating wave of pain blasted through me.

I dropped to my knees. I couldn't keep standing, even if I wanted to. Crackling energy blistered beneath the spot, and I could feel it sizzling the nearby nerve endings.

"What. The. Hell?" My question came out through clenched teeth. There was no end to the pain—no light at the end of a very dark tunnel. My fingers clawed at the wooden flooring until finally the intensity lessened. "If that's what happens just from touching the damn thing, how am I going to survive removing it?"

I hated how weak I sounded . . . how small my voice was.

Aunt Millicent was uncharacteristically quiet until she finally broke the silence. "I've never experienced this strength of magic before."

Her confession terrified me.

"Never?" I croaked, my throat dry.

"It's very old." There was an undeniable fear in her tone that overshadowed the reverence she usually felt for power and magic. I almost wanted to ask her more questions, but then some hidden switch inside her flipped, and she was back to being the arrogant witch I knew. "But that won't stop me from removing it."

She touched the mark one more time, the gesture almost like a caress.

"What do you need?" Micah interrupted. "I can get it for you."

My aunt looked about at the items that surrounded us. "I need something sharp to cut with." Then, as if to clarify, she corrected herself. "An athame. It has to be imbued with power for it to work."

That made my heart race quickly.

"Do I want to know?" I asked skeptically.

"There's always a price when it comes to power and using your gifts. Sometimes it's small, but in a case like this, a great sacrifice is needed."

Blood. She meant blood would need to be spilled to fuel the spell. Blood magic was something I'd never practiced. In fact, everything about that branch terrified me. I'd rather willingly watch every scary horror movie ever produced . . . nonstop . . . in the dark . . . alone . . . than perform anything remotely connected to it.

Micah returned from the table that held my grandfather's tools. Handing my aunt the athame our family's patriarch used most, he lingered close just in case. We were still somewhat leery of her newfound sense of family and loyalty.

Twice bitten, twice shy.

"I'm going to cut my palm and then yours, Sedona." She let go of one of my hands, careful not to let go of the other. "Just for a moment. When I've completed the task, we'll hold hands again, and I'll recite the incantation, then remove the mark from your body. The magic won't like that we're interfering with the spell's intention, but this is the only way. You ready?"

Time was going so quickly that I didn't have a moment to pause and argue. The pain was growing stronger and stronger, making it hard not to wince with each beat of my heart. The spirit inside was angry it'd been discovered.

"Yes." I bit my bottom lip as she sliced across my palm.

"Now me." She repeated the motion. Then she squeezed my fingers, and in a tone I rarely heard, she said, "I love you, Sedona. I'm sorry I wasn't the aunt I should've been. I was wrong to push you so hard. I just hope that this will make up for my foolish pride."

Her words stoked up fear. They sounded more like a goodbye than an apology.

"What do you mean?" I asked, feeling edgier by the second. I glanced over at Micah, who was staring at my aunt like he'd never seen her before.

That's when it dawned on me.

She *was* saying goodbye.

As the words for the spell left her lips, I heard the truth—she was taking my place—welcoming the spirit to leave my body and enter hers.

"No!" I screamed, trying to let go of her so the connection would break. I didn't care if the magic bounced back and hit me with all its might. I wasn't even thinking that my reaction might kill me. All I could see was the peaceful face of my aunt as she accepted responsibility.

She clung to my hands, refusing to drop them.

I struggled to slip from her grasp and failed.

All the while, I watched in horror as I felt a malevolent energy push against my skin and then burst out of my body. A black form appeared beside us in the pentagram. At least, that's what it looked like to me. Whatever it was, it wouldn't be able to go far. It was trapped in here as long as the circle held true.

"Micah, go get Saundra." She was in over her head and would need the high priestess to come help. "Find her and explain what happened. Tell her to come quickly."

Indecision warred in his eyes. "I don't want to leave you."

I loved him for that.

"Trust. Isn't that the foundation of a successful relationship?" I threw him the best smile I could muster.

"Doesn't mean I like any of this." His weary smile helped soothe my own exhaustion. I felt beat up.

"We're going to be okay. Promise." I looked nervously at my aunt, who had closed her eyes. I didn't like how quiet she was. "Now go. Please."

A deep, guttural sound erupted from my aunt's mouth. "No. Wait."

Her eyes flew open, and she stared vacantly, as though she was blind. I'd never seen her look like this before, and her voice . . . it wasn't her own.

It belonged to the one responsible for this very ugly and nasty piece of magic.

"My work is done here. Consider this another warning. Get in the way again, and everyone you love will die."

The message was directed to Micah as Aunt Millicent's mouth moved effortlessly—her eyes blank.

"What are you?" I asked, needing to know who was threatening us. I grabbed my aunt tightly, tempted to shake her hard so the spirit would answer. "Who are you?"

My blood ran cold as I became its focus. "I am but a messenger. They are coming."

Before either of us could speak, my aunt began to convulse. She was fighting against the spirit—and from the looks of it, she was losing.

"Micah, I need you!" I cried out. I was desperately trying to channel every ounce of energy I possessed, mentally sorting through all the magical lessons I'd received in the hope I could remember something—anything—that might help. I felt so unbelievably helpless, and for the first time ever, regretted my stubbornness in fighting against learning more.

Aunt Millicent had been right.

She said I would regret not exploring my powers. She'd warned me that the day would come when I'd be facing a challenge and lose.

I was in that situation now, and there wasn't a damn thing I could do.

Except break the connection.

If I ended the spell and stopped the flow of power, the spirit couldn't stay inside her. He'd be cut off and too weakened to hold his position.

It was time to face the consequence.

If I survived, I would make sure I honored the legacy my family had passed down and not ignore it any more.

I took in a deep breath.

I looked to Micah.

"Go get Saundra Beaumont," I repeated again. Without another word, he left the room, and I whispered after him, "I love you. Forever."

Then I let go.

As I felt the electricity that had been part of the spell dissipate, I watched the residual energy from the mark be pulled out from my aunt, forming a grotesque mouth that opened wide in a ghoulish cry.

"They will come, and you will die. Praise be to the one I serve."
Then in an explosion of black, the marking disappeared.
Aunt Millicent crumpled to the side.
A price had been paid—a sacrifice made.
She was dead.

# CHAPTER 14

$\mathcal{M}$y aunt's funeral was beautiful.

She would've been tickled pink by those who attended to pay her and our family respect. After the services, everyone had come to Shelf Indulgence for some light refreshments.

I walked around in a daze, numb with grief and denial.

She'd sacrificed herself for me. It had never been her intention to have me remove the threat. I could see that now. She'd opened herself up and taken on the mark herself. She'd wanted to spare me any further pain.

The mysterious attacker had killed her just for spite. I'd scoured the magical books I'd inherited to see what had happened, and the same answer kept coming back to me. The blood exchange shouldn't have resulted in her death. The spell was messy, but solid. It would've provided one hell of a kick, but never to this extent.

No, the more I looked at it from different perspectives, the more I knew the truth.

Aunt Millicent didn't deserve to die.

My head demanded justice.

My heart demanded vengeance.

I saw the side glances from those my aunt admired. They were members of the coven she had dedicated her life to. Even Roman Bishop had come to pay his respects.

"I'm sorry about your aunt, Sedona. She was a great woman." His words were all polished and sophisticated. I had a feeling this was the façade he presented to the world and was nothing like who he truly was. I'd heard whisperings. In a town like Havenwood Falls, people talked, and he was definitely a favorite topic to gossip about.

Roman Bishop was a man you never wanted to cross or get on the bad side of, and I was pretty sure he didn't care who Millicent Mathews was at all. This was all merely a formality—what you said at a funeral when you didn't have anything real to say.

"Thank you, sir," I answered respectfully.

He nodded brusquely and then walked away.

"People are starting to leave." Micah placed his hand at my elbow, letting me know that he was there. "Then I'll get you home."

Home was now Micah's house. I hadn't felt safe enough to return to the apartment, and I didn't have the heart to be upstairs. It was too soon. My feelings too raw. He and Holly had made sure to pack a few of my belongings and see that Lavender was brought over from my apartment.

Right now, all I wanted to do was curl up with my cat and sleep. Anything to avoid reality.

"I don't want to be here anymore," I whispered, after looking around at those who still remained. I didn't have the heart to listen to any more apologies over my loss of another family member, or how much the person would miss my aunt.

They were empty words that wouldn't bring her back.

"Breathe, sweetheart."

I leaned into him. "What would I do without you?" It was hard not to feel lost. I was an orphan now—my family gone. The weight of that almost suffocated me. "I can't stay. I need to go."

Tears were already falling as I fled Shelf Indulgence.

If only I had the courage to keep going.

IT WAS LATE when I arrived at the house. Lights were shining through one of the windows, showing at least someone was up.

My phone had blown up with texts and missed calls from Micah. I finally replied that I was okay, that I'd just needed to clear my head a bit.

The front door clicked closed behind me, and when I turned around to catch my breath, I was surprised to find not just Micah, but Holly and Maxwell sitting in the living room—all looking at me.

"Umm, hi?" I said with a small wave of my hand. It reminded me of an intervention I'd seen in a TV show. The way they studied my every move left me feeling nervous. Reading the atmosphere in the room, I could feel the love and concern they shared.

"Come in and talk with us," Maxwell replied, the aged ghost floating behind the couch Holly was sitting on. The poor girl looked tired, and a pang of guilt went through me for not coming home sooner.

"I kinda lost track of time," I continued, wanting to shake whatever this feeling was. Since seeing my aunt die before me, I'd been terrified to use any of my gifts. I hadn't been good enough—strong enough—to keep us all safe. "So I'm sorry."

"We understand, sweetheart." Micah stood up and came to where I was standing. Wrapping me up in his arms, he held me tight against him. The spell was truly gone, and I was back to feeling like regular old me. "But we do need to discuss what happened."

Tears filled my eyes again. Why would he want to rehash something that obviously hurt my heart?

"Please, it's too soon." I just couldn't find the words to form the sentences needed. It was all too much.

He rubbed the sides of my arms. I felt little comfort. "I know, but it's important. The magicked marking gave us a warning."

And there it was. The real reason behind this discussion. It wasn't so much about how I was reacting to the death, but more for the bomb he was about to level me with.

"Please don't say it," I cried. I was barely hanging on to my composure. If he uttered the words I knew were coming, it would completely break me.

His brows furrowed briefly. "I think we need to come up with a plan. Something is coming. Whether it's this Collector Austin was working for, or something else, we need to come up with a plan for when it arrives."

I hiccupped from the force of the sob that ripped from me. "You mean you're not leaving Havenwood Falls?"

I frantically looked over to Holly and Maxwell for confirmation. Sadness was the only thing I could sense radiating from them.

"Do you think we should?" The sincerity in his eyes spoke volumes. That wasn't what caught my attention, however.

"We?" I felt like I was stuck in a movie toward the end without a clue of what had happened beforehand. He'd said we—not just him and Holly.

"Do you really think I'd just leave you here?" Micah's eyes grew round. "Didn't you hear me say that I love you?"

I had heard it, but with everything in chaos, the sentiment had been shoved to the side. Wiping away my tears, I needed to tell him how I felt. "I love you, too. I also know how important it is to keep Holly safe, so I understand if you need to leave."

"We'd better not be leaving Havenwood Falls," came the indignant complaint from Micah's younger charge. Holly stood up and came toward me. "I finally feel like I can have a home here. I can go to school and live like a normal teenager." She folded her arms across her chest and defiantly glared at Micah. "So you can go, but I'm staying here with Sedona and Maxwell."

He didn't say a word for what seemed like a lifetime. "Do you feel the same way?" He'd directed his question to my ghostly friend.

I could tell Maxwell was chuffed about being included. "I haven't always approved of the men in Sedona's life, but you . . . you make her happy. Plus, I've developed a soft spot for a pretty young brunette with a voracious appetite for reading."

Holly blushed at the compliment. "I'd say you're outvoted, Uncle Micah." We all knew they weren't related, but she hadn't given up the family endearment. "Three against one."

"Count again."

Even I had to look at him quizzically.

He grinned. "I mean it. It's not three against one. I want the same thing. I thought I'd have to convince Sedona here."

All eyes turned to me. I was so freaking happy right now, but there was still the bigger picture to consider. "But will you be safe if you stay?"

"Would we be safer if we left?" he countered, much to my annoyance.

"I'm being serious here. I love you so much, Micah, and can't imagine my life without you. But I won't claim happiness for myself at someone else's expense." I turned to Holly. "All I want is for you to have a chance to be normal. Magic is a weighty responsibility."

Holly came and hugged me. "And who better to help me learn my own powers than a badass empath who loves me?"

"This means you'll need to let go of your aversion to exploring your gifts," Maxwell chimed in, his eyebrow cocked as if to challenge me to disagree.

He was right. Things would definitely be different now. I'd already made the decision to follow my aunt's counsel and not hide away.

"So you'll stay in Havenwood Falls," I stated.

"And you'll live here with us," added Holly. Micah grinned in response.

"I'll continue helping out when I can," Maxwell contributed.

Holly wore a huge smile. "And I'll work at Shelf Indulgence after finishing school for the day. I can't wait to attend Havenwood Falls High."

That made Micah pause. "We still need to discuss that."

As they bantered back and forth, a new sensation settled over me. It wasn't replacing the grief I felt over what was lost or the apprehension I still had for the future. Threats still seemed to lurk around every corner, hiding in shadows.

It was contentment.

It was knowing that even when it felt like it, I wasn't truly alone. My friends had become family as well, and they surrounded me with their love and support. I still had the Beaumonts, and more than ever, I felt the need to reach out and be better at communicating with them.

Micah was at the center of that.

My angel.

I'd learned a lot over the past few months.

I'd faced many challenges.

But one thing was for sure—falling in love could be deadly for an empath.

But—as my mother realized before me—it was worth the risk.

# ABOUT THE AUTHOR

International and #1 Multi-Genre Bestselling Author Belinda Boring is known to many readers as the Queen of Swoon and also the Queen of Cliffhangers. Her Mystic Wolves series has topped many charts along with receiving several awards and nominations such as Paranormal Book of the Year, Best Debut Book, as well as being in the Top 3 Best Rated on Amazon. With additional titles like Bittersweet Melody, Bittersweet Symphony, Enchanted Hearts, Loving Liberty, and Broken Promises, it's easy to see why readers are captivated by this swoon-worthy author!

A homesick Aussie living amongst the cactus and mountains of Arizona, Belinda Boring is a self-proclaimed addict of romance and all things swoon-worthy. It wasn't long before she began writing, pouring her imagination and creativity into the stories she dreams. Whether urban fantasy, paranormal romance, or romance in general, Belinda strives to share great plots with heart and characters that you can't help but connect with. Of course, she wouldn't be Belinda without adding heroes she hopes will curl your toes. Surrounded by a supportive cast of family, friends, two adorable Chiweenies, and the man she gives her heart and soul to, Belinda is living the good life. Happy reading!

You can find Belinda on Social Media:
Official Website: www.belindaboringauthor.com/
Facebook: www.facebook.com/BelindaBoringAuthor
Twitter: twitter.com/BelindaBoring
Instagram: www.instagram.com/BelindaBoring
BookBub: www.bookbub.com/profile/belindaboring
Amazon: www.amazon.com/Belinda-Boring/e/B005C1IRFC/

# ACKNOWLEDGMENTS

I wanted to say a quick, but VERY heartfelt thank you to everyone who has supported and stood by me throughout this year. I'm grateful for your love and friendships. I'm grateful for the inspiration you bring into my life and the way you embrace each and every one of my stories and characters.

I love writing within the Havenwood Falls world. Paranormal romance is one of my greatest loves—both to read and write—so I feel like I have the best of both worlds. There aren't enough words to express how much I appreciate author Kristie Cook and the exceptional authors I write alongside with. I remember reading countless quotes and articles about 'finding your tribe' and how much that can help as an author. Without a doubt, I've found my tribe, and I ADORE each and every single one of these talented writers. I cherish the friendships I've been able to make. You guys are the cream of the crop!

Thank you to those who work behind the scenes as I write:

My amazing author coach, Jessi Gibson. She helps me to keep focused when I have a STRONG tendency to squirrel. I love having her in my corner—cheering for me and keeping me accountable when I start doubting myself.

My faithful beta readers, Cindy Mayberry, Julie Engle, Julia Lucero, Susan McCray, and Stephanie Krause. Your feedback means a lot. Thank you!

The best writing partner a girl can have, Stephanie Garza. Our video writing sessions are some of the best memories I have, and I'm so grateful for you. We've written a lot of words this year. I can't wait to see what 2019 holds.

My family: Thank you for always asking how my writing is going and being excited when I finish a story. It might not seem like much, but to me, it is. I love you all!

My incredible husband, Mark. You're the reason behind it all. Whatever I did to deserve you . . . I'd do it a thousand times again and again. You always seem to know what I need, when I need it. You help me remember my words. You listen to me when I'm stuck and have to talk the scene through. Most of all, you never complain when we listen to Hamilton and *In The Heights* on repeat. You get me. You support me. You give me the space I need to be creative. Me and you forever . . . *that would be enough*! << shameless plug of a Hamilton lyric.

Lastly, because we save the best for last, right? All my love and gratitude to you all—those who pick up my books and agree to take the journey with me and my characters. Thank you for entrusting me with your time and imagination. Thank you for embracing my characters. You guys are AMAZING!

As always, don't be afraid to take a risk and dare to fly!

Happy swooning!

Bels xxx

# AFFLICTION MINE

## C.J. PINARD

~ A Havenwood Falls New Adult Novella ~

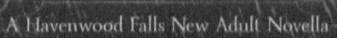

# HAVENWOOD FALLS

# AFFLICTION MINE

USA Today Bestselling Author

# C.J. PINARD

# BOOKS BY C.J. PINARD

Paranormal Fantasy:

Enchanted Immortals 1

Enchanted Immortals 2: The Vortex

Enchanted Immortals 3: The Vampyre

Enchanted Immortals 4: The Vixen

BSI: Bureau of Supernatural Investigation

Enchanted Immortals Box Set: 4 Books + Novella

New Adult Contemporary Romance:

Patriotic Duty (Duty & Desire, #1)

Tour of Duty (Duty & Desire #2)

Boots Beneath My Bed (Duty & Desire #3)

Playing the Field (Duty & Desire #4)

Romantic Suspense:

Antihero (Imperfect Heroes, Book 1)

Above Protection (Imperfect Heroes, Book 2)

Beneath Broken (Imperfect Heroes, Book 3)

Beyond Love (Imperfect Heroes, Book 4)

Paranormal Romance:

Unscathed (A paranormal romance novel with Tim O'Rourke)

Soul Rebel (Death's Kiss #1)

Soul Redemption (Death's Kiss #2)

Soul Release (Death's Kiss #3)

Kovah: Soul Seeker (A Death's Kiss Novel #4)

Lotus (Daughter of Darkness) Lotus's Journey Part I

Watcher (Daughter of Darkness) Lotus's Journey, Part II
Guardian (Daughter of Darkness) Lotus's Journey, Part III

The Lunar Effect (The Ayla St. John Chronicles, #1)
The Lunar Curse (The Ayla St. John Chronicles, #2)
The Lunar Secret (The Ayla St. John Chronicles, #3)
The Lunar Magic (The Ayla St. John Chronicles, #4)

Reverse Harem Fantasy:
Four Princes (Rothhaven Trilogy, #1)
Four Kings (Rothhaven Trilogy, #2)
Four Heirs (Rothhaven Trilogy, #3)

*This is for all the Havenwood Falls authors. Thank you so much for sharing your characters with me—with us. You've created a world I want to live in.*

# CHAPTER 1

## KARSON

*T*he backpack was getting heavy, and I shifted it to my other shoulder as I wondered just where the hell this Greyhound bus was. It was supposed to depart at 10:20 a.m., but as of yet, it wasn't even here in the station.

"Karson! Hey, dude!"

I turned around and spotted my coworker, Dex, waving at me.

*Oh, God, what does this guy want?* I wondered as I watched him approach.

"Happy new year. Where you going, man?" he asked, staring at me as he took a swig from a black and green can.

"Going out of town. Why are you here?" I asked, keeping it vague so he'd go away.

"Same. Goin' to see family. You know." He shook his head before taking another swig of his caffeine-loaded drink as he measured me with a curious stare.

Seriously hoping this pothead wasn't on the same bus as me, I smiled tightly at him and said, "Great. Well, see you next week." I turned and headed toward the vending machines that lined the back of the Greyhound station.

Just as I was about to choose a bag of jalapeño-flavored potato chips, the loudspeaker announced that the bus to Montrose was leaving. I quickly shoved my dollar bill into the machine and willed the bag to drop so I could board the damn bus.

Once I snatched the chips from the bottom of the machine, I hustled to the boarding area, presented my ticket, and found a seat in the back, just wanting this stupid trip to be over with. I had other shit to attend to, and dealing with my "cousin" and his weird-ass request wasn't what I had on the agenda for the holidays.

Still . . . I literally couldn't remember when I had last been to Havenwood Falls. A part of me wondered why most of my childhood was absent from my memory, but I knew it had to do with the sleepy Colorado town. Had I really grown up there?

I pulled out my phone and clicked on the email app, deciding to re-read the cryptic message for the hundredth time.

*Karson,*

*This is going to sound weird as hell, but hear me out. I need you to return to Havenwood Falls like, yesterday. I know you're thinking, "Return? When was I there?" Well, you have been here. You grew up here. You don't remember because the town is full of witches and other supes and shit. You leave, you don't get the luxury of remembering it at all. The witch bitches are gonna have my ass for telling you this, but I don't have any fucks left to give at this point, so here goes.*

*My pops, your uncle, is in a bad way. He used his affliction to piss off the Court and was sent to prison. Why am I telling you this? Because he's gotta do six weeks in jail here before they release him back to us. Before you ask why you should care, here's why: My dad's a loose cannon. In his late 40s and still ain't learned shit about shit. I need you to help me put a leash on him once he gets out. The Kane name has been muddied enough. Oh, and also, your dad is here (they're brothers), and he's been asking about you. It's getting old, and you need to come home. Of course, you prob don't remember your dad, but still.*

*Fuck . . . I know this email is so damn weird to you, but you have to trust me, cuz. Head up to Havenwood Falls, and you'll see. Once you get here, your memories will return. All of them. It'll take a hot minute, but I promise it'll happen. It's gonna be a trip, bro. Take a bus to Montrose, and when you get off, there will be a special bus to Havenwood Falls at the stop there. Hop on it, and don't ask any questions. I'll swing by and get you at the coffee shop, which is the last stop for the bus. We'll talk then. Reply with your itinerary, dude. I need you here pronto.*

*Jalen*

My head was spinning. The email had literally come out of nowhere yesterday, and the only reason I sat on this damn bus right now was pure, unadulterated curiosity. I hit reply on the email and told him I was on the bus heading to Montrose, but had no idea when I'd actually reach Havenwood Falls, as there was no online schedule to the place that I could find.

But the part of the email that touched on getting my memory back and the mention of my father had definitely sweetened the deal. As a twenty-four-year-old living on my own, I'd always taken care of number one. Nobody had ever been there to help me. I knew I had parents, but I could never get ahold of them. They never answered my texts or calls. I looked down at my phone and clicked the *Contacts* icon. Sure, I could click on *Dad*, but I knew it would go to a generic voicemail box.

It always did.

Hell, I couldn't even remember what my parents looked like or their names.

Then the email from this Jalen guy came in, promising me answers. It would have been a cold day in hell before I'd turn that down. I had no idea if he was shitting me or not, but hell, I'd take the chance. I had to. What did I have to lose, really? I was tired of wandering aimlessly, no matter how busy I was, always wondering if I had a family.

Half of me was hopeful this Jalen character was telling the truth and could fill in the missing pieces I felt had been absent from my brain. The other half of me was terrified that someone was playing a joke on me—that someone was running a hustle, and I would, yet again, be caught up in some shit I should have just walked away from. I had been lucky the guy hadn't pressed charges that night in the bar when I let my temper get the better of me over a stupid game of pool.

I pushed that from my mind and continued to click. I had to clear out my emails, because once I reached this mystery town, I knew I'd have no time for shit.

The next email to pop up on my phone was from a particularly needy client. Willing my eye to not twitch before I opened it, I took a deep breath and began to read:

*Karson!*

*I want a Smurf. I need a Smurf! On my ass, or maybe my inner thigh ;) I know you can pull it off, can't you, cutie? ~Angel*

I swallowed down my irritation and decided not to even reply. I deleted Angel's email and hoped she'd get the hint that I didn't want to tattoo her.

*Ever.*

A few weeks ago, she'd come into my shop in downtown Colorado Springs, tagging along with a friend. The friend was pleasant enough, just wanting a small tattoo of something to commemorate her father's passing. It was an easy tat, but what wasn't easy was the friend, Angel, who'd sat and stared at me as I worked. Sure, she'd pretended to be looking through the photo albums of my designs, but I knew she was checking me out. I could feel the weight of her stare as I tatted her friend.

When the friend's tattoo was done, she had been very happy with it, and paid me and thanked me profusely. Angel, though, asked me for my number. In deflection, I'd referred her to the front counter, where Dex would have given her a business card with the email address to our general box.

The crazy bitch used it, too. She'd sent me no less than six emails with photos of tattoos she wanted, and then suggested we meet up "in private" to talk about them.

Shouldn't I have been flattered? I guessed I should have. But at this time in my life, I didn't want to deal with such entanglements. Angel was hot, but I wasn't into pushy women. I was the one who called the shots.

I eventually drifted to sleep, and was awoken hours later when the bus driver indicated over the loudspeaker the stop we'd just reached: Montrose.

# CHAPTER 2

## KARSON

*T*he cold air hit me like a slap in the face as I hopped off the bus and looked around. A truck stop of some kind greeted me. There were gas pumps and a large, convenience-type store with a red and yellow logo.

Not seeing any buses marked Havenwood Falls, I adjusted my backpack and wandered into the store. I needed to take a piss, anyway. The restrooms were clearly marked, and after I used the facilities, I went to wander around the shop, wondering what I should do next. I was starving, so I bought a premade sandwich and a bottle of Mountain Dew, along with a bag of beef jerky. I spied a small sitting area, and made my way toward it to eat my dinner. The bus ride had taken twice as long as it would have if I'd driven, and I'd only had the chips.

On my way to the tables, I passed a rack of brochures boasting all Colorado had to offer for recreation and tourism. A brochure for Telluride caught my eye. Something about the way the mountains in the photo were positioned in a box canyon intrigued me. Flicking my gaze away from it to make sure I wouldn't run into anything as I walked, my plan was to set my food down and come back for it. But as my gaze shifted back to the brochure, I thought my eyes were playing tricks on me; for where I could swear it had read "Telluride," it now read "Havenwood Falls."

*What in the hell?*

Of course, I immediately snatched the pamphlet from its resting place and quickly made my way to the tables, never taking my eyes off it. I blindly unwrapped my sandwich and bit into it as I set the pamphlet down on the table and unfolded it. Its glossy photos called out to me. As I stared at it, a knowing feeling began to swirl in my gut. I'd seen that canyon before. Everything inside of me said I had been there before. I knew it deep down in my soul.

I opened the first page of the brochure, and my stomach began to turn over even more. Photos of familiar scenes seemed to jump off the page and smack me in the face. I knew that ski resort. I knew that inn. I knew those waterfalls. I knew that town square. And I most definitely knew that fucking tattoo shop.

My eyes scanned every inch of it, and when I flipped to the back, bright yellow writing caught my eye: *Buses to Havenwood Falls depart daily at 12 noon and 12 midnight.*

A glance at my watch showed 8:57 p.m.

Looked like I had three hours to kill, because come hell or high water, I would be on that bus.

~

AFTER SURFING THE WEB, checking social media, and people-watching, a couple hours had passed, and I was getting anxious. I grabbed my bag, got up, and wandered over to the corner of the store.

I approached a store employee who was stocking coffee mugs bearing various Colorado logos and pictures. "Excuse me, can you tell me where the Havenwood Falls bus stops?"

She turned around, a mug in her hand. She dipped her eyebrows in confusion. "I'm sorry, I don't understand what you're asking me."

She seemed nice enough, but her response frustrated me. "Havenwood Falls—you have a bus departing at midnight. Does it meet out front? Is it marked?"

She shook her head. "I . . . I don't know where that is, so I can't help you. But maybe my manager knows. I can go get him—"

I pulled out the pamphlet and practically shoved it in her face. "See?"

She narrowed her eyes at it, then looked at me. With a shake of her head, she said, "That says Telluride. That bus meets out back. It's clearly marked."

I pulled the brochure back to my face to see it did, indeed, say Telluride on it.

*What in the . . . ?*

Feeling like I was going crazy, I checked my watch to see it was 11:51 p.m. I left the store and went around to the back, where a large bus depicting a mountain scene with *Havenwood Falls* written on it sat idling, no passengers on board, just one driver seated up front. I looked around to see if anyone else was in the parking lot, but it was deathly quiet.

I suddenly realized I didn't have a ticket, but I approached the bus anyway. The door was open, so I stepped inside and looked at the driver. He smiled at me with warm, brown eyes and waved me on, his face crinkling at the corners of his eyes. "Welcome!"

"Um, hi. Thanks. Where is this bus headed to?" I asked cautiously, remembering how the lady inside the truck stop couldn't see the brochure the same way I had.

"Well, where do you want to go?" he asked jovially, his pale skin looking almost sickly under the one orange light illuminating the parking lot.

*Here goes nothing.* "Havenwood Falls?"

"Well, you've come to the right place, elf. Choose a seat, and we'll be on our way!"

I blinked at him a few times before quickly checking my reflection in the large overhead mirror at the front of the bus. I was glad to see my glamour hadn't slipped, as the driver had given me a strange look. Sighing, I pushed a stray blond strand from my forehead and looked at him.

The old driver grinned at me and then looked down at the newspaper he'd been reading. At that moment, the only thought I had was to exit the bus and just run. Hitchhike, Uber . . . something, and get the hell out of Montrose and go back to my mundane life. But something even stronger than fear was pulling at me to stay on that bus.

So without another glance at the driver, I took a seat in the middle of the bus, set my backpack on the seat next to me, and blew out a breath. To my surprise, the driver closed the door, put the bus in gear, and began to drive. I glanced at my phone to see it was midnight on the dot.

Feeling weird that I was the only passenger, but too tired to give a shit, I used my backpack as a makeshift pillow and quickly fell asleep.

∾

THE FIRST THING I felt was cold. As I blinked my eyes open, I could see I was still seated on the bus, I was alone, and it was dark outside. The door was folded open, but the driver was gone. I wiped drool from the corner of my mouth and stretched.

After wearily grabbing my bag, I made my way down the aisle, and off the bus. As I stepped down, I could see I was in front of the coffee shop Jalen had told me about. The January air was chilly as hell, and I was only in a hoodie and jeans.

With my breath pluming out in front of me in foggy puffs, I hurried toward the shop and hoped it was still open. But judging by the darkness behind the windows, I wasn't optimistic. So I wasn't surprised when I tried to pull open the front door to Broastful Brew and it was locked up tight.

The hissing sound of air brakes caused me to turn my head. I saw the bus's doors close and its wheels turn, pulling away from the coffee shop.

"Shit," I murmured, wondering what I was going to do now.

What had I been thinking? I had hopped on this bus, without even waiting for a reply from Jalen, and now I was stuck, at two in the morning, in a strange town in the bitter Colorado winter cold.

I pulled my cell from my pocket, and—surprise, surprise—I had no cell service. "Awesome," I grumbled.

As I looked around, I could see I was on some kind of main street in the tiny town. There were tons of little shops lining the street. I saw a stoplight, a park, and briefly wondered where the alleys between the shops led to. With nothing else to do, I began to walk west, hoping the town also had some kind of motel nearby I could hole up in so I could regroup and figure out just what the hell I was doing in this godforsaken place.

What had I been thinking?

# CHAPTER 3

## KARSON

*I*gnoring the cold, I continued to walk down the dark streets of this strange town. But . . . was it so strange? I wasn't sure. There was an air of familiarity about it that I couldn't deny. I wasn't scared or stressed. In fact, I felt sort of at ease, despite not knowing where the hell I was or where I was gonna lay my head down for the rest of the night.

As I passed by a planter box set next to a tree, I saw it empty and sighed. I couldn't wait for springtime and all the flowers that would bloom once more.

I continued walking and lifted my gaze when I could see someone approaching. He was tall and imposing—and he wasn't alone. Two others flanked him, and they were walking right toward me on the sidewalk. I looked left, then right, wondering if I should just remove myself from this situation. But there was nowhere I could go.

As the three got closer, their white hair and pointed ears shone under the almost full moon, and I relaxed.

"Karson?" someone called out.

I stopped walking and adjusted my bag on my shoulder. "Jalen?"

"Damn," I heard him say under his breath. "Yes."

The three approached me quickly. They were definitely elven, with their pointed ears, pale skin, and white-blond hair. We could always sense each other.

Jalen put his fist out. "Sorry I wasn't at the coffee shop to get you. I wasn't expecting you."

I bumped it with my own, and said, "I replied to your email, like, hours ago."

He held up his phone, its bright light almost blinding me. "The cell service here sucks donkey balls, man. I went home and checked my emails on the laptop with the Wi-Fi and saw it just now."

*What in the hell have I gotten myself into?* I wondered. Shitty cell service wasn't going to work for me.

"Okay . . . well, I have a shitload of questions."

He laughed and shook his head. Shoving his hands into the pockets of his plain black hoodie, he said, "Like what?"

I flicked my gaze between him and his two compadres. "First off, who are they?"

"Oh. Damn. I forgot your memories are fucked. This is Tarron." He pointed to a beefy-looking dude who couldn't have been older than eighteen—and then he patted the other on the back. "And this is Gavin."

Gavin nodded, and I could sense he was the strong, silent type. He wore jeans and a denim and cotton jacket, and looked like he'd rather be at the dentist.

Tarron slightly jutted his chin at me in greeting. "What's up, cuz?"

I furrowed my brow in confusion, and put my attention back to Jalen. "You got a place I can crash?"

He grinned. "Of course."

As they started to walk, I followed. After a turn off the main street, we weaved our way down a few side streets. We finally found ourselves at the end of a cul-de-sac at a mundane-looking two-story house. Jalen opened the front door with a key, and we all followed him inside. It was a simple structure, average-looking, with nice living room furniture, a kitchen beyond that, and a steep staircase to the left.

"There are rooms upstairs. I'll show you yours," Jalen said as he began to climb the stairs.

Tarron, Gavin, and I followed him up. I felt this strange mix between apprehension, weirdness, and complete comfort stirring inside of me.

Jalen pointed to a closed door. "You can crash in there."

"Thank you," I said.

But as soon as I touched the doorknob, something flashed in my brain. I fell to my knees, a pain like no other searing my head, and everything went black.

*She took a long drag from her cigarette, the smoke smell making me nauseous. After she blew it out, she looked at me. "You know I love you, Kar-Kar. Right?"*

*I nodded my little head. "Yes, Mommy. Please don't leave me in here, Mommy."*

*"You know why I have to, baby. If it doesn't hurt, you won't learn."*

*I felt confused. "What does that mean, Mommy?"*

*Her pale face smiled at me, a cruelness behind her eyes I had become used to. "I love you, Kar-Kar."*

*She closed the door, and I heard locks engage before I could ask anything more. I walked to the window and looked out to see the sun was quickly setting, and I hoped I wouldn't be left in here for days and days like I had been so many times.*

*And I didn't even know what I'd done to deserve it—just like all the times before.*

"Shit, what's wrong with him?" I heard a voice say.

I blinked rapidly to see the three elves looking down at me. Embarrassed and confused, I stood quickly and shook off the . . . memory? "I'm . . . I'm okay."

Jalen measured me with a serious stare with his lavender eyes that were so much like mine. "You sure, dude?"

I nodded.

He looked at the other two, then back to me. "You know we're all related, right?"

I stopped in my tracks and looked at him. "You mentioned we were cousins in your email, but honestly, man, I don't remember much of my childhood. It sucks."

"There's a reason for that," Tarron replied, his arms folded over his massive chest covered in a blue and silver Havenwood Falls High hoodie.

I glanced at Jalen, then Tarron. "Why's that?"

Gavin, who had been mostly quiet this whole time, replied, "Magic, dude. You grew up here, but you left. Fuckin' witches put a spell around this place. You leave, your memories do, too. It sucks, but we all get why they do it."

"Witches . . ." I parroted. "There are witches here?"

The three of them burst into laughter. Finally, Jalen said, "Get some sleep. I'll be in the next room. There's a lot to discuss. And we'll do it tomorrow over pancakes and bacon."

The three of them left, and Jalen closed the door on his way out.

I glanced around the small room. One double bed, a dresser, a closet, and posters of my favorite female fitness model took up the entire wall of one side of the room.

I couldn't ever remember feeling this exhausted. I was so confused as to what was going on, where I was, and what I was feeling that I just couldn't process it. So after throwing my bag on the floor, taking off my jacket, and kicking off my shoes, I flipped the light off and fell onto the bed, passing out.

∽

"He needs to come with us," I heard a voice whisper.

"No, fuck that. We need to get going," another voice said, trying to whisper, but failing miserably.

I blinked my eyes open and flipped back the covers. The room was strange to me, but I immediately recalled where I was. Still in yesterday's clothes, I slogged out of bed and went to see who was arguing outside the door. The voices had stopped, so I opened the door.

Two elves whipped their heads toward me.

"What's with all the noise?" I asked, stifling a yawn and scratching my head.

"Jalen's in jail, dude," Tarron replied, a look of stress coloring his young face.

I looked at Gavin, but pointed to Tarron. "Jail? You guys are shitting me, right?"

I couldn't explain the comfort and familiarity I felt in the presence of Gavin, but it was there.

"No, we're not shitting you. You remember us yet?" Gavin raked a hand through his hair.

Confused, but wanting to roll with it, I asked, "No. Should I?"

"Like I said," Gavin replied, "all in due time. But first things first. Meet us downstairs in ten."

He waved for Tarron to follow him down the stairs.

There was nothing worse than going to bed utterly confused, then waking up the same way. Sleeping was supposed to reset your brain. Make things clearer in the morning. But, apparently, that wasn't the case in Havenwood Falls.

After locking the door, I stripped off yesterday's clothes and wandered into the bathroom attached to my room for a shower.

# CHAPTER 4

## KARSON

"*S*o what happened?" I asked as we rode in Gavin's Nissan sports car. I was sitting in the front seat, and Tarron was in the back.

Gavin lifted a shoulder and let it fall. "Dunno. After we all went to bed, I got a call from Jalen saying he'd been arrested and was in jail. I asked him why, but he just said he had to go. That was a few hours ago."

"Weird," I said, shaking my head.

"Get used to it." Tarron laughed.

"Ow!" A sudden burning pain in my neck caused me to slap my hand over it. I yanked the visor down and stared wide-eyed in the mirror at the tattoo of a phoenix that most certainly hadn't been there before. I was pretty tatted up, but chose to never get them on my neck.

Taron and Gavin started laughing.

"What in the hell is going on?" I asked, pointing to the tattoo and looking at them both incredulously.

"Your tat is back, man. That means your memories should shortly follow," Gavin responded.

"Finally," Tarron muttered from the backseat.

"What does this mean?" I asked, still confused, and the tattoo still burning like it was fresh.

Gavin held his arm out, and I stared at a tattoo of some kind of

Celtic symbol. Tarron leaned forward and pulled up his sleeve to show me one he had on his forearm, a tree with roots extending down to his wrist. "Every resident gets a tat. Everyone. Even temporary ones. Ugh. Ya know what, just wait and pretty soon I won't have to explain shit."

"Fine," I said, huffing out a breath.

*No wonder I left this weird-ass town.* I looked again in the mirror and wanted to ask who had done the tattoo, as it was actually pretty awesome and quite badass, but I didn't.

We pulled up in front of the sheriff's station. It seemed pretty quiet, with two squad cars and a few unmarked vehicles in the front.

We wandered inside and spoke to a woman manning a desk. Gavin said, "Here to see Jalen Kane."

Without looking up, the woman kept her eyes on the computer screen and pointed at the door we'd just arrived in. "Just got taken to court."

"Crap," Gavin murmured.

"Is that bad?" I asked as we went back outside.

"I think I know what this is about," Tarron said. He glanced at me, then to Gavin. "Witches."

Gavin waved at us to follow. "That's what I was thinking, too."

I didn't ask. What would be the point? I'd find out soon enough. My head already felt like it might explode.

It was a short walk to the large, white building with the words *City Hall* boldly displayed on top. With bare trees and dead grass in front, I thought maybe in summer it looked much nicer with everything green. The sky was getting darker with bloated white clouds, and I could feel that it was going to start snowing soon. We walked to an unmarked door in the back of the building. There was an oddly familiar symbol of a half moon and a mountain above it. We went down a steep flight of stairs and through a room, which led to a large courtroom.

A panel of men and women sat at the front on a raised dais, and the one in the middle, an elegant-looking woman with silvery-white hair, seemed to be in charge. Jalen was sitting in front of them, his hands resting on a table.

The three of us took seats in the back of the courtroom as quietly as we could.

"This is just a preliminary hearing," said an older lady in a business suit, her graying hair in a bun. "The charge is breach of confidentiality among the supernatural; specifically, circumventing the systems put in place to protect the town by means of electronic hacking. How do you plead?"

I pulled my phone out and discreetly hit the email icon. I went to pull Jalen's email up, but it was gone. Not even in the trash. I looked in the sent items, and my reply had disappeared, too. Looking up, I realized the panel members were all supes, and suddenly realized what was going on. *He's here because of that email he sent me.*

I stood, but Gavin put his hand out to block me. "What are you doing?" he hissed.

"Move," I said, looking down at him menacingly.

His jaw ticked with annoyance, but he eventually moved his arm.

I slid out from the bench and approached the front. The panel members looked at me. A lady with dark brown hair smiled. "Welcome back, Karson."

*How does she know my name?*

Jalen turned and looked at me. "Go sit down. This isn't your problem."

I ignored him and looked at the panel. "Look, if he hadn't sent that email, there's no way I would have come back here. Can't you cut him a break?"

The panel members murmured amongst themselves, and the man spoke. He had a small bit of amusement dancing in his eyes. "Son, it's clear your memories have not returned, or else you would have known better than to approach the Court out of turn. So we will cut you some slack there. However, had we wanted to call character witnesses up, we would have. This is just a preliminary hearing, like I already said."

I had nothing to say to that, so I clapped my cousin on the shoulder and went to sit back down next to Gavin and Tarron.

"Mr. Kane, how do you plead?"

"Guilty, sir."

"Very well. Court will convene in three days for sentencing. The defendant shall remain remanded until the Court can ensure the internet wards are back in place and have been tested and reinforced. Court is dismissed." The man pounded his gavel.

Jalen looked at me apologetically as a young woman with glasses escorted him from the room.

The panel began to disperse, and I looked at Gavin and Tarron. "What now?"

Tarron looked at his watch. "I've already missed first period. I gotta go to school. I'll be over right after, as long as Willa doesn't have any plans."

He hurried out of the courtroom, and I looked at Gavin. "Willa?"

"His girlfriend. She's a wolf."

I made a face. "Really?"

He chuckled as we walked out of the room. "Yeah. Very weird, I know. But it works. Tarron's not full elven anyway."

"He's not?" I asked as we made our way down the hallway.

"No, he's . . . ya know what? You'll know soon enough," Gavin replied, shaking his head. "Let's go get something to eat."

"Now you're talking in a language I understand."

Gavin snorted.

# CHAPTER 5

## KARSON

*E*ggstravaganza was the coolest little breakfast shop I'd ever been in. Okay, well, maybe I had been here before, but I wouldn't know until, apparently, my stupid memories came back. Still, the place felt slightly familiar, just like every place else I'd been to so far in this town. The server set the check down. I grabbed it and insisted on paying, since Gavin had been chauffeuring me around town.

"Thanks, man," he said after I paid and we walked out. "Where do you want to go now?"

I wasn't sure. I measured him with a stare and said, "I hate to ask another question, but do you have a job or somewhere you need to be? It's Monday."

He chuckled. "Don't *you* have a job to be at?"

"The tattoo shop is closed on Sundays, Mondays, and Tuesdays. I'm good."

He nodded as we stopped outside a shop window displaying ski gear and clothing. "To answer your question, which you already know, I work doing online trading and stuff. With my boyfriend."

I lifted an eyebrow. "Well, that's awesome. Where's he now?"

"My boyfriend?" he asked, then started walking.

"Yes."

"In Denver. As you know. I only come here once a month so I don't forget this place. I grew up here, like you—with you. We're cousins. I'm Jalen's brother. But again"—he sighed—"you already know this."

I laughed. "Is there anything I can do to speed up the memory process thing?"

He shook his head. "Nah, it takes about twenty-four hours for elves. Last time I checked, anyway. In fact, you're lucky they didn't boot you out today for disrupting Court. Though there would be no use in that. No need to try to hide anything from you."

Again . . . weird. But okay. We kept walking, and I wasn't sure where we were going, but I was enjoying looking at the town, the familiarity mixed with newness kind of cool.

We passed by a building, a sign reading *Tragic Ink* in the second-story window. I pointed at it. "Tattoo shop?"

He nodded. "Don't go in there."

"Why not?" I asked.

He huffed. "I love you, man, but if you ask one more question, I'm gonna burn you."

"You can't use affliction on other elves," I stated matter-of-factly.

"Oh, I won't need that to inflict pain. Now, no more questions." He looked up at the sky. "It's cold as hell. You like video games?"

"Uh, yeah."

He grinned. "Let's go back to the house. Jalen's a video game tester. He's got every game you can think of."

I nodded. "Sounds cool. But aren't we . . . I mean, uh"—I needed to word this in the form of a non-question—"we should go bail him out first."

Gavin shook his head. "No bail in Havenwood Falls, man. He's gotta sit there till sentencing."

*All righty then.*

WITH JALEN in jail for at least three days, I wondered what I was supposed to do. I'd told my boss that I'd be back by Wednesday. Obviously, that wasn't going to happen.

Gavin and I had been playing *Call of Duty* and *PubG* for hours, eating junk food, when we decided to take a break. I looked outside and could see the sun was beginning to set.

"Can we go visit Jalen?" I asked, the bottle of Mountain Dew paused at my lips.

Gavin screwed off the lid to his water and looked at me. "Yeah, I guess. But why?"

This confused me, but I was careful not to ask another question. "I need to talk to him is all. About y'all's dad. He told me to come here because he needed help with him once he gets outta prison."

Gavin chuckled and took a swig. "He did not summon you here to help with our dad. That shitbag is beyond help."

My eyebrows hit my hairline. "Did you just call your dad a shitbag?"

He nodded. "Sure did."

"Okay. What about my parents? Where are they? I think I need to see them."

Gavin rolled his eyes. "Your dad is . . . Your mother . . . Fuck. When your memories are back, you can . . . I can't answer that."

We stared at each other for a few seconds, the tension in the air growing thick. "Okayyy. Well, tell me then, why do you not care that your brother's in jail?"

He set the bottle on the counter and put the lid back on. With a shake of his head, he looked at me. "You. Are. So. *Annoying.* Without. Your. Memories."

This pissed me off. The smug look on his face. The blasé attitude about his brother and my mental state. I was always a goal-minded person, so being here in this remote mountain town, seemingly without a reason, was driving me crazy.

"That doesn't make any sense!" I snapped. I wanted to fold the guy's teeth back with my fist. Instead, I turned around and punched the first thing I could see. Which, unfortunately for me, was an oven set into the wall of the kitchen. When my fist made contact, I watched as the black glass splintered and began to spiderweb.

As if in slow motion, I looked down at my fist and could see blood covering my knuckles and the bones of the top of my hand looking not quite right. Instead of being straight and symmetrical, the middle two were sort of askew. Then came the pain.

"Fuck!" I yelled, shaking out my bloodied hand.

Gavin raced over to me and looked down at my hand, then into my eyes. "Looks like a trip to the hospital is in your future, you dumbass hothead."

"I'm fine," I gritted, trying not to pant or pass out at the pain.

He scoffed. "Your hand is broken. You're not fine."

"It'll heal," I came back.

Gavin snatched a dishtowel and filled it with ice from the freezer, then handed it to me. He snatched his keys from the counter and demanded, "Get in the car."

I shook my head. "No. I'm fine. I'm sorry about the oven. I'll pay to have it fixed. This ice pack will be just fine. I'll be okay."

"If you don't get your stubborn ass in the car by the time I count to ten, I'm gonna call Tarron over here, and we're going to drag your ass to the hospital. And trust me, you don't want that."

The pain in my hand was getting worse, and I was trying to smile in spite of it. "I'm not afraid of a high school kid."

"Don't let the baby face fool you," Gavin said, shoving me toward the front door.

Deciding I wasn't going to win this fight, and hoping the hospital bill wasn't going to break my bank account, I let Gavin corral me to the car.

I wasn't sure why I was fixated on her braids, but I was. Their auburn color was almost mesmerizing. Or maybe I was using them as a focal point in order to not cry out in pain. *Scottlin*, the name sewed onto her white doctor's coat read.

Yeah, my hand was broken. The middle two bones were fractured, and it was for this reason I sat here waiting for someone to come and get me so they could put my hand in a cast.

"Are you in any pain?" the pretty redhead asked me.

I shook my head slowly. Of course I had to put on a brave face and lie through my teeth. "It's not too bad."

She lifted her gaze to mine, and I almost choked on my own breath. Her eyes were so blue, I thought maybe the sky outside the window was reflecting off them.

"So how did you do this, Mr. Kane?" Scottlin asked sweetly, her voice like a soft melody floating on a breeze.

It seemed I had two choices here: The truth, or something way cooler. After staring into her face, I decided on something in between. "I punched something."

She laughed and shook her head. "Well, that's pretty evident."

"Is it?" I asked, just anxious to keep her talking. She had a sweet disposition about her, but she also had that hot nurse thing going on.

"It is. It's not easy to break the metacarpals when the hand isn't balled into a fist. Unless something falls down on it and crushes it, of course."

When she lifted those baby blues to mine, I could hardly remember a word she'd said. "Huh?"

Laughing again, she said, "Keep your arm still and stay here. I'll be right back."

I wanted to laugh. Really, where was I gonna go?

She came back a couple minutes later with something that looked like a board and a roll of tape. I looked at the device, then back into her face. I could see a light smattering of freckles there.

After grinning at me, she slid the board under my arm. "You wanna do this the hard way or the easy way?"

I looked at her. "The easy way. You've got an easy button, right?"

She grinned and, seeming to produce a syringe out of nowhere, she lifted the sleeve on my right arm and tore open an alcohol swab. I watched as her brow furrowed.

"What?" I asked. "I'm not afraid of needles."

She pointed to my tattoos. "That's obvious."

Then she swabbed a small section above the skull on my shoulder. After pushing the plunger home, she removed the needle and quickly put a Band-Aid on it.

"Let's give the meds a few minutes to kick in."

I couldn't stop staring at her. "Are you going to stay and keep me company?"

I immediately felt relaxed and happy, like I'd taken a hit off a joint.

She bit back a grin. "You're funny."

"And you're pretty," I replied quickly.

"Thank you," she said quietly. "I'll be right back."

I watched her leave and wished she wasn't wearing the medical smock so I could check out her ass.

"She's got a boyfriend," Gavin said from the corner of the room, where I had forgotten he was seated. He was looking down at his phone, typing something.

"Really. Is he hotter than me?" I asked, now feeling totally high and not caring about filtering my mouth.

Gavin chuckled. "I'm only saying this because I like dudes and not because you're my cousin, but fuck no. He's a total dweeb."

"Human?" I asked.

Gavin looked toward the door and then back to me. "Keep your voice down!"

I furrowed my brow. "I was."

He laughed again and shook his head. "No, you weren't. And yes, the dude is human."

"No, is the hot nurse human?"

He glanced toward the door again, then back to me with his lavender-colored eyes. "Not sure. Also, she's not a nurse. She's a nurse practitioner."

Cocking my head to the side, I asked, "What's the difference? Hot nurse is a hot nurse."

"Oh, my gods. You without your memories is bad enough, but you loaded on pain meds is like, torture."

"I'm not loaded," I practically slurred.

"A nurse practitioner is almost like a doctor. I think. Something like that."

Just then, the cutie with the braids came back in. "How are you feeling, Mr. Kane?"

"Hey," I asked, "are you a doctor?"

She grinned and looked at my hand. "No, but kind of close."

"Do you know me?" I asked.

"Oh, brother," Gavin groaned from the corner.

She looked into my eyes. "No, should I?"

I blew out an exaggerated breath. "I don't know. My memories are . . ." I made circles near my temple with my finger and whistled.

She looked alarmed and shot a look to Gavin. "He's from here?"

I looked at Gavin, and now there were two of him as he said, "Yes, just got back into town early this morning."

She flicked her gaze to me and then pulled out a flashlight. As she shined it into my eyes, her light ginger brows furrowed together. She clicked the light off and returned it to her pocket. Then she glanced at Gavin again. "Pain meds mixed with the spell is never a good idea. I wish I had been informed."

"Oh, no," I slurred, putting my hand on her arm. "I'm okay. I really am." I reached up and fingered a braid. "You're sooo pretty."

She shook her head and looked at Gavin, concerned.

"I need to lie down." I let my top half fall back on the gurney I had been sitting on. The last thing I heard was the nurse's beautiful voice saying, "After I'm done, get him home. Then call me."

# CHAPTER 6

## SCOTTLIN

*A*s I slogged into the house, exhausted as usual, my phone vibrated. I wearily pulled it from the pocket of my scrubs and could see I had a text.

**Len: Can I come over?**

**Me: Sorry, not tonight.**

I closed and locked the door behind me, then set my purse, keys, and jacket on the dining room table. Glancing at the microwave clock, I could see it was past eleven p.m.

*Why do I work so many hours?*

Shaking my head, I headed toward my room and stripped off my scrubs. I put them in the special hamper I used for my medical clothes. Then I wandered into the bathroom and turned on the water before lighting the two vanilla-scented candles on the vanity. I guessed I was an odd one—I preferred to shower in the dark and quiet. It helped me unwind, I supposed.

Once the water was heated, I stepped into the shower and groaned as the heat pounded my stressed muscles. With the flats of my hands against the wall and the water cascading over me, I closed my eyes and willed the relaxation of the shower to melt all the troubles of the day away.

I hadn't been working at the Havenwood Falls Medical Center very long, which was why I was on ER duty. And I was okay with that. It had been barely a year since I'd gotten my degree to become an NP, and I knew I had to pay my dues. However, the ER could be a sad and stressful place.

But it wasn't the sad or stressful that now invaded my brain. It was the smoking hot elven guy with the broken hand I'd worked on. The way his lavender-colored eyes had pierced me while we had been talking. The strain of his black Guns N' Roses T-shirt over thick, muscular, tattooed arms. It was all I could do to keep eye contact with the guy.

I turned around, grabbed my strawberry-scented shampoo, and squirted some into my hands. While working it into my hair, I thought more about Karson Kane. He had apparently just returned back to town after a long time away, and didn't have his memories back. Then, like an idiot, I went and injected him with ten milligrams of morphine to relieve his pain. Huge no-no. Narcotics combined with powerful witch spells had to be considered very carefully when used.

I should have asked him more questions.

I should have been more thorough.

I should have asked his elven friend about Karson's situation beforehand.

*Dammit! I should have known better.*

I was glad that, at least, I had found out about his memories before I had decided to heal him magically. Still, I wish I would have known he had just returned to town and was still an amnesiac.

Deciding that self-loathing was too much of an energy-suck, I rinsed off and stepped out of the shower. Once toweled dry, I padded into my room and slipped on a black tank top with *Book Nerd* written in blue across the chest and a pair of comfy black yoga pants.

After combing out my wet hair, I sat on the bed and looked at my phone, staring at the text from Len asking me if everything was all right. I felt bad for ignoring him. Truth was, I had been delaying the inevitable with him for quite some time. We'd been dating about six months, but I just wasn't feeling it. It was one of those things where you knew the other person was way more into you than you were into them. And I felt bad about that. Really bad. But I couldn't force what wasn't there. Len, a volunteer firefighter and EMT who worked for the town, had asked me out one day after he'd brought a patient into the ER. He had been cute and charming, and I'd agreed to meet him for coffee.

Since then, we had been seeing each other, but we had never become serious—and there was a reason for that. There was no chemistry. I didn't give myself to just anyone, and when sparks were lacking, there was no way I was going to.

It was for this reason that I had been dreading doing what I had to do—break up with him. But I wasn't going to do it over text, and I was certainly too exhausted to meet with him in person. *Tomorrow*, I told myself. *I'll deliver the bad news on my lunch break.*

Frowning, and with my stomach in knots, my thumbs typed out a reply:

**I'm fine. Let's meet for lunch at Napoli's at noon tomorrow.**

His reply was immediate: **I'll be there, beautiful.**

I groaned. This was going to completely suck.

My knee bounced up and down as I sat in a corner table at Napoli's Pizza. I wasn't hungry, and knew I wouldn't be able to eat, but I had to order something while I waited for Len to show up. I was fifteen minutes early, and, as he was always late, I knew I would be sitting here for a while. *Good.* It would give me time to formulate what I wanted to say, because as of now, I had nothing but pure lameness planned.

"What can I get ya?" I heard an accented voice ask.

I looked up to see a young, olive-skinned girl standing there in a Napoli's T-shirt and jeans. My eyes flicked to her nametag.

I smiled. "Hi, Zara, can I get a coffee and a water please?"

"Absolutely, miss," she replied, smiling at me.

Her British accent was a little odd-sounding in Havenwood Falls, but then again, nothing about this place was normal. Staring unseeing at the menu, I went over a million different ways to word what I had to say to my boyfriend in my head. Nothing sounded good, and I grew frustrated. Unfortunately, for once, I was out of time, it seemed. I heard the bell above the door chime and looked up to see Len walking in. He smiled immediately when he saw me.

*He does have such a nice smile . . . Maybe I should give it more time.*

*Stop, Scottlin. Just stop!*

I stood when he arrived at my table. He hugged me, then kissed me on the cheek like he always did. After he sat down, Zara returned with my drinks and asked Len what he wanted.

*Diet Coke with a lime.*

"Diet Coke with a lime," he replied, smiling.

Zara grinned. "You got it, love."

"I wasn't aware we had any people from England living here. Well, besides Dr. Lewis's family," I said quietly as she walked away.

Len chuckled. "She's American. She's from Havenwood Falls. She just loves to speak with a British accent. Maybe she wants to be an actress?"

My eyes widened. "Seriously? Well, someone give that girl an Oscar. She had me convinced."

Len chuckled. "Right?"

I cleared my throat and looked down at the menu again. "You going to get pizza, or something else?"

When he didn't answer, I looked up at him over my menu. He was staring at me, his chocolate-brown eyes almost studying me.

"What?" I asked.

"What, what?" he countered. "You asked me here. You never ask me to lunch. Plus, you know it's my day off, or else I wouldn't have been able to meet you at all."

I sighed, set the menu down, then folded my hands over it. "We need to talk."

"You're breaking up with me," he deadpanned.

Chewing the side of my lip, I began to nod slowly when Zara returned with his soda.

"You ready to order?" she asked, still in character.

I shook my head. "No, not yet."

Sensing the tension, she simply nodded and flounced off.

Len made a scoffing noise and looked down at his own hands. "I'm not stupid, you know. I know this has been a long time coming."

"I'm sorry," I squeaked. "But it has."

His gaze met mine once again. "No, I'm sorry. I fell much harder than I should have. For you."

"Len, it's not your f—"

He put a hand up. "I know it's not. But you can't force what's not there."

"You took the words right out of my mouth," I whispered.

He looked pained, but somehow relieved, too, as he said, "You're a beautiful girl, Scottlin. You'll find someone. I'm just sorry it isn't me."

This hurt my heart even more, and I felt like a total jerk. "I'm sorry."

"Can we stay friends?" he asked. "Still have lunch?"

This made me happy. I thought guys hated it when you friend-zoned them. "Yes. I would love that."

Zara returned to take our order. I wasn't sure I could eat, but I decided on a house salad and a slice of cheese pizza. Len got a calzone, and once she walked away, he started a conversation about the upcoming election in Havenwood Falls, and how strange it was that a Stuart always won the mayor's seat. I don't think we'd ever had such an easygoing interaction before.

I felt relief I didn't deserve.

# CHAPTER 7

## KARSON

*I* woke the next morning feeling like I'd drunk a fifth of Jack. Groaning, I rolled over and looked for the alarm clock that wasn't there. Opening my eyes further, I realized I wasn't at home, but in a strange bed. Light from a window illuminated the room, and once I located my phone, I plucked it from the nightstand. It was after ten a.m., and I wondered how I'd gotten here and why I'd slept so long.

Jalen's house. The hospital. The cute redhead.

I pulled my hand out from under the comforter and examined the cast covering it. "Shit," I groaned.

So it had been real. I'd punched the oven in the kitchen and broken my hand. What in the hell was going on? Just then, I put my good hand to my neck, remembering the phoenix tattoo. I got out of bed and rushed to the bathroom to stare in the mirror. Sure, I'd inked that bird with its flame many times on many people, but I'd never thought of getting a phoenix tat myself. I opened the door to my room and wandered down the stairs. There was nobody around. Shrugging, I opened the refrigerator and found a box of pizza with a few slices in it.

I could eat cold pizza, but I couldn't do a no-coffee morning. While I munched on a slice, I rummaged through the cabinets and located some coffee pods, plunking one in the single-cup maker.

Looking around at my surroundings, I could tell the house was older, but it had been furnished and decorated nicely. Ironically, it was how I would decorate a house if I had one. As of now, I only had a one-bedroom apartment in Colorado Springs that wasn't worth spending too much money on.

Speaking of . . .

I'd been here well over twenty-four hours, and I was still confused as hell. Maybe Jalen had been lying in his email. Maybe he'd said all that stuff to get me into town, playing on my loneliness.

But . . . how would he have known about me or my life?

I was getting a headache from this shit.

The blue lights lit up the coffee machine, and I slammed the lid down, placed a coffee mug with the words *I Love Havenwood Falls* printed on it, and pushed the button to start the blasted machine. I definitely did not love Havenwood Falls at the moment. I just wanted to go home.

*But you are home* came a voice. Inside my head.

Irritated with all my fleeting thoughts, I watched as the machine spit out the black liquid, and as soon as the cup was full, I picked it up and carried the mug upstairs and had drunk most of it by the time I reached the bathroom. I took a shower, cautious not to get my cast wet.

After drying off, I stared at myself in the mirror, my purple eyes gazing back at me.

"Who are you?" I whispered.

Of course, I knew who I was. My name was Karson Eli Kane, I was twenty-four years old, and I worked as a tattoo artist. I lived in Colorado Springs. I liked women, and they liked me. I was damn good at what I did, and I had a few friends and a super cool boss.

Looking down at my cast, I shook my head. But where did I go to high school? Where had I grown up? Who were my parents? Had I had a happy childhood with a dog or a cat? What about siblings—did I have any? The fleeting memory of that weird blackout I'd had came back to me, but when I tried to remember exactly what it had been about, the images vanished, like a vapor.

I looked down at the tattoos covering my arms and could still see the small, circular scars under them. You had to look closely to see them, but they were there. I just couldn't remember how I got them or what they were from.

Sighing, I left the bathroom and threw on a Metallica T-shirt with a thick hoodie over it. After sliding on my jeans and shoving my feet into boots, I quickly scrubbed my teeth and threw some goop into my hair to make it stand up the way I liked. Some hair stuff had gotten onto the silver hoop in my right ear, and I wiped it off.

I headed downstairs and out the door, not having ever seen another member of the household. Of course, I knew Jalen was in jail, and that was where I was headed—to get some damn answers. I just hoped it was visiting hours by the time I got there.

∼

ON FOOT, I walked out of the neighborhood and soon found myself on the main street of the town. The strange feeling of not knowing where I was, yet knowing exactly where I was, was completely odd. I felt like I had some kind of war battling inside my head.

The storefronts, shops, cars, and streets were comforting and familiar, yet I couldn't remember where I was supposed to go to reach the jail. Was it inside City Hall?

*Oh yeah, it's at the sheriff's station. Where was that again?*

As I passed a small pizza shop, I casually glanced inside. I could see a few people having lunch. That's when she caught my eye: the gorgeous nurse practitioner from the night before. She ran her fingers along her hair that lay over her shoulder as she laughed at whatever the guy she was with had said. I paused to watch them as he reached over and grabbed her hand. She looked down at the interaction and seemed to frown briefly.

*Damn. Guess Gavin was right about the boyfriend. It would have been nice to take her out and get to know her. Guess that's not going to happen.*

Before I turned to walk away, our eyes met. Hers widened momentarily when she spotted me, then she smiled. I didn't think she'd recognize me. She motioned for me to come into the restaurant, but . . . fuck that. I already had some dumb little schoolboy crush on her. I had no desire to meet her boyfriend, or husband, or whoever the hell that was.

Looking away, I quickly made my way toward the jail. I reached City Hall first and stopped short as I looked at the massive structure.

"Karson," a high-pitched voice said from behind me.

I turned around to see Scottlin standing there with her hands in her pockets and a friendly smile on her pale face. Her bright indigo eyes looked extra striking against the cloudy gray sky.

"Uh"—her gaze flicked down—"how's your hand?"

My eyes lazily drifted down to it, then back to her gorgeous face. I looked at her strawberry braids and wondered how fun it would be pull them while . . .

"I can see you're busy," she cut into my thoughts.

Jerking back to reality, my eyes widened. "No."

Her ginger brows furrowed. "No . . . what?"

"Shit." I shook my head. "No, not busy. And fine. My hand's fine."

No, it wasn't. It was throbbing something fierce in this cold-ass weather. But no way was I gonna puss out and tell her that.

"Really?" she asked, taking another step toward me. I noticed she wore green medical scrubs under her oversized brown jacket, which had white fur trim around the collar and sleeves.

"Yes, really."

"Can I take a look?" she asked, with a lopsided smile on her cherry-red lips.

I shook my head. "Nah, I'm good. But . . . could you tell me where the jail is at?"

We were within touching distance now. And, oh, how I wanted to touch her, but knew there was no use in doing that.

"It's on the other side of City Hall."

"Thanks," I replied, turning to continue walking.

"Why are you going to the jail?" she asked.

I stopped and turned around, thrusting my hands into the pocket of my hoodie, the cast barely fitting inside. "Why do you care? Isn't your man waiting for you back there?"

*God, Karson, could you sound any more insecure?* I turned around and walked away.

"If you're referring to the guy in Napoli's, he's . . . just a friend."

"Famous last words," I murmured. I figured while I was making an ass of myself, I might as well win an Oscar at it.

She laughed at my stupidity. "He's an ex. Not that it's any of your business."

Turning around, I could see her walking back toward the restaurant. I longed to run after her and rub my thumbs over her cheeks—ones that looked to be turning red from the cold. But, of course, I didn't. I let her go and headed toward the jail.

# CHAPTER 8

## SCOTTLIN

*Y*eah, I was a really bad person. A total ass.

The second I'd seen Karson Kane's gaze piercing mine from the other side of the window, I'd excused myself, jumped up from my seat in Napoli's, and bolted for the door. I couldn't believe I'd even remembered to grab my coat from the back of the chair.

Len must have picked up the tab and left, because by the time I arrived back there, he was gone, and the table we'd occupied was clean and ready for more patrons.

*Yep, I'm an ass.*

With a shake of my head, I walked back toward the Havenwood Falls Medical Center, knowing I'd taken a lot more than an hour lunch break. But if my boss tried to give me any crap about it, I'd remind him that I never took lunch breaks. Sure, I'd go down to Coffee Haven and grab something every once in a while, but I always ate it in my small office where I was probably typing my patient notes into the computer. I hadn't actually left the facility for a lunch break in . . . well, ever. Not in the almost year I'd worked there. I hadn't even finished my lunch before taking off after Karson, but thankfully, the four bites of pizza and half a salad I'd managed were enough. And now, as I sat in my office, I needed to finish my notes before I had to head back into the ER.

I typed what I had jotted down about Karson's case.

*Subject is a twenty-four-year-old elven male. He presents to the ER with hand pain. Suspects fracture. Subject reports he struck a glass oven door with a closed fist no less than one hour prior to arriving at the ER.*

I lifted my gaze from the page and stared at the door to my office. Why had he punched something? Was this guy a hothead?

I finished my notes and decided, while I was taking one-hour-and-fifteen-minute lunches, that I could break another rule today and maybe look him up in the hospital's computer.

After a few keystrokes into the part of the computer only we supernatural staff had access to, his name popped up right away. Karson Eli Kane: Elven. Date of birth, hair and eye color, parents' names and race (both purebred elven). He didn't have much else in there. Born and raised in Havenwood Falls. No significant medical history or problems. Everyone in town knew about the Kanes, but I had never personally met Karson. I was thinking maybe it was time I asked around about this guy.

I sat back in my chair, my pencil to my mouth, and pondered this. *Why do I give a crap? He's just some hot guy I treated.* Sure, he had acted a little macho, like the broken hand hadn't hurt, but I had seen that plenty of times, especially in male supes. Men—they just couldn't seem to embrace pain.

They weren't like us women. We not only embraced pain, we bathed in it and made it our friend. We wallowed in and clung to the agony like it was our long-lost friend. And for what? Why did we do this? I wasn't sure, but I definitely did not want to think about pain right now. My breakup with Len—which had gone way too easily, I might add—was still fresh in my mind. The pathetic part was that I should be feeling pain. I should be feeling guilty. I should be feeling a loss.

Except for a little guilt, I felt none of these things.

The only thing I felt was a draw to the tall, sexy blond elf who'd come into my ER yesterday. I thought about our interaction in the town square earlier and couldn't believe he was the same guy. One had been broken and in need of help. The other had been cocky, moody, broody, and a little emotional, if I was being honest.

*Move on, Scottlin. You're twenty-four. There are lots of fish in the sea.*

Pushing thoughts of him from my mind, I clicked on the next patient file and began typing. I definitely needed the distraction.

~

I ENDED up staying way too late at the hospital. It seemed like the work just never ended, and I had always been the type who liked to finish what I started before leaving for the day. But after almost a year here, it was clear that was never going to happen.

You wouldn't think a small town like Havenwood Falls would have such a high amount of ER visits, but we did. The problem was, while the human ailments were easy to fix, it was the supes who came in with odd injuries or symptoms that sometimes left us scratching our heads. Like this one, as I began to type, since dictation was forbidden here, in case humans overheard us:

*Subject is a seventeen-year-old female, suspected wolf, but no lycan characteristics have presented as of yet. Patient claims to have fevers daily, but no other symptoms. Ran routine tests, including CBC . . .*

With a yawn, I saved the file, put it into the queue, and began to shut down the computer when a notification popped up that Karson's lab results were ready from when the nurse had taken his blood upon his admission to the ER.

*Just read it later,* I told myself.

Of course, I couldn't help myself and clicked on it. I casually read over the results and was about to close the file when something caught my eye.

I squinted at the screen. My eyes widened. How in the heck did he have molomorphine in his system? That was only for vampires!

There was only one answer: Someone had prepared ten milligrams of molomorphine into the syringe—not the regular morphine I'd ordered. I'd need to check the nurse's schedule to see who'd prepared it. In the meantime, how was an elf even functioning on molomorphine? I scanned Karson's medical record and could not find a phone number. All patients admitted into the emergency room were supposed to leave one. Yet more incompetence of the ER admin staff I was going to have to bring up with the hospital administrator.

*Let it go, Scottlin. Let it go.*

I took a deep breath and tried to rein in my inability to let go of control. "Just think of another way around this," I murmured.

Remembering reading in his file that he was a cousin to the Kanes, I knew I could easily find a phone number for one of them.

Those boys were constantly getting hurt. I specifically remembered last winter when Jalen Kane thought he could jump off a gondola while it was still several feet in the air and just ski down the hill. Unfortunately for him, it hadn't worked out that well, and a broken ankle was his reward. Lucky for him, the elven healed quickly—not as quickly as vampires or wolves, but with some help from me, he avoided wearing a cast altogether.

I grinned at the memory and went into the hospital's database to find Jalen's phone number. I found it quickly and dialed his cell first, but it went straight to voicemail, as if it were dead. Next, I tried what was listed as a home number. After two rings, somebody picked up.

"Hello?" answered a deep male voice.

I cleared my throat. "Hello, may I speak to Karson Kane?"

After a long pause, the voice said, "He's not here. May I take a message?"

"Sure, but who am I speaking with?" I asked.

"Gavin. I'm Karson's cousin. And you are?"

"I'm Scottlin Glover. I'm a nurse practitioner here at the Havenwood Falls Medical Center. Karson was recently treated in our ER, and I'm calling to follow up with him."

Gavin chuckled. "Yeah, I know. Dumbass punched the oven. It's all cracked now."

I furrowed my brow. "Okay, well, do you possibly have a phone number I could use to reach him?"

"Sure. Hang on." I could hear the phone rustling, then he came back and recited a number very quickly.

"Seven-one-nine area code?" I asked.

"Yes," he replied. "That's his cell."

"Thank you, Gavin."

"No problem."

I hung up and dialed his number. The 719 area code was southern Colorado. Where had this guy come from?

# CHAPTER 9

## KARSON

*J*alen stood inside his cell, metal bars separating us. He looked happy to see me. I gave him a quick fist-bump, then slipped him two flowers I'd swiped from a vase at the hospital yesterday.

"Thanks," he said, popping them into his mouth and chewing quickly.

I folded my arms across my chest as I measured my "cousin" with a hard glare. "Now. You wanna tell me just what the hell is going on here?"

Jalen had the decency to look embarrassed. "I'm sorry, man. I didn't anticipate this." He gestured around the jail with his eyes. "Dad's getting released soon, and I just needed a little help."

I blew out a breath and raked my fingers through my too-long hair. "Help with what? Do I look like a damn social worker? What can I do?"

"No," he said, looking as if he was about to snap. "I just . . . I needed you here." He looked down. "What happened to your hand?"

All this cryptic talk and odd, unfinished conversation was working my last nerve. I ignored his question. "Look, dude. I don't know you at all. You send me this weird-ass email to get me to come to this weird-ass town, and once I get here—"

Jalen cut me off. "What are you talking about? Are you seriously standing there and telling me you still don't remember this place?

What's wrong with you, Karson? You were born and raised here! Your memories should have returned by now. Something isn't right."

I stared at him incredulously and then took a few steps back, preparing to leave. "I still have no idea what you mean, so I think I'm just gonna go catch a bus back to the Springs and get on with my life. I have a shitload of clients waiting for tats, and I don't have time for these bitch-ass games."

"Wait!" Jalen said, sounding desperate.

I stopped and turned around. "What?"

"You don't remember anything? Nothing at all?"

I needed to come clean and tell him that yes, some of the things in the town felt familiar to me, almost comforting. But I couldn't explain it, and I doubted he could, either. So I changed the subject. "When are you getting out of here?"

"Don't know. I'll be here at least two more days, though," he replied.

I sighed. "What am I supposed to do in the meantime?"

He blew out a breath and jutted his chin at the phoenix. "Tattoo returned, I see."

"Yep. Weird as hell, since I don't remember getting it."

"You will. Just strange that you haven't remembered us yet. Something is wrong. You should probably go find—"

"Visiting time is over," a deep voice bellowed.

I glanced at the deputy, who sat at a nearby desk with a Styrofoam cup in his hand. I looked back at Jalen. "That's my cue to leave."

"Find a witch. They can figure out why your memories haven't returned," Jalen called out.

"Shut the hell up!" the deputy snapped, getting up from his desk and rushing over to Jalen.

I watched wide-eyed as he unlocked the cell door, tossed him onto the stone bench, and told him there'd be consequences if he didn't keep his mouth shut.

The deputy then locked the door, mumbled something about the Kanes, looked at me and snarled, "Get out of here!"

I backed out of the sheriff's station and sprinted down the road that would lead me to my cousins' house.

If that was who they truly were.

∾

As I slowed to a stroll on the snowy, icy streets, plumes of breath clouding as I walked, I pulled my cell from my pocket. Before I could swipe the screen to check it, it suddenly rang in my hand with an unknown number.

"Hello?"

"Karson Kane?"

"Yeah, who's this?"

"Hi, Karson, it's Scottlin." She cleared her throat. "From Havenwood Falls Medical Center. I treated you earlier . . ."

Like she needed to explain who she was. How could I forget that hottie? "What can I do for you?"

"Well, I've come across something in your medical file that needs to be re-checked. Can you come back to the medical center?"

Figuring I had nothing else to do, I shrugged a shoulder. "Sure. When?"

A long pause, and she replied, "Uh, now, if you can."

"Fine. I'll be there in a few." I ended the call and turned around. I knew I needed to head west to reach it. How I knew that, I wasn't sure. I just did.

My head was swirling with all kinds of things. My conversation with Jalen, which had gotten me nowhere. All the work I was missing out on back home and how I would pay my rent next month. Jalen's alarm at how I hadn't "gotten my memories back."

That disturbed me. I was an elf. I knew that things weren't as they seemed. After all, my ears were pointed, but nobody could see that. They were glamoured from humans. Magic. I knew there were witches and vampires and wolves—God, so many wolves in Colorado. But we supes kept to ourselves and never mingled or bothered with the other species except when we had to. Hell, I even had a special ink for the vampires who came in for tats. I had to use a very small needle and work very quickly to tattoo them, or else the ink would spread, then disappear on their skin. But I had found a way to get it to stick because I was awesomely talented that way. Also, there may have been a little magic involved.

The vampires and other creatures who came into the shop to see me knew what I was. They always did, but it was obviously never discussed. Occasionally, I would get small talk from one, asking me where I was from. But I could never tell them because I couldn't remember. It was like the back of my mind had all this information stored, but the front of it was clouded with a thick blanket of fog and wouldn't allow the information to come forward.

I had been musing as I walked, and now found myself in front of the Havenwood Falls Medical Center. I entered in through the front door and made my way to the emergency room.

A cheery young girl—witch—in scrubs greeted me with a smile on her face. She slid some jet-black hair behind her ear that had fallen out of her hair clip. "Hi. Can I help you?"

"Yeah. Looking for Dr. . . . I'm looking for Nurse . . ." I furrowed my brow. "Got an employee named Scottlin here?"

Her pretty face lit up. "Yeah, she's our nurse practitioner on call. I'll let her know you're here. Name?"

Oh yeah. "Karson," I grunted.

I watched as she picked up the phone and punched some numbers. "Yes, ma'am. A, uh, Karson is here to see you." Pause. "Will do."

She hung up and looked at me once more. "Go down the hall, last door on the right." She gestured toward the wide wooden door that seemed to lead into the offices area of the hospital.

I thanked her and pushed open the door, hoping Scottlin could give me some answers. It was, after all, the only reason I agreed to come back here. I couldn't be here in this town not understanding why everyone expected me to remember them, but feeling so at ease and comfortable here at the same time.

Nope. Nope. Nope. I was gonna get some answers. Today.

I found a door with a plaque displaying her name and knocked twice.

"Come in," I heard her call out.

I twisted the doorknob and pushed the door open. She sat behind a desk wearing a white medical coat, her hands folded together over the top of the desk.

"Have a seat." She glanced at the chairs in front of her desk.

I obeyed, sitting in one of the plush, red chairs.

Piercing me with a stare, she asked, "How are you feeling?"

Caught off guard by her question, I simply lifted a shoulder and put on an impassive mask. "Fine. Why?"

"Your memories return?" she asked.

I stared at her long and hard for a moment before replying, "No."

"Nothing at all? Don't you think that's a bit strange?" she countered.

I snorted. "Lady, this whole town is strange. Jalen told me in an email that I was born and raised here. That my memories of the town would return. Well, they haven't. So I'm beginning to think this whole weird-ass place is just a figment of my fuckin' imagination."

She laughed softly and looked down at something on her desk. "It's not, Mr. Kane. I can assure you."

I huffed. "Scottlin, look at me."

She lifted her sapphire gaze questioningly to meet mine.

"Don't call me Mr. Kane. Just Karson. Okay?"

"Okay," she replied, staring into my eyes.

# CHAPTER 10

## SCOTTLIN

*I* bit back a smile. *Wow, bossy, this one.*

"Do you know me?" he asked, still piercing me with those gorgeous purple-blue eyes. They reminded me of the sky at night during a storm, where you could only see its color when the lightning illuminated it briefly. Probably because the storm behind his gaze was just as violent and beautiful.

I shook my head, remembering he'd asked me that before. Right after I had administered the narcotic. "I don't, but I know your cousins."

"Are you from here?" he asked, and I noticed he was absentmindedly rubbing his hand over the cast.

I glanced back into his eyes. "My family moved here when I was ten. I was raised out by the falls, and was homeschooled by my mom and grandmother. I didn't meet a lot of people, really, until I went to college."

He nodded. "So what did you need to see me for?"

I looked down at his hand, then back to his face. I had to keep my eyes trained on his in order not to stare at his full lips. "Your hand is bothering you, I can see. Being elven, you should heal quicker than most."

Karson raised an eyebrow at me. "How did you know that? I thought you were human."

*Only partially.* I pointed to the computer screen. "It's in your medical record."

He lowered his voice. "So the humans around here know about us?"

There was no way to answer that without getting complicated, so I said, "No, not really. Only supes can see those notations in your record. To a normal human, that part would read your race, such as White, or Hispanic, or whatever."

"To answer your question, yes, it still hurts, but the cold isn't helping."

I got up, walked to the cabinet, and pulled open a hand warmer pouch. I shook it to activate it, then wrapped it in a small hand towel. I placed it on his hand and told him to hold it there. I wished I could just heal him now, but I wasn't taking that chance. Not with his amnesia still in effect.

He looked up at me from where he sat, and his features softened. "Thank you. That feels better already."

"You're welcome." I smiled warmly at him. "I'll give you a few more before you leave. You shouldn't be walking around in this cold anyway. You don't have a car?"

"I do, but it has a busted transmission. I'm saving up to fix it. So I walk or Uber everywhere back in the Springs. Took a Greyhound to get here."

"I see," I replied. "Well, I wanted to let you know that I believe you received a pretty large dose of a narcotic yesterday when you came in. The nurse grabbed the one infused with magic for vampires, called molomorphine. Vampires heal pretty quickly, but there are times they need something immediately for the pain, so that was our, ah, special blend, if you will. It should *not* have been used on you, and I wanted to apologize for the mix-up. You seem to be feeling okay, though?"

"That might explain the brain fog. I thought it was just this memory problem that was doing it. And being in a strange place that doesn't feel so strange sometimes."

I licked my lips and measured my words carefully. "Actually, I have reason to believe the narcotic might be affecting the memory spell. The wards the witches put around the town are quite complex, and very specific. Sure, they affect each person differently, but eventually, everyone remembers. And maybe you will, too, and just need more time, but I can't help but think the molomorphine you received is delaying their return. Magic messing with other magic. I could send you to see Addie, or we can wait and see what happens."

He nodded and almost looked relieved. Then I noticed a new tattoo on his neck that wasn't there yesterday. "Resident tattoo?"

He put his hand to his neck and nodded. "Just appeared outta nowhere."

I rolled up the sleeve on my right arm to show him the shadowed blue butterfly on my inner wrist. "Here's mine."

Karson sat forward in his chair and looked at it. "May I?"

I nodded.

He gently took my wrist and brought it close to his face. Then he rubbed his thumb over it. The motion caused my entire body to break out in goosebumps, and I resisted the shudder that wanted to overtake me.

"Beautiful." He looked up at me.

"Thank you. Addie does good work."

He let go of my wrist and sat back in the chair. "You've mentioned her twice now. She's a tattoo artist and a witch, or what?"

I laughed. "I guess you could say that. She's kind of in charge of the town wards and keeping our little place here a true haven. She works with the Court."

He nodded, but said nothing. I could tell he was trying to figure everything out.

"Would you mind if I did a quick exam?" I asked.

He lifted a shoulder and let it fall. "No, go ahead."

I stood up and went around the desk, coming to stand in front of him.

"Do you need me to stand up, or what?"

"No, you can stay seated." I pulled my flashlight from the pocket of my lab coat, bent slightly, and shone it in his eyes quickly. Normal pupil dilation. I replaced the flashlight, then removed the stethoscope from around my neck. "Please sit up as straight as you can."

Karson did as I asked, and I listened to his lungs and his heart. The heartbeat was a tad slow, but he was a big guy—about six foot two and over two hundred pounds—and he still obviously had the narcotic in his system. I removed the stethoscope and put it back around my neck. Then I knelt down in front of him and felt his throat. No swelling. Without getting up, I looked at him and asked, "Are you in any pain?"

He shook his head slowly. "Just the hand, but it's already feeling better."

I nodded and slowly stood. When I was almost to my full height, I lost my balance and almost fell right on Karson.

*Oh, God . . .*

He caught me around the waist and steadied me. So there we were, me looking down at him in the chair, his hands on my hips, both of us not moving.

I snapped out of his hypnotic gaze and shook my head. "Crap. I'm so sorry!"

He chuckled, and it was the first time I'd seen him smile genuinely. "Don't worry about it."

I looked down at his broken hand. "I hope that didn't hurt you."

Staring at me, he slowly shook his head.

After clearing my throat, I said, "Well, would you like to go see one of the witches, or would you like to wait it out and see if your memories come back on their own?"

He stood up, so now he was towering over me. "I want to do something about this now. Otherwise, I'd rather just leave this town. I don't feel like I have a reason to be here."

"Very well. Since you know where City Hall is, go around the back to a metal door, then go downstairs and you'll find Addie Beaumont. She'll help you." I went around my desk and began to sit to finish up my paperwork.

"No."

I froze mid-sit and cocked my head to the side. "Excuse me?"

"You're coming with me."

I laughed and sat down. "I have to work."

He looked at his watch. "When do you get off work?"

"When I finish," I quipped.

Karson sat back in the chair. "Then I'll wait. Or if you want, I can help."

"No, you can't," I replied, biting back a smile. Not that I would protest having this gorgeous specimen sitting in my chair for the next couple of hours, but there was no way I'd get any work done when all

I wanted to do was go sit in his lap and run my fingers over his full lips.

"I appreciate the help, but I have a few more patients to see, plus I'm on call for the ER. So unless you're a medical professional moonlighting as a tattoo artist, I doubt you could be of much help. If you want to wait in the waiting room, there are TVs in there."

He stood up. "Your shift ends at what time?"

Being specific, very smart. "Four."

"I'll see you at four, in the waiting room."

# CHAPTER 11

## KARSON

*I* glanced at my watch: 3:58 p.m. The TVs had definitely helped pass the time. I ate a protein bar from the vending machine and drank a bottle of water while I waited. I was still starving, though. I also realized that four p.m. would indicate exactly thirty-eight hours since I arrived in town. I was excited to meet this witch Addie and hoped she could give me some answers.

I also kinda wanted to find the dumb nurse who'd mixed up the meds and throttle her. My brain was still foggy, but I was grateful the irrational anger I felt earlier had subsided. I had no business being pissed off at Scottlin for having a boyfriend. It was none of my business, even if I did feel like she had been flirting a little with me in her office earlier.

Not that I minded.

She was so beautiful, I had no doubt she had a few guys chasing her. I didn't need to be another one. I had enough crap to deal with anyway. I pulled out my phone and scrolled through it, not that I got very far with the crappy signal.

"Hi."

I looked up to see Scottlin standing there in her green scrubs and furry coat. She plunked a knit hat on her head, and in her hand she held a puffy black nylon jacket. She thrust it at me. "Here."

I stood up and stared at it. "Whose is that?"

"Yours, now."

I didn't take it. "Okay, but where did you get it?"

"Lost and found, unclaimed six months. Look at it—it's barely been worn."

I dragged my gaze away from her bright blue eyes and down to the jacket. It really did look new. Shrugging, I took it from her and put it on. Perfect fit. And very warm. "Thank you."

"There are gloves, too. If you want, we can go find you a pair."

I shook my head. "Nah. I'll use the pockets. Besides, I could only wear one anyway." I held up my cast.

She shook two hand warmer pouches to activate them, and slipped them into the pockets of my jacket. Her closeness made me squirm a little—in a good way.

"Those will keep your hands warm."

"Why are you being so nice to me?" I asked, smirking down at her.

She lifted one shoulder. "Because I like you." She began to walk toward the front doors of the hospital and out of the ER.

I followed her. "You think I'm gonna sue you for the meds mix-up, and are just trying to stay on my good side, aren't you?"

She tipped her head back and laughed, her breath coming out in foggy clouds in the cold air. "No. That just goes to show you how much you need your memories. The Court of the Sun and the Moon doesn't entertain such petty and frivolous lawsuits."

*Wow.* "You're shitting me. And misdosing someone isn't petty."

She stopped walking when we reached a small red Honda. She disarmed it with a beep. I used my good hand to open the driver door for her.

She stood in the open door and said, "When there's magic involved, it changes the game. Thank you for opening my door." She paused and stared up at me. "Now get in."

I didn't have to be told twice. As I sat down, she started up the engine and hit a bunch of buttons to turn on the seat warmers and heat.

She flipped on some classic rock, which made me happy, then began driving slowly down salted but icy streets until we reached City Hall. She hummed along to "Love Bites" by Def Leppard, which made me smile.

She parked in the back, and we both got out. After walking down a short path, we came upon that same plain gray door we had used to go to Jalen's hearing. It looked like some kind of maintenance entrance. Once inside, we immediately descended the steep flight of stairs that led to the courtroom.

As I was sitting in the ER waiting room, it had suddenly hit me that Scottlin had to be a witch. I wasn't sure why I had at first thought her human, but she had said only supes could see the patient's true race in the medical records, not to mention her extensive knowledge of magic. And hadn't Gavin mentioned something about her not being fully human, anyway? Argh, my brain was in such a fog. But . . . I knew she wasn't a vampire, shifter, elf or other kind of fae, or a wolf, as those were very easy to spot. That left witch or some variation of it. Maybe she was mixed-race?

Once at the bottom of the stairs, after walking down a long hallway, we were in some kind of small reception area. Scottlin went to the only desk in the room, which was unmanned, and rang a bell sitting on it. As we waited, I looked at Scottlin as she removed her cap and gloves. Hair that had escaped her braids was sticking up in places, and I reached over and smoothed them down for her.

"Thanks," she replied. Her cheeks were already red from the cold, so I wasn't sure if she was blushing or not.

I stared down at her. "You're a witch, aren't you?"

"Scottlin Glover, so nice to see you!"

We both looked over to see a gorgeous woman with multiple tattoos and long light brown hair smiling at us. The tiny diamond stud in her nose glinted under the harsh lights of the windowless office.

"Hi," Scottlin said as they hugged briefly.

The woman turned her attention to me. "Karson. What have you been up to? Happy to be back in Havenwood Falls? Seems like you've been gone forever!"

I shook my head. "Addie, I presume?"

She furrowed her brow. "We went to high school together, Karson . . ." She looked at Scottlin. "What's going on?"

"His memories haven't returned. It's been—"

"Thirty-eight hours," I finished.

Addie adjusted her dark-framed glasses and cocked her head to the side slightly. "Well"—she shrugged—"magic affects everyone differently. That said, there's usually something by now, a glimmer of memory, especially since you grew up here." She smiled. "Why don't you have a seat." She indicated a chair in front of her.

I obeyed, keeping my eye on the witch. I never did trust them very much. I listened as Scottlin explained about the mix-up with the medication, both of them staring at me the whole time.

Addie's brows rose. "It can take time to re-acclimate to our town and the magic. That can be disorienting all on its own. But adding in magic meant for vampires? That's a recipe for a major shitstorm."

Scottlin chewed her lip. "It was an accident, I can assure you. The nurse has been counseled, and she's very sorry. I couldn't get her to stop crying."

I wanted to throttle that nurse a little less now.

"But it's not unfixable. In fact," Addie said, reaching into her pocket and plucking out a small vial of powder, "I think I can fix this right now."

It took all I had not to jump up and scream like the Broncos had just won the Super Bowl.

Addie pulled up another chair and sat directly in front of me. She glanced back at Scottlin and said, "I think once the medication is out of his system completely, his memories will start coming back slowly. I'm just gonna speed that along for him."

"You don't have to talk about me like I'm not here," I commented.

Addie had the grace to look embarrassed. "Sorry. This is a teachable moment for me, so I had my instructor's hat on. I meant nothing by it."

I looked at Scottlin. "So you are a witch."

She nodded. "Half."

I looked at Addie, and she smiled. "Ready?"

"Fuck yes, I'm ready."

Addie chuckled. "Same ol' Karson." She shook some of the shimmery purple powder from the vial into the palm of her hand, then handed the vial to Scottlin. Her smile faded, and she closed her eyes. She began chanting low in what I assumed was Latin, then her eyes popped open. With her hand cupped in front of my face, she pursed her lips and said, "Close your eyes."

I did as I was told, then I heard her blow. I inhaled in surprise as I felt the powder go up my nose and down my throat. I instinctually began to cough and sputter. "Holy shit, that's gross!"

Both women laughed.

I opened my eyes and saw them both standing there, staring expectantly at me. But no magical rush of memories exploded into my brain.

"Well?" Scottlin asked. "Anything?"

"Nope," I replied, as I stood up and swiped my hand over my face, not wanting to be sparkly.

Addie smiled. "Don't worry, it won't be long now."

"What was that, some kind of memory-restoring fairy dust?" I asked.

She laughed. "No, just a spell to clean that stuff out of your system quicker. You may be peeing a lot this evening. Or sweating. Or both."

"Awesome," I murmured.

"What now?" Scottlin asked.

Addie put the vial back into her pocket. "Take him home, let him rest." She looked at me and adjusted her glasses again. "Are you staying with Jalen?"

"Yeah, but he's in jail."

"I know. Because of you."

My eyebrows hit my hairline. "Hey now. I wouldn't go that far. He wrote me the email, not the other way around. I didn't ask to come back here. I was pretty much coerced."

Addie shook her head, frowning. "You shouldn't have left to begin with, Karson. We all told you not to, but you let your pain guide your decision, not your logic. Now you're paying the price for it, aren't you?"

The way she said it didn't seem scolding or rude, but more motherly or sympathetic. "I have no idea what made me leave, but I can't wait to get my memories back to find out."

"Now, that, I wouldn't be too quick to want to remember," Addie said with a grimace.

# CHAPTER 12

## KARSON

*A*fter thanking Addie, we left City Hall, and Scottlin drove me back to Jalen's house.

I sat in the car for a little bit and looked at Scottlin before I said, "Thank you."

She smiled. "You're welcome. Please let me know if your hand gets worse. You can reach me at the medical center."

I looked at her phone sitting in the middle console. I picked it up and swiped the screen. I went into her contacts and added my name and number, then sent myself a text.

She said nothing, just watched the interaction curiously. I felt my phone vibrate in my pocket before I said, "I'll text you."

Scottlin laughed. "Well, okay then. A guy who takes charge. Nice."

I bit back a smile and resisted the urge to finger her hair. "Like that, do you?"

She pursed her lips together, and I wanted to kiss them. "Get out of here, and get some rest. Oh, and please let me know if your memories return?"

"I will." I still longed to touch her, but decided I'd better not. Her hands were still gloved, so kissing one wouldn't have had the same effect. "Drive safely."

"Thank you."

I got out of the car and watched her drive off before carefully making my way up the icy path toward the front door. Looking up into the darkening sky, I could see snow clouds begin to move in. I sort of hated this time of year. January always seemed to be the darkest. Dark when you got up, and dark when you got home.

With a sigh, I opened the front door, which had not been locked, and was hit with the smell of pot. After hanging my coat on a hall tree in the entryway, I went into the kitchen.

Gavin came waltzing in with a joint in his hand. He looked at me expectantly, then slowly asked, "Where you been, man?"

"At the hospital, mostly. Went to see Jalen, too."

"How is he?" Gavin asked, before bringing the joint up to his lips and taking a long drag.

I looked at it, then him. "Not happy."

Gavin chuckled, then choked on the smoke. "Shit." He coughed some more. "You want some?" He held it out to me.

I rarely touched the stuff, but my hand was starting to throb again. "Sure."

I took a drag from it and held the smoke in while I stared at my cousin through the haze.

Gavin grabbed a glass from the cabinet and filled it with tap water. After taking a long drink, he said, "You remember me yet?"

I shook my head and blew the smoke out of the side of my mouth. "Nope."

"What the fuck, man." He finished the water and set the glass in the sink. "I think we need to take you to see Addie."

I handed him back the blunt. "Already done. The cutie from the hospital took me down there."

"Who? The redhead?"

I simply nodded. Then I went into my day and told him everything, the drug relaxing me and making me chatty, like a chick.

The joint had been discarded, and he now stood with his arms folded over his chest. "That's a trip. Maybe we should go see your dad. Might stir something up?" He pointed to my head.

My brow furrowed. "It might, but I don't remember my parents at all, still."

Gavin frowned. "True. It's just your dad, though. Not your mom."

"Where is she?"

He raked his long fingers through his white-blond hair and shook his head. "We'll talk about that later. Hopefully, I won't have to, though."

This was the second cryptic thing I'd heard about something unpleasant regarding my past, and yet, I couldn't wait to remember what it was.

*I think.*

"Probably not a good idea to see my dad if I can't remember him. Might make it weird. Don't you think?"

Gavin nodded. "You're probably right. Let's order pizza and play some Fortnite."

"Yes to the pizza. Not sure about Fortnite. Isn't that for kids?"

He chuckled. "Nah, it's fun, c'mon." He ordered the pizza while I set up the game.

We played for hours, until we couldn't keep our eyes open any longer.

~

*"KAR-KAR, you know Mommy has to go. You don't need to cry every fuckin' time," she slurred.*

*"What the hell, Lyn. He's only ten. Stop talking to him like that." I heard my dad's voice, but did not look up from where I was curled into a ball in the corner of my room.*

*"I'm not crying!" I gritted out, with my head still tucked down so my dad couldn't see my bloody nose. I had toilet paper stuffed in my nostrils, and I probably sounded like I was crying. But I wasn't.*

*"Whatever," my mom said, then blew smoke through her mouth. The smell made me queasy. "I'm outta here. You deal with your stupid-ass kid."*

*I heard the front door slam before slowly looking up. Dad's massive frame took up the doorway to my room. He looked at me sympathetically and said, "I'm sorry, kid. She really is a useless mother."*

*His words stung. My little heart and brain couldn't understand why I was angry at him for saying bad things about Mom. She had just backhanded me so hard, I had flown across the room, landing on my video game console. My back ached where the corner of it had dug into my skin and muscle.*

*I stood up and shrugged, not knowing what to say.*

*Dad came toward me. I looked up at his thinning blond hair and into eyes so much like mine. "Let's go get some burgers."*

*I pulled the toilet paper out of my nose and threw it onto the floor. "I'm not hungry."*

*"Yet you're going to go with me, anyway. We'll go to Burger Bar. I know you love their milkshakes."*

*He was right; I loved them. I went into the bathroom attached to my room and said, "Where did Mom go?"*

*I heard him audibly sigh. "I don't know, kid."*

*Now I wanted to cry. "Is she coming back?"*

*"Eventually. She always does. Now wash that blood off your face and get your shoes on."*

I BLINKED MY EYES OPEN, and everything was blurry. Wet tears slid down my face and into my ears. I sat up and looked around the room. It was the exact same one from my dream—just the furniture was different.

God, I hated my mom. That bitch . . . I was so glad she was dead.

*Whoa! Oh, my God . . .* "Oh, my God!"

My mom. Chasing that next high, she'd died taking mushrooms especially poisonous to our kind two years ago, right here in this house. My dad was devastated. I couldn't handle it. More tears sprang to my eyes.

"I'm the one who found her," I said to no one in particular. The pain in my chest slammed into me with the same savagery it had two years ago. I put my good hand over it and closed my eyes, trying to stay the pain and battle back emotion. Damn, remembering kinda sucked. I took a deep breath and closed my eyes, willing the agony away.

*Screw crying over her.*

I threw back the covers, flew out of my room, and went downstairs. It was quiet. I glanced at the clock on the microwave: 5:52 a.m. Too early to knock on Gavin's door with the good news. I went back upstairs, used the bathroom, and sat back on the bed in my room. I picked up my phone and texted the only person I could think of—Scottlin.

**Me: I remember!**

I set the phone down and let my memories flood in. Going to high school with Gavin and Addie. God, I had such a crush on her back then. Everyone else had crushed on her BFF Michaela Petran, but I'd thought Addie was way cuter. Finding my mom on the bathroom floor in a pool of her own mushroom-filled vomit. Me trying to rouse her. Screaming at her to wake up. Slapping her in desperation. Yelling for Dad. Jalen and Gavin coming running. Rushing her to the HFMC, blinded by tears.

But it had been too late.

Anger and sadness invaded my heart. I looked down at my arms, and it was no longer a mystery why I had all those circular burn marks all over them. The tattoos covered them up just fine, but I shouldn't have had to sleeve my arms and tattoo my chest just so I wouldn't have to look at them. I should have been able to get the tattoos for art expression, not memory suppression.

I pushed my mother from my mind and immediately wanted to go see my dad. I *ached* to see him. I shouldn't have left him the way I did. But at the time, I just had to leave. I distinctly remember feeling like the box canyon town was literally closing in all around me, trying to suffocate me, coffin me.

I looked around the room and had to think hard for a minute as to why Jalen and Gavin were living in the house I grew up in, and not my dad. He had been living here when I left. Things must have changed.

My phone chimed.

**Scottlin: That's amazing! I'm so happy for you.**

**Me: Sorry if I woke you, I had to tell someone, lol**

Since there was no way I was going back to sleep, I got up and went into the bathroom for a shower. My phone buzzed again.

**Scottlin: You didn't. I'm already at work. Came in early to get paperwork done. Somebody distracted me yesterday ;)**

I grinned at her flirtation and then stripped out of my T-shirt and shorts. I went to text her back, my fingers hovering over the phone.

Fuck it.

**Me: Can I take you out somewhere tonight to celebrate?**

I started up the shower and waited for it to get hot. And for her to text back before I got in. *Buzz.*

**Scottlin:** That would be great. Burger Bar?
**Me:** Sounds perfect. What time you off?
**Scottlin:** 4 again
**Me:** See you there at 5. I would pick you up, but . . . you know
**Scottlin:** LOL yes I know. Do you need a ride?
**Me:** Nah, I'll manage
**Scottlin:** Have a good day
**Me:** You too

I was smiling like a jackass all throughout my shower. I got my memories back, I was gonna get to see my dad today, and I had a date with a hottie tonight. It was going to be a great day.

# CHAPTER 13

## KARSON

"Gavin Fuckhead Kane, birthday July second. Loves shopping, gaming, and vampires. Gay as fuck."

He chuckled as he strolled into the kitchen, looking down at his phone. He lifted his eyes to me. "Memories returned, I see, asswipe?"

"Yep," I replied, before spooning more Froot Loops into my face.

"Fuckhead isn't my given middle name, you know," he replied facetiously, checking his hair in the reflection of the microwave door.

"Well, we gave it to you. And we've been calling you that for so long, I can't remember your real one."

"Henry," he replied with an eye roll. He went to the fridge, pulled out a box of orange juice, and splashed some into a cup.

I looked at his pressed khaki pants, his sweater over a collared shirt, and his shiny shoes. "Where you headed?"

"Time to go back to Denver. I only stay here a day or two a month, so I don't forget this place, then leave."

"That's right," I murmured.

"Yep. Anyway, got a meeting later with my boss. Plus, I miss Beckett."

I wrinkled my nose. "You still dating that vampire?"

"Yes, asshole."

I laughed. "Okay, well, good thing I got my memories back before you left."

"Yes, thank the gods. You were working my last nerve." He grabbed the keys to his little Nissan sports car and headed toward the front door.

"Hey, before you go, why are you and Jalen living in my house? Where's my dad?"

"Oh, I just stay here when I come back to town. Jalen moved in when his dad went to prison. Hasn't moved out yet. Your dad remarried and is living near the falls with a witch named Regina."

I lifted an eyebrow. "Seriously?"

"Yep, his address and phone number's on the fridge. He lets Jalen stay here as long as he pays the utilities and keeps the house and yard up."

"I have more questions, but I'll get them out of Dad. I'll see you later, I guess?"

He opened the front door and moved his backpack to his other shoulder. "Will I? Or are you going to leave again?"

I lifted a shoulder. "Not sure, but I doubt it. Don't have much in the Springs except a job and a crappy apartment. I don't even have a car."

He smiled and clapped me on the shoulder. "Good decision. Take care."

I gave him a quick man-hug and lightly pounded him on the back. "Be safe."

Gavin nodded and walked down the two front steps and toward his car. After he'd driven off, I closed the front door and went to the fridge to find my dad's info. I found the paper easily enough and pulled out my cell phone. Shit, did this town have Uber yet? Guess I was about to find out . . .

I pulled up the app, waited for it to find my location, and waited some more. Then I imputed the address from the paper. It took a good three or four minutes, but I finally got notified that my driver was on his way.

"Jakeel in a"—I put my face closer to the screen and blinked— "1999 orange Lincoln Town Car? Huh. Didn't know they came in orange." Then I glanced at the app again to see it wasn't Uber at all, but something called "Luber."

*Where had that app come from . . . ?*

I went back up the stairs to my room and opened my closet door.

Inside was a dresser where I knew I had warm gloves and hats. I also remembered leaving a wad of cash in there, having cursed myself for leaving it when I was halfway down the mountain the last time; I'd been too stubborn to go back for it. I skipped the gloves since I could only wear one, found a warm scarf and set it on top of the dresser, then opened the bottom drawer and felt around for an envelope taped to the top of the inside of the drawer. My fingers located it.

*Yes!*

I opened up the envelope, and the two thousand dollars I'd left there was all still intact. God, if I had known this was here, I'd have a working car right now. I remembered I had stormed off with about that much in my bank account, but it had dwindled quickly.

My phone buzzed in my pocket, so I pulled it out and looked at the screen: **Your driver is arriving.**

I shut the drawer and closet, threw the scarf on, and pounded down the stairs while shoving the envelope into my pocket. After grabbing the black coat Scottlin had given me (I liked it better than the wool one I knew was inside the hall closet where we kept the coats), I flipped the curtain back to see an orange hearse idling in front of the house.

*What in the . . .*

My phone rang with a strange number. "Hello?"

"Karson?" said a man's voice, which was a little on the high side.

"Yeah?"

"This is Jakeel. I'm your Luber driver. I'm out front, pal."

I tilted my head to the side and looked at the orange monstrosity. "In a hearse?"

"Yes, sirree. See you soon." He hung up.

I shook my head and went outside, leaving the door unlocked because I hadn't had time to go dig for a house key. Slipping into the backseat, I noted it was nice and warm in the car.

"Hey," I said to the driver.

"Howdy," he replied cheerily as he used the old gear-lever-type shifter to put the car into drive. He was a tiny man with about four strands of hair combed over his bald head. He had an unlit cigar between his lips, which were covered on top by a thick, brown mustache. The cold gray day did nothing to dull the sparkle of his green and red Christmas sweater.

"So this is quite a bit a ways out from here," he replied, pointing with heavily jeweled fingers to the map on his smartphone, which I noticed was mounted on some kind of contraption that looked like it was built from beige PVC piping. It was bolted to the dash and floor, and double-sided Velcro tape held the phone to the top of it.

"That's fine. I'll pay whatever," I replied quietly as I watched the car leave my neighborhood. "I just don't have my own car, obviously."

He chuckled. "That's no problemo. I'm the only Luber driver in the town, so you're stuck with me if ya need a ride-o back. So, are ya a newbie in town?"

I bit back a smile. "Nah, I'm from here. Just got back."

"That's super duper! Are you enjoying being back?"

Oh, geez. I wondered if he'd stop if I gave one-word answers. But I was probably stuck using him for a ride back later, so I'd better be nice. "Yep, it's good to be home."

He smiled at me through the rearview mirror. "I bet it's awesome-sauce! I love Havenwood Falls."

He turned a knob on the radio and began to sing along to "Bohemian Rhapsody" by Queen. I just chuckled and sat back while I watched the scenery go by. We walked down the main street, and I smiled at all the familiar shops and restaurants. I couldn't wait for that milkshake tonight at Burger Bar.

# CHAPTER 14

## KARSON

*T*he hearse's tires crunched over gravel after we turned off the main highway. I stared at the nearly frozen waterfalls trickling down the mountain to my left. They emptied into the Mathews River below, and memories of playing and fishing in that river when I was younger brought a smile to my lips. I also had especially fond memories of going to the Paddle Fest every year; it had been my favorite part of summer. My dad had taken me several times. My mother, of course, was never there.

I shoved her out of my mind and looked up when the car came to a stop. I briefly wondered if I should have called first, but I wanted to surprise Dad.

"Okeydokey, we're here, Karson."

In front of the car sat a cozy, quaint-looking house with ivy crawling up its walls and smoke billowing out of its chimney stack. A cobblestone path led to a big wooden front door with a gnome's head as a knocker. A large RV and small SUV beside it.

I handed Jakeel a five-dollar tip and thanked him. "I may need a ride back. I'll let you know."

"Sounds swell. You take care now. Toodle-oo!"

As I went to exit the car, I noticed Jakeel was sitting on what could only be described as a child's booster seat. He had some kind of special pedals that stuck up really far from the floor so he could reach them. He was tiny, like a little person. He was so odd, I couldn't quite tell if he was human or something else.

I closed the car door behind me and walked slowly up the cobblestone path. *God, I hope somebody's home, or I'm stuck.*

I used the door knocker and pounded three times. My eyes widened as I spied a planter box full of peonies. I never saw them in winter. I carefully plucked one and quickly popped it into my mouth. "Thank you, witches. Mmmm."

Now shifting from foot to foot for warmth, I didn't have to wait long until the door opened slowly and a middle-aged woman stood there. She was pretty, with curly blond hair and a friendly smile. She held a dishcloth in her hands and was drying them on it. "Hi, can I help you?"

I swallowed the flower. "Uh, is Ellis Kane here?"

She furrowed her brow, then her eyes went wide. "Karson?"

I nodded. "Yes."

She opened the door wider to let me in, and beamed from ear to ear. "Oh, my goddess. Ellis is gonna freak out." She hugged me. It was awkward because I didn't know her.

"Ellis!" she yelled, after she broke the hug. Seeing my face, she said, "I'm sorry. I'm Regina. Your dad's wife. I like tea, photography, gardening, and awkward hugging."

I chuckled. "Nice to meet you."

"What, woman? I'm not done fixing—"

I turned around when I heard my dad's voice. His eyes went wide. He dropped the wrench from his hand, immediately rushed over to me, and wrapped his huge arms around me. "Karson. Son. I'm so fuckin' happy to see you!"

"Language, Ellis," Regina corrected with a grin. "I'll make some tea."

I looked up at him, and the only thing I could think to say was, "I'm so sorry, Dad."

He shook his head. I could see his face had gained more lines, and more silvery threads had popped up along his temples. Otherwise, he looked exactly the same. "No, I'm sorry. I shouldn't have fallen apart like that when your mom died. I should have been stronger for you."

"It's okay. It was immature, me leaving like that. I won't do that again."

He put his arm around me and led me to a quaint dining room. He indicated for me to sit. I took off my jacket and scarf and set them on one of the chairs before doing so.

Dad sat next to me right as Regina arrived with steaming cups of tea. I wasn't a tea drinker, but the warmth looked inviting.

"Where have you been?" was his first question.

"Colorado Springs."

"What do you do there?" he asked, lifting the tea to his lips.

"Tattoo artist."

"Figured. You make a decent living?"

I nodded. "I do okay."

"What brought you back here? Surely, you couldn't remember this place. How did you get back?"

"Jalen," I said. "Sent me an email that sounded really weird at the time. I followed my gut and took a bus to Montrose, then boarded the Havenwood Falls bus here. Got in almost three days ago."

"Okay, first off . . . three days ago? Why didn't you come see me sooner? And those little shits didn't even call?"

"Just got my memories back this morning."

I launched into the story, and knowing Regina was a witch, I wouldn't have to hide anything.

"Addie fixes everything." Regina smiled.

"The hell happened to your hand?" Dad asked.

I looked down at it. "Well, the oven door might need replacing." I grinned sheepishly. "I sorta punched it and broke it."

"Kid, you have got to learn to control that temper."

"I know," I murmured.

"Now, how did Jalen send you an email about this place and not get his chops busted by the Court?"

"Well, about that. And why he didn't call you. He's, uh, in jail."

Dad raked his fingers through his hair. "Shit."

"We need to help him. He risked his neck for me. He said Uncle Will gets out of prison soon and he needed my help. Why would he need my help?"

"My brother is a hothead, like you. Just don't use your affliction on people. Almost killed that guy, he did."

"I know. I remember that. I'm surprised he's getting out at all."

"He's lucky the guy didn't die, really. But in the big picture, it wasn't intentional. Will was just pissed."

I nodded. "What now?"

"Before I answer that, are you back? Like, to stay?"

"Yes," I replied. "I got nothing there I can't leave behind. My car don't even work."

"That sucks," he replied, chuckling. "So you need a vehicle, then?"

"Yes, I had to Uber here. I mean, Luber."

"What the hell is Luber?"

"Like a taxi," I came back, laughing.

He got up and went to a keyholder mounted to the wall and plucked up a set. He tossed them at me. "You can have the Harley. And stay at the house. There's a spare house key on that ring, too. Just get yourself a job soon, 'cause it don't look like Jalen can pay the utilities and shit right now."

My face lit up. "Thanks, Dad. Where's the bike?"

He jutted a thumb behind him. "In the shed out back."

"But . . . I don't have a motorcycle license. Just a regular one."

Dad chuckled. "Sheriff K don't give a shit. You just gotta watch out for Deputy Conall."

I smiled. "That's true."

Regina asked if I wanted more tea, and I shook my head.

"Let's go see the bike," I said excitedly, standing up.

Dad grinned and set his teacup down. He'd had the Harley for at least ten years and never rode it. And judging from the crossover SUV and the RV parked out front, I doubted the thing had seen road in a while.

We exited through the back door of the kitchen, with Regina fussing at us to put on our coats. We quickly shrugged them on and walked a small garden path to a large tool shed that was almost as big as my studio apartment back in the Springs.

Dad produced a key from the pocket of his work pants and used it to unlock the padlock holding the door secure. He opened the doors, and I peered inside, squinting in the darkness before Dad flipped a light switch.

"Fancy," I said, then whistled through my teeth. The shed had epoxy-painted floors, fully finished and painted walls, and electricity.

He laughed. "Regina calls it my man cave."

"It totally is one. I'm a bit jealous."

He made a scoffing noise. "You and Jalen got that whole house with a garage back home. Make your own man cave."

I looked at my dad's amused eyes. "I just might." I glanced around to see tools neatly hung on a board against one wall and a lawnmower in the corner. "What, no bathroom?"

"I ain't no plumber," he replied.

That was true. He was a mechanic who dabbled in residential electrical work and carpentry. He sometimes subcontracted for McCabe & Sons Construction.

I went over to the bike and pulled the sheet off it. My eyes went wide. The 2008 Harley Nightster glinted under the overhead lights. "Dad, this thing looks brand new."

He grunted. "That's because it practically is. I think I've ridden her a dozen times, maybe. She'd just be collectin' dust if I left her in here. She's yours."

*Holy shit!*

# CHAPTER 15

## SCOTTLIN

*I* replaced the cap on the lip gloss and checked my reflection one last time. With my hair down, it was kind of wild, and I always felt like Carrot Top because I could never control its unruly curls.

"It's just burgers, Scottlin. Calm down," I said to my reflection.

I resisted the urge to pull my hair back into some kind of clip or braid, but instead pushed it all behind me so it cascaded down my back. I finished applying some mascara and blush, then threw the makeup back into the drawer in my bathroom. I quickly spritzed some body spray on and then checked my phone: 4:42 p.m.

The drive to Burger Bar was only five minutes. Should I be early?

*God, why am I so nervous?*

I blew out a breath and went into the living room of my small apartment. I located my knee-high boots quickly enough and slipped them on. After smoothing down my flowery black shirt and making sure my jeans didn't have anything on them, I shrugged on my jacket and threw on a scarf.

On the car ride over, I had to tell myself to just chill. There was no reason to be this anxious. I wasn't this nervous when I went on my first date with Len. *So what gives?* Probably because Karson was twice as hot as Len. I giggled to myself. That was most definitely true.

When I arrived, I saw Karson in the parking lot, sitting on a shiny black-and-silver motorcycle in blue jeans, a dark-colored tee, and a black leather jacket. Did he just buy that motorcycle today?

*Who cares?* He looked smoking on it.

He glanced up from where he'd been looking at his phone and smiled when he saw me pull in.

I parked and killed the engine, but before I could exit the car, he had my door open and a hand out. I glanced down at it, then him, then put my hand in his.

He hoisted me up and then closed the door for me. "Lock it," he instructed.

*So bossy.* I laughed and hit the fob to create the satisfying beep. "Happy?" I asked with a smirk.

"I am now," he said, looking down at me.

Karson placed his hand on the small of my back and ushered me toward the front door of Burger Bar. He opened the door for me, and we waited in line at the counter to order. It smelled delicious in here. My stomach somersaulted with hunger.

I was really beginning to like what I saw in Karson. Despite his tough exterior, he really did behave like a gentleman. I was anxious to see what else he was going to impress me with.

We both decided on bacon burgers and shakes, then found a table to wait for our orders. It wasn't long until Shayna Collins, a girl who worked with me at the hospital, but also worked here waitressing part time, skated over to us and set our trays down in front of us.

"Anything else?" she asked.

"Nope, looks good," Karson replied.

She winked at him, then looked at me before skating off. "Enjoy your dinner, doc."

Karson looked at me. "You know her?"

"Yeah, she works at the hospital."

"She always call you doc?"

"All non-medical staff call everyone in a white lab coat that," I replied, amused.

He laughed and unwrapped his straw. "I see."

"New bike?" I grabbed a fry and used it to point toward the windows, where night was beginning to descend, the parking lot lights popping on one by one.

He picked up his burger with his good hand, then pierced me

with his intense stormy gaze. "Yes and no. Dad's had it ten years and never rides it, so he gave it to me today when I went to see him."

My eyes went wide. "Really? Wow. That was super cool of him."

He grinned. "Yes, it was. I'm having the best day I've had in two years."

I tilted my head to the side. "Yeah? Why's that?"

"Because I woke up with my memories—not all of them good, but that's a story for another time. Then I got to see my dad for the first time in forever, and meet his cool new wifey. Then he gave me a Harley. A fuckin' Harley, Scottlin. I had always been envious of that bike, and he had never let me ride it, except one time. Now it's mine!"

I loved the excitement on his face and in his voice. He was so damned cute.

"And to top off my day, I have a date with the most gorgeous girl in Havenwood Falls."

My eyebrows practically hit my hairline. I absentmindedly began playing with my hair as I felt heat creep into my cheeks. Compliments were hard for me to accept, but I could never figure out why. "I . . . I . . . Uh, thank you." I managed a smile.

His gaze roamed my face and head, and he pointed at my hair. "I like the curls. Why do you always wear those braids?"

I shrugged. "It gets in my way at work. And when I'm not at work, I'll end up messing with it. Easier to keep it tamed, I guess."

He chuckled and pointed at my right index finger, which had a strand twisted around it. "Like that?"

I immediately put my hands into my lap, chagrined. "Yes, like that."

He laughed and bit into his bacon cheeseburger.

"So, besides riding around on your Harley, what do you plan to do while you're in town?" I asked.

He set his burger down. "I'm not 'in town.' I live here."

I lifted an eyebrow and bit back a grin. "Really? You're staying?"

He nodded. "Oh, yeah. I should have never left."

This excited me way more than it should have. I slid some hair behind my ear. "I'm very happy to hear that."

"Yeah? Why's that?" he asked with a mischievous glint in his eye.

"You guys still good?" Shayna asked, seeming to show up out of nowhere.

We both replied in the affirmative, and she skated off.

I wasn't sure how to answer Karson's question, so I shoveled a French fry into my mouth to avoid it. Goddess, this place had amazing food. Then I made sure the bacon was crispy before I lifted the burger and bit into it. I had to resist the urge to let my eyes roll back in my head.

After I set the burger down, I heard chuckling.

I looked up to see Karson touching his chin. "You have a little . . ."

Mortified, I quickly wiped my face on the paper napkin. *I suck at dating!* "Thanks. There's no ladylike way to eat a burger here, it seems."

He took a long pull from the straw of his milkshake and said, "I don't expect ladylike behavior while eating bacon cheeseburgers. Nobody here does."

I asked him a question I knew I might regret, but I was feeling kind of empowered at the moment. "And when do you expect ladylike behavior?"

His burger paused at his lips, then he set it back into the basket. After a quick glance around the quickly crowding restaurant, he pierced me with a smoky look. "Not in the bedroom, either, if that's what you meant."

I pursed my lips to keep from grinning and simply nodded. "Duly noted, sir."

"Don't call me sir. Not in public, anyway."

Thinking the conversation was bordering on inappropriate, but secretly loving it, I decided we could continue it later. So I changed the subject. "Tell me about your past."

He bit into his burger and chewed a bit before swallowing. I did the same, patiently waiting.

"What do you want to know?" he asked after swallowing.

I daintily wiped my lips with the napkin before staring at him across the table. "Pretty much everything."

# CHAPTER 16

## KARSON

*W*hat was I going to tell her? I wasn't sure. I was too distracted by the mass of red curls lying on her breasts and the way her cherry-red lips moved when she spoke. How was I supposed to concentrate on anything she had asked?

To keep from getting too aroused in the restaurant, I began to talk. "Uh. Okay. Well, I was born here. Went to school here. Graduated from HFHS six years ago. Worked right out of high school at HF Ink. Rowdy's an amazing teacher."

"I remember that place," Scottlin replied. "But he closed up shop a couple of years ago."

This surprised me—that would have been right after I left—but I didn't say anything.

"So you already had some kind of artistic talent before you started tattooing?"

I nodded. "Yes. I used to draw and sketch to pass the time while I was . . ." *Locked in a room with no food or water for days.* "Bored."

Scottlin smiled, and it was beautiful. She only knew the good, not the bad. And I would keep it that way. Her pretty smile made me happy, and encouraged me to keep going.

"Anyway, Rowdy must have seen a talent in me of some kind, because he taught me everything I know about tattooing. How the ink worked. How to keep a steady hand. How to talk to clients. Everything."

"He did beautiful work," Scottlin agreed. "Did he do any of yours?"

"My first one. It's on my calf. I'll show you later." I winked at her.

She grinned and cleared her throat. "I only have the butterfly." She held out her wrist. "Because they made me, of course. It's sorta for my dad. He died when I was a baby. Or so I'm told."

This interested me. "You don't know?"

"My mom said he died on the pass out of town. Snowy day on his motorcycle. He was human, so I believe it's possible."

That answered the question I was going to ask anyway. I lowered my voice. "So your mom's a witch, and your dad was human?"

She nodded. "Yep."

I swirled my fry in the ketchup on my plate. "Do you have full witch powers?"

She shook her head. "No. But my mother is a healer, and I have been blessed with that gift. When a case comes into the hospital, and I can't diagnose it, I cheat a little and use magic to find out what's wrong. Other than that, and having the advantages supes have around here, that's it for me."

I was impressed. "Well, that's a cool superpower to have."

Just then, the bell above the door chimed, and three pale men dressed in black clothing walked in.

I watched closely as they didn't order any food, but took a booth near the back. They eyeballed me as they walked past.

"What?" Scottlin asked as I met her stare once more.

"Nothing," I murmured, biting my tongue.

She glanced back at the group, then to me. "They're no more vampire by choice than you are elven. Ignore them. I do."

"See, that's where you're wrong. They chose to become that." I jabbed my thumb behind me toward where they sat.

Scottlin shook her head and smiled tightly at me. "No, some of them didn't. They were born that way."

I knew this. The moroi . . . they were literally born into that life, and I had no problem with them. But the ones seated in the back of Burger Bar weren't them. They were the ones who had *chosen* to be turned.

"I know," I said. "But not them."

"Just don't stare," she commented. Then her face darkened. "They have bad tempers."

I looked into her eyes. "You know them?"

"One. Treated him when he was first turned. He didn't know what was happening and came to the ER."

My eyebrows hit my hairline. "Some vamp turned him without his permission and then left him on his own?"

"Oh, yeah. The Court took care of him."

"Good," I said, finishing up the last of my burger. We changed the subject and chatted some more about anything and everything.

After a few more minutes, I asked, "Are you ready to go?"

She nodded, and we got up to leave. I noticed the vampires weren't in the restaurant any longer and wondered how they'd snuck out without me noticing. This was why I didn't care for them. Much too slippery.

I held open the door for her, and we made our way outside. I wasn't sure where we would go next, but I didn't want our date to end. I looked up to see the vampires hovering around my bike. "Shit."

Scottlin glanced up at me, then to where I was looking. "What are they doing?"

"Stay here," I told her, as we were still in front of the restaurant under the lights.

I strode purposefully toward them, and they looked up when they saw me approach.

"This yours?" one asked, a smirk on his pasty face. He was tall and thin with black hair and thick sideburns.

*Let's try polite first.* "Yeah. I'm gonna need you to move so I can leave, though."

"Where did you get this?" another one asked. He was shorter and thicker than the other, with long blond hair tied back into a ponytail.

"None of your business. Now move. *Please.*"

"No," the taller one said. "Can't we take her for a little test drive? Been in the market for a Harley, and this is just perfect."

"It's not for fucking sale." I put my hands on my hips and began to concentrate on the magic inside me. I could feel my chest growing warm, and my head was starting to float with anger.

The tall one slung his leg over the seat and sat down. He stroked the handlebar like a lover. "Oh, come on. How much you want for it?"

I slowly walked toward them and got within six feet of the bike. I couldn't take on three vampires by myself, but I could make them hurt. I looked at the one sitting on my bike right in the eye and pushed all the rage and magic out of me, delivering a sting to his brain.

"Dammit!" He put his hands to his head and doubled over.

Using his weakness to my advantage, I yanked him by the coat and tossed him onto the ground of the parking lot.

He quickly rose up onto his knees, cradling his head.

I turned and looked at the other two, who were staring in horror at their friend, and looking confused.

"Fucking elves!" the vamp said, still gripping his head.

The magic still poured out of me, aimed right at him. "It'll stop once you're a good distance away. Now get the fuck outta here before it spreads to the rest of your undead body."

The two picked up their friend, and the three rushed off at vampire speed. I hoped someone in the restaurant would tell the Court they'd used supernatural speed in front of humans.

Scottlin came over and put her hand on my arm. "Are you all right?"

I looked down into her pretty face and instantly relaxed. "Yeah, I'm fine."

"Let's get out of here." She went toward her car. "Follow me."

I got on my bike, started it up, and followed her out of the parking lot.

～

SHE COASTED into the parking lot of the Annex, where movies were shown the second Saturday of every month during the winters. *But wait, it's like Wednesday.* I pulled up next to her and killed the engine to my bike. After putting the kickstand down, I went over and opened her door for her.

*Love Bites* by Def Leppard was blasting out of the speakers again, and she looked at me sheepishly and turned it down. "Oops."

"You've got that song on repeat, or what?" I teased.

She shut off the engine and just smiled in acknowledgement as she went to get out.

"I haven't seen a movie in forever," I said as I helped her out of the car. "But they don't show movies here on Wednesdays."

She nodded as I closed her door. "There's a special screening tonight. I heard some patients talking today about it. I hope this is okay? It's too cold to do anything else."

"I agree." I grabbed her hand as we walked toward the entrance. The place was brimming with people, and I didn't care who saw us holding hands. She squeezed mine when we reached the front and saw people staring at us.

We approached the small ticket booth and I looked at the sign.

"Hmm. Looks like they're showing *Death Race Four*. Is that okay?" She looked up at me.

I chuckled. "Uh, yeah, but it's not like we have a choice. You sure you wanna see that?"

"Why not?" She smiled. "I really liked the first three."

I bought us tickets for the show, and once we were seated, we had about twenty minutes to kill.

She looked over at me and said, "So how often do you have to use your, uh"—she glanced around briefly and lowered her voice—"superpower?"

# CHAPTER 17

## SCOTTLIN

*I*t was a legitimate question, but he was staring at me like I had two heads.

I bit back a smile. "What?"

He licked his lips and looked around the theater. There wasn't anyone seated on either side of us, but there were people in front of us.

"To answer your question, not often. Very rarely. I've never used it on a human. Only"—he cleared his throat—"those people."

I nodded.

"I also want you to know that if the guy had been by himself, I wouldn't have used it. I would have just yanked him off and probably beat his ass. But between the hand and the fact that there were three of them, that was the quickest way to give him a healthy dose of respect for . . . my kind."

Made sense. "I hope you don't think I was judging you. I had just never seen a, uh, person of your race use that . . . uh, what's it called?"

"Affliction."

"Well, it's a handy trick," I commented.

"We're only supposed to use it in self-defense, if I'm being honest. So that was just a preemptive strike before the self-defense would have had to come into play. That's how I think of it, anyway."

"I agree," I said, meaning it. "Do you realize your eyes flashed red when you were doing it?"

He nodded. "Yeah. But I'm told if you blink, you'd miss it."

The screen was blank, and people were still filing in and taking seats. I was glad we had some time to talk.

Karson reached over and grabbed my hand with his good one. His touch made me feel warm inside, and the way he pierced me with his intense eyes made my stomach feel like a swarm of butterflies was about to burst up and out through my mouth.

"I'm gonna kiss you."

Right as the lights dimmed in the Annex, I nodded absently as his face closed the distance between us. His beautiful lips that I had been longing to touch finally connected with mine, and all I could see when I closed my eyes were stars shooting from behind my lids. The butterflies increased their speed in my stomach, and something warm and delicious began to blossom even lower.

Then his hand was on my face, his strong fingers stroking my jawline as he cupped my cheek. When his lips moved in perfect sync with mine, I swooned. When he slowly licked the seam of my lips, demanding entry, I felt like I couldn't breathe. When his tongue mingled with mine, I never wanted the moment to end.

Suddenly, the screen flickered to life and exposed us. Reluctantly, Karson broke the kiss. His beautiful lips glimmered under the light from the screen, and I could tell he was trying to catch his breath. I was sure my face reflected the same.

"You . . . you . . . are an incredible kisser," I said breathlessly.

He grinned, and those butterflies picked up speed again when his hand stroked my face. "That wasn't my best performance." He looked around the Annex again. "Audience and all."

I reached up and grabbed a strand of my hair. I just couldn't leave it alone when it was down, and being nervous didn't help. "Well, I can't wait for an encore."

We held hands like teenagers throughout the entire movie.

"THAT WAS REALLY GOOD," I lied as we made our way back to our vehicles, hand in hand.

"No, it wasn't," he replied, chuckling.

We both laughed as we reached my car, our breath creating

plumes in the cold January night air. "You're right. They need to stop with those movies."

Karson gently pushed me up against my car and then boxed me in with his arms. "I really want to throw you on the back of my bike and take you to my place, but I'm not going to. I'm gonna be a gentleman and leave you with this."

He leaned down slowly and nipped my bottom lip with his teeth before pressing his lips to mine. The kiss was searing and toe-curling, and so much better than the one in the theater, if that was possible. I instinctively wrapped my arms around his neck as he pressed his hard body into mine. Soon, his hands found my waist, and he ran them up and down over my hips as our tongues and lips continued their dance. It didn't even bother me that the one in the cast was heavy on my hip.

Kissing him felt so natural, but thrilling. His body molded perfectly against mine, but felt exhilarating at the same time. My fingernails raking through the short hair on the back of his head had him groaning into my mouth, and I could feel how much he wanted me, the evidence pressed into my belly. I reached his ear and stroked my fingers over it and the hoop there.

"Good night, Scottlin," he whispered, sounding pained as he pressed his forehead against mine and pierced me with his stormy gaze.

"Good night, Karson," I whispered, wishing the night didn't have to end.

He pushed off me and opened my car door after I'd disarmed it with a beep. He closed it after I got in, then I watched as he went to his bike and slung his leg over the seat. He pulled his phone from his pocket and began typing awkwardly with one finger.

Was he texting another girl so quickly after our date? I frowned and pushed the button to start the car. Before I could put it in gear and drive off, my phone lit up.

**Karson: Text me when you get home so I know you got there okay.**

I grinned and went to look at him out the window, but he was already zooming out of the parking lot.

~

I WISHED our date could have lasted longer, but I was glad when I got home. I was tired from work and the excitement from earlier. The movie had relaxed me, and Karson's kisses had definitely been a rush.

As I put my purse and keys down, I smiled, thinking about the night we'd had. Aside from the vampires, it had been almost perfect. But even with the incident in the parking lot of Burger Bar, it had been kind of cool to see an elf use his abilities. These types of things fascinated me. All magic did. I just wished I was a full witch so I could do all kinds of cool things, too.

I reached for the pack of matches on top of my fridge and lit a candle. I remembered my mother flicking her wrist to light candles in our home as I was growing up. I didn't have that talent. That being said, I wouldn't trade my natural healing abilities for parlor tricks. Curing ailments and healing people was so much more satisfying and made me feel like I had a purpose in life.

After lighting the vanilla-scented candle, I went into my room, stripped out of my clothes, washed my face, and settled onto my sofa to catch up on whatever I had recorded. My phone chimed with a text.

**Len: I miss U**

I huffed and ignored the text. Responding to it would only encourage him further, and I couldn't do that to him. I didn't miss Len. The connection just hadn't been there, nor was I interested in exploring another go at our relationship. He didn't make my stomach dance with butterflies, or cause heat to spread to my core like Karson did. I needed passion in my life, not mundane.

I set the phone on the end table and sat on the sofa. After picking up the remote, I found what I needed to continue my binge-watching of the newest series I'd become obsessed with, when I heard my phone chime with another text.

If that was Len, I was gonna snap . . .

**Karson: You make it home okay?**

Oh no! I was supposed to text him.

**Me: Yes. Sorry**

**Karson: I'll punish you later for making me wait. Sleep well, beautiful**

I smiled.

**Me: I will. You too. xxoo**

God, we were already being sappy. And we hadn't even slept together yet.

# CHAPTER 18

## KARSON

*S*itting in the back of the courtroom, I could do nothing but observe. Memories of five years ago, when Uncle Will had been sentenced for assault, flooded me. He hadn't liked the punishment doled out to him, and had used his affliction to sting a Court member. Unfortunately for everyone involved, the man had fallen and hit his head, almost dying. Thank the gods he'd survived.

But I wasn't here today for my uncle. I was here to see if his son was going to suffer the same punishment as his father. After dressing in jeans, a hoodie reading *Welcome to the Jungle*, and my black boots, I'd taken my bike to the courthouse so I could hear Jalen's fate.

There were very few people in the galley of the windowless courtroom. Addie Beaumont cleared her throat and began speaking. "Jalen Andrew Kane, please stand."

We stood as ordered, and once the Court members took their seats, she instructed us all to sit, which we did.

I looked to the defendant's table to see Jalen stand up, a bit of white-blond stubble covering his jawline.

Mathilde Augustine, a witch on the Court, began, "The charge is breach of confidentiality among the supernatural; specifically, circumventing the systems put in place to protect the town by means of electronic hacking. The defendant has pled guilty."

Jalen nodded.

Mayor Barbie Stuart, a busty blond woman in her forties, pierced my cousin with an icy stare. "Well, Mr. Kane, what do you have to say for yourself before you face sentencing?"

As Jalen seemed to be grasping for words, I felt an overwhelming need to speak up. When my cousin stammered and seemed frustrated, I could hold back no longer. I stood up in the galley of the courtroom and, remembering how I was scolded before for interrupting, I raised my hand. "May I speak on behalf of the, uh, defendant?"

The mayor narrowed her eyes at me, then glared at my cousin. "Is this what you want?"

Jalen nodded. "Yes."

Mayor Stuart, still with an impassive face, nodded slightly. "Very well. Karson Kane, you may speak."

I stood and went to stand near Jalen.

"Mr. Kane, how long have you known the defendant?" Mathilde asked.

"My whole life," I replied, smiling slightly at my cousin.

"You got your memories back!" Jalen blurted.

I nodded and grinned, but the entire Court narrowed their eyes at him.

"Do not speak unless you're spoken to!" Mathilde snapped.

Jalen shrunk down in his seat a little bit and mouthed, "Sorry."

She turned her attention back to me. "I see," she continued. "And has he always been sneaky and deceitful?"

I shook my head. "Not in the least. In fact, not ever. Jalen's a good dude."

"Do you trust him to keep your innermost secrets?" she asked, a smirk playing on her wrinkled lips.

I nodded slowly, then looked at Jalen. "I trust him with my very life. He risked everything to get me to come back to Havenwood Falls, and I will be forever indebted to him. Please . . ." I stared hard at Mathilde and Mayor Stuart, hoping I could get through to them. "It took almost three days to get my memories back, but thank f— the gods that they did. I needed to be back here. I needed to see my family again. There was no other way for him to get me to come home but to break the rules." I looked at my cousin once again. Then I noticed a redheaded breath of fresh air enter the courtroom and take a seat near the back.

I grinned subtly at Scottlin, but continued. "I was lost, completely lost, until I received that email. When I was angry and grieving, I left this town. I let my emotions cloud my judgement." I stopped to heave in a big breath and then blow it out. "But it wasn't the right decision. I've been wandering aimlessly for two years—until I received that email." I looked over at the Court members seated at the dais. "Yes, he hacked your system. Broke your laws . . . these rules." Then I looked at Mathilde Augustine. "But he didn't hurt you, or this town. Nobody found out about us. We're all okay. Right? His dad's in prison. His mom is dead. You blame him for wanting some family around when he was stressed about Uncle Will getting released soon?"

Mathilde's brow furrowed. "William Kane has a bit still left to serve. Why would you think he was getting out so soon? He almost killed a Court member. We don't take kindly to that."

"But he didn't kill him. He used his affliction because he was angry. He didn't want to kill him," Jalen blurted out. "My dad looked devastated that day, I could tell. He'd just wanted to sting him a little. Not kill him."

The memories of what happened to Mihail Petran, a moroi vampire, came flooding back to me. I noticed the Petran seat was empty today. Because of the history? I set my jaw and looked at Mathilde. "He's right. Uncle Will was devastated."

Barbie Stuart pounded her gavel and glared at me. "No speaking out of turn!"

I clamped my mouth shut and nodded slightly in acknowledgment.

Jalen whispered something to me, and I said, "We were under the assumption that Uncle William was getting released soon. Is that not the case?"

Mathilde replied, "He has served his five years, but he got into some trouble while on the inside, so his time in supernatural prison has been extended a bit. He also will still need to serve six weeks in the sheriff's jail."

Jalen looked as frustrated and angry as I felt. "How much longer?"

Mathilde looked down at a paper in her hand through her glasses. "An extra month."

I breathed a sigh of relief. So did Jalen.

"We need an hour recess to make a decision on your punishment, young man. Reconvene at thirteen hundred hours. Court is dismissed." Mayor Stuart pounded her gavel.

I gave my cousin a hug.

"Thanks for doing that for me."

Nodding, I clapped him on the shoulder. "It was the least I could do. I just hope it helps."

"Well, I appreciate it."

"I'm going to grab food. Can I bring you something?"

He nodded. "Yes, please."

"I'm going to get sandwiches. Any requests?" I asked.

He shook his head. "Nope, I'll take anything."

I made my way to Scottlin and smiled down at her. "Thanks for being here."

She leaned up on tiptoe and pecked me on the lips. "It's my lunch break. I've been taking long ones lately, so why stop now?"

Chuckling, I grabbed her hand and led her out of the courtroom. "I'm headed out to get lunch for Jalen and me. You're joining me."

She laughed. "Of course I am."

We left the courthouse hand in hand and walked to Daily Knead.

# CHAPTER 19

## KARSON

*I* shouldn't have eaten the whole sandwich. Now, as I sat in the courtroom waiting for the stony-faced Court to dole out its punishment, my stomach was in knots and so not agreeing with being full.

Scottlin seemed to sense my unease, and she squeezed my hand while seated next to me.

"Will the defendant please rise," Addie said.

Mayor Stuart removed her reading glasses and pierced Jalen with her light gray stare. "You knew what you did was blatantly wrong. Permission to contact your cousin and bring him back home would have been granted if you'd only asked, and we could have taken proper measures. Instead, you chose to rebel and break our rules, potentially putting our town's people at risk. That said, in light of your cousin's testimony, combined with the fact that we are already housing one Kane in prison, I hereby sentence you to three days of jail, which have already been completed, a one-thousand-dollar fine, and one hundred hours of community service, to be completed within six months."

Jalen nodded, looking relieved.

"One more thing, and listen to me good. If you ever use your hacking skills to break the wards again, it'll be supernatural prison for you. And you don't want that. Trust me. Are we clear?"

Jalen swallowed hard and nodded. "Yes, ma'am. Won't happen again."

She pounded her gavel. "Court is adjourned."

Addie approached him. "The wards were a bitch to put right again. Don't do that shit again."

He smiled sheepishly. "I won't. Sorry. Can I get my stuff now?"

She nodded. "Of course. Follow me."

"Meet you out front," I said to him as I led Scottlin toward the door that would take us to the stairwell leading up and out of the secret part of City Hall.

JALEN LOOKED DRAINED as I dropped him off at home. I knew he was anxious to charge his phone and sleep in his own bed. I, however, did not want to sit around at home, and decided I should probably go find myself a job. I grabbed my keys and took a short ride through town.

With my bike idling outside of Tragic Ink, I took some deep breaths and pulled my phone from my pocket. I hit the contact icon for the tattoo shop in Colorado Springs and waited while it rang.

Dex answered.

"Hey, it's Karson."

"Hey, dude. When you coming back? Keep getting people in here looking for you."

"About that." I raked my fingers through my hair. "Is G there?"

"Nah, he's gone for a few days, man."

"Can you tell him I won't be coming back?"

Dex gasped. "What? Why?"

I decided to make a long story short. "I moved back home."

"Where's that? I thought you said you didn't know when I asked you last time."

"I, uh, suddenly remembered. Take care, man."

I ended the call, not wanting to talk about it any longer. We only worked in cash there, so it wasn't like I had a final paycheck to look forward to. Thank the gods for the small stash of cash I'd found at home to get me by. I had a few things in the apartment, but I'd take a day trip to Springs to get that stuff later.

Now, with both hands on the handlebars, I stared up at the second story over Howe's Herbal Shoppe, where Tragic Ink was, and saw the lights on.

"Here goes nothing," I whispered to myself, not knowing what to expect, since Scottlin told me Rowdy had closed HF Ink and this was now the only shop in town.

After passing the smelly herbal store, I rounded the corner and climbed the stairs. The door chimed above my head as I entered. The smell of incense and the sound of heavy metal music playing made me smile.

I was surprised to see Gwen Facharro, a friend from high school I had art class and a lot of detention with, sitting in a chair, tattooing something onto the upper arm of a human with a shaved head and lots of muscles.

"I'll be right with you," she said without looking up.

"It's fine. I'm not in a rush." I smirked.

The needle immediately halted, and Gwen looked up. Her eyes went big, and her mouth dropped open.

"Excuse me," she barely spit out to the customer before setting the gun on the tray next to her, yanking off her gloves, and rushing over to me.

She squealed as I picked her up and gave her tiny ass a hug. "Karson!"

"I'm back, baby," I said, staring into her pretty green eyes. "I love the hair, by the way," I added.

She raked her fingers through her hair, as short and as pale as mine. "Thanks."

"You work here now?"

She nodded. "Own it, actually. Opened it a couple years ago."

"I was gonna go see Rowdy, but I heard HF Ink is closed."

She nodded. "Yeah, Rowdy died."

My eyes widened. "He died?"

"Yes," she replied, frowning. "Sucks."

Deciding I'd get details later, I said, "Look, I won't beat around the bush. I need a job."

"Thank fuck," the human blurted, and we both looked over at him. He was smiling at us and said, "It took me, like, six weeks to get this appointment because she's the main game in town."

"Oh, shut it, Hank," she said. "You know I hate people."

Hank and I both laughed.

"What do you say?" I asked, hopeful.

"Of course you're hired. If Rowdy trusted you, so do I. Plus, I've seen your work on folks around town. It's good stuff." She sighed. "Besides, Hank's right. I've been swamped, plus with all the traveling I've been doing . . . but you know I don't have the patience to be peopling, anyway. But, with you here, it'll be nice to have an extra set of hands."

"Sweet!" I said, my stomach stirring with excitement. "That was easy."

She punched me lightly in the arm. "You knew I'd hire you. But, uh . . ." She pointed at the cast on my hand.

I smiled, embarrassed. "Yeah, Karson's temper for the win."

She snorted and made her way back to Hank. After sitting, she grabbed a fresh set of rubber gloves from a box and put them on. "Right. You angry asshole."

"I'm better now, I swear. And the hand . . . cast comes off in two weeks. It's my strong hand, though. Unfortunately."

She glanced at me briefly, then picked up the gun. "Got some new ink, I see."

"Yeah, I worked at a shop in Springs. I see you don't have any more room for any new ink." I jutted my chin at her sleeved-up arms and shoulders. As she was in a black tank top, I could see most of them. They were badass, and she had done them all herself. Well, except her registry tat, of course.

She grinned. "So what brought you back to town?" She put the needle to Hank's skin to continue the shading she was doing on his upper arm.

I launched into the entire story, leaving out the memory issues for the sake of the human in the room. She glanced at me a couple of times when parts of the story didn't quite make sense, but I knew she understood.

After sitting and visiting with her for about half an hour, and watching her amazing work on Hank, I left the shop, happy things seemed to be working out for me.

Bored, I drove my bike to the Havenwood Falls Medical Center to see Scottlin. As I entered the ER, I stopped short when I saw her standing behind the counter of the nurse's station, talking to the same guy I had seen her eating with at the pizza joint. This time, though, the man wore an EMT uniform and was leaning over the counter, reaching up to finger one of her braids. She smiled at him and laughed at something he'd said while moving back and out of his reach. When he put his hand on top of hers on the counter and she frowned at it, the rage I was suppressing came bubbling up.

I stalked toward the counter and smacked my good hand down on it. This caused not only Scottlin and the guy to look up, but everyone around to startle.

"Karson," Scottlin said, smiling tightly at me. "I didn't expect to see you here . . ."

"Who's this? A *friend*?" I asked her, but was looking into the guy's brown eyes.

He stood up straight and was just a couple inches shorter than me. He lifted his chin and said, "Who the hell are you?"

"Karson, let's go into my office, okay?" Scottlin said, coming around the desk and grabbing me by the arm.

"Nah, I'm good," I said, feeling the magic inside of me begin to stir. I wanted to sting on this guy so bad, it hurt. For no other reason than he was looking at Scottlin in a way that only I should be looking at her.

The EMT put his hand on his hip and looked past me at Scottlin. He pointed at me. "Who is this asshole?"

That was it. Without thinking, I reared my left arm back and smashed my fist into his cheek.

The guy swore in pain and then took a swing at me.

I stepped back before he could make contact, then turned on my heel and stormed out of the hospital. "Fuck!"

Scottlin didn't even yell out my name or try to stop me.

As soon as I located my bike, I hopped on and rode off with no destination at all.

# CHAPTER 20

## KARSON

"*D*ude, you need anger management or something," Jalen said, the video game controller in his hand, the game paused on the screen after I told him everything.

I plopped down next to him. "No shit."

"You said she told you that guy was just a friend or something, didn't she?" He stared at me.

I looked back at him and was happy to see he looked rested, the dark circles that had been under his eyes gone, and he'd shaved and gotten a haircut. "Yeah, I guess."

"You're the one who's gonna be in court next. That dude could charge you with assault. And you'll be in even bigger trouble with the Court since he's human. You could have really hurt him."

I snorted. "I probably did."

"Let me know if you need bail money," he joked with a sardonic laugh. He threw me the extra controller and changed the game so we could both play.

I welcomed the distraction, and we ended up playing for a good three hours, during which time I didn't check my phone once. We had a nice catch-up about how I'd gone to see my dad, how he'd given me the bike, and how Gwen had hired me at the shop.

I got up to get something to eat and plucked my phone out of my pocket to see I had no texts or calls.

*Great.*

I sighed in disappointment that Scottlin hadn't responded to the apology text I'd sent after leaving the hospital.

After pocketing the phone, I found a couple frozen dinners and heated up the oven to get them going for us. I obviously wasn't going anywhere tonight, even though I should be apologizing to Scottlin in person. She was already off work, and I contemplated going to her apartment and begging for her forgiveness.

I ran the idea by my cousin. He shook his head. "Nope, nope, nope. Chicks need time to cool off. She'll probably slam the door in your face, bro."

"Because you're such an expert on women? You're twenty-six and still single."

"First off, asswipe, you asked me. Second, I'm single for a reason." He used the controller to kill three zombies heading toward his avatar.

I snorted. "And why's that?"

"Because women are too much work. Especially the elven chicks. God, they're moody."

I sat back on the couch and folded my arms across my chest. "Where are there female elves in this town? Our moms were the only ones."

Jalen cleared his throat. "I have to leave Havenwood Falls to find them, but they're out there."

"So date a human. Or a witch or something."

"Fuck those witches. And humans . . . too much work to hide what we are."

I shook my head. "I disagree. There's nothing to hide. Our ears are glamoured from them around here, and aside from the quick healing and affliction, we're just like them."

"And all the delicious flowers," he said, laughing. Then he went back into the zone, chopping off the head of a zombie who was ambling toward his character. The oven beeped, and I got up to put the dinners in. I shook my head at the cracked door that I had caused and vowed to research tomorrow how to replace the glass. I'd YouTube it if I had to.

After I set the timer, I checked my phone. No texts.

I began to pace the living room where Jalen continued to furiously press the buttons on the controller. I was too distracted to play, though. I checked the time on my watch and saw that it was nearing seven p.m.

"Fuck it," I said, heading toward the front door. I snatched my coat off the rack and called out to Jalen, "Don't let the TV dinners burn. They'll be done in about fifteen."

He laughed and said, "She's gonna slam the door in your face, and I'm going to eat both dinners. Byeeee."

I flipped him off. After closing and locking the door behind me, I fast-walked to my bike, hopped on, started it up, and headed toward Scottlin's apartment to try to do the right thing.

~

"Go away, Karson," Scottlin said weakly, muffled behind the door.

I put my forehead against the door and said, "Please just let me in? I want to explain. Please."

No response greeted me.

"Scottlin, I'm sorry. I have a temper. I just want to talk to you. I didn't mean to do that. You've just . . . dammit." I raked my fingers through my hair. "I just lost it when I saw that guy with you. I want you all to myself. I'm selfish, but I promise I'm not a jealous asshole. It's just that I've got all these fucking feelings for you and obviously need to learn how to express them better." I sighed, then knocked. "Can't we just talk? Please? I miss your pretty smile and beautiful laugh. I need to know you don't hate me."

I heard no movement from behind the door. There was just nothing. I waited and knocked for five more minutes, but the door never opened. I looked down when I saw a small slip of paper slide out from under the door. I picked it up to see Dr. Espensen's card.

*Okay, I can take a hint.*

Defeated, I slowly made my way down the stairs and out to the parking lot, tossing the business card into a nearby trash can. After starting up my bike, I looked up at the window to Scottlin's apartment and saw her face staring down at me for just a split second before she flicked the curtain back into place. With a heavy sigh, I lifted my facemask with the skull on it over my mouth and nose to protect from the cold. I should probably wear a helmet, but I didn't give a shit as I steered my way out of the icy parking lot.

As I rode, I internally kicked myself for fucking things up with Scottlin. We'd barely gotten started, but I knew she was into me. Until my temper reared its ugly head. It had been ruining things for me since I was a teen, and I needed to get a handle on it. I knew my life would never change for the better until I dealt with all the shit with my mom, and the two years of my life I lost because of it.

But how?

I was never one for counseling or therapy, even though I knew I should probably talk to someone. I just wasn't sure where to start. I wasn't sure I would even go through with it, and of course I'd just impulsively thrown away that business card.

Then Scottlin's pretty face materialized in my mind. Her beautiful blue eyes. Her pretty smile. Her soft-spoken and caring mannerisms. Her silky hair. Her beautiful mind. Maybe if I got some help for my temper, she would give me a second chance. Maybe I could prove to her that I wasn't an impulsive asshole.

I reached my house quickly enough and found Jalen right where I'd left him—and true to his word, he'd eaten both dinners.

Without turning around, he said, "She slammed the door in your face, didn't she?"

I threw my jacket and mask onto the dining room table, then plopped down next to him. "No, she never even opened the door."

"You shoulda listened to me, man." He chuckled.

I picked up the extra controller. "I need to kill something."

He grunted and switched the game back to zombies.

"So where is Uncle Will imprisoned at, anyway?" I asked, wondering why he hadn't suggested visiting him.

"Supernatural prison."

I resisted the urge to roll my eyes. "No shit? Where's that?"

He lifted a shoulder as his character dodged a zombie and then did a roundhouse kick to its head. "Through some portal near the falls. They took him off in cuffs, and I haven't seen him in five years."

I shuddered as my avatar used its machete to chop off a zombie's head. "I wonder what kind of prison it is?"

"I tried asking around, but I only got vague answers. Some island the fae run in another part of the world. I'm not sure. I asked if I could visit, and they laughed at me."

I hit pause on the game and looked at my cousin.

He stared at me expectantly.

"Tell me this. What's the real reason you wanted me back here? Do you really need help with Uncle Will once he gets out, or what?"

Jalen let out a sigh and set his controller down. "I don't know, man. I missed you. Gavin only comes here a couple days a month, my mom's fuckin' gone, and I miss my dad. I just don't know what to expect when he gets back. Plus, you had been gone way too long. After you took off, I thought, 'Oh, he'll come back before the lunar cycle. He's not that stupid.' But you *were* that stupid. Thank the gods you never changed your email address or I would have never fuckin' found you. Your cell number was disconnected almost immediately."

"You waited two years to get in touch with me, though . . . kinda weird."

He nodded. "Yeah. I was going to earlier, but Gavin said to give you time."

I thought about what he said, and Gavin had been right. A month or six after I left would not have been enough time for me to have learned my lesson. I would still have been that angry guy who didn't know how to grieve the abusive mother who didn't deserve to be grieved.

I thought about today and how I'd messed things up with Scottlin because of my temper. *I guess I still am that angry guy . . .*

"You did the right thing," I assured him. "Now . . . I need to do the right thing."

I went over to the laptop and booted it up as I walked with it back to the sofa. "I need to talk to someone."

"What, like a shrink?" he asked, surprised.

"Your mom died in an accident, and that sucks. But she didn't do horrible things to you. I gotta get a grip on my shit." I typed "grief counselors" into the search bar.

Jalen threw the controller down and turned all the way to face me. "What in the hell are you talking about?"

Looking up from the computer, I took a deep breath and looked into my cousin's eyes. He'd been my best friend my whole life, and should have known these things, but never did because I never said shit about it when we were kids.

"You sure you wanna know, man? Because once I tell you, you can't unhear this shit."

"Fucking spill it. Now."

"Okay . . ." With more bravery than I felt, I word-vomited everything that happened to me for as long as I could remember—which started about age four. The cigarette burns. Being locked in closets and rooms for hours and sometimes days. The verbal abuse. Her forcing vodka down my throat just to get me to stop crying and go to sleep. The way she told me she hated me so many times when she was drunk, or high, or both. I went on for half an hour, barely taking a breath in between stories. Once I was done, my eyes blurred with unshed tears from letting it all out . . . but it had felt good. So good.

My cousin's eyes were glistening, and he turned away and sucked in a deep breath. "What the fuck, man? Where was your dad?"

"Working," I replied bitterly. "Always fucking working. He knew she was an addict, but didn't know about all the things she did to me —just some. And I haven't even told him half the shit I just told you, but he knew enough right before I left Havenwood Falls after finding her dead. I'm sure that's why he never came looking for me. He just knew."

"Well, that sucks, and now I'm pissed off." He leaned forward and rested his forearms on his basketball shorts.

I clapped him on the back. "It's okay. What sucks is . . . when I lived in Springs, I didn't have to deal with this bullshit because I forgot all about it."

"Well, that's one positive to you having been gone, I guess," he murmured. "Now I feel kinda bad bringing you back."

"Well, don't. Because the problem is, I always had pain in my chest . . . in my soul. I always knew something was terribly wrong, but I could never pinpoint what it was, because I couldn't remember. I couldn't go see a doctor, because what would I tell him? I couldn't go see a shrink, because they'd just want to know about my past and why I was so wound up and in pain. So the not remembering kinda backfired now. It sucks to relive all this shit, but it's kinda freeing to talk about it, too."

Jalen stared at the ground, his hands folded together over his legs. "I guess I can understand that."

I looked down at the laptop and clicked on a few sites, saving them to call later to see if there was someone in this town I could talk to.

# CHAPTER 21

## SCOTTLIN

*I* sat on my bed with my fingers in my ears and the volume on the TV in my bedroom up loud. I couldn't take listening to Karson's pleas that were breaking my heart, or the pounding on my door. I just hoped he'd leave soon, before one of my neighbors called the cops on him. He definitely didn't need any legal trouble, and it seemed the entire Kane family attracted that stuff like flies on honey. I was glad slipping him the business card had the desired effect and got him to leave. Hopefully he was off to get some real help.

I'd had to beg Len to not call the sheriff on Karson. He had wanted to press charges, but I convinced him not to. I told him he was a patient who'd developed a little crush on me, but didn't elaborate further. I was a coward for not telling him how deeply I'd fallen for the guy, and how I had been thinking about a future with him in it after just one date. No, I couldn't hurt Len like that. We had agreed to be friends, but the man still looked at me the same way he always had—with longing and admiration. I couldn't take it.

I'd had to put my professional mask into place as I had treated his very bruised but thankfully not broken cheekbone. Karson had only opened up a small cut with his knuckles, and I was surprised he could do that much damage with his weak hand. He was lucky he wasn't sporting two casts at this point.

The boy had a temper . . . and I didn't want anything to do with someone like that. I wasn't sure why he was so angry—and at the most peculiar of times, too—but I supposed it wasn't any of my business. He had been fun, but there was no way I was going to waste my time with someone with anger issues. He was way more drama than I was ready to take on.

But hadn't I known he was kind of a loose cannon from the first day I met him? Why had he punched that oven? I just figured he had been frustrated over the fact that his memories hadn't returned. But to punch something that hard over something like that—who does that?

*Somebody deeply hurting, that's who.*

I squeezed my eyes shut and tried to block out Karson's beautiful face and all the sweet and kind things he'd ever done and said to me. All the pain I'd seen floating behind his stormy gaze that I had ignored and had brushed off as something about his race.

Breathing out a calming breath, I slowly reopened my eyes and stared unseeing at the TV. I had obviously never fallen victim to the memory wards around the town, and I never planned to. If Karson had grown up here, he had to have known that his memory would be gone if he stayed away too long.

So why had he?

I took my fingers out of my ears and was met with only the sound of the TV. I picked up the remote and muted it.

Silence. Deafening silence. Karson had left.

Because I was a masochist, I looked at my phone. No other texts from him. I hadn't responded to his apology earlier because I had been so furious. Since I'd calmed some, I contemplated texting him back. But what would I say? *I forgive you? It's okay?* No, neither of those things applied here. I threw my phone down in frustration and unmuted the TV. I needed to sleep on this.

~

"GOOD MORNING, DOC," Shayna said with a grin.

"Good morning," I replied, the large steaming cup from Coffee Haven warming my hand.

I made my way to my office. After hanging up my coat, I went around and sat at my desk. I pushed the button to boot up my computer and opened my daily calendar. A list of appointments greeted me, along with the blocks of hours I would be on call in the ER. One appointment caught my eye, flashing like a beacon: *2:00 p.m. Cast Removal – Karson Kane.*

I heaved a sigh. It had been almost two weeks since Karson had punched Len. He had sent the apology text, then a few days later, another about him missing me. I had ignored that one, too. I hoped that ignoring him would make his beautiful face and eyes fade from my memory.

But they hadn't. Not even remotely. I woke every day thinking about Karson, and thoughts of him would consume me as I lay down at night to go to sleep, with no break in between—even while I was working. It was absolute torture. I kept telling myself that it would fade eventually. That I would get over him and find someone else soon. A nice, normal man, who was not hotheaded or violent. And I believed the words I constantly told myself.

In my head, they made sense. *I could do this.* But in my heart . . . those stirrings just wouldn't let him go. He had embedded himself into my very soul, and the pain in my chest wasn't going to ease up any time soon. There was something about Karson that was different from the men I had dated before, and I was kicking myself for letting him in so easily and so quickly. No, that list wasn't very long, but I had been in relationships, and none of them had felt as fiery or passionate as this one had.

What was wrong with me? Two kisses and a couple of dates, and here I was practically panting over a guy I barely knew. I certainly hadn't gone all the way with him, but goddess . . . I so wanted to.

*Snap out of it, Scottlin!* I screamed at myself. *Yes, let's get out of la-la land and live in reality. Bad boys are no good for you. Find yourself a man who is stable and sweet.*

The phone in my pocket vibrated. I pulled it up and looked at the screen:

**HFMC-ER: You're needed in the ER STAT**

Without more time to dwell on Karson, I raced out of my office, slammed the door shut behind me, and went into the ER to face the latest emergency.

I stopped short when I arrived to see a woman lying on a gurney with her throat looking like raw hamburger. A nurse ran around me and placed a cloth against the woman's neck, then climbed on top of the gurney to hold it there while the EMTs pushed her into a room.

I spotted Len as one of those EMTs, but paid him no mind. The bruise on his cheek was nothing more than a fading yellow annoyance, and it seemed he was also in the zone, just trying to help the young woman.

"What's your name?" I asked the girl as I ran alongside the gurney.

"Lily," she whispered. "He was so strong. Help me. I'm scared."

I lifted the cloth on her neck and could see her throat had been ripped open. The bleeding had stopped at her carotid, but the exposed skin and muscle showed telltale signs of a wolf's bite.

"Take her to room four. I'll tend to her," I demanded angrily.

"What can I do?" Len asked, looking at me with fearful eyes.

I shook my head. "Nothing. I got it from here."

The nurse who had hopped on the gurney jumped down, and I looked at her. "Can you give the patient sixty milligrams of Toradol IM, times one dose now and one gram of Rocephin IM, times one dose now?"

"On it," the nurse said, scurrying out of the room to get the meds.

I looked down at Lily, who was definitely human and didn't look a day over twenty-one. I smiled at her. "It's going to be okay. Can you tell me what happened?"

Her eyes fluttered shut as if she was going to lose consciousness. "He was so strong."

She'd already said that. I tried a different approach. "Where were you today, Lily?"

Her eyelashes flickered and then opened, coffee-colored irises meeting me. "The falls. He was so cute . . . so beautiful. I thought he was into me . . . then he turned into a monster . . . Oh, God . . ."

She began to sob, then eventually fell into unconsciousness, and I knew I had to report this to the Court. But first, some pictures. I pulled my phone from my pocket and opened the camera app. After I snapped half a dozen pictures of her injuries, the nurse came in and administered the medication I'd ordered.

"Anything else I can do?" she asked.

"Yeah, try to find out her last name and address. I'll stay with her to make sure she's stable."

"I think she had a purse. On it." The nurse left the room.

When I was sure the door was shut tightly, I placed my hands over Lily's cheeks and closed my eyes. My hands began to grow warm with magic, and as I felt it swirling inside me, I let it rush out of my fingertips. A faint yellow glow only someone supernatural could see began to light up her face.

I leaned down and whispered into her right ear. "You were attacked by an animal out by the falls. You shouldn't go out there alone. There was no boy. You were by yourself."

Still unconscious, Lily heaved in a big breath, and then let it out again.

I removed my hands and sighed. After carefully removing the makeshift dressing, I tossed the bloodied thing in the trash and then cleaned the wound carefully. It had healed a lot, but not completely —which was my objective. She couldn't walk out of here with no wounds. And she most certainly couldn't go around telling people a man turned into a wolf. I was pretty sure I had removed any werewolf venom she may have had in her system, as I knew some wolves could create other ones like we read about in folklore, and in this case, I didn't know what wolf had done this. Better safe than sorry, I say.

I covered her up with a blanket from the warmer and left the room. I instructed the nurse to start a transfusion, then get her into a room in the ICU, which I knew she probably didn't need, but it would make sense medically to do so.

All was quiet in the ER, but I was drained. I went back to my office, shot off a quick email to the Court that I needed to speak to them, hung up my lab coat, and grabbed my purse. *Coffee Haven, here I come.*

# CHAPTER 22

## KARSON

*M*y calendar app chimed on my phone. I pulled it off the nightstand and looked at it: *2 p.m. cast removal.* Freaking finally.

But how awkward was that going to be? I would have to see Scottlin, and she would probably make someone else do it. I wanted to see her badly . . . but I couldn't take that look of rejection and disappointment on her face.

I flung back the covers, took care of business, brushed my teeth, and went downstairs to see it was all quiet. *Jalen must still be in bed.* I wandered into the garage. After flipping on the light, I was relieved to see that Dad's tools were still sitting on his giant workbench.

I looked down at my cast, then wandered to the group of saws. "Electric or hand saw?"

Then I saw a new toy Dad must have gotten recently. A Dremmel electric hand saw with a three-inch blade. After putting on a thick work glove, I picked up the tool. It was lightweight, and I could use it with one hand. I flicked the button, and the thing whirred to life.

"You're not doing what I think you're doing, are you?"

I turned to look at Jalen.

"No, but you are," I said with a wicked gleam in my eye, holding up the saw and clicking it off.

Jalen chuckled and walked toward me. "Uncle Ellis bought that when I was replacing some baseboards last year. It's a cool little tool,

330

and I know it can cut through plaster. But are you sure it's safe to take that off? What if your hand is still fucked up?"

"I have an appointment today to get it taken off, but I don't want to see her, so I would rather just avoid some awkward shit if I can."

He nodded. "I hear you."

Before I lost my nerve, I handed the gloves to my cousin and laid my arm down on the workbench. I felt a little better knowing Jalen had already used the tool and knew how to handle it.

"What, now?" he asked, looking at me.

"Yes, now, before I chicken out," I said, taking a deep breath.

He lifted a shoulder and let it fall. "Okay, dude."

I watched him put on the gloves and a pair of safety goggles. He clicked the button.

"Ready?" he asked.

"Yep."

With one hand, Jalen held my arm flat on the bench, and with the other, he slowly began to saw through my cast, starting at the end, near my forearm. It didn't take long for me to feel heat from the saw, and I prayed it wouldn't touch my skin.

I looked down to see that he had successfully cut all the way through to the bottom of the plaster. Occasionally, he would set it down to try to pry the cast apart with his hands. Once he reached my hand, though, the plaster was thicker, and he had to use the tool again.

"Hold very still," he said quietly, tilting his head.

"Just do it, man," I said, wanting the thing off.

He nodded and began to run the saw over my wrist and toward the junction between my thumb and forefinger. He was almost there when we heard, "What the fuck are you clowns doing?"

We both startled, and the saw bit into my bare skin.

"Fuck!" I yelled, pulling my hand away. Blood began to seep out of the plaster as my dad ran toward me.

"Are you guys stupid? What did you think was gonna happen, trying to get this thing off yourself?" Dad said, handing a paper towel to me.

"I almost had it," Jalen snapped, turning off the saw and jerking his gloves and glasses off. He threw them down on the bench. "You scared us!"

Dad used all his strength to pull the cast the rest of the way off. It shimmied off like a really tight glove. He tossed it onto the bench and looked at the cut, which was bleeding pretty badly. "That's gonna need stitches. Put some clothes on. I'm taking you to the hospital."

I groaned and kept the paper towel wrapped around my hand as I went inside to try to change.

"You and I are gonna have a talk later," I heard Dad say to Jalen.

~

"WHAT WERE YOU DOING THERE, anyway, Dad?" I asked as we pulled up to the front of Havenwood Falls Medical Center. I was trying to do anything to distract myself from thinking about the look Scottlin was gonna give me when she was forced to, yet again, fix my stupidity.

"Ironically," he said, shutting off the ignition and piercing me with his purple eyes, "I was coming over to get that saw. Regina wants crown molding in the dining room, and it's the perfect size."

"Sorry," I said sheepishly.

He just grinned. "The saw still works, I'm sure. But you completely defeated the purpose of removing the cast by winding up here anyway." He pointed to the hospital.

"Let's get this over with," I griped, getting out of the car and cradling my hand while trying to close the car door with my hip.

We walked inside, and thankfully, the ER was empty, save for a couple of staff. I went up to the desk and told Shayna, "I need to see a doctor."

She smiled at me. "Hey, Karson. You're a couple hours early for your appointment, though."

My dad chuckled, and I wanted to elbow him in the ribs. I ignored him instead, and said, "Yeah, about that . . ." I held up my blood-soaked hand.

"Eek!" she said, then picked up the phone and hit some buttons. "Scottlin, you're needed in the ER."

*Great . . .*

"Imma grab a coffee from the machine. Want one?"

I looked at Dad. "Yeah, and something to eat before I pass out."

He nodded and went toward the machines. While Shayna walked

away from the desk, I noticed a vase of roses on it. I took a quick look around, pulled one out of the vase, popped the flower off the stem, and shoved it into my mouth.

*Mmmm.*

Just then, Scottlin came out in her green scrubs and white medical coat. She looked absolutely stunning, even if she did sport the braids that I wished she'd take down. She was looking down at an electronic tablet in her hand. "What do we have today—" We locked eyes, and after her initial surprise, hers just looked . . . pained. "Mr. Kane, you're early today."

I cringed at the formality with which she'd addressed me.

I was still chewing the rose, and she looked at me funny. "What's in your mouth?"

I shook my head, and swallowed hard. "Nothing."

"Okay . . . well, what are you doing here?"

"First off, please don't call me that. Secondly, I don't need the cast off"—I shoved my hand up toward her—"but I think I need some stitches."

Her features immediately softened. "Oh, Karson, what did you do?" She sighed. "Follow me." I obeyed, subtly sniffing the strawberry scent she left in her wake as she led me into a small room. "Sit."

I sat on the medical table with my feet dangling over the edge while Scottlin closed the door. I swallowed hard. We hadn't been alone in a room together in a while.

"Let me see," she quietly commanded. I held my hand out. She slowly unwrapped the bloody paper towel and set it on the metal table full of tools that stood next to her. She examined the cut, which had stopped bleeding, but was gaping open, and said, "How did this happen?"

I pierced her with a look that said *Do I have to?*

She bit back a smile. "You removed the cast with a saw, didn't you?"

I shook my head. "Nope. Jalen did."

"You couldn't wait a few hours for your appointment?" she asked, turning away to rifle through some drawers.

With her back to me, I decided I had nothing to lose by being honest. "I didn't want to see you."

She froze mid-rifle and paused before saying, "That's

understandable." She found what she had been looking for and turned back around. "And how did that work out for you?"

*Ouch.*

I lifted my chin. "Obviously, not well. So let's get this over with, or else I'll end up begging you to give me a second chance. Again. Which clearly *won't* work out for me."

# CHAPTER 23

## SCOTTLIN

*I* kept my face impassive and pretended that his words hadn't cut me deep. Just seeing the sexy man again was painful. I thought I was over him, had moved past all of this, but just hearing his voice and seeing him hurt had me right back at square one. All I wanted to do was fix his wounds, then take him home to give him some more TLC.

*In the bedroom.*

But I knew that was not best for me. So in response, I said, "I'm saying this as a professional, and not as an ex . . . whatever." I set the suture kit on the tray and looked straight into those stormy purple eyes of his. "You need to learn to control your impulses. Hitting things, punching people, removing casts with very dangerous tools." I looked at all the tattoos on his arms, which were hot, but I had to wonder if those had been impulsive, too. "It's not good for you. Make better decisions, Karson, then maybe we can talk about . . . us."

He looked wounded for a minute, so I decided I wasn't going to use sutures. I was going to heal him so I could send him on his way. The longer I spent alone in this room with this heat crackling between us, the more my resolve would waver. I might agree to give him another chance, and nothing would change with him.

"Thank you," he said quietly.

"How is your hand feeling without the cast?" I asked, trying to ease him into what I was about to do without freaking him out. Sure, he was a supe, but he probably hadn't dealt with being healed supernaturally before.

"Hard to say, feels weak, but I haven't had my coffee yet." He grinned faintly at me.

Just then, someone knocked on the door.

"Come in," I called out.

"Can I just give him this?" a large man carrying a cup of coffee and a muffin asked.

"This is my dad, Ellis," I said. "Dad, this is Scottlin."

"Nice to meet you," I said, rubbing my hands together on my lap.

"Can he eat this in here?" his father asked.

"I don't know. He's pretty accident-prone," I replied, swallowing down a smile.

Dad chuckled. "No, he's not. He's just a hothead."

*Even his dad sees it.* I just smiled.

"I'll set it down here, and you can have it when you're done with that." He set the coffee and muffin on the counter and poked his head around my shoulders. "Ew," he said before walking out and closing the door behind him.

I chuckled and then pierced Karson with a serious stare. I placed both hands over his injured one. "Stay still, okay?"

He nodded, not breaking eye contact.

My eyes slid closed, and I brought the warmth from my very center up through my chest and into my hands. I didn't need to open my eyes to know they were glowing yellow. Karson's gasp was enough. When I felt the warmth start to fade, I opened my eyes and looked down at the cut.

Completely gone.

I glanced up at him, and his eyes were wide. "So cool!"

I pressed a finger to my lips. "Shhh."

"Why didn't you do that when I broke my hand?" He cleared his throat. "I mean, seems like it would have been easier."

I got up because his beautiful lips and stormy eyes were starting to break my resolve, and I felt like I couldn't breathe. I turned my back to him and threw his bloody paper towels in the trash. "Because you thought I was human. And . . ."

"And what?" he asked eagerly.

I slowly turned around. "I thought maybe wearing that cast could serve as a reminder to, you know, cool your jets, like my grandpa used to say." I smiled weakly. "Plus, there was too much magic going on as it was."

He nodded and held up his hand. "I guess. But thanks for using your juju on me this time."

"I won't hesitate to the next time you come in here."

He stood up and gave me a half grin. "Next time?"

I folded my arms over my chest and simply nodded.

Karson cleared his throat. "Okay, anyway. Um, do you know of any, like, counselors here in town?"

I cocked my head to the side. He didn't seem like the type who talked about his feelings with strangers. "Yes, I know a couple." I cleared my throat. "And I do believe I already gave you a card."

"Um, I, uh, don't have that card anymore."

This didn't surprise me. "You looking for a certain type of therapist?"

He nodded. "Yeah, trauma, PTSD, mommy issues, that type of shit."

*Mommy issues?* "Yeah, Dr. Espensen. I'll get you another card when we're done."

"Thanks."

God, he was being so sweet and calm. And now he was asking for psych help?

We said nothing else, but I could feel the weight of his stare on me as I finished up jotting notes into his chart. He sat there, still looking at me. I wanted to go sit on his lap, lay my head on his chest, and let him wrap his arms around me.

But, of course, I didn't.

"Let's get you an X-ray to make sure that hand has healed properly, then once you're clear, you can go.

He scooted off the table and lifted his hand. "Thanks."

I pointed to the counter. "Don't forget your breakfast."

He grabbed the items, and I led him out and toward my office. He stood just inside the door as I rummaged through my drawer until I found Dr. Espensen's card. I handed it to him. "Talk to her. She's great."

"Appreciate it," he murmured, shoving it into his jeans pocket.

"Hey. Are you okay?" I asked, meaning it.

"Hopefully, I will be one day, once I get my shit straightened out." He turned and walked out of my office. I was going to follow him to show him where to go, but figured he could read the signs.

I sat down and sighed. Maybe I'd misjudged him? He had a sweet and soft side, but I already knew that. Clearly, he was dealing with some deeper issues that I hoped he could get help for. Half of me wanted to know what they were; the other half just didn't. It was his business, and I hoped talking to someone would help him out.

*Mommy issues.*

Curiosity got the best of me. I turned to my computer, typed in his name, and found his medical history again. I noted his mother's name, Lyn Kane, and looked her up. *Deceased, December 2016. Overdose.*

With a heavy sigh, I stared at my cup of almost-gone coffee and used my desk phone to dial Alex, my closest friend.

"Hello?"

"Girl, I need coffee," I said.

She laughed. "I'm actually studying at Coffee Haven right now, but I'm almost done. I gotta run a few errands after this. You want the usual?"

"Yes, please. And a scone. I don't care what kind."

"You got it."

"Thanks." I hung up the clunky phone, and my cell vibrated in my pocket. I got up before even looking at it, heading toward the ER to deal with the next emergency.

"Ahh," I said, sipping the hot, caffeinated nectar.

"You're addicted," Alex said, sitting on the bench with me outside the hospital. It was chilly, but we were bundled up, and the sun was shining. It glinted off the sparkly snow piled up on the grass surrounding the medical center.

"I know." I sighed.

Alex twisted the clunky ring she always wore on her thumb and stared hard at me with her mocha-colored eyes. "What's wrong? Something's wrong."

I chewed my lip and broke her stare. "Karson came into the ER today."

"Is he okay?" Alex asked.

I laughed, but there wasn't much humor in it. "He had his cousin use a saw to get his cast off."

"Dumb boys," she replied with a snicker.

"Right? Well, he said some things that pulled on my heartstrings a little, ya know. Hinted at a second chance."

She placed her hand on mine, and I stared down at the contrast between her warm caramel-colored skin and my freckly whiteness. "And are you going to give him one?"

I shook my head. "Nah. I can't. He's got things he needs to fix first."

"Don't we all," she replied. "But I'm sure it's hard."

I nodded. "Yeah, it is. He's so cute and sexy, and I'm so attracted to him."

"Sex does not a relationship make, girlfriend," she replied. "But it can be fun for a while."

"I wouldn't know," I replied dryly. "Never had one of those types of relationships. I just seem to attract the boring ones or the damaged ones."

"Who's damaged?" Alex asked, lifting her chai latte to her lips.

"Karson just said he had some issues and needed to talk to someone, so I referred him. He didn't elaborate, and I didn't ask."

"Well, could it be his issues are what's causing his anger?"

Uh oh, the doctorate degree Alex was working on was about to start coming out.

I shrugged. "Not sure."

"Well, they're probably connected." She stood up. "I gotta go, kiddo. Holler at me later if you want to go get a drink or something."

Like I ever went to bars. I could only imagine the kind of guy I would pick up at one.

# CHAPTER 24

## KARSON

The next day, I found myself looking up at the small house-turned-office with a wooden sign reading *Havenwood Falls Psychology & Counseling* swinging in the wind. I walked up the three rickety steps and blew warm air into my hands before knocking on the front door. It opened quickly, and an older lady dressed sorta hippie-chic opened it up. She smiled warmly at me with kind brown eyes.

"Hi, I'm Julie Espensen. You must be Karson?"

I shook her hand. "Yes."

"You can hang your coat over there. Then have a seat," she instructed, after leading me down a hallway to an office with a large oak partners desk in the corner and a plush blue sofa opposite it. On one wall hung many framed certificates. On her desk were multiple photographs of children and adults.

I hung up my coat and sat down, feeling nervous and just wanting to bolt. I wasn't sure I had made the right decision coming here. But I also knew I couldn't keep going on the way I had been.

"So, Karson, what brings you in?" she asked, pushing a curly gray strand of hair behind her ear as she smiled at me. I noticed she had rings on almost every finger.

I swallowed and licked my lips before saying, "I've, ah, been told I need some anger management therapy or something."

She began scrawling on a notepad in her lap. "I see. And do you think you need anger management?"

I shrugged. "Yeah. I tried running away, and that didn't work. Came back just as angry. My dad says I'm a hothead."

"And do you think you are?"

"I guess."

She jotted some more notes. "Tell me about your childhood."

And there it was. I knew she was going to ask, just like they always did in the movies. Deciding not to fight it, I took a deep breath and began talking about my earliest memories of my mother. I didn't think she got a word in edgewise, as she furiously jotted down notes while I spoke. Then I told her about my leaving Havenwood Falls, and what had gone on since my return, leaving out the memory glitch, since I was pretty sure the doc was human.

I glanced at the clock and could see forty minutes had gone by. *Wow.*

I was proud I hadn't shed a tear, but I had to hold a few back a couple of times. The weirdest thing, though, was that I felt like a huge weight had been lifted off me. Even more so than when I had told Jalen about it.

Dr. Espensen talked to me some more in her mild-mannered way, said some things about guilt, and tried to help me understand that none of what happened to me as a kid was my fault. We set an appointment for me to come back in a week. I paid her cash for the visit and left through the front door with a little bit of a spring in my step.

AFTER ARRIVING HOME, I glanced at the clock on the microwave to see it was nearing five p.m. It was a Friday night, and I was feeling restless. I plunked my keys and phone onto the dining room table and went to the living room to find Jalen—surprise, surprise—playing video games. Well, he was a video game tester, after all, but didn't he ever get sick of it?

I parked my ass on the opposite side of the couch and looked at the screen. Some kind of robot-looking creatures were chasing humans through the streets of a big city.

"The fuck is this?" I asked, intrigued.

"Brand new," he said as his avatar ran into a nearby building and began climbing the stairs.

"Have you left the house today?" I asked, trying not to sound judgy.

He shook his head. "Nope."

"Wanna go out tonight? Go shoot some pool at the Knuckle?"

He shook his head, stopped the game, and tossed the controller onto the sofa. "Nah, got a date. Not taking her there."

I lifted an eyebrow. "With who?"

He stood and stretched, and I noticed he was still in his clothes from yesterday. "I'll tell you if I get a second date. If not, don't worry about it, man."

I also stood and grunted. "I wasn't worried."

He wandered to the staircase, I presumed to shower and get ready.

"Hey, Jalen."

He turned around before his foot hit the top stair. "Yeah?"

"Can I move in?"

He laughed. "It's your house, and of course. You already have. You staying for good?"

I nodded. "Yes, nothing for me back in Colorado Springs."

Jalen smiled, and it was the first time since I returned that he seemed genuinely happy. "You got a job?"

"Yep, remember I told you Gwen hired me at Tragic Ink? Gonna start next week."

"Awesome," my cousin replied as he sprinted up the steps.

I went into the kitchen and wondered what I was gonna do with myself for the rest of the night. I could go to the Dirty Knuckle by myself, but that would be kinda sad. It sucked that none of the friends I grew up with could hang out with me—either they'd left town, or they were in serious relationships. Some were even married.

I turned on the satellite radio console we kept in the kitchen and pushed the button for the classic rock station. As Metallica began to bleed from the speakers, I opened the fridge and pantry to search for shit to cook. As usual, there wasn't much, but I found sauce, noodles, and sausage to make spaghetti. As I sang along and banged my head to "Enter Sandman," I thought about Scottlin. Even though I had just seen her yesterday, I missed being near her. I missed talking to her. She was so sweet, almost innocent-like. She was funny in a subtle way, and I had mad respect for what she did for a living. But I couldn't be mad at her for not wanting me.

As I was browning the sausage over the stove, I clenched and unclenched my hand several times. The people at the hospital had called to say my X-rays looked great, but I still felt weak in my right hand. I supposed it would get better soon as my healing ability kicked in—but it would also take time. At least the cut was gone, thanks to Scottlin's magic.

I dumped noodles into the boiling water and almost dropped the package as I heard Def Leppard begin to croon through the speakers. Reminded immediately of her, I closed my eyes and listened to them belt out "Love Bites."

I had the urge to go over and shut off the damned radio, but I couldn't bring myself to do it. So I did what any fool would do: I opened the music app on my phone and downloaded the song so I could torture myself with it any time of the day or night.

I poured the sauce over my cooked sausage and stirred it around, wishing I had something better to distract myself with. Half relieved and half sad that the song had ended, I blew out a breath and went to the fridge to grab a Coors to go with my spaghetti. Just before I cracked it open, Jalen walked in. He was all cleaned up in jeans and a fitted T-shirt with his wool jacket over it. His hair had goop in it, and he had put on cologne.

"Smells good," he said.

"It's gonna taste even better," I replied.

"See ya," he said, leaving.

I was jealous of him. I leaned my ass against the counter with the beer in my hand. Then an idea hit me.

After turning off all the burners, I grabbed my keys and flew out the door. As the icy wind blasted through my hair, I pushed the throttle on the bike faster so I wouldn't lose my nerve. It seemed I was doing a lot of brave things today.

The sun had set, and the night had taken over. As the day had been a tad warmer than usual, a light rain began to fall, and I was grateful it wasn't snow. As I drove, I looked up at the snowcapped mountains. The moon was full, and heavy clouds drifted through a star-shot sky.

Once I reached Scottlin's apartment complex, I killed the engine to my bike, then walked around to where her apartment was and looked up through raindrops falling into my eyes to see the light on.

The parking lot was so quiet. What I was about to do was risky, but it had to be done. I wasn't here out of boredom; I was here because seeing Scottlin yesterday had stirred things inside me that I thought I had pushed aside. Because I had to try to get her back, no matter the cost.

At the end of the day, I knew I wasn't fooling anyone. I knew there wouldn't ever come a day where I wouldn't miss her or think about her. Because I lacked the nerve to walk into the apartment building and risk having her not open the door like before, I was going to lean on the cheesy, romantic—yet seemingly effective—moves of an old 1980s movie.

I pulled the phone from my pocket and found *Love Bites* on the playlist. After turning the volume on my phone all the way up and plugging it into my Bluetooth speaker, I pushed play and let the song float from it.

With the phone in one hand and the speaker in the other, and happy they were waterproof, I held them high above my head with my face upturned toward her apartment window, the raindrops now turning to freezing rain. The pellets assaulted my face in hard, cold stings.

I didn't care.

Then, for good measure, I even sang along. Loudly and badly.

A couple of dogs barked and howled. A few lights in the complex flipped on, but I paid them no mind. I was anxiously awaiting movement from the curtain in Scottlin's window.

I was starting to shiver, but I persevered, continuing to sing along.

Finally . . . *finally*, I saw the curtain move and a pale face peer out. Our eyes met. Hers went wide, while I just kept singing like a fool.

"Shut up!" a male voice yelled from somewhere. I ignored him.

The curtain on Scottlin's window flicked closed, and it wasn't long until she stormed out the front door of the building, looked around, and yelled, "Karson! What do you think you're doing?"

I continued to sing about not wanting to touch her too much, and how making love to her might make me crazy.

She looked around, the rain quickly soaking her. "Karson!"

I muted the phone, shoved it into my pocket, and set the speaker on a nearby planter, all without breaking eye contact. I stalked hungrily toward her, and when I was within a foot, I looked down into her face, which was quickly becoming streaked with rain.

I sighed. "I miss you, Scottlin."

Her eyes went wide again, and when I reached out and grabbed her face with both hands, she gasped, but did not pull away. I stared deep into her eyes. "I'm sorry. I'm so fucking sorry. I'll do anything for a second chance. Anything. Don't make me grovel, baby. *Please.*"

Without waiting for an answer, I leaned down, pressed my lips to hers, and captured her mouth. She didn't resist at all, but instead put her arms around my neck and kissed me back under the chilly, hard-falling rain.

A few catcalls and whistles could be heard, but we ignored them.

"It's freezing out here," she said. "Come inside."

I didn't have to be told twice. I snatched the speaker from where I'd set it, and she led me by the hand into the warmth of her building. We quickly walked up the stairs together, and as soon as I closed the door to her apartment, she turned around and pierced me with a look I couldn't decipher, water dripping off her nose and chin. Confusion and hope mixed with a little lust was the only way to describe what was going on behind those blindingly beautiful blue eyes of hers.

I walked over to her and put my arms around her. "I'm sorry. A thousand times over, I'm so sorry. Please let me make it up to you."

"It's not me you need to apologize to. It's Len," she replied quietly, untangling herself from me. She used her hand to dry off her face and push her hair away.

"Done. Tell me where to find him, and I'll do it right now," I replied, meaning it.

"I don't know where he is now, but I'm gonna hold you to that."

"You have my word." I could see her hair was out of the braids, and I took a step closer to push some behind her ear so I could look at her face. "I can't do this without you."

She flicked her gaze back and forth between my eyes. "Do what?"

C.J. PINARD

I let out a deep sigh. "I'm getting help for my anger. For the shit from my childhood. Dr. Espensen is great. I'm so glad you gave me her card."

Her eyes went wide. "You already saw her?"

I nodded. "Yep, called the same day. I talked to her this morning."

She smiled, and it was so beautiful. "I'm so glad, Karson, I really am." Her smile then fell. "Because I can't be with someone who can't control their anger. Your temper is gonna be your downfall." She turned around like she was trying to hide emotion.

I couldn't take it any longer. Her cherry-red lips were too tempting, so I touched her shoulder and turned her around. Without asking, I claimed her lips again, just before she gasped in surprise. She melted into me and sighed in pleasure.

With nothing left to be said, I picked her up while I continued to kiss her. I spied the one and only bedroom in the apartment, and I made my way toward it while running kisses along her jaw, cheek, nose, and mouth.

"Karson," she gasped when I set her down on the bed.

I removed my jacket and threw my keys to the floor. "What, beautiful?"

"I don't know—"

I froze. "If you don't want this, just say so now, and I'll leave. But Scottlin . . . just know that I can't stay away from you. You're an addiction I haven't been able to kick. You're like nobody I've ever met, and I think I'm falling in love with you. Please say you feel the same?"

I was damn near breathless now. I'd never wanted anyone so badly in my life, and by the way she sucked her bottom lip between her teeth, and the blue flame of desire burning behind her gaze, I knew she couldn't deny how she felt any more than I could.

Slowly, she nodded. Then she took me by surprise. She rose from the bed, pulled her tee over her head, slid her black pants off, and stood in front of me in nothing but lace panties, milky white skin, and the most beautiful body I had ever laid eyes on.

I wasn't sure I'd ever disrobed as quickly as I did in that moment, but once my clothes were off, I stalked over to her like a hungry animal, picked her up, and kissed her as she wrapped her legs around me.

Once she was under me, we let go of our inhibitions and loved

346

each other for hours upon hours. I showed her how much I'd missed her, and she accepted all I poured into her. I wasn't sure we even slept that night. And if we didn't . . . it was totally worth it.

As I looked down into her sleeping face, I knew in that moment she'd attached herself to my soul. And if she ever stopped looking at me the way I looked at her, it would destroy me. Because there are things worse than death, and not having the love of my life as a part of my forever would be just that.

Scottlin was beautiful, the complete package, and she had wrecked me in the most perfect way possible.

I wouldn't have it any other fucking way.

# EPILOGUE

## KARSON

FEBRUARY 14

*A*s we all sat eating a nice dinner at the Fallview Tavern, we discussed whether or not we wanted to go to the Cupids & Cuties Valentine's Day event. It was, after all, at Whisper Falls Inn, the owner being Michaela, the daughter of Mihail Petran, whom Uncle Will had stung and almost killed five years ago. He'd passed since then, but not because of what Uncle Will had done. Still, we weren't sure how cool the Petrans were with the Kanes. None of us had attended the event since.

"I think it'll be fine," Scottlin said.

"We'll only have to stay for a little while," Jalen added, before shoving a carnation he'd plucked from the centerpiece on the table into his mouth.

Scottlin made a face. "Did you just . . . eat a flower?"

I chuckled. "They're like a delicacy for us."

"Gives us a little tiny buzz," Dad commented before taking a swig from his beer.

"Um, well, that's interesting," Scottlin said.

Regina chuckled. "I have to watch my flowerbeds around this one." She elbowed her husband in the ribs.

"So what do you think? Think we should go?" I asked. "I have a gift, like a peace offering." I lifted up the small bag containing a bottle of expensive wine that Scottlin had helped me pick out at Sanguine Elixirs—a special blend for vampires.

"Yeah, let's just stay there for an hour and leave. We have to head out to the falls later, anyway," Gavin said.

I smiled. It was good to see him again for his monthly visit.

After a short drive, we arrived at the inn. My arm around Scottlin, we entered the lobby. For the special occasion, I'd forgone the band tee in place of a red button-down shirt and some black slacks. Scottlin wore a deep red dress that reached her feet, and some kind of white furry thing around her shoulders. Her hair was up in some twist thing. She looked stunning.

When we stepped inside, the party was in full swing, as we'd arrived about an hour late. I was a little relieved nobody was handing out those stupid gold-tipped arrows that were supposed to lead you to your "one true love." I'd already found her, and that would have just been fucking awkward.

The ballroom was already crowded with people dancing and standing around, talking with drinks in their hands. Jalen and his date, along with my dad and Regina, all went separately to the bar or to talk to people.

"Want to dance?" I asked my beautiful girlfriend.

"Sure."

As I led her out onto the dance floor, we got a few looks and smiles, but nobody said anything. Over the past month, we'd made no secret of our relationship. I held Scottlin close as we danced, reveling in the feel of how perfectly she fit against me. I didn't fail to notice that Mihail's sister-in-law was hovering in a corner, staring at us.

Scottlin looked up at me. "Why is Madame Luiza staring at us?"

I sighed. "From what I understand, she's all that's left—if you could call it that—of that generation of Petrans. She's a ghost."

"Oh. Awkward. Nothing like having a ghost staring you down."

I chuckled. "Yeah. But I can't wait to see Uncle Will tonight."

She nodded. "You dropping me off first?"

"I'd like you to come," I said hopefully.

She rested her head on my chest. "I'd like that."

Michaela Petran and her boyfriend Xandru Roca greeted us, and they were nothing but friendly and welcoming. It made me feel better. As I looked around at my cousins and Dad, I could see they were a little relieved, too.

~

AFTER WE HAD all changed out of our party clothes, we stood on a large outcropping of rock, the powerful falls rushing all around us. I held Scottlin's hand firmly in mine. My dad and Regina, along with Jalen and Gavin, stood near the entrance to the falls. This was the day we'd been waiting for. This was why Jalen had wanted me to return to Havenwood Falls.

But had that been the only reason? No, I didn't believe it was. That being said, I didn't think it really mattered anymore. Uncle Will was coming back to us, and this was a very important day.

We all turned to look when a strange light shimmered before our eyes, and from out of it stepped my Uncle Will, hands bound in glowing supernatural bindings and wearing a yellow jumpsuit. His hair was longer than I remembered, and a long, white-gray beard and mustache framed his mouth. He was escorted by two muscular Seelie guards.

A woman I hadn't noticed before came forward, put her hands on my uncle's head, and whispered something. He closed his eyes, and we saw her hands glow yellow. Once he popped his eyes open, he blinked rapidly, looking around.

"I think she's restoring his memories," Scottlin whispered.

When William spotted Jalen and Gavin, his dulling purple eyes went wide, then filled with unshed tears. "My boys," he cried.

Gavin and Jalen tried to rush up to him, but the Seelie guards put their arms out to block them. "Please stand back."

I frowned. My cousins couldn't even embrace their father, whom they hadn't seen in five years?

"It's not right," Scottlin whispered, her warm breath on my ear.

"I agree," I replied.

Uncle Will kept his eyes trained on his sons as the guards passed him off to two Havenwood Falls deputies. After the Seelies disappeared through the portal, which quickly vanished, the deputies put him in an unmarked white van. When they drove away from the falls and toward town, Scottlin and I quickly mounted my bike and followed. The others were right behind us in their cars.

The white van stopped at the sheriff's station, and I respected them enough to park my bike at a distance and stand back as they escorted Uncle Will inside. When Jalen and Gavin got out of the car and went into the jail area, Scottlin and I followed. We knew he had to spend six weeks in Sheriff Kasun's jail, and had accepted that.

Once Uncle Will was uncuffed and then secured in a cell, a deputy spat tobacco into a Styrofoam cup and pierced us with an authoritative stare. "You have ten minutes, elves. Make it count." Without another word, he left the cellblock and disappeared though a door.

My uncle stood gripping the thick bars of his cell, the same one Jalen had been in weeks ago.

"Dad, we've missed you so much," Jalen said, fighting back emotion as he hugged his dad through the hard metal bars.

Gavin hugged him next, followed by Ellis. I gave him a quick one, too.

Will grinned at his sons. "I've missed you so much."

"Good to have you home," my dad said to his brother.

"I need to see him. I need to apologize," Will said, and we knew whom he meant. He sat down on the bed inside the cell.

"He passed away a few years ago," I said.

My uncle looked shocked. "Probably from what happened in court. It wasn't right, what I did."

"No, it wasn't. He was already circling the drain, trust me." Dad said quickly.

Uncle Will nodded, his brow furrowed. I could tell he would never forgive himself.

"Totally sucks you have to stay here," Jalen grumbled.

Will looked up and smirked. "Boy, I can do six weeks standing on my head here compared to where I've just been."

"And where is that?" Gavin asked, crossing his arms over his turquoise polo shirt.

Will looked at his other son. "You don't wanna fuckin' know, kid. Just be here in six weeks when I get out so we can go party at the Knuckle. Then . . . you'll have to get me drunk as fuck if you want me to talk about that place."

Gavin nodded, and I remembered him calling his dad a shitbag. Now that I had my memories back, I knew why—they'd always had an extremely strained relationship. Still, Gavin had shown up here, so that said something.

Uncle Will looked at Scottlin, then drifted his gaze to me. "What you been up to, boy? Still a hothead?"

I glanced down at my beautiful girlfriend, my arm around her delicate shoulders, then back to my uncle. "Nah, not anymore." I kissed Scottlin's nose, then looked at Uncle Will. "Welcome home, asshole."

~

We hope you enjoyed this story in the Havenwood Falls series featuring a variety of supernatural creatures. The series is a collaborative effort by multiple authors.

Read the book where we first meet Scottlin - *Defying Gravity* by Kallie Ross. You can also read about Addie Beaumont, starting with *Forget You Not* and *Lose You Not*, then continuing with her own story in *Break Me Not*, all by Kristie Cook, as well as *The Collector: Awakening* by Kristie Cook, R.K. Ryals, Belinda Boring & Nadirah Foxx. Read about Karson's cousin Tarron in *Written in the Stars* by Kallie Ross.

Also try the YA line, Havenwood Falls High; the historical line, Legends of Havenwood Falls; the darker, sexier side of town, Havenwood Falls Sin & Silk; the local supernatural college, Sun & Moon Academy; and the short story holiday anthologies.

Stay up to date at www.HavenwoodFalls.com

# ABOUT THE AUTHOR

C.J. is a USA Today bestselling author living in Colorado. Lover of red wine, wearer of fabulous shoes, and die-hard Niner fan, she's also an editor at heart. She's the author of over thirty novels and short stories that contain both contemporary/new adult and paranormal romance that are a little bit badass, a little heart-wrenching, and sorta funny (to her, anyway). Almost all of her books contain law enforcement or military undertones, since strong, brave, alpha men and women are her weaknesses. When she's not writing, she can be found working at a very strange day job, which may or may not have some mild influences on her gripping stories—so strange, in fact, she may just write a book about it one day.

You can find her on Facebook, Instagram, and Twitter, or on her website, www.cjpinard.com

# ACKNOWLEDGMENTS

Thank you Heather, Kallie, Kristie, and Michelle for letting me use your amazing characters. Thank you, Liz, for your amazing copyediting skills. And lastly, thank you Kristie for creating this world, and then editing Karson and Scottlin's story so it was perfection for Havenwood Falls.

# AN EXCERPT

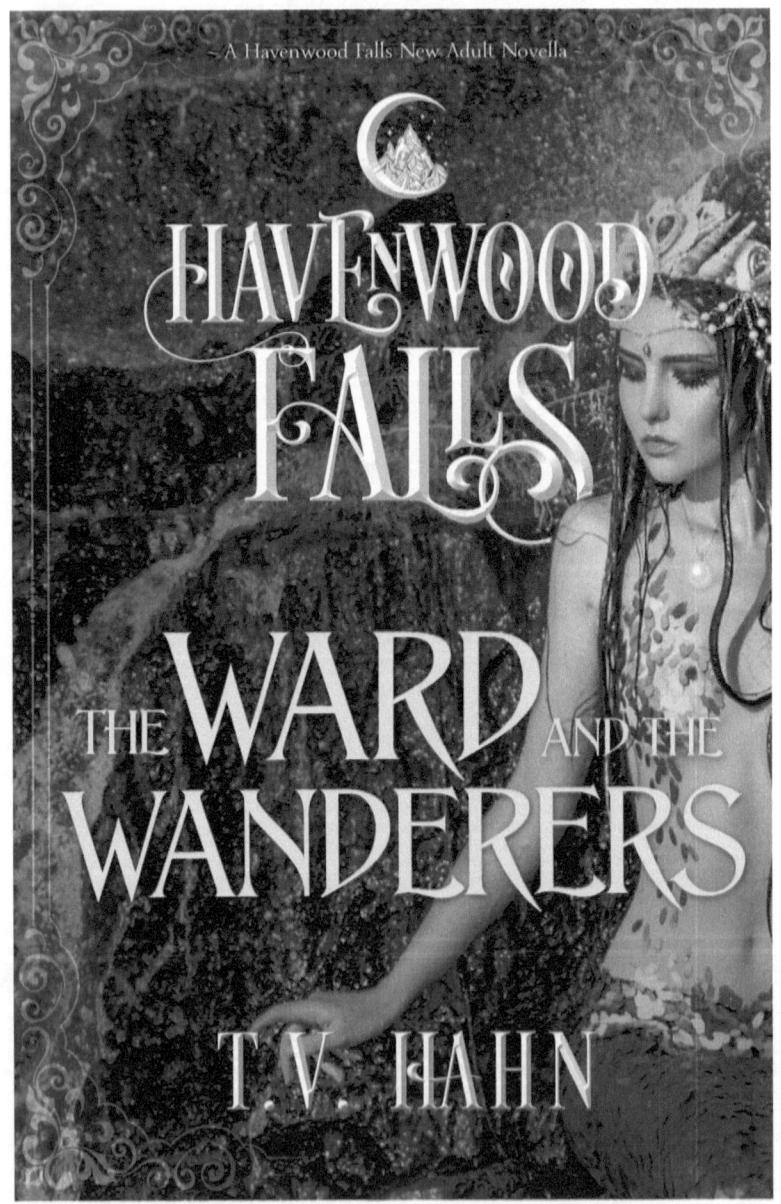

~ A Havenwood Falls New Adult Novella ~

# Havenwood Falls

# The Ward and the Wanderers

## T.V. Hahn

### *The Ward & the Wanderers* (A Havenwood Falls Novella) by T.V. Hahn

**In this sequel to *The Winged & the Wicked*, Teeny Weeny is off to save her little mermaid friend in another Teeny Weeny Fairy Tale.**

Teeny Weeny Tahini's life had always been quiet and simple, just the way she liked it. At least, until a year and a half ago, when her owl-shifter nephew Mat came to town with trouble on his heels. She and her extraordinary friends saved the day, but their happily ever after was short-lived. Now, the spring faerie has been haunted not only by nightmares, but also her past.

Compelled to travel thousands of miles to her ancestral home, Teeny Weeny leaves the safety and security of Havenwood Falls for the Isle of Gwynf'l, off the coast of England. Coralie, her long-time mermaid friend, is in danger, and the only way to save her is to take her back to Havenwood Falls. A series of obstacles combined with personal dilemmas from Teeny's past make it a foreboding journey, but one she must endure.

Traveling with a mermaid isn't easy, and the return trip could be racked with more problems because of the town's protective wards that only give her a lunar cycle away from her safe haven. Teeny Weeny and Coralie, not to mention a few uninvited travelers, race against time before they lose all memories of the place they now call home.

# THE WARD & THE WANDERERS

## BY T.V. HAHN

"FATHER, NO!"

"Siobhan, stay out of this. Your brother has disobeyed the code, and for that he must be punished."

My mother stood beside my father, crestfallen and bereaved.

Grenfold stood firm, silent, accepting of his fate. If he only knew.

My father chanted the code. "We, this family of fae, are of earth and air. When sea mixes with earth, it becomes mud. When sea mixes with air, tears fall from the heavens. You have brought both to this family. To be true, from this day hence, no longer are you fae, a prince. For your crime I extol, from this day forward, your life, a troll."

With that, King Ian—for he acted as king now, and not as a loving father —waved his royal wand above my brother's head, and the glowing orb at its tip touched my brother's brow. The first sounds Grenfold made since the commencement of this ghastly ceremony— which was unfairly replacing our usual festive Rites of Spring—were of such pain and agony that nothing human could compare to what my once beautiful brother was suffering. I knew this because over the years, as an empath, I had felt human pain, and this was something far beyond it.

The decibels and frequencies of my brother's cries were otherworldly as his body was transformed. The graceful, perfect frame of the handsome prince made a grotesque crunching of bones as his back disintegrated into a warped spine. My brother's cries and the horrific crackling of cartilage rocked the Isle of Gwynf'l to its core. His hands and feet became gnarled and twisted. His gorgeous golden locks fell in clumps from his head to be replaced by a wiry configuration of corkscrew strands, and even those had a resonance that I could taste as acrid and fuzzy on my tongue. His bright hazel eyes became like lumps of coal placed in a bed of gray clay, as his handsome features distorted. His nose became a long crooked probe with crusty warts, and his mouth turned and twisted, totally malformed, filled with protruding and decayed teeth.

After this horrible transformation was complete, my father, the great King Ian, ordered the troll to find a rock to crawl under.

And so he did.

My mother, the kind and generous Queen Rose, was so heartbroken, she turned ill and died within a few short months after Grenfold's departure.

Such is the price one pays for love. It didn't seem right that a gift of love should be so painful, so costly.

~

The tinkling of the shopkeeper's bell rang sweetly in the dining room of Broastful Brew as I entered and slowly closed the shop door behind me, accidentally allowing a brisk March wind to add a bit of chill to the café. I trudged into the toasty coffee house and made my way to the back table, where my best friend, Barbie Stuart, the mayor of Havenwood Falls, sat sipping a simmering cup of coffee.

Havenwood Falls was no ordinary Colorado town. Oh sure, it looked like your typical frontier Victorian village one could find nestled in just about any canyon in the state, with the sun rays glistening off the golden aspens' fluttering leaves and the scent of pine wafting in the cool breeze. I could assure you, however, that was just a façade. Behind the brick and mortar, wood shingles, and gingerbread lattice work was a town full of supernaturals, from vampires and demons to werewolves and angels. In fact, I was one of them, a spring fae.

Not all of the townsfolk were supernaturals. The ratio varied from time to time, ranging between forty and sixty percent supes. I think it depended on how the stars aligned, but I could be wrong. There could be something much more mysterious behind the mix.

Regardless, the town was founded by the Old Families, one of which was mine. We were—and yes, some of us are still quite alive and kicking—supernaturals looking for a safe haven, where our supernatural abilities would not subject us to prejudice, as we discovered would happen just about anywhere else.

The founders created the town and the government known as the Court of the Sun and the Moon. All of the Old Families had one member sitting on the Court. I held my family's seat, although I was basically the wallflower of the group most of the time.

The Luna Coven created most of the magic that protected Havenwood Falls, including something the town referred to as the "memory ward." As soon as a visitor traveled outside of the twenty-five mile radius of the town's limits, their memory of our little haven vanished. The residents got a bit of a reprieve on this mystic cloak, in that we could exit town for one complete moon phase—twenty-eight days—before our memories of Havenwood Falls disappeared.

I found Havenwood Falls serene and comforting, and really never had any reason to go anywhere outside of its protective borders. Others—a Roca here and a Bishop there—seemed to have a necessity to come and go frequently.

I withdrew the chair from the table when the mayor looked up at me. She was visibly startled at my appearance.

"Siobhan! You look dreadful! Is it the spring equinox that's bothering you? I've never seen you look so . . . well, so bad." Barbara, a dear friend and a member of another Old Family, invited me to join her.

Barbie had listened to me recount my family tale every spring for what seemed like a hundred years, and may very well have been. We met regularly at Broastful Brew. Unlike the bustling Coffee Haven, where the younger folk liked to hang, Mabel's coffee shop was quite sedate and the perfect place for us two to congregate.

Barbie's stature was so starkly different from mine, me being only four foot five, the town's mysterious palm reader and potion mixer, lovingly (I think) known as Madame "Teeny Weeny" Tahini. By contrast, Barbie's six-foot frame was not enough to intimidate, her bouffant beehive hairdo—which she sometimes dyed in various pastel colors according to her whimsy so it looked like a wand of cotton candy—added at least six more inches to her height.

Tahini was not really my surname. It was McFeeny, but being a palm reader and all, I felt Tahini gave it a much more exotic allure for my trade, and it rhymed with McFeeny. For that matter, it rhymed with Teeny Weeny, too.

Normally I was very cheerful and lighthearted, or so I'd been told. Barbie always said I had a childlike nature of wonderment drifting about me. However, this day my faerie glamour wasn't sparkling, dark circles rimmed my eyes, and my generally shiny long brunette hair was in a fizzled mess around my shoulders. I'd noticed the ghastly reflection in the glass door before I entered.

"I haven't been sleeping well, Barbie. I've been bombarded with nightmares. I can't make anything of them. It's just so weird for me. The Rites of Spring dream—I'm used to that. For so long, I've relived that moment, and I have wished I had the power to break my father's curse."

Barbie nodded with understanding, but she raised one eyebrow, as if she thought differently about my wish.

She wrapped her large soft hands around my tiny wringing fists, trying her best to comfort me.

"You poor dear," she said soothingly. "Maybe these nightmares stem from that awful incident with that Pisik cat-shifting witch and your poor nephew Mat. You are not so accustomed to commotion."

I smiled weakly at my friend's attempt at assonance—word play had always been one of my favorite forms of dialogue. But not so much today, or for the last week or so, for that matter.

"Tell me about the nightmare. It might help to talk it out. Maybe between the two of us, we can fathom its meaning," she prodded.

"Well the first one—" I started.

"First one! There's more?"

"Nightmarezzz," I exaggerated wearily, emphasizing the plural, then continued. "The first one starts out in the dead of winter. The snows have already fallen heavily in the canyon. I have effervesced and flown up to Peacock Lake. The triplet falls are frozen solid, and the lake is like a shining mirror. I'm barely able to discern any of its radiant colors. I am enjoying the crisp, fresh smell of the whiteness. The air is so clean, the scent of the pines is outright singing to me at

Small's Falls. I am listening to the soft chords of the sunlight passing through the icicles on the falls' ledge, spraying the colors like a prism, a harp strumming angelic psalms across the lake. It's peaceful and serene, and I am enjoying the scenery."

I paused, then continued, "Suddenly, black irregular spots begin to appear across the snowy landscape. They grow bigger, dripping upon the land, as if something black and evil is clawing at the snow-laden mountains. The blackness runs like spilt ink, and the spots begin to run into one another, growing larger. The smell is so acrid, sticky, like the smell of crude oil, but worse, like deeper than those bowels of the earth. It is a smell so strong that I wake up drenched in sweat, unable to shake the odor from my nostrils and way too afraid to try to go back to sleep."

Barbie sat unblinkingly as she pondered the dream's description and sipped her coffee. Mabel had brought my usual pot of hot water and favorite chamomile tea in a bag. I half-heartedly bounced the teabag up and down in the pot, but I was just not really inclined to actually pour the tea into my cup.

"Not sure I can make much of that. *Yet*." Barbie went on, "Normally, it doesn't sound like much to make such a sweat over—sorry, no pun intended. However, you do have that ultra-synesthesia thing going on. You know, where you *feel* smells so strongly, and *hear* colors so vividly, and a bunch of other mixed up senses, that it's perfectly understandable. Maybe it's connected to the next dream. Tell me about that one?"

There were not too many folks in town who knew the mayor had a talent for interpreting dreams. Maybe it was just her curiosity in netherworldly ways, or maybe an inheritance she had yet to expose.

Barbie was supposedly human, but I had my doubts, having known her for so long. Even with our long friendship, I had just learned some of her secrets at her last Thankshannamas gathering, when she thought she had lost her dragon pendant, a family relic that evidently gave her strength and agelessness when she wore it. I had noticed long before that she never changed, except, of course, for the mound of cotton candy that topped her crown. From time to time, her hair color had been pale blue, pale pink, pale yellow, pale purple, pale whatever, a pastel rainbow of sorts. The pale yellow must've been her favorite, at least when in public, but every now and again, she would get a little adventurous. And each color smelled like . . . well, pale blue like blueberry, pale yellow like lemon chiffon, etc. At least to me, which was yummy.

I remembered when she had it almost a lavender color, but lavender was not the scent I'd picked up. I'd had a hard time identifying it.

"Welch's grape juice," she'd remarked.

That was it! It smelled like grapes. Did she soak that magnificent head of hair in a vat of Welch's grape juice, or was it just her inspiration? I didn't know. Maybe someday she'd tell me.

But like I said, Barbie had never changed—other than the color of her hair—for decades. On the other hand, she had never exhibited any supernatural powers either, in public or to me, other than that ancient talent of dream interpretation. Then again, she did seem to have some superhuman strength, or I could be imagining it. Since she's so much larger than I am, her own human abilities might just be that strong in comparison to me having to use my faerie dust to accomplish something similar, like picking up beings twice my size, as an example.

She'd held so many different positions in town and on the Court, but had always been a major presence. And she was never without the dragon pendant (which most folks thought represented the high school mascot) that hung precariously from a silver chain around her neck, with its tail always pointing to a voluptuous cavern of cleavage, as she was very well-endowed.

As to her requesting me to tell her about the *next* dream, I obliged.

"So the next time, I dreamed I was sipping a delightful cup of tea in front of the blazing fireplace in the parlor of Whisper Falls Inn. Madame Luiza is sitting with me in her ghostly form, and we are having one of our lovely chats about the town's ancient history, and the miscreants that once inhabited our wonderful village, and the few who still do. You remember what it was like? We are having such fun, as Luiza describes so many of the colorful characters and their doings and misdoings. She saw and knew so much. It is always fun talking with her."

Barbie nodded her lemon-chiffon head, recollecting those chats herself, but waved her large beautiful hands in a come-forward gesture, begging me to continue.

So I did.

"The fire in the hearth suddenly crackles loudly, and fiery sparks fly out of the fireplace. We stand up immediately, trying to bat at the tiny sparks that could alight and place the entire inn in peril. Of course, Luiza is a ghost, so her batting is totally useless. A swirl of black smoke emits from the embers and circles throughout the room, thickening the air, making it nearly impossible to breathe. I am grasping at my chest, trying to gasp at least one more ounce of oxygen into my lungs before the horrific smog-like smoke takes over. There is a similarity in the smoky stench and that oily odor from the previous dream. At this point, I wake up, once again dripping with sweat, the pungent smell still burning in my nose and an ominous, dull ringing tone tolling in my ears."

Barbie sympathetically shook her head and patted my hands. "It's interesting that these dreams start out so . . . well, so dreamy. Then they kind of catch you off guard and take a sudden turn. So that's something to keep in mind. It might be that your dreams are foretelling the fortune teller something. Maybe you need to keep your guard up. Seems like you need to be on the alert."

"Yeah, you might be right, because the next one is like that too," I confided.

"Next one? You mean there's even more?" The mayor grimaced, realizing suddenly why I looked so miserable.

"One more, actually."

Barbie's brow raised higher than I thought capable, so I continued.

"I am back on the Isle of Gwynf'l with my parents and my brother, before, well, you know, before Father changed him. It is a beautiful day, and we are having a faerie picnic on the shore by the Bay of Gwynf'l. Mother has baked our favorite faerie cakes of honeysuckle honey and daisy flower flour. The pixies are skipping along the mollusk shells scattered on the beach and breaking out into their familiar wrestling matches in the sand. The waves are bright aqua topped with marshmallowy sea-foam, and they are gently lapping the shore. There are mountainous fluffy clouds in the sky, and they send sound waves of comforting lullabies and happy Irish ditties toward the sandy dunes that buffet the beach.

"I spot a waterspout forming out in the sea, and I am mesmerized by the sight of the swirling funnel, so magnificent in its perfect Fibonacci spiral. The funnel, though, is moving quickly closer and growing darker and larger. It is suddenly totally black as it reaches the shore, and a giant wave crashes over all of us, smelling like . . . Well, like before—oily, inky, black. And I awoke as soaked as if the wave had actually hit me, and this time I began to vomit from the odiferous air that surrounded me."

"This is not good, Siobhan! You should have called me earlier. We will have to be vigilant, since I am sure these are *warning* signs."

"But there's something else, also," Barbie continued. "I don't know if it's the smell or the black thing, maybe both. I will have to think more about this. No matter what, if you have another dream, you are to call me pronto, regardless of what time it is, understood?"

I nodded in acquiescence to Barbie's order, but my hands were still wringing one another and my teacup still remained empty.

"Drink your tea, hon. It'll help calm you. I have to run. I have a meeting at City Hall with a new visitor. I mean it about calling me!"

I shakily tried to pour the steeped tea from the pot into my cup as Barbie bent over to kiss the top of my head. I struggled to wiggle a few fingers in toodle-oo style, but it probably looked like a very disheartened farewell.

I did finish my tea at the Brew, albeit slowly, since my cup rattled every time I tried to lift it from the saucer, and I was fearful I would spill tea all over the place. I thanked Mabel for letting me sit so long, brooding. I guess today, it could be called Brooding Brew.

Purchase *The Ward & the Wanderers* where books are sold.